W9-BLZ-159

Murder
in the
Family

Also by Cara Hunter

Close to Home
In the Dark
No Way Out
All the Rage
The Whole Truth
Hope to Die

Murder in the Family

CARA HUNTER

wm

WILLIAM MORROW

An Imprint of HarperCollins*Publishers*

This is a work of fiction. Names, characters, places, and incidents are products of the author's imagination or are used fictitiously and are not to be construed as real. Any resemblance to actual events, locales, organizations, or persons, living or dead, is entirely coincidental.

HarperCollins books may be purchased for educational, business, or sales promotional use. For information, please email the Special Markets Department at SPsales@harpercollins.com.

Published in the United Kingdom in 2023
by HarperCollins Publishers Ltd.

FIRST U.S. EDITION

Library of Congress Cataloging-in-Publication Data
has been applied for.

ISBN 978-0-06-327207-1

23 24 25 26 27 LBC 12 11 10 9 8

For my agent, Anna Power, for her wisdom,
patience, humour and unfailing insight.
I couldn't have done any of this without her.

Murder
in the
Family

The Times, 8 November 2023

TELEVISION

And then there was one

Christie-worthy final twist gives **Infamous** a killer climax

ROSS LESLIE

The latest series of **Infamous** bowed out yesterday with a last-gasp twist that didn't just bring the house down but the whole theatre with it.

It's been the standout hit of Showrunner's autumn season, never out of the streamer's top ten shows since the first episode aired on 3rd October, and generating the sort of water-cooler debates those of us who remember a terrestrial-only world look back on with wistful nostalgia. As I said, back when it first launched, it must have taken guts to hold out for a gradual episode drop rather than cave to the prevailing box-binge culture, but boy, it paid off. Not least because it allowed real-life off-screen events to be incorporated into last night's double-episode series finale.

This season's format was a first for the Infamous franchise, and I suspect, for many of the viewers, but however innovative it might have felt, the closing sequence of last night's final episode proved that what we'd been watching all these weeks was, in fact, a very modern reprise of the time-honoured And Then There Were None scenario, first created by Agatha Christie, and re-invented by every new generation of crime novelists ever since, most notably by the late great PD James, but also, more recently, by the likes of Lucy Foley and Sarah Pearse. A small group of strangers, cut off from the outside world, who begin to turn on one another in the face of the horrifying realization that there is a killer among them, hiding in plain sight.

For so it proved last night. And no, of course I'm not going to tell you who. Let's just say I won't be the only member of the audience who's promptly re-watching the entire series, to see how I could possibly have missed it...

★★★★★

@RLeslieTV

Ten months earlier

Showrunner

January 9, 2023

New Season of 'Infamous' sees British Film-maker Revisiting His Stepfather's Murder, Unsolved for 20 Years

Filming On-Location in London, 'Who Killed Luke Ryder?' Will Include Never-Before-Seen Home Video Footage, Interviews with Family Members, and Exclusive Access to the Crime Scene

'Infamous: Who Killed Luke Ryder?' Set to Debut Tuesday October 3 (9:00 p.m.–11:00 p.m. EST) on Showrunner

In Season 7 of the global hit 'Infamous', film-maker Guy Howard will take viewers through the case that traumatized him as a child, and has haunted his family for two decades. In October 2003, when Howard was 10, his stepfather, Luke Ryder, was found dead in the garden of the family home in an upscale district of London. Despite a lengthy and high-profile investigation by British law enforcement, no charges were ever brought, and the case remains unsolved.

In a new format for the 'Infamous' franchise, producer Nick Vincent of Dry Riser Films has brought together key players in the original case, along with acknowledged experts in the fields of Crime Scene Investigation, forensic psychology, police investigation, and the law, to revisit the crime and attempt to identify the perpetrator, who still remains at large. Participants include:

Alan Canning
Detective Inspector, Metropolitan Police (Ret.)

Mitchell Clarke
Journalist, covered the case for the London press in 2003

Hugo Fraser KC
Leading UK criminal prosecutor

Dr Laila Furness
Forensic psychologist

JJ Norton
Crime Scene Investigator, South Wales Police

William R. Serafini
Detective, NYPD (Ret.)

After months in development, the seven-part series will follow the work of this team, as they re-examine original testimony, re-interview witnesses, and interrogate the 2003 evidence in the light of subsequent developments in forensic science. They will also interview family members who have never before spoken on camera about the events of that night.

Showrunner Head Of Factual, Garrett Holbeck, said, ‘We are all excited about the pace and tension this new format brings to the show, and my hope is that we will not only offer viewers a first-hand insight into this important case, but perhaps find some long-overdue closure for the family.’

The first episode of ‘Infamous: Who Killed Luke Ryder?’ is set to air on the twentieth anniversary of the murder, Tuesday, October 3 (9:00 p.m.–11:00 p.m. EST) on Showrunner. Subsequent episodes will appear in instalments.

'Infamous' is an award-winning series produced by Dry Riser Films for Showrunner TV Inc, which first aired in 2014. An acknowledged leader in the field of true crime, 'Infamous' has previously covered notorious and unsolved crimes such as the death of JonBenét Ramsay, the disappearance of Lauren Spierer, the murder of Peter Falconio in Australia in 2001, and the Camilla Rowan 'Chameleon Girl' case in the UK. The series is renowned for its incisive reporting, in-depth analysis, and exclusive access to those closest to the crime.

Nick Vincent's Dry Riser Films is an innovative and leading-edge creator of entertainment and documentary programming. Previous projects include 'The Red Lanterns: Journeys in China' (2016), produced and directed by Dominic Cipriani; 'The Real Homeland: Inside the CIA' (2018), produced by Rudy Assad; and 'Catching Colombia's Drug Lords' (2019), produced by Beth McVeigh. 'Infamous' is produced by Nick Vincent, edited by Fabio Barry, with research by Tarek Osman. Cinematography on S7 will be by Zach Kellerman and Mary-Ann Ballinger, with graphics by Medium Rare Creative, and music by Pangolin Sound Studios.

Guy Howard studied Film and Media Studies at the University of Thanet in the UK and has worked on a number of British TV projects. This is his first major feature.

Media enquiries
Xanthe Malthouse
Dry Riser Films Ltd
xanthe@dryriserfilms.com

Notes to editors:

Further information about participants is given below. Interviews and/or backgrounders can be arranged with any of the participants on request. Please contact Xanthe Malthouse for details.

Professional resumés of participants to follow:

ALAN CANNING

Retired Senior Police Officer

Experience	**Metropolitan Police Service (MPS)** **Detective Inspector, MPS Brent** 2009-2022 Handling of major crimes and serious incidents in the London Borough of Brent Planning and allocation of police resources on an incident-by-incident basis Implementation of MPS policies and standards Liaison with Council officers and community groups **Detective Sergeant, MPS Hayes and Harlington** 2001-2009 **Uniformed Sergeant, MPS South Croydon** 1995-2001 **Detective Constable, MPS Brixton Hill** 1990-1995 **Uniformed Constable, MPS South Croydon** 1984-1995
Education	**Police Training College,** Hendon, 1984 **Carlisle Road Secondary School,** Croydon, 1972-1984 6 'O' levels, 5 CSEs
Personal	Date of birth: 5th May 1967 Marital Status: Married Children: None
Hobbies	Golf, reading, travel

MITCHELL CLARKE

FREELANCE JOURNALIST

WHO I AM

I was born in Ladbroke Grove in 1982 and I've never left. My father was Jamaican, my mother from Grenada, both of them proud members of the Windrush generation. The values they taught me have shaped who I am and what I'm loyal to: my race, my class, my friends, my values. I tell the truth, like it is. In black and (occasionally) white.

WHAT I DO

NEWS

Hard-hitting fearless reporting, whoever, and whatever I'm covering.

FEATURES

Well-researched, in-depth and compelling stories born of a long and deep association with my neighbourhood and my community.

My work has appeared in the local and national press for 30 years, from the **West London Evening News** to **The Daily Mirror,** and **The Voice** to the **New Statesman**.

He/him

The Lawyer Hot 100, 2022

#thelawyerhot100

Hugo Fraser KC

Appearing in this list for an unprecedented fourth time, Fraser continues to impress as one of the most charismatic and sought-after silks at the Bar, and shoo-in candidate to lead his Chambers the next time that slot becomes vacant. Considered by many to be one of the leading KCs of his generation, Fraser never shies away from demanding and high-profile cases, and excels at presenting fiendishly complex evidence in an effective and telling manner. Known not just for his Eton education but his taste in expensive suits, Fraser is gutsy, creative and unashamedly clever. Small wonder he stands head and shoulders above his peers.

Laila Furness

Forensic and Clinical Psychologist

Profile

Registered Forensic Psychologist, Health & Care Professions Council

Member of The British Psychological Society (BPS)

BPS Register of Approved Psychological Practice Supervisors (RAPPS)

Current role

Founder and lead practitioner

Furness Associates, Oxford

Areas of specialism

Forensic psychological evaluation

Pre-trial assessments and the provision of expert testimony, especially in relation to violent 'serial' offenders

Personality and family dynamics, and trauma work

Academic qualifications

Diploma of Forensic Psychology, British Psychological Society, 2009

ClinPsyD Doctorate in Clinical Psychology, 2002

MSc Research Methods in Psychology, 1999

BA(Hons) Psychology, 1996

Experience

I have previously worked for HM Prison Service in both Secure Adult Units and Young Offenders' institutions, and as part of NHS clinical teams in London, Liverpool and Derbyshire, dealing with issues such as drug and alcohol dependency, personality disorders, and child sexual abuse.

Selected Publications

'Dissociation in Criminal Forensic Psychology', *The Psychiatrist*, Summer 2020

'Beyond Mindhunter: Profiling Current Approaches to Serial Killers', *Clinical Psychology Journal,* Winter 2016

'Crime and PTSD', *British Journal of Psychiatry*, June 2013

'Cognitive Analytic Therapy in the Treatment of Serial and Violent Offenders', *American Papers in Forensic Psychology*, Fall 2006

'Towards a more Humane Understanding of Dissociative Personality Disorder', *The Psychiatrist*, Summer 2004

'Far Gone: Dealing with Grief and Absence', Paper presented at EABCT conference, Manchester, 2002 (as Laila Khan)

CURRICULUM VITÆ

→MY NAME IS JJ NORTON AND I'M A FORENSIC INVESTIGATOR

I've worked in this field for over 20 years · I took a BSc in Forensic Science at the University of Birmingham, followed by an MSc at the University of Huddersfield · I've worked for Greater Manchester Police, Gloucestershire Constabulary and am currently with South Wales Police ·

MY SKILL SET

- DNA analysis
- Blood spatter analysis
- Forensic
- Ballistics
- Fire scene investigation
- Toxicology
- Digital forensics
- Forensic anthropology
- Entomology

NEED TO KNOW

I was once a blue-gloved hand in an episode of 'Silent Witness'

I have attended 378 autopsies, including one of a man killed by a falling grand piano, three people struck by lightning, and one half-eaten by a killer whale.

I flirted with the idea of becoming a priest before settling for forensics.

I am a member of Mensa

I once had a pet tarantula

I am a black belt in Tae Kwan Do

I never watch true crime TV

William R. Serafini Jr
Investigation Services

PROUD TO HAVE BEEN ONE OF NEW YORK'S FINEST

"Everything you could want in a PI"

Satisfied Customer

Experience

I did 30 years as a Manhattan Detective with the NYPD. In that time I investigated in excess of 350 homicides, 250 sex crimes, and countless thefts, home invasions, arsons, drug crimes, and street muggings.

I've attended thousands of crimes scenes and dealt with almost as many offenders. I've been commended for bravery six times, shot three times (once nearly fatally), and married twice (once, also, nearly fatally).

I've worked alongside the FBI, the Met in London and Europol.

Add all that up and there's very little I don't know about Crime Scene Investigation, criminal profiling, victimology, or investigative procedure, and if I don't know it myself, I'll definitely know a guy who does.

Why hire me? Because I'm not a quitter.

I'll get the job done even if I die trying. Well, perhaps not quite that but you get my meaning.

Skills

- Honesty
- Integrity
- Candor
- Persistence
- Good Judgment
- Initiative
- Courage
- Discretion

- end of press release -

Kick-off email from Nick Vincent, 31st March 2023

Date: Fri 31/03/2023, 14.05 **Importance: High**

From: Nick Vincent

To: Guy Howard, Hugo Fraser, Alan Canning, Mitch Clarke, Laila Furness, Bill Serafini, JJ Norton

CC: Tarek Osman, Fabio Barry, Dry Riser production team

Subject: Infamous: Who Killed Luke Ryder? Shooting schedule

Great to finally meet you all in person last week. It's always useful to get a sense of each other before filming, though as I said, we'll play the opening ep with introductions, so we can give viewers your backgrounds without making it too much of an info dump (unlike the press, the audience won't have seen your resumés!).

Feel free to question each other at that stage (experience, expertise etc) as your interactions – both positive and negative – will be a key part of the ongoing on-screen dynamic. It's also a good way to make sure the viewers understand the differences between UK and US criminal and legal procedure (→ Alan/Bill/Hugo).

As I explained, the first ep will require some re-hashing of information you clearly already know, to get the audience up to speed, but thereafter it will be much more free-flowing. The research team are still working on certain specific elements of the investigation which we deliberately aren't going to brief any of you about – it's crucial this doesn't look 'rehearsed'. We want you to look genuinely surprised if – as we hope – we get significant new evidence along the way. And of course this is very much an active investigation – we may end up somewhere very different even from what we currently envisage.

We've had to tweak a few logistical things for next week so I've attached an updated schedule. Any questions, just ping me or Tarek an email/WhatsApp.

See you Monday.

Nick

Text messages between Amelie and Maura Howard, 1st April 2023, 9.56 p.m.

Is he really going through with this?

Looks like it. Look, I know how you feel but it's a big deal for him

He may never get a chance as big as this again

So he says

You don't have to do it Am. In fact I really don't think you should

I don't think *any* of us should do it

Mum would HATE it

Yeah well she's not exactly going to notice is she

That's not the point and you know it

Guy's going to do it whatever so there's no point us two arguing

OK. Just keep me posted OK?

If they find anything?

How likely is that?

You never know with those fuckers

Crashing in about in other people's lives not caring how much damage they do

Look I've got it OK? Trust me – I won't let anything bad happen

Promise?

Promise x

Voicemail left for Peter Lascelles, 2nd April 2023, 10.03 a.m.

Peter? It's Alan Canning. Long time no speak, as they say. You might have picked up that I'm going to be involved in this new Showrunner series rehashing the Luke Ryder case. Would you be free for a quick chat this weekend? I think it might be useful. And not just for me.

Talk soon.

0.52 -0.11

Speaker **Call back** **Delete**

Episode one

Filming

DRY RISER FILMS Ltd
227 Sherwood Street London W1Q 2UD

CAST
Alan Canning (AC)
Mitchell Clarke (MC)
Hugo Fraser (HF)
Laila Furness (LF)
JJ Norton (JJN)
Bill Serafini (WS)

UNIT CALL 0900
Camera ready: 0930

Sunrise 0637
Sunset 1937
Weather forecast 13°, cloud

CALL SHEET

Infamous:
Who Killed Luke Ryder?

Monday 3rd April 2023

Ep 1: ON-SITE
DAY 1 of 3

Producer	**Nick Vincent**
Director	**Guy Howard**
Film editor	**Fabio Barry**
Researcher	**Tarek Osman**
Prod asst	**Jenni Tate**
Location manager	**Guy Johnson**

Breakfast on set from 0830
Running lunch from 1245
Exp wrap 1730

Location: **Dorney Place**
2 Larbert Road
Campden Hill London W8 0TF

Notes:
Some parking on site – must be reserved in advance
Nearest tube Holland Park
Emergency contact number 07000 616178

CREW

TITLE	NAME	PHONE	CALL	TITLE	NAME	PHONE	CALL

TITLE SEQUENCE: ARTHOUSE-STYLE B/W MONTAGE OF IMAGES AND SHORT CLIPS: CRIME SCENE, CONTEMPORARY NEWS COVERAGE, FAMILY PHOTOS

THEME SONG – 'IT'S ALRIGHT, MA (I'M ONLY BLEEDING)' [BOB DYLAN] FROM THE SOUNDTRACK TO 'EASY RIDER' [1969]

TITLE OVER

INFAMOUS

FADE IN

WHO KILLED LUKE RYDER?

FADE OUT

BLACK FRAME, TEXT APPEARS, with VOICEOVER – Narrator (female)

On the evening of Friday October 3, 2003, police were called to an affluent address in West London.

The caller was a child, who was in so much distress the first responders weren't sure what to expect.

An accident? Domestic violence? Maybe a burglary?

What they found was a body.

In the garden, at the bottom of a flight of steps, the face and head brutally beaten.

There was no-one else in the house. Just two traumatised teenage girls and their little brother, asleep upstairs.

FADE OUT

CUT TO: Guy in sitting room at Dorney Place. French windows, slightly old-fashioned furniture, view of garden beyond. Guy is slightly built, with arresting light-blue eyes and longish dark-blond hair. He has a single earring, a silver wrist chain, and a heavy aviator-style watch with a chrome strap. He's wearing a white shirt and jeans.

NICK VINCENT (Producer) – off

And you were that little boy.

GUY HOWARD

Yes I was.

NICK VINCENT (Producer) – off

And the girls were your sisters?

GUY HOWARD

(nods)

Maura was 15, Amelie was 13, and I was 10. It was Maura who called 999.

NICK VINCENT (Producer) – off

She found the body?

GUY HOWARD

Yes.

NICK VINCENT (Producer) – off

And who was it?

GUY HOWARD

Luke Ryder. My stepfather.

CUT TO: MONTAGE of contemporary newspaper headlines under vox pops/news broadcasts/clips as follows:

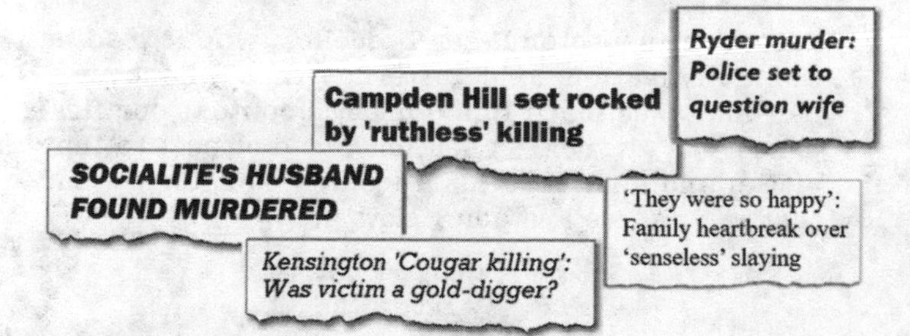
Ryder murder: Police set to question wife

Campden Hill set rocked by 'ruthless' killing

SOCIALITE'S HUSBAND FOUND MURDERED

'They were so happy': Family heartbreak over 'senseless' slaying

Kensington 'Cougar killing': Was victim a gold-digger?

NEWS ITEM 1

More than two weeks after the body of 26-year-old Luke Ryder was found savagely beaten in the garden of his wife's house in Campden Hill, the Metropolitan Police seem no closer to finding out who did it. Mrs Ryder was at a party that night, and the only other person in the house was her 10-year-old son. It was only when her daughters returned from the cinema at around ten thirty that the horrific discovery was made.

VOICE 1 (woman on street)

It's been absolutely ghastly. *Ghastly.* I have friends who are still afraid to go out on their own, never mind at night. A crime like that - it just doesn't happen round here.

VOICE 2 (man on phone-in)

Of course it was the wife - who else could it have been? Who else even had a motive? And as for getting into that house without anyone noticing, no chance. If you ask me, he was playing away and she caught 'im at it. Wouldn't be the first time, now would it.

NEWS ITEM 2

As if a brutal and apparently senseless killing weren't enough, the Metropolitan Police are now coming under fire from campaigners who say that Caroline Ryder is being unfairly targeted because she's an older woman in a relationship with a much younger man.

Detective Inspector Peter Lascelles, who is leading the investigation, said yesterday that 'whenever a murder takes place in a domestic context our first priority is always to question those closest to the victim and eliminate them from our enquiries, and that is what we are doing now'.

VOICE 3 (friend of Caroline)

I've known Caroline Ryder for ten years and she would never do something like this. She just doesn't have it in her. And despite what the papers are insinuating she and Luke were very happy. I know, because I saw them together only a few days before he died and there was absolutely no tension at all.

And as for the idea that she would kill Luke and leave her own *children* to find the body, well, anyone who knew her would tell you it's just inconceivable. Absolutely inconceivable.

NEWS ITEM 3

It's come to be known as the 'Cougar Killing' though, and more than a decade on, there is still no evidence to suggest that Caroline Ryder murdered her much younger husband, and she has certainly never been charged. Nor, indeed, has anyone else.

CUT TO: Interior as before, Guy.

NICK VINCENT (Producer) – off

So now its 2023 and it's been nearly twenty years since all this happened. Why are you revisiting it now?

GUY HOWARD

Because I want to know the truth. Because that's what I do, as a film-maker.

And because my family has lived with this thing hanging over our heads for almost two decades and until someone finds out who did it and puts him away none of us will ever have any peace.

NICK VINCENT (Producer) – off

I believe your mother is also unwell?

GUY HOWARD

(nods)

She's been diagnosed with early onset dementia. She's only 60. This case - Luke's murder - it's destroyed the whole family, but my mother most of all.

NICK VINCENT (Producer) - off

So this film - you want to vindicate her? Is that why you're doing it?

GUY HOWARD

I want to find the truth.

(pause)

Whatever that truth turns out to be.

MONTAGE: shots of the Campden Hill area. Four-storey brick and stucco frontages with railings along the pavement, tall windows with wrought-iron balconies, trees, wisteria. Expensive cars parked in the street, mothers pushing buggies, dogs.

VOICEOVER - narrator

And the search for the truth starts here.

It's probably the most expensive part of London you've never heard of. This isn't Mayfair, or Belgravia, or South Kensington. It isn't even Chelsea. It's Campden Hill, London W8. The smash-hit '90s film starring Hugh Grant and Julia Roberts catapulted neighbouring Notting Hill to international fame, but Campden Hill and its elegant, leafy surroundings still remained largely anonymous, much to the relief of its super-rich and super-private residents.

These days, $10 million will barely buy you an apartment in W8, and one of these Victorian villas could easily hit double that. But this house - *this* house is in a league of its own.

Cut to drone FOOTAGE over Dorney Place showing the size of the plot and extent of the garden.

When Dorney Place was built, way back in the 1760s, this area wasn't even part of London. In fact, it was barely even part of a village. There was an old Jacobean mansion, Campden House, which gave its name to the area before going up in smoke in 1862, and a scatter of smaller buildings around it, but that was about it.

Voiceover continues over IMAGE of old Campden House, followed by camera panning over 1810 map of London showing Kensington and Knightsbridge as villages.

If you walked up Campden Hill back then you'd be surrounded by green fields, and the chimneys and steeples of 'London' would be just a distant blur.

IMAGE of Dorney Place in the early 1900s.

Dorney Place didn't start out with that name; it didn't even start out as one house.

Some time in the mid 1850s two adjoining cottages were knocked together into one much larger house, and the new owner started 'developing' it, adding new wings, an orangery and a stable block, and by the end of the century it had become a very desirable gentleman's residence.

MONTAGE: Sequence of Victorian-era photographs of the house: people in summer clothes having tea, playing tennis; exterior shots of front elevation, courtyard, various interior shots including drawing-room, entrance hall, morning room.

And all this at a time when as the London we know now – the London of railway stations and shopping streets – was just starting to emerge.

By 1900, the green fields around Dorney Place had long since disappeared. Roads had replaced the lanes, and shiny new terraces had surrounded the garden on all sides. So much so, that you couldn't even see the house from the street.

And the same is still true today.

Camera tracks up the street to the Dorney Place entrance then zooms in. NB No security camera is visible.

There's this discreet gateway onto Larbert Road, but even when the gates are open you can't see more than a few yards down the drive. There's no name, just the number 2, and an entry keypad. If you didn't know the house was there, you'd almost certainly miss it.

With so much housing springing up around it in the late 1800s, it's some sort of miracle that Dorney Place survived at all. Even back then, developers would have been knocking the door down – always assuming they could find it – and you can imagine what a site this size would be worth today. But survive it did, and by the First World War ownership had passed to the Howard family.

Camera pans round to Guy, standing by the entrance.

GUY HOWARD

My family.

Cut to MONTAGE of home videos showing Guy as a child: on a swing, with a puppy, playing with other children in a paddling pool. Various adults are visible in the background, including Caroline and Andrew Howard.

VOICEOVER – GUY HOWARD

I was born in Dorney Place. So were my older sisters. It was a fabulous place to grow up. The house was a bit of a rabbit warren inside, at least upstairs – loads of staircases and passageways and attics and odd corners where the house had been extended over the years. For a kid like me it seemed like an enchanted castle – there was even a basement we pretended was a dungeon, though it was actually Dad's wine cellar.

In the summer, when the trees were out, you couldn't even see any other houses, so it was like we had a secret garden where you could almost forget you were in London at all. The grounds were so big my sisters even had a pony. OK, it was just one of those little Shetland things, but it was still a pony. In *London*. All their friends would come round and take turns riding it. Made them super-popular at school, I can tell you.

IMAGES of the Howards's wedding with text below 'Andrew and Caroline Howard', then various family portraits with the children as babies, toddlers, in school uniform, and as a family.

My parents married in 1987, it was Dad's second marriage. He was 39, Mum was 24.

CUT TO: Howard family tree

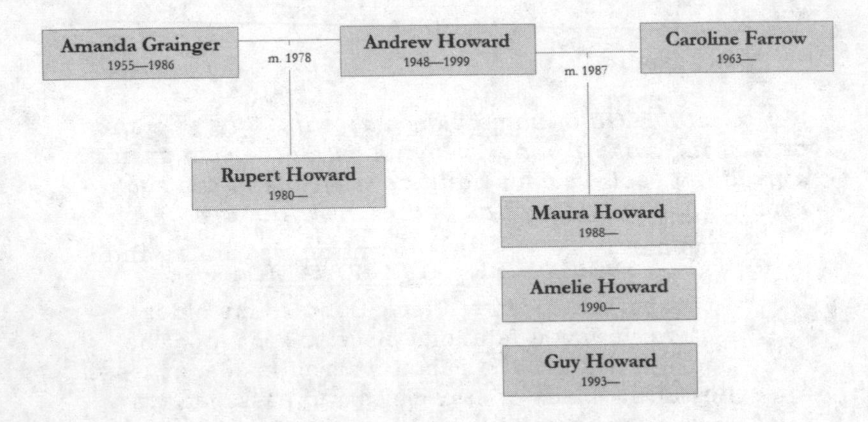

Maura was born a year or so after they married, Amelie in 1990, and me in 1993. We had an older half-brother too, though he was at school most of the time. Eton.

I remember my parents entertaining a lot – there were always people in the house in the evenings. We'd get sent upstairs. The girls used to sneak out sometimes to look, but I just found it all completely boring.

RECONSTRUCTION: Two small girls looking through banisters at a group of adults drinking in a large hall below. 'Caroline' animated and laughing at one end of the room, 'Andrew' reserved and silent at the other.

The following day the place would stink of smoke, there'd be a stack of empty bottles by the bins, and Mum would 'have a headache'. I don't know if she actually enjoyed all that hostessing – most of the people who came weren't what you'd call 'friends'. They didn't really have any friends, at least not any joint friends. Dad would play golf with men who never got invited in, and Mum would go out during the day and tell us she was seeing her 'ladies who lunched'. We never saw them at the house either.

The people who came for the dinner parties were business contacts of Dad's. Bankers, lawyers, finance people. He was 'something in the City'. At least that's what Mum used to say whenever it came up. I had no idea what that meant, of course – it was years before I discovered what he was really doing. All I knew, as a child, was that he was hardly ever home, except on weekends, and not always then.

But when he was around he was always prepared to make time for us. Though I obviously didn't think about it in those terms then. I just remember him playing with me.

CLIP of Guy playing cricket with his father in the Dorney Place garden. Guy bowls to his father and Andrew deliberately skies the ball so Guy can easily catch it. Guy runs around cheering and Andrew sweeps him up and gives him a hug. Caroline and the girls are watching, the girls on a rug and Caroline in a garden chair. Caroline is wearing a large hat that shades her face and has a glass in her hand. She looks distracted.

That's the summer of 1999. The Millennium Dome had just been opened, Bill Clinton's impeachment trial had failed, and there was a war in Kosovo. But that's not how I know it was 1999. It's because we didn't have another summer. Not as a family. By that Christmas Dad was dead.

RECONSTRUCTION: B/w FOOTAGE of small boy sitting on a sofa as adults swirl about him. PoV is such that only the bottom half of the adults is visible. Low lighting so the figures cast long shadows.

It was like an asteroid hit – completely out of the blue. Years later Mum told me he'd been ill for a while but no one had ever said anything to us at the time. It actually happened when he'd taken me to Holland Park one weekend, just the two of us. He had a massive heart attack and that was it. At least that's what they told me later – to be honest, I don't remember anything about it. I mean I must have *seen* it, but I have no memory of it. But I do remember everyone kept asking me if I was OK.

Anyway, after he died the house filled up with people – his sister and her kids who we hardly ever saw. Men in suits we'd never seen at all. And Rupert. Our half-brother. That's the first real memory I have of him.

CUT TO: Maura Howard, sitting room at Dorney Place. She's 35 now, slender, well-groomed in a shabby chic sort of way. She's wearing a pale turquoise shirt, long silver earrings and a matching pendant. She has the confident manner of her class but seems fragile all the same; there are dark circles under her eyes and she fidgets with her necklace as she speaks.

<u>MAURA HOWARD</u>

Rupert would have been 19 then. Still at school, technically, but only because he was 'doing Oxbridge'—

<u>GUY HOWARD – off</u>

For our American viewers, that's sitting the entrance exams for Oxford and Cambridge, so staying on an extra term.

<u>MAURA HOWARD</u>

Right. Anyway, he was still way out of our league and patronizing the arse off us, for no other reason than because he could. Not that I realized that at the time. I just thought he was 'sophisticated'. Mum only ever used that word about people she approved of.

(laughs)

But maybe it was just the tie.

I do remember envying Rup – that he was going to university and not having to live at home and get told what to do all the time. He'd passed that magic line that separates kids from grown-ups.

(takes a breath)

And of course he was a pall-bearer. For Dad. Son and heir, and all that.

(looks directly at Guy then turns away)

CUT TO: Guy, same room, different angle.

GUY HOWARD

No one really explained to us about the funeral. I remember there was a huge row the day before between Mum and Dad's sister, Alice. I found out later that Alice didn't think we should go. That we were too young. And looking back, she was right.

The girls were 11 and 9, but I was only 6. Old enough to know something really bad had happened but way too young to process it properly. All those people in black, that weird car they took him away in, the hole in the ground. It was like one of my kids' books come to life. *The Hobbit* or something. But not in a good way.

I don't remember Rupert talking to me much. I didn't expect him to – I might have been miserable and lost and confused, but I was just a kid. I didn't matter. Why would he bother with me?

It was only years later that I realized he knew exactly what I was going through, because it had happened to him. He was the same age as me when his mother died. And that happened out of the blue, too, just like Dad. And yet he never talked to me about it. I was his brother, but he never sat me down and asked if I was OK, never even gave me a hug.

(looks down)

CUT TO: Maura.

MAURA HOWARD

Things went to shit a bit after that. The house emptied out until there was only us. Us and Mum. She'd have 'meetings' with some of the suits, and she still went out to her lunches. But there were no more parties.

She smoked a lot, had more of her 'headaches'. The staff looked after us. The housekeeper – I can't remember her name, she left soon after – and the woman who came to clean and do the laundry. Mum hated doing that so she always got someone in. Beatriz, that was her name. We liked her. I guess she spoiled us a bit. Especially Guy.

And then, of course, there was Rup. One way or another we started seeing a *lot* of Rup.

CUT TO: MONTAGE: Rupert Howard as a child – at Dorney Place, with his parents, at Eton, as a young man at Cambridge.

VOICEOVER – narrator

Rupert Howard was born in 1980, Andrew's only child with his first wife, Amanda. He was barely 6 when his mother died in a car crash. There were rumours she'd been drinking, but the official verdict was an accident caused by icy roads.

Caroline had been the Howards's au pair, and there was quite a scandal when Andrew Howard married her within weeks of his wife's death.

CUT TO: IMAGE of diary page of the Daily Mail.

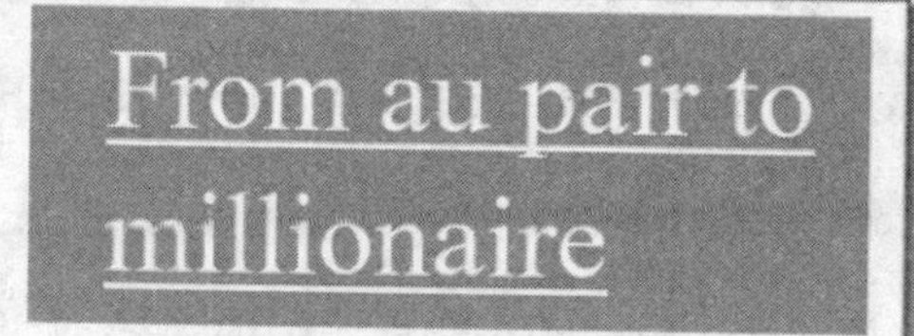
From au pair to millionaire

By JANET ARDEN FOR THE DAILY MAIL

For the daughter of a builder brought up in Hull, Caroline Farrow is certainly constructing a very desirable life for herself in one of London's most elite postcodes.

After scarcely two years working as live-in childminder to millionaire City supremo Andrew Howard, 39, the 24-year-old is set to upgrade to lady of the house.

'The wedding is set for this summer,' a source tells me. 'They are very mindful of appearances, naturally, given what a short time it's been since Amanda died.'

VOICEOVER narrator

Many people – perhaps unsurprisingly – concluded that Andrew must have been having an affair with Caroline long before Amanda died, something he always denied.

Some even suggested that the car accident may not have been an 'accident' at all. Not that they said so in public, of course. That's not how things are done in London W8.

Whatever the truth of it, the newly-weds had only been married a few months when rumours began to circulate that all was not well at Dorney Place.

Caroline told friends that Rupert was 'acting out' and 'sullen', and while Andrew seems to have made every effort to smooth things over, Rupert started spending more and more time with his mother's side of the family, and when he turned

13 he was packed off to Eton and only made occasional visits home in the holidays.

CUT TO: Rupert Howard, in a City office. He's wearing a suit and glasses, and a bright orange and red MCC tie. He looks very like his father.

RUPERT HOWARD

If you're asking me if I liked her, then no, of course I didn't *like* her. I hated her. I was very close to my mother and I resented Caroline, as fiercely and irrationally as any 6-year-old in that situation would.

Did she deserve it? Probably not. But I never warmed to her, and I never trusted her. And the older I got the more convinced I became that I was right not to.

CUT TO: Guy watching FOOTAGE of Rupert's last comments on a laptop. He smiles dryly.

GUY HOWARD

It doesn't surprise me that he said that. He's always made it pretty obvious what he thinks.

(shrugs)

I guess I might feel that way too, if I was in his position.

NICK VINCENT (Producer) – off

How are things between you two, these days?

GUY HOWARD

We don't see each other much. He wants to stand for Parliament at the next election so he spends all his time out in the wilds of Shropshire schmoozing the local Tories.

But to answer your question, we get on. We agree to disagree. Mainly by avoiding the elephant traps.

Like anything to do with the F-word.

F as in Family.

NICK VINCENT (Producer) - off

Is that why you decided not to interview him on camera yourself? Why you wanted someone else to do that?

GUY HOWARD

(shifts in his chair)

This film is about getting to the truth. And that means some aspects of it are better done by other people. Not me.

NICK VINCENT (Producer) - off

But given what you said just now about the family being an elephant trap, some people might be surprised that Rupert agreed to take part in this at all.

GUY HOWARD

You'd have to ask him. But I suspect he'd tell you he has nothing to hide.

CUT TO: Rupert.

RUPERT HOWARD

(smiles and spreads his hands)

Me? I have nothing to hide. Nothing whatsoever. I wasn't even in London the day Luke died. And before you ask, I don't feel guilty about Caroline.

(pause)

Luke, though. That's another matter. I do feel guilty about Luke. You could say the whole thing was all my fault.

CUT TO: Crime scene PHOTO, the face blurred out. The body is sprawled on its back on a flight of steps; there are cracks in some of the slabs, and a spade and several other workman's tools visible at the top left. It's obviously been raining but there's still a large blood stain around the head.

NARRATOR

Luke Ryder had been married to Caroline Howard for just over a year when he died. He was 26, and a native of Kalgoorlie, Western Australia. The only paid work he'd ever done that we know of was as a barman, first in Sydney and then in Greece.

The odds of someone like him even crossing paths with Caroline Howard were vanishingly small. And yet he did, and two years later he was dead.

No one has ever been charged with the killing of Luke Ryder. The case that gripped the public, baffled the police, and changed the lives of his three young stepchildren forever remains unsolved.

But with the twentieth anniversary of the murder now approaching, and with so many recent advances in DNA and forensics, perhaps it's time to take another look.

Perhaps it's time to bring Luke Ryder's killer to justice, and give the Howard family some closure.

CUT TO: Dining-room at Dorney Place. The team are seated around the table, along with Nick and Guy. Nick is unshaven, with shoulder-length dark hair going grey. He's wearing a blue cotton shirt, and has various beaded and plastic bracelets on his left wrist. Guy is in a black T-shirt.

There are papers and photos on the table, glasses of water, a cafetière of coffee, laptops. There's also a white-board and pinboard propped on easels; the latter has some of the images we've already seen (exterior of the house, entrance gate, family tree, etc).

CLOSE-UP as camera pans over the pictures, finishing with a series of shots of the family.

NICK VINCENT (Producer)

(looking round at those seated at the table)

And that's where you guys come in. If we're going to solve this case we need an A-team, and that's what we've got – I don't think there's any aspect of the criminal justice system we don't have covered round this table.

There are smiles, some muted laughter.

And as you can see, we're here at Dorney Place, where the murder took place. It's the first time anyone but the police or the family has had access to the house, which will give us a unique opportunity to walk the scene and maybe – after all this time – work out what actually happened that night.

(gesturing at the cafetière)

The coffee's better than at the studio, too.

(More laughter.)

And amazingly enough this is actually the first time we've all met together in the same room. So we're going to do that cringe-making thing everyone does and go round the table introducing ourselves. Perhaps you can start, Alan?

In next SEQUENCE camera moves to each team member as they speak, name and title appearing on screen.

First CLOSE-UP is on Alan. He's in a dark jacket and tie, glasses and a slightly creased white shirt; he has short salt-and-pepper hair and a thin face. He talks in a rather staccato way and seems ill-at-ease.

As he speaks there are video-only CLIPS of news items from some of his cases, with Alan speaking to camera, being questioned by the press, etc.

ALAN CANNING

I'm Alan Canning, a retired detective inspector from the Metropolitan Police, specializing in homicide. I have over thirty years' experience in criminal investigations, and I was working at the Met when this case occurred, though I never worked on that team.

Camera moves to Hugo. He's in his early fifties but doesn't look it. He's wearing a suit with wide pinstripes, a pink shirt and a spotted navy and white tie. There's a red silk moiré lining visible inside his suit jacket. He's smooth, confident, perhaps a little superior.

HUGO FRASER

I'm Hugo Fraser KC, which for those outside the UK stands for King's Counsel. It basically means I'm a senior member of the Criminal Bar in England and Wales, and I've been both defending and prosecuting offenders of all varieties since 1997.

Camera moves to Mitchell. He's in his forties, with a shaven head, glasses and a short beard which is going grey. He's in a denim shirt with a patterned silk scarf.

MITCHELL CLARKE

My name is Mitch Clarke and I'm a journalist. I've contributed articles to the national and London press for nearly twenty years.

NICK VINCENT (Producer)

Though that's not quite the whole story, is it?

MITCHELL CLARKE

(picks up a pen and starts playing with it)

No. I was also the first reporter on the scene on the night of the Ryder murder. In fact, I was there even before the police.

GUY HOWARD

And how that came to be the case is something we're going to look into in a lot more detail as we get into the investigation.

Laila?

Camera moves to Laila. She's in her late forties with olive skin, impeccable but understated make up, and short grey hair; she's wearing a green satin blouse, a silk scarf and a clutch of gold bracelets. She clearly takes a lot of care over her appearance.

LAILA FURNESS

I'm Laila Furness and I'm a forensic psychologist. I've worked alongside the Met, and at various UK prisons including Broadmoor. My speciality is serial killers.

GUY HOWARD

To be clear, there's never been any suggestion that Luke was the victim of a serial killer.

LAILA FURNESS

(nods)

You're right, there hasn't. But as the police officers among us will know, you have to assess *all* potential theories of a crime before you focus on one single line of enquiry.

BILL SERAFINI

I'd agree with that.

CAMERA MOVES to Bill. He's a big man, in every respect. Imposing physically, and with considerable presence. He has a genial demeanour but he's clearly not someone you'd want to cross. His suit is a little too small for him. He has a stars-and-stripes pin in his lapel.

BILL SERAFINI

My name is Bill Serafini, and I'm a retired NYPD detective.

MONTAGE of old photos of Bill. In uniform, receiving a medal, in plain clothes with a badge.

Murder, rape, arson, child abduction, gang crime, you name it, I've investigated it.

(smiles)

Not personally of course. I had thirty-plus years on the force and now I work as a private eye. Private investigator, as you British folks would say. Anything else you want to know, feel free to ask.

NICK VINCENT (Producer)

Thank you, Bill. And finally, JJ.

CAMERA MOVES to JJ Norton. He's in his forties, with short dark hair and glasses; he's wearing a black shirt with ornate silver tips on the collar points. There's a tattoo on the inside of his left forearm. It looks like a barcode but it's actually his DNA profile. He has a stainless steel water bottle in front of him.

JJ NORTON

I'm JJ Norton. And no, I'm not going to tell you what JJ stands for. As for the boring stuff, I dig about at crime scenes for South Wales Police, which I've been doing for the last five years. Before that, basically more of the same.

GUY HOWARD

(addressing the team)

You all know why this case is so important to me, but this is the point where it stops being 'my' case and starts being yours.

I'm making this film, but I'm not 'directing' it. Where this story goes next is down to you, and where your investigations take you. Whatever place that proves to be.

From now on, the only time I'll be in front of that camera—

(points)

—is as a witness. Or if there's some other, very good reason. And the same goes for Nick, too. It's your gig now.

CAMERA PANS round the team, and by the time it pans out again Guy and Nick have gone.

BILL SERAFINI

(looks round the table)

So - are we going to get started?

People shift in their chairs, reach for their papers. There are one or two glances between them. Evidently Bill has made an assumption of authority.

In my experience, it's always best to start a cold case review with a summary of the facts—

ALAN CANNING

I'm happy to do that—

BILL SERAFINI

(interrupting)

With respect, Alan, I think at this stage we need a fresh pair of eyes. Your input is going to be invaluable, clearly, given your knowledge of Met procedures, but right now we need a clean slate. No preconceptions.

So, how about you, JJ? This case hinges on the forensics, after all.

JJ NORTON

(wryly)

Don't they always. But happy to oblige.

(pulls his papers towards him)

OK, so what do we know?

We know that Luke Ryder was married to Caroline Howard. That they hadn't known each other very long, and the marriage had been, shall we say, 'controversial', not least in her own family.

We know that Luke was alone in the house the night he died, babysitting Guy. Caroline was at a party and the two girls were at the cinema in Notting Hill Gate.

We know that it was raining heavily by the time the police got there, but there were still some dry patches of paving under the body, suggesting the rain started *after* he fell.

Continues to speak over RECONSTRUCTION. B/w, video only. It's dark as the camera pans the garden up to the house. No windows are lit upstairs, only one or two downstairs. It starts to rain, the droplets catching the light.

CUT TO: Team. There is now a timeline on the pinboard.

Timeline – 03/10/03

PM	**8.15**	**Caroline drops off girls at cinema**
	9.05	**Caroline leaves for party**
	10.20 approx	**Starts to rain**
	10.30	**Girls arrive home, go into kitchen**
	10.45	**Maura finds body in garden**
	10.47	**999 call**
	10.52	**Maura attempts to call her mother**
	10.56	**Police and ambulance attend**

JJ NORTON

We know that the call to the emergency services was made at 10.47, by Maura Howard, and first responders attended at 10.56.

We know, from Met Office records, that it began to rain at approximately 10.20 that night, and the pathologist estimated that Luke Ryder had been dead for around an hour by the time the paramedics arrived, giving a window for time of death at between roughly 9.20 and 10.20.

We know that he had an injury to the back of his head that could have been the result of a fall. But the actual cause of death was extensive blunt-force trauma to his face and the front of his skull, and that was definitely *not* the result of a fall.

Aside from that, we know there were no signs of a break-in, and that the main entrance to the property had an entry keypad, which meant the gate would only open if the visitor knew the code, or if someone *inside* the house let them in. There were no security cameras on the street outside, however, so we don't know who came or went that evening.

So what we're left with, as I see it, and with due deference to the law enforcement professionals at this table, is a whole lot of questions.

CAMERA PANS out as he gets up and goes over to the whiteboard and picks up the pen. The board rocks slightly as he writes.

Starting with just the most obvious:

One: *Means.* The police never conclusively identified the murder weapon. Did the killer bring it with them, or was it just something seized in the garden in the heat of the moment?

Two: *Opportunity.* Who could have got into the garden that night? Was it someone Ryder knew –

someone he let in? Or someone who already knew the entry code?

It's worth noting that there was no mud inside the house and given the weather the previous few days and the state of the drive, anyone coming in from outside would have had very muddy shoes. Which makes it very unlikely that the killer went into the house. But for some reason we can only guess at, Luke went *out*side, despite the cold weather. And that's where he died.

And finally the factor I personally think is the most significant—

Three: *Motive.* Who had a reason to kill Luke Ryder, and why?

LAILA FURNESS

I agree. Motive is key. But what I'm missing in all the papers we've had on the case is any real sense of who Luke Ryder actually was. I think we need a much clearer picture of the victim before we can even start assessing who might have wanted to harm him.

BILL SERAFINI

(looking round the room)

Well, I think we can all agree on that.

Switch to NARRATIVE mode.

MONTAGE of library FOOTAGE of Australia in the mid '70s, the opening of the Sydney Opera House, people on beaches etc.

VOICEOVER - narrator

Luke Ryder was born in Kalgoorlie, Western Australia, in June 1977. His parents were Brian and Maureen Ryder, who emigrated to Australia from the south of England in the early 1970s - by no means the first Brits to go looking for sun, sea, and a new life Down Under, then or now.

But whereas most such families end up settling in the big coastal cities of Sydney, Melbourne, Adelaide and Brisbane, the Ryders found themselves in a small town in the middle of the Australian outback, a day's drive from anywhere.

MAP of Australia, slow zoom to Kalgoorlie

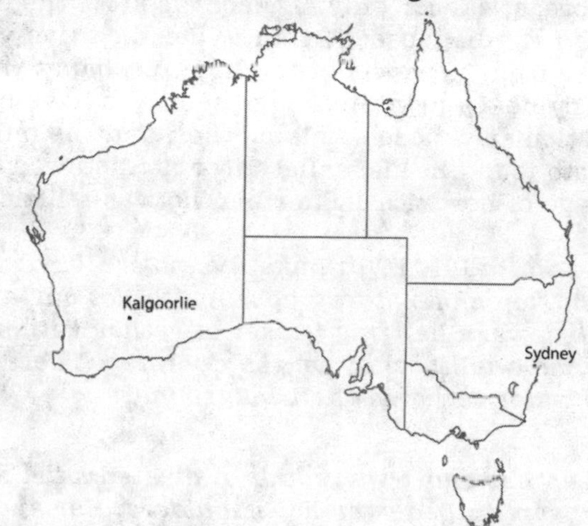

Library pictures of the town of Kalgoorlie in the '70s. Faded colour. Sparse development, old fashioned cars, men with long sideburns and moustaches drinking in bars.

<u>VOICEOVER - narrator</u>

Brian Ryder's parents were Victor and Florence Ryder, who were the owners of a thriving family business on the outskirts of Guildford. But there seems to have been a falling-out before Brian left England, possibly associated with his marriage.

Brian appears to have cut all ties with his family after he left England, and even if he'd wanted to stay in touch, long-distance telephone calls were hugely expensive at the time, so communications would have been confined to the odd letter that took weeks to arrive.

Brian had trained to be a mining engineer, which would account for the family's choice of the thriving mining town of Kalgoorlie as their new home.

But the hoped-for fresh start turned to tragedy: when Luke was eleven, Maureen Ryder succumbed to breast cancer only six months after the disease was first diagnosed. Brian Ryder died five years later from cirrhosis of the liver, probably brought on by heavy drinking. Luke seems to have been particularly close to his mother, and the only photo found in his wallet after he died was this image of her with Luke when he was a little boy.

Black-and-white PHOTO of Luke Ryder as a boy with a woman outside a one-storey house with net curtains at the windows, a hanging basket of rather withered flowers, and a milk caddy on the doorstep. There's a concrete water tower in the background.

The woman has short wavy hair, a pleated skirt and a pale cardigan draped over her shoulders. Her arm is around a small boy in a short-sleeved white shirt and short trousers.

<u>VOICEOVER – narrator</u>

At 17, Luke was left all alone in the world, with no family nearby, and no prospects: the disruption to his schooling brought on by his mother's illness had left him without any formal qualifications. All he was interested in was motorbikes, and when the family home was sold after his father's death, he took the money, bought a Ducati, and ran.

Straight to Sydney. It was 1994 and the city was just getting into its stride.

Library FOOTAGE of Sydney at the time. Bars, beaches, bikinis, and surfing; lots of surfing.

Sydney and Kalgoorlie were like night and day. The country's largest city was the fun capital of Australia, bright, colourful and buzzing – a melting pot of people from all over the world who'd brought their food, music, and culture with them. It had a lively and growing rave scene, a laidback easy-going approach to life, and – as Luke soon discovered – some of the best waves in the world.

Luke had never surfed before but he didn't let that stop him. Within a few weeks he was spending as much time as he could on the beach.

Library FOOTAGE of surfers.

It was about this time he picked up the nickname 'Easy'. Given his surname, you might have expected that would have happened a lot sooner, but life had never been exactly 'easy' for Luke in Kalgoorlie.

But now, things were different. He had a job at a local bar, he was fit, he was tanned, and he was meeting more girls in a single week than he'd done his whole time in Kalgoorlie. Life was good, life was 'easy'.

And it might have carried on that way, if he'd stayed.

But he didn't.

After a couple of years he was on the move again. First to Bali, then Cambodia and the Lebanon, and after that Greece, where he picked up bar work while island-hopping in 1999.

And that's where he met Rupert Howard.

CUT TO: Rupert, same interior/set-up as before.

RUPERT HOWARD

It was the summer after my 'A' levels, and Dad had stumped up some cash for me to go interrailing in Europe for a couple of months. It was a Thing back then. Cheap and cheerful and it felt like an adventure even though you were rarely in any sort of real danger. You met a lot of random people, lived on bad carbs and never got enough sleep. I had my first shag, my first joint, and my first pass-out drunk hangover, so it was pretty memorable all round. I'd told Dad I'd go to Italy and look at 'Art'—

(makes air quote marks)

-but somehow that never happened and I found myself in Greece, in Cephalonia to be precise. A tiny fishing village called Assos. And the first bar I walk into, there he is. Big smile, 'Hello, mate, fancy a beer?' and that was it. Friends.

For life.

(pause)

As it turned out.

MONTAGE of photos from that summer: Rupert and Luke at the bar, on a boat, drinking, smoking, laughing. There are girls in every picture, but never the same ones twice.

I went back to Eton in September to sit my Cambridge entrance and Luke stayed on in Assos. I don't remember him saying what his plans were, but things were always a bit fluid where he was concerned. I didn't hear from him and I didn't expect to. He wasn't the letter-writing type and you have to remember there was no Facebook back then. In fact, I doubt there was a single person in Assos who even had an internet connection.

The next time I saw him was in London three months later. New Year's Day. The first day of a new millennium. That's not a date you're likely to forget. Though I'd hardly been celebrating – it was only a week or two before that my father had died.

I think if Luke had turned up at any other time I'd have been pretty cool with him. I mean, we've all had holiday friendships, haven't we: they don't tend to travel well. A bit like retsina.

But what with Dad dying and the weather being crap, and everyone else having a great time except me, seeing him was just a reminder that life wasn't always that shitty.

We went out and got pissed and I paid because he didn't have any money, and then he kipped on the floor because he didn't have any money, and what started out as just a couple of nights turned into a couple of weeks. I wasn't living at Dorney Place by then – I'd never felt that comfortable there, to be honest, and it was even worse after Dad died. Hashtag 'awkward' as the kids would say now.

Anyway, after I found out I'd got into Cambridge after all (which, frankly, was as gobsmacking to me as it was to my teachers) I went off travelling again. And this time, Luke came with me.

NICK VINCENT (Producer) – off

So when did he meet Caroline?

RUPERT HOWARD

(shifts in his seat)

That wasn't till my first Christmas vac.

NICK VINCENT (Producer) – off

So that would have been December 2000.

RUPERT HOWARD

Right. She had a drinks thing on Christmas Eve she invited me to – I doubt she really wanted me there but she didn't exactly have a choice, not when all her friends were going to be there. Appearances, don't you know.

Luke was staying with me in Earl's Court so he came along too. I was surprised he wanted to, to be honest – it really wasn't his sort of thing, but then again he was never one to turn down free booze.

I thought we'd raid the bar and be in and out in an hour, but when I went looking for him around nineish I found the two of them in the kitchen. Him and Caroline. And no, before you ask, nothing was *happening*, they were just talking.

I mean really *talking*. I'd never seen him like that around girls before.

(laughs)

Though you could hardly call Caroline a 'girl'.

NICK VINCENT (Producer) – off

Had he ever shown any interest in women like that before?

RUPERT HOWARD

(raising an eyebrow)

By which you mean older women, I presume? And no, never. To be fair, you didn't tend to see women Caroline's age in the sort of places we'd hang out, and even though there'd been older women customers at the bar in Assos he'd never made much effort with them. Polite but perfunctory, if you get my drift.

NICK VINCENT (Producer) – off

So what made this so different?

RUPERT HOWARD

(spreads his hands)

Your guess is as good as mine. When he finally got round to telling me that they were seeing each other I actually laughed. I thought he was pulling my chain.

I mean, yes, she was an attractive woman. For her age. I could even have seen him having a quick fuck just because it was right there on a plate, but—

(hooks fingers in the air again)

—a 'relationship'? Actual *marriage*? No way.

NICK VINCENT (Producer) - off

How do you explain it then?

RUPERT HOWARD

(raises his eyebrows)

Search me. I don't know, maybe he had Mummy issues? After all, his mother had died when he wasn't much more than a kid.

Maybe it really was *lurve*, but I don't buy it. I never did. And of course everyone thought it was the money. That he was just a gold-digger.

NICK VINCENT (Producer) - off

And you agreed?

RUPERT HOWARD

(laughs disdainfully)

What do you think?

CUT TO: MONTAGE of images of Luke Ryder's wedding to Caroline Howard. They're artistic shots, mostly black and white, clearly done by a top-class photographer. The ceremony is in the Dorney Place garden, with chairs set in a semi-circle around a flower-covered pergola. Caroline wears a silk dress just below the knee and carries white roses. Luke is in a pale suit and open-neck shirt with a white rose in the buttonhole. He has short blond hair and he's smiling in every picture. Rupert is a rather tight-lipped best man, and Caroline's daughters appear in several shots, wearing identical bridesmaids' dresses. Their expressions are hard to read. Guy only appears in the background of one shot, kicking at a stone urn, his head turned away.

NARRATOR

Luke Ryder and Caroline Howard were married in the garden of her house in the summer of 2002, in front of a small group of family and close friends. The honeymoon was in the Maldives, and when they returned three weeks later there was nothing to suggest that the new couple weren't as blissfully happy as they appeared on the surface.

But that didn't stop the gossip.

CUT TO: Madeleine Downing, sub-captioned 'Friend of Caroline Howard'. She's late sixties, with well-styled grey hair and a grey cashmere sweater a few shades darker. She's sitting in a country-style kitchen with a rack of copper pans and dried herbs hanging over a central wooden table; there are gingham tablecloths drying on a red Aga, and a sleeping black Labrador.

MADELEINE DOWNING

Yes, people did talk. I suppose it was inevitable. I know it's become quite fashionable since, but women dating much younger men wasn't quite the thing back then. Though if you ask me most of the women who bitched about Caroline behind her back were just plain envious: Luke was very good-looking, and *really* fit – in both senses of the word. All that working out he did.

And he wasn't at all full of himself, either – he was very sweet, and very attentive. Who wouldn't want a partner like that? And as for the age difference, I just kept reminding people what Joan Collins said when she was asked about the young guy she married about the same time – 'if he dies, he dies'.

(laughs)

And in her case the age gap was thirty years or something. With Caroline it was only fourteen. That's not all that much, not these days. And in any case Luke always struck me as very mature for his age. Caroline used to call him an 'old soul'.

GUY HOWARD – off

There was speculation in the press at the time of his murder that he might have been cheating on her – that infidelity might have given her a motive to kill him. Did you ever see any suggestion of that?

MADELEINE DOWNING

Absolutely not. She certainly never said anything to me.

GUY HOWARD – off

But she did talk to you about their relationship?

MADELEINE DOWNING

Sometimes. I mean, they had the odd row, of course they did. All couples row. But she certainly never gave me any reason to believe there was anything seriously wrong.

GUY HOWARD – off

A lot of people thought he was a gold-digger. Did you?

MADELEINE DOWNING

(looks uncomfortable)

No, I didn't. I don't think money mattered that much to him. I mean – look at the way he'd been living the previous few years. Surfing, bar work – they're hardly the career choices of someone who aspires to a five-star lifestyle, now are they?

And in any case Caroline wasn't interested in swanky hotels or expensive restaurants. That sort of thing wasn't important to her.

CUT TO: Abigail Parker, sub-captioned 'Friend of Caroline Ryder'. She's in a dark suit, glasses, and a white blouse. She's evidently in her workplace: a desk, filing cabinets, a computer.

ABIGAIL PARKER

I think money was *incredibly* important to her. It was all about status. Being the 'chatelaine' of Dorney Place. Even if she did only inherit it by marriage. And quite apart from that, any building that old is always needing work done on it – roof, plumbing, just general maintenance. That house positively *ate* cash.

GUY HOWARD – off

But my father left her well-off, didn't he?

ABIGAIL PARKER

Well, yes and no. I mean, yes, compared to most people. But she had significant outgoings, like I said. And there were school fees too. Though there was no question of sending *you* to Eton; she simply couldn't afford it. Though Luke wasn't exactly a pauper. He might have been living like a beach bum but he had a big inheritance coming his way from his grandparents.

GUY HOWARD – off

Did he really? Hadn't there been a big falling-out years before? That's what Luke led people to believe.

ABIGAIL PARKER

You're right, there had. But Luke reached out to them soon after he got married. It turned out his grandfather had died a few years earlier, but his grandmother was still alive and very spry by all accounts. And given Luke was the only grandchild he could reasonably expect to inherit the lot.

I think he kept it quiet that he'd contacted her because he didn't want people to think he'd gone up there with a begging bowl. Scrounger is never a good look.

GUY HOWARD – off

But Mum knew?

ABIGAIL PARKER

Of course she knew. She was the one who encouraged him to do it in the first place.

(laughs)

In fact, you could say that if anyone was a gold-digger in that marriage, it was Caroline, not Luke.

GUY HOWARD - off

But that couldn't have been a motive for my mother to kill him, could it? If he died before his grandmother the cash wouldn't go to Mum. She wouldn't get anything. She had a vested interest in keeping him alive, at least until the old lady pegged it.

ABIGAIL PARKER

(suppressing an expression of distaste)

Well, that's one way of putting it. But yes: the inheritance couldn't have been a motive. And that was no doubt what the police concluded, too.

CUT TO: MONTAGE of pictures of Luke and Caroline: at the wedding, on honeymoon on the beach, in the garden at Dorney Place, with Guy and his sisters. None of the children is smiling. Camera zooms out and we realize these photos are scattered across the table in front of the team.

BILL SERAFINI

So, I think we can all agree the picture's more complex than we thought?

LAILA FURNESS

And Luke is a far more complex personality, too. Having lost his mother so young and his father soon after, I suspect he was struggling with a lot of unresolved issues around grief and abandonment. But on the surface he appears to have been remarkably care-free and easy-going.

BILL SERAFINI

As well as remarkably good at falling on his feet. Sounds to me like he had a talent for reading people. Working out who to gravitate to.

HUGO FRASER

Who to use, you mean. What you're describing is a self-centred manipulator, and a pretty blatant one at that. And he was all the more effective at it for the baby face and looking like he didn't care.

ALAN CANNING

He certainly seems to have 'managed' Rupert into footing most of his bills.

JJ NORTON

So maybe there were other people he'd come across who weren't so accommodating. People who thought they'd been, in Hugo's word, 'used'?

ALAN CANNING

Never underestimate the power of money as a motive for murder. If thirty years' experience of policing have taught me anything, it's that.

And of course, if he was killed by someone he knew - someone he'd pissed off - it would explain how they got access to Dorney Place that night.

HUGO FRASER

What more do we know about Ryder's associates? Presumably we'd only be looking at people he encountered in London. That can't be a very big cohort.

LAILA FURNESS

(sifting through her copy of the case file)

There's very little here that I can see. Three or four people came forward in response to the police appeal, all of whom were cleared. The police don't seem to have unearthed anyone else of any significance.

HUGO FRASER

Well, if you'd been swindled by a murder victim you'd hardly come forward to the boys in blue, now, would you? You'd be offering yourself up as a suspect.

BILL SERAFINI

But it's something we need to look into, for sure. A young guy his age must have had more acquaintances than just this list - drinking buddies if nothing else.

We need to find those people.

JJ NORTON

I don't disagree, but in my opinion, our first priority should be the forensic evidence. Talking my own book, I know, but we need to know more about the injuries, what that tells us about the weapon, and what we might be able to deduce from that about the assailant.

Did he know his killer, as seems likely given where the murder took place? And if he did, was it a premeditated attack or a moment of impulsive violence? And either way, what lay behind it - anger, passion, jealousy, revenge, what?

General nods and murmurs of agreement round the table.

BILL SERAFINI

OK, I suggest we start by expanding on the timeline for that day - who was at Dorney Place and when, just to get that all straight in our minds. And then get you to take us through the forensics, JJ - does that work for you?

JJ NORTON

Sounds good.

CAMERA TRACKS Bill as he gets up and pins up a map and a second sheet of paper next to the existing time-line.

BILL SERAFINI

OK, so this is what the earlier part of that day looked like in Dorney Place.

Timeline – 03/10/03

AM	8.35	Caroline leaves to drive Guy to school; girls go on foot
	9.00	Cleaner arrives (Beatriz Alves)
	9.15	Caroline returns to the house
	11.15	Caroline leaves for lunch
PM	2.00	Alves leaves
	2.45	Caroline returns from lunch
	3.30	Caroline leaves to collect dry-cleaning, pick up Guy
	4.15	Girls return from school
	4.45	Girls leave for party
	7.00	Girls leave party and return by 7.15, have pizza

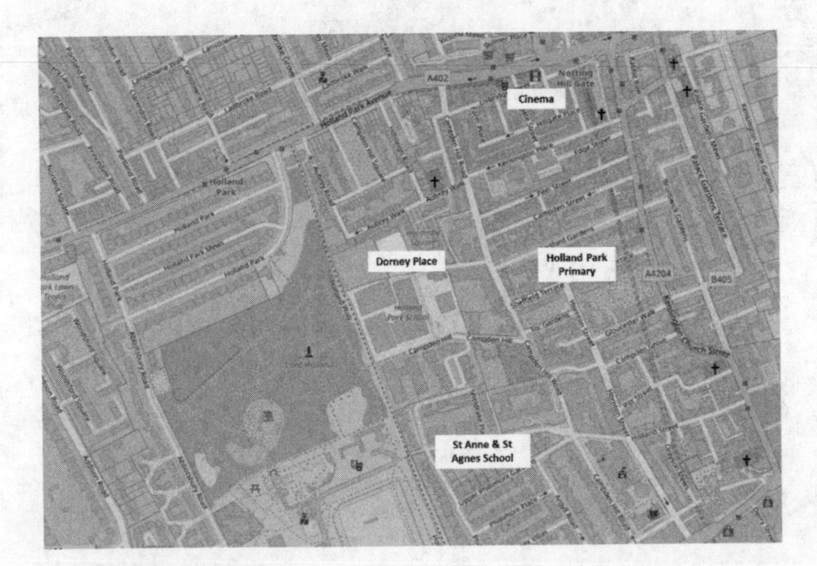

BILL SERAFINI

October third was a Friday, so all three kids were at school. Caroline drove Guy to Holland Park Primary, while the girls walked to their own school, which was three blocks away in Bicester Street—

ALAN CANNING

It's pronounced 'Bister'.

BILL SERAFINI

Really? I never can get my head round the way you folks mess with the English language.

(realizes what he's just said and smiles)

I guess that's what you Brits call irony, huh?

Anyway, they all left Dorney Place around 8.35 a.m., leaving Luke alone in the house.

JJ NORTON

Do we know if anyone came round or called during that time?

BILL SERAFINI

The cleaning woman, Beatriz Alves, arrived at just gone nine, but she told the police she didn't see anyone come to the house between then and when she left at two.

She also didn't notice anything out of the ordinary in Luke's manner - she said he was polite but not particularly chatty, which was apparently par for the course. He certainly didn't seem upset or agitated. Not according to her, at least.

HUGO FRASER

Which suggests to me he either wasn't expecting anyone to come to the house that evening, or if he was, he certainly wasn't expecting it to turn nasty.

BILL SERAFINI

Right. And of course the police checked the LUDs for the house—

LAILA FURNESS

Sorry - LUDs - what's that?

BILL SERAFINI

Apologies - it's just shorthand for phone records. In the US, at least. Though judging by the looks on your faces, evidently not here.

ALAN CANNING

So what calls were made to the house that day?

BILL SERAFINI

Two.

Picks up a marker pen and adds handwritten notes to the timeline.

One was at 9.46 a.m., and lasted one minute twenty seconds; the number was listed to a local dry-cleaning firm, who later confirmed that they'd called to say Caroline's cleaning was ready to collect. Luke answered the phone, and again, he apparently seemed perfectly normal.

The second call was at 2.37 p.m., and lasted two minutes thirty-three seconds, and was from a payphone. The police established that the phone in question was on the King's Cross station concourse, but were never able to identify the caller.

HUGO FRASER

That's too long for a wrong number.

BILL SERAFINI

I agree.

LAILA FURNESS

Was Luke alone in the house at the time?

BILL SERAFINI

Good question, hold that thought.

Meanwhile, back to the timeline: Caroline comes back from dropping off Guy at school at 9.15, then is in the house until 11.15, when she goes out to run some errands and then go for lunch. She confirmed that Luke was in the house that whole time, and, again, seemed perfectly normal. Nor did Beatriz Alves notice any tension between them, but she probably wasn't in the same room very much, since she was cleaning and doing laundry.

(turns to the timeline again)

Caroline gets back from lunch at around 2.45; again, Luke seemed fine, and certainly doesn't mention the mystery call from King's Cross station. She goes out again at 3.30, first to collect her dry cleaning, which was confirmed by the police, and then pick up Guy from school.

In the meantime Maura and Amelie get back home around 4.15, and get changed before heading out to a party thing at one of their friend's.

LAILA FURNESS

(smiling)

'Party thing'? I can tell you don't have kids.

BILL SERAFINI

(grinning back)

Is it that obvious? Anyway, there were a dozen or so girls at this whatever-you-call-it, and Maura and Amelie were there until around 7.

CAMERA TRACKS Bill as he turns and pins up a series of PHOTOS next to the timeline; Maura and Amelie are shown with several other teenage girls in a bedroom: fairy-lights around a mirror, a dressing-table stacked with make-up and nail varnish, a dreamcatcher on the wall, a scatter of brightly coloured cushions just visible on the bed.

The girls are making faces at the camera, striking poses, and taking turns wearing a pink Stetson, a lime-green feather boa, and various pairs of high-heeled shoes while they experiment with different make-up and hairstyles. They're obviously having a whale of a time.

The girls get back to Dorney Place around 7.15, and have pizza in the kitchen with Luke and Guy.

HUGO FRASER

Who have presumably been at home that whole time.

BILL SERAFINI

Yeah, either in the garden or watching TV inside. There'd been heavy rain that morning but it was sunny in the afternoon, and Luke played cricket in the garden with Guy for an hour or so. At least until it got dark.

LAILA FURNESS

Sounds like Caroline wanted the two of them out from under her feet. Especially if she was going out that evening.

BILL SERAFINI

Maybe. Apparently Luke had been intending to go to the party *with* her, but changed his mind at the last minute. We know that from Caroline's statement to the police, and it was also confirmed by Beatriz Alves, who was supposed to babysit but got a call from Caroline's cell at 8.30 that night telling her not to come after all.

HUGO FRASER

So it's possible Luke changed his mind about going out as a result of that mystery call from King's Cross?

BILL SERAFINI

Yup.

(gesturing at the timeline for the evening)

Like I said, Caroline took the girls to the movies in Notting Hill at around 8.15, then came back to find her husband in the sitting room watching TV, at which point he tells her he's not going to the party after all.

LAILA FURNESS

And that was OK with her?

BILL SERAFINI

(shrugs)

Evidently. She gets changed, comes down just after 9, at which point he's still watching TV and having a beer. And that's the last time she sees her husband alive—

JJ NORTON

According to her.

BILL SERAFINI

(nodding meaningfully)

According to her.

LAILA FURNESS

And what does Guy remember about that evening? I mean, I've read the transcript of the interview the police did at the time but I just wondered if he's remembered anything else since – given he was the only other person in the house when Luke was killed.

BILL SERAFINI

(looking past the camera)

You want to pick that one up, Guy?

CAMERA TRACKS Guy who comes round into shot and takes a seat. He leans forward, elbows on his thighs.

GUY HOWARD

To answer your question, Laila, no, I haven't remembered anything else. I know I played cricket with Luke in the garden that afternoon. He was rubbish, incidentally, especially for an Aussie, which always pissed me off because it meant he never wanted to play for very long.

And then we had the pizza. It wasn't a school night so Mum'd said I could stay up until ten because there was something I wanted to watch on TV, but Luke sent me to bed at 9.30.

(gives a wry smile)

I didn't even get to see the end of my programme.

HUGO FRASER

Did he say if he was expecting someone? Is that why he wanted you out of the way?

GUY HOWARD

No, and I don't know, in that order.

JJ NORTON

Did you hear anything after that? The doorbell? Voices?

GUY HOWARD

No, nothing. The next thing I remember was being woken up by Mum and the house being full of people.

BILL SERAFINI

(checking the file)

Which according to the police, would have been just after midnight.

HUGO FRASER

(studying the two timelines)

So based on what we've just heard, the time of death narrows to between 9.35, after Guy went up to bed, and 10.20, when it started raining.

BILL SERAFINI

Exactly.

JJ NORTON

So what happened when the girls got home?

BILL SERAFINI

Why don't we ask them?

CUT TO: Maura Howard, as before, in the sitting room of Dorney Place.

MAURA HOWARD

We got back around 10.30. The lights were all on and nothing seemed weird or anything.

GUY HOWARD - off

The main gate was shut?

MAURA HOWARD

Yes.

GUY HOWARD - off

And the front door was definitely locked?

MAURA HOWARD

Of course it was - there's no way we wouldn't have noticed that. But I had a key so we didn't ring the bell, just went in.

GUY HOWARD - off

Again, there was no sign of anything being wrong?

MAURA HOWARD

No, not at all. We went to the kitchen to get a Coke, and then I headed out to my room—

GUY HOWARD - off

The one above the old stable block - the one Mum had when she started working for Dad.

MAURA HOWARD

Right.

GUY HOWARD - off

So what happened next?

MAURA HOWARD

(taking a deep breath)

I found him. I mean, I knew something was wrong, as soon as I went outside. I could see - it.

(swallows and looks away)

I knew it was a body. It was raining really hard and it wasn't easy to see, but I still knew.

GUY HOWARD - off

What did you think had happened?

MAURA HOWARD

I'm not sure I was thinking much, right then.

(shrugs)

I guess if I was thinking anything it was that someone had fallen on the steps. Mum was always going on about how they were dangerous and what with it raining—

GUY HOWARD - off

Did you recognize him? Did you know it was Luke?

MAURA HOWARD

(shaking her head)

No. Not to start with. It just looked like a bloke. A bloke in black. It wasn't till I got closer that I realized it was him.

GUY HOWARD - off

You could tell, even in the dark and in the state the body was in?

MAURA HOWARD

It wasn't that—

She stops and looks down; she's visibly distressed and breathing hard, trying to compose herself. After a few moments she starts to speak again, but doesn't look up.

It was the clothes. I recognized the jacket. The black denim one. It had a silver logo thing on the collar. It was the one Mum bought for him.

GUY HOWARD - off

So what happened next?

MAURA HOWARD

I ran. Or at least I wanted to but my legs were all numb and I kept slipping in the mud. As soon as I got inside I called out for Amelie and told her to check on you. I was worried something might have happened to you as well.

GUY HOWARD - off

And then you called 999?

MAURA HOWARD

(hesitates then nods)

Right. And shut the doors. In case whoever it was had attacked him was still outside.

GUY HOWARD - off

You called Mum as well?

MAURA HOWARD

I rang her mobile but she didn't pick up. And then the police arrived and everything went to shit.

For, like, *forever*.

(looks away)

CUT TO: Team.

LAILA FURNESS

Poor kid. She was only 15 at the time. That's no age to have your life turned upside down.

HUGO FRASER

That mention of Caroline's mobile started me thinking - I assume Luke must have had one too.

Were there any odd calls either to or from either of them that day?

BILL SERAFINI

(shaking his head)

Nothing the police couldn't account for.

(looks round the room)

So, any other questions at this stage? No? In which case I think it's over to you, JJ.

CAMERA SWITCHES to JJ who opens his file and starts laying out PHOTOS from the crime scene on the table. Some of the pictures have already been shown: close-ups around the body showing blood spill (the clothes are clearly visible but the facial features have been blurred for camera); new wider-angle views show the body in relation to the house.

JJ NORTON

So as we can see, Ryder was wearing the black denim jacket Maura just referred to. Also jeans, a T-shirt, a pair of black loafers, and a Breitling Avenger watch that Caroline had given him as a wedding present.

HUGO FRASER

(appreciatively)

Nice piece.

JJ NORTON

And if it looks familiar that's because Caroline gave exactly the same model to Guy as a twenty-first birthday present.

He taps his keyboard and a body map appears on the screen.

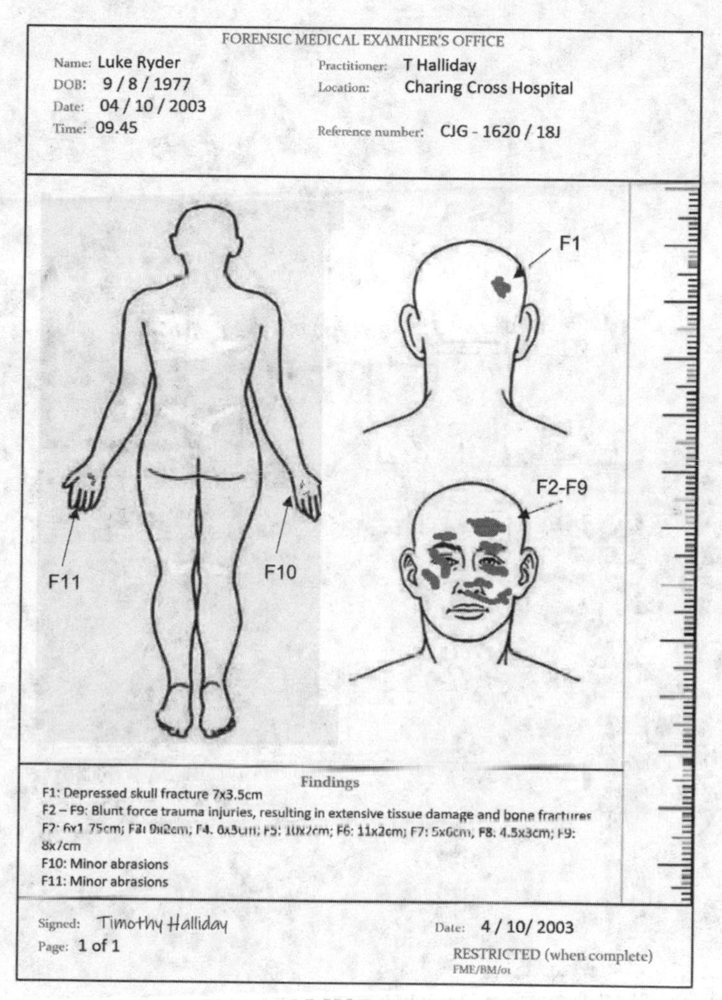

FORENSIC MEDICAL EXAMINER'S OFFICE

Name: Luke Ryder
DOB: 9 / 8 / 1977
Date: 04 / 10 / 2003
Time: 09.45

Practitioner: T Halliday
Location: Charing Cross Hospital
Reference number: CJG - 1620 / 18J

Findings

F1: Depressed skull fracture 7x3.5cm
F2 – F9: Blunt force trauma injuries, resulting in extensive tissue damage and bone fractures
F2: 6x1.75cm; F3: 9x2cm; F4: 6x3cm; F5: 10x2cm; F6: 11x2cm; F7: 5x6cm; F8: 4.5x3cm; F9: 8x7cm
F10: Minor abrasions
F11: Minor abrasions

Signed: Timothy Halliday
Page: 1 of 1

Date: 4 / 10/ 2003
RESTRICTED (when complete)
FME/BM/01

JJ NORTON

OK, so to recap, the body was found at approximately 22.45, and at that point Ryder had been dead for around an hour. We're going to go outside shortly and see for ourselves, but if you look at this diagram here—

(turns to site plan)

—you can get a sense of the lie of the land.

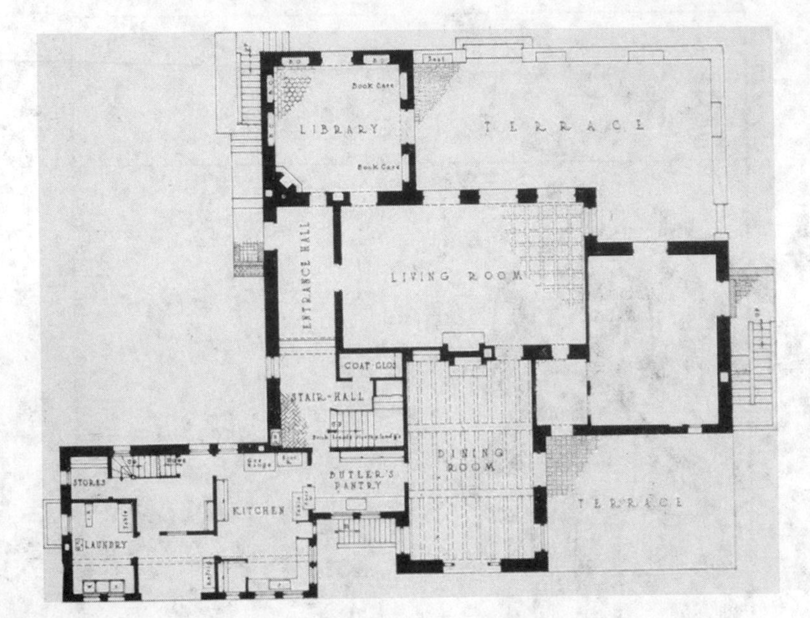

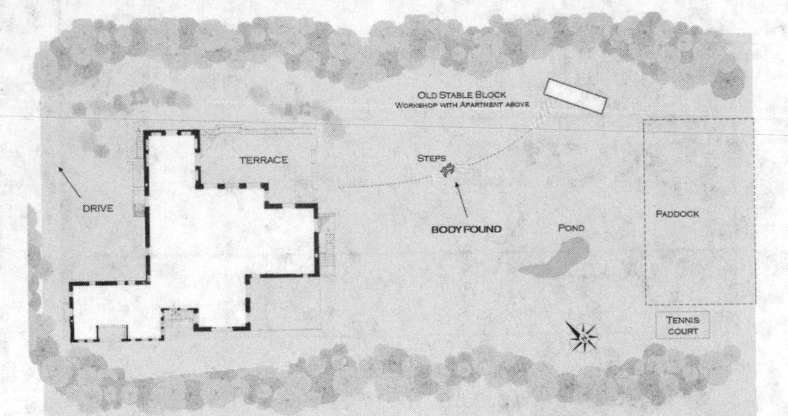

<u>JJ NORTON</u>

There's a tennis court *here*, a paddock *here*, and these buildings along *here* are the old stable block, which the Howards converted into a workshop and storage. That's where Ryder kept his motorbike.

The lofts above had been knocked together into a self-contained apartment for Caroline when she first started work for the Howards as their au pair, and as we've just heard, by the time of the murder Maura Howard had moved into those rooms.

There's actually quite a steep slope away from the house towards the stable block which you obviously can't tell from this, but that's why there are those flights of steps - the garden is basically laid out in terraces.

(puts down the plan and looks round)

As I said earlier, there was no evidence that the assailant was ever inside the house, and the doors were all locked when the girls got home. Nor were any identifiable footprints found in the garden - the weather saw to that.

ALAN CANNING

And in any case, it was October, the weather was bad and it was only 8° - anyone coming to the house could quite easily have been wearing gloves and a mack, and that would have all but eliminated any DNA transfer, even without the rain. And being dressed like that wouldn't have aroused any suspicion either, not given the weather.

JJ NORTON

So either Ryder realized there was an intruder in the garden and went outside to investigate, which seems rather unlikely, or the person was someone Ryder knew—

MITCHELL CLARKE

Like the cryptic King's Cross man. Or woman—

JJ NORTON

—and for some reason Luke didn't want to let them in the house and elected to talk to them outside, despite the weather.

LAILA FURNESS

That's not so odd, though, is it? The absolute earliest he could have been killed was just after nine thirty, and by that time he must have known Maura and Amelie could be back any minute. If he *was* meeting someone even remotely suspect, I can easily see him wanting to keep that fact from the girls.

BILL SERAFINI

(nodding meaningfully)

Especially if he didn't want *Caroline* to find out. The girls wouldn't keep anything shady from her – especially if they could use it to get back at Luke.

LAILA FURNESS

Exactly.

HUGO FRASER

But on the other hand, Luke kept the motorbike in the workshop, which would have been reason enough on its own for him to be in the garden, whether he was expecting someone or not.

JJ NORTON

In theory, yes, but he kept that workshop padlocked and when they found him he didn't have the key on him – it was still in the house. Which pretty much eliminates any possibility that he was ambushed on his way out to work on the bike.

And just for the record, none of the tools from the workshop were missing, and none bore any trace of blood or biological material.

LAILA FURNESS

Which brings us to the possible weapon.

JJ NORTON

Right.

He starts to hand out the autopsy images; the details are blurred to camera.

These aren't for the faint-hearted, that's for sure. As you can see, there's an injury to the back of the head which was definitely serious enough to have knocked him out, and also some minor abrasions to the hands consistent with a fall down stone steps. But the damage to the face and the front of the skull could not possibly have been accidental.

BILL SERAFINI

(scanning the images)

This was sustained and it was brutal.

JJ NORTON

(going up to the body map and pointing)

There were eight separate and distinct blows to the face, which were unquestionably the cause of death. Brain matter was clearly visible at autopsy.

LAILA FURNESS

Classic overkill. That's not random. It's personal. *Very* personal.

MITCHELL CLARKE

All the more so if Luke was already out cold – that rules out any element of self defence. The killer must have really wanted him dead.

HUGO FRASER

So if the weapon wasn't one of Luke's tools, what did the police think it was?

JJ NORTON

They weren't able to identify it conclusively. Either something similar to a hammer that he brought with him, or something random like a lump of rock or broken paving from the garden.

And as you can see from the photos, the repair work being done on the steps meant there was indeed quite a lot of broken paving to choose from at the time.

MITCHELL CLARKE

It's quite tough to walk round London with a hammer under your jacket without anyone noticing. Just saying.

JJ NORTON

Right. And I think that's why the police tended more towards the rock theory. But if that's what it was, the rain put paid to any chance of identifying it.

BILL SERAFINI

(working through the crime scene photos)

What you said about the repairs - I assume everything being used for that work was tested? Shovels and the like?

JJ NORTON

Absolutely.

HUGO FRASER

(looking at the plan)

There's a large pond only a few yards away, which to my mind has 'disposal site' written all over it. Especially if the weapon was just random garden detritus.

JJ NORTON

Right, and yes, the pond was drained at the time. The bottom was lined with chunks of rubble and broken slabs, so another random chunk would have been next to impossible to identify, even at the best of times. But with all that water it was absolutely a non-starter, in evidentiary terms.

LAILA FURNESS

Was there any debris in the wounds or hair that would tally with the rock theory?

JJ NORTON

Good question. The answer is yes, but not enough to be definitive. Given the victim was outside and had fallen down several steps there was always going to be a degree of contamination.

ALAN CANNING

The point about the rock theory, surely, is that a woman could wield something like that just as easily as a man.

BILL SERAFINI

(nodding meaningfully)

And Caroline was only twenty minutes' walk away.

LAILA FURNESS

Did the friends she was with say whether she slipped out at any point?

BILL SERAFINI

'Not that they noticed'.

But it was drinks, not dinner, so people weren't seated. There were also at least thirty or forty guests, so it wouldn't necessarily have been obvious if she'd disappeared for a short time.

LAILA FURNESS

But by the time she got back to the party it would have been pouring down – she'd have been pretty wet. Not to mention covered in blood. Surely someone would have noticed that.

BILL SERAFINI

Which is precisely what her lawyers said to the detectives on the case. But we're going to try to run down some of the people who were there that night, to see if they might be willing to talk to us.

HUGO FRASER

(making notes on a yellow legal pad)

So as at now, our list of suspects looks like this.

Caroline – the most obvious, given that murders of this nature are invariably the work of an intimate partner. *But* she had a fairly decent alibi, as well as no apparent motive. None, at least, that has yet been uncovered.

Rupert – likewise has no obvious motive, and also insists he wasn't in London, though I think we'd be advised to double-check that.

And last but not least our mystery King's Cross caller, who was never identified, far less found.

But if there really was someone out there who had a big enough grudge to want to kill Ryder, we're going to have to look damn hard, because the police don't seem to have found them.

(looks round the table)

I mean, frankly, who else is there?

(silence)

MITCHELL CLARKE

(looking up)

Me.

FADE OUT

– end credits –

Wrap-up email from Nick Vincent, 6th April 2023, 10.11a.m.

Date: Thu 6/04/2023, 10.11

From: Nick Vincent

To: Guy Howard, Hugo Fraser, Alan Canning, Mitch Clarke, Laila Furness, Bill Serafini, JJ Norton

CC: Tarek Osman, Fabio Barry, Dry Riser production team

Subject: Ep 1 wrap-up and next steps

Just to say thanks again for managing to keep the big reveal about Mitch under your hats until the last frame. Nothing like a cliff-hanger to keep 'em watching. But from now on, if something comes up during filming you didn't already know about, just come right out and say so. All adds to the drama!

We film again on the 17th, and obviously the main focus this time will be on Mitch, and how he found himself in the frame. In the meantime we've set up an i/v for Alan and Bill with Peter Lascelles, the original lead investigator. He's long retired but by all accounts still sharp. He was in two minds about doing it when we last spoke, but looks like he's agreed now. He lives in Devon now, so it will probably involve a jaunt down south.

As ever, any questions, just give me a shout

Nick

Date: Fri 7/04/2023, 14.05 **Importance:** High

From: Tarek Osman

To: Fabio Barry, Mel@MediumRare.com

Subject: Visuals for Ep 2

As discussed, I've attached some stills Mitch has given us from around 2003. As predicted the Met are refusing to release footage/transcript of any of his police interviews, so we're going with plan B and filming reconstructions.

I've also tracked down some more news footage of the original investigation though of course none of that features Mitch.

Best,

Tarek

Text messages between Amelie and Maura Howard, 7th April 2023, 7.33 p.m.

How's it been?

Like I expected, I guess. Weird going back in the house tho

?? You've been there for months

In my own room, yes. Not the house. It's like a fucking time warp in there. Seriously

Your room is just like it was the day you left. Guy's is the same

It's freaking me out

What about the interviews?

They've been rehashing a lot of that stuff about Mum and Amanda. The crash

What's that got to do with anything?

Guy says it's 'context' 😏

But I guess it was always going to be part of it. And who bloody cares now anyway, after all this time?

Easy for you to say

Look, I know that I'm doing OK? It'll be fine I promise

I don't think Rup's exactly covering himself in glory btw

Covering his arse more like

Twat

Yup. As per. So you just chill OK? Everything's under control

Episode one

Broadcast

October 3

The Times, 4 October 2023

TELEVISION

The mysterious affair at Dorney Place

Can Showrunner's new series finally solve an infamous crime?

ROSS LESLIE

Infamous: Who Killed Luke Ryder?
Showrunner

English Mystics: Samuel Palmer
BBC4

Showrunner's new season kicked off last night with a new series of **Infamous**, this time focusing on a genuinely 'infamous' cold case from 2003. The brutal murder of 26-year-old Australian Luke Ryder took place in Campden Hill, only a few miles from where I was living – fresh from university – at the time. I still remember the anxiety the killing generated, especially for my female housemates.

There were hundreds of officers on the investigation at the time, and it's hard to believe every possible lead wasn't checked and rechecked. There have been a number of true-crime documentaries about the case since, none of which has offered anything new. But now, prompted by the 20th anniversary of the murder, we have Who Killed Luke Ryder? directed by the victim's stepson, Guy Howard, which gives the production unprecedented access to both the family and the murder scene. If anyone can unearth something, he can.

Unlike previous series of the Infamous franchise, Who Killed Luke Ryder? also adopts a new format, bringing experts together to re-examine the case in 'real-time'. True crime reality TV, if you like. Judging by the cliffhanger at the end of last night's opening episode, it certainly shows promise.

The second episode of **English Mystics** focused on the 19th-century painter Samuel Palmer

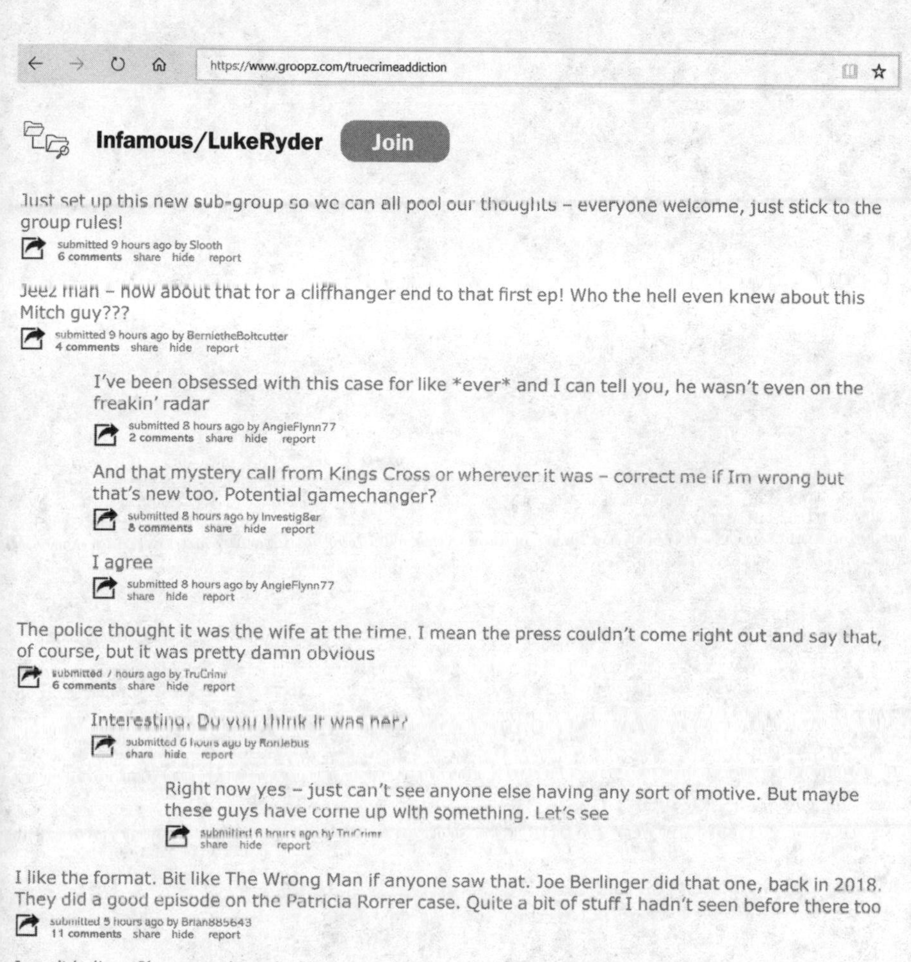

https://www.groopz.com/truecrimeaddiction

Infamous/LukeRyder Join

Just set up this new sub-group so we can all pool our thoughts – everyone welcome, just stick to the group rules!

submitted 9 hours ago by Slooth
6 comments share hide report

Jeez man – how about that for a cliffhanger end to that first ep! Who the hell even knew about this Mitch guy???

submitted 9 hours ago by BerniethеBoltcutter
4 comments share hide report

> I've been obsessed with this case for like *ever* and I can tell you, he wasn't even on the freakin' radar
>
> submitted 8 hours ago by AngieFlynn77
> 2 comments share hide report
>
> And that mystery call from Kings Cross or wherever it was – correct me if Im wrong but that's new too. Potential gamechanger?
>
> submitted 8 hours ago by InvestigBer
> 8 comments share hide report
>
> I agree
>
> submitted 8 hours ago by AngieFlynn77
> share hide report

The police thought it was the wife at the time. I mean the press couldn't come right out and say that, of course, but it was pretty damn obvious

submitted 7 hours ago by TruCrimr
6 comments share hide report

> Interesting. Do you think it was her?
>
> submitted 6 hours ago by RonJebus
> share hide report
>
> > Right now yes – just can't see anyone else having any sort of motive. But maybe these guys have come up with something. Let's see
> >
> > submitted 6 hours ago by TruCrimr
> > share hide report

I like the format. Bit like The Wrong Man if anyone saw that. Joe Berlinger did that one, back in 2018. They did a good episode on the Patricia Rorrer case. Quite a bit of stuff I hadn't seen before there too

submitted 5 hours ago by Brian885643
11 comments share hide report

I can't believe I've never heard of this case before! Absolutely fascinating. And that house! OMG! Never even knew there were houses like that right in the middle of London. How much is that sort of pile even worth? $$$$

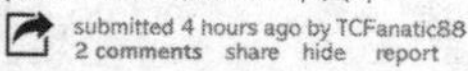

submitted 4 hours ago by TCFanatic88
2 comments share hide report

> Follow the money. Just sayin
>
> submitted 4 hours ago by TruCrimr
> share hide report
>
> > I agree. Has to be a factor. With one hell of a capital F
> >
> > submitted 3 hours ago by Brian885643
> > share hide report

Episode two

Filming

DRY RISER FILMS Ltd
227 Sherwood Street London W1Q 2UD

CAST	CALL SHEET	
Alan Canning (AC) Mitchell Clarke (MC) Hugo Fraser (HF) Laila Furness (LF) JJ Norton (JJN) Bill Serafini (WS)	**Infamous: Who Killed Luke Ryder?** Monday 17th April 2023	Producer **Nick Vincent** Director **Guy Howard** Film editor **Fabio Barry** Researcher **Tarek Osman** Prod asst **Jenni Tate** Location manager **Guy Johnson**
UNIT CALL 0845 *Camera ready: 0915*	**Ep 2: ON-SITE** **DAY 1 of 3**	*Breakfast on set from 0830* *Running lunch from 1245* *Exp wrap 1730*
Sunrise 0559 *Sunset 1950* *Weather forecast 3°, cloud*		***Cast note:** Outside shots to film first, dress appropriately*

Location:	Notes:
Dorney Place **2 Larbert Road** **Campden Hill London W8 0TF**	*Some parking on site – must be reserved in advance* *Nearest tube Holland Park* *Emergency contact number 07000 616178*

CREW							
TITLE	NAME	PHONE	CALL	TITLE	NAME	PHONE	CALL

TITLE SEQUENCE: arthouse-style b/w montage of images and short clips: crime scene, contemporary news coverage, family photos

THEME SONG – 'It's Alright, Ma (I'm Only Bleeding)' [Bob Dylan] from the soundtrack to 'Easy Rider' [1969]

TITLE OVER

INFAMOUS

FADE IN

WHO KILLED LUKE RYDER?

FADE OUT

BLACK FRAME, TEXT APPEARS, with VOICEOVER – narrator (female)

October 3, 2003: Luke Ryder's badly beaten body is found by his 15-year-old stepdaughter in the garden of his wife's home, in an upscale district of west London.

There was no one else in the house, no signs of a break-in, nothing had been stolen and there was no apparent motive for the brutal attack.

As far as the public were concerned, the police were making little progress.

What they didn't know was that a man had been taken in for questioning within hours of the body being found.

That man's name was Mitchell Clarke.

FADE OUT

CUT TO: team standing outside the gate of Dorney Place. The weather is cloudy but clear and obviously cold for April, as they're all in coats and scarves.

BILL SERAFINI

So, Mitch, the end of the last episode was probably a real shock for our viewers. Why was this never made public at the time, do you know?

MITCHELL CLARKE

Well, I was never actually arrested for the murder, and I guess the police were wary of being seen to target a black guy. Especially in that part of town. You have to remember that in 2003 the Macpherson inquiry was still pretty fresh in people's minds.

BILL SERAFINI

(to camera)

For our US viewers, this was an investigation into how the Metropolitan Police handled the murder in 1993 of a young black man called Stephen Lawrence.

The findings were published in 1998, and accused the Met of being 'institutionally racist'. That was pretty explosive at the time, right?

MITCHELL CLARKE

Absolutely.

BILL SERAFINI

So talk us through what happened to you - how did you end up involved? You were already a journalist, right, even though you were only in your early twenties?

CUT TO: MONTAGE of stories with Clarke's by-line, interspersed with images of him around the time of the murder. Images continue under Mitch's next speech, then cut back to Bill.

Black schoolboy, 14, latest victim of rising gang violence

By Mitchell Clarke

The teenager who died after a knife attack near Burnley Road on Friday night was named yesterday as Jackson Turner, 14, of Ely Close, Westbourne Park.

Turner's mother, Carol, denied that her son had been involved in any gang activity, and warned other parents in the area to keep a closer watch on their children. "Jackson was a good ... in any tr...

Teachers at Oakley Park Community College confirmed that Turner had had a good record of attendance until very recently, and staff had been expecting him to sit five GCSEs.

West London Gazette
January 2002

Opinion: What has MacPherson really changed?

By Mitchell Clarke

and until concerns like these are addressed, very little is likely to improve in the short ...

Every black man I know has been stopped and searched at least once, including several friends who were at university at the time. But that, it seems, is not how the police see us.

The Voice
June 2001

Drug and knife crime 'endemic' says Met chief

By Mitchell Clarke

Senior Met officers now accept that the level of drug and knife crime on London's streets is reaching 'almost unpoliceable' levels, sources said yesterday.

Areas of West London were singled out as being of particular concern, with racial tension and increasing levels of gang membership cited as among the principal causes.

'More effective strategy' urgently needed

Speaking at a charity event, Deputy Commissioner Fordham stressed his own and his force's commitment to giving the people of London a policing service fit for the 21st century.

The event, held at St Anne and St Agnes School, was part of a campaign to raise money for Save the Children's work in Africa.

Ladbroke Grove Evening News
March 2003

MITCHELL CLARKE

I was 21 in 2003. And I was freelance – I wasn't attached to a particular paper until a lot later. I was living in Ladbroke Grove and that's where most of my stories were coming from.

BILL SERAFINI

Ladbroke Grove's right next door to Campden Hill, but in every other respect it's very different, right?

HUGO FRASER

A world away, and even more so back then. About as poles apart as two places could be that are barely a mile from each other. You're talking drugs, violence, gun and knife crime. Not a pretty picture.

MITCHELL CLARKE

(looking at him)

And almost all of that was - and *is* - the direct result of deprivation, poor housing, even poorer education, and yes - sorry, but I have to say it - endemic *and* 'institutional' racism. Those stories need telling.

HUGO FRASER

(holding up his hands; he's wearing designer leather gloves)

Hey, I'm not disagreeing. Look at me. I'm hardly your average WASP.

BILL SERAFINI

So how did you find out about the Ryder case, Mitch? Doesn't sound like your usual beat.

MITCHELL CLARKE

It wasn't. But like many local journos I kept a watching brief on police radio traffic—

CUT TO: Library FOOTAGE of police scanner; CLOSE-UP as user tunes in, picking up snatches of police dialogue.

BILL SERAFINI

You listened in, right? To get the inside track on what was going down?

MITCHELL CLARKE

And I heard them calling a car to that address and I just had a hunch. Bad shit just doesn't happen round here.

(gestures round at the street)

I mean, look at this place.

Anyway, I had nothing else on, I was close by, so I came over on spec.

BILL SERAFINI

And what did you find when you got here?

<u>MITCHELL CLARKE</u>

Well, as you can see, the house isn't even visible from the road - it took me about five minutes just to find this bloody gate. I parked up over there, on the other side of the road, and when the squad car arrived and got buzzed in, I got out and followed them up the drive on foot.

<u>ALAN CANNING</u>

Which, of, course was unlawful—

<u>MITCHELL CLARKE</u>

Technically, yes.

<u>ALAN CANNING</u>

Not just technically. Actually. That's why you ended up—

<u>BILL SERAFINI</u>

(interrupting)

Whoa, we're getting ahead of ourselves. Go back to when you first went up the drive. The police didn't realize you were following them?

<u>MITCHELL CLARKE</u>

I guess not. It was pretty dark. And pissing down. Their windows had probably steamed up as much as mine had.

<u>BILL SERAFINI</u>

What happened next?

<u>MITCHELL CLARKE</u>

Well, why don't I show you?

CAMERA PANS to show the gates. They start to open, and the team follow Bill and Mitch up a gravel drive lined with tall hedges. It bends to the right, and after a few moments the house becomes visible. Even though we've seen numerous pictures of it before, it's still impressive.

MITCHELL CLARKE

(stopping and pointing)

The cops parked up over there, on the left, then went up to the door and rang the bell. I waited about here, where they couldn't see me. I knew there was no way anyone was going to let me in, but I figured I might still be able to see something through the windows—

BILL SERAFINI

So the curtains were open?

MITCHELL CLARKE

Right. So after they went in, I started off round the back.

They start moving again, crossing the drive to a path round the right side of the house and emerging onto the terrace at the rear. Someone can be heard to say 'wow'. The gardens stretch away before them; the old stable block and the steps where Luke's body was found are clearly visible. There's no sign of life, however, apart from two pigeons squabbling on the lawn.

LAILA FURNESS

Is there anyone living here at the moment?

BILL SERAFINI

Caroline was, until her third husband died last year. She's living in Somerset now. Maura moved back into her old room a couple of months ago, to keep an eye on the house. But otherwise, no. There's no one here.

(he turns to Mitch)

So back to 2003. What happened when you got here?

MITCHELL CLARKE

Well, it was pretty dark – the only light was from the windows and it was pouring with rain. But I could definitely see something at the foot of the steps over there. But I couldn't see what, just a dark shadow. Like a pile of old clothes.

BILL SERAFINI

Which is pretty much what Maura saw, too. Let's take a closer look, shall we?

THE CAMERA FOLLOWS as they walk across the lawn to the stone steps. The PoV is low, catching the crunch of their feet as they leave a trail of footprints in the frosty grass.

BILL SERAFINI

You must have realized pretty quickly that it wasn't just a pile of old clothes.

THE CAMERA ZOOMS in on where the body was found, then morphs slowly into a RECONSTRUCTION of the night of the murder, with the body lying in the dark and the rain, before morphing back out to daylight and the present day.

MITCHELL CLARKE

Right. It was like something out of a horror movie. The state of his face, blood everywhere. The rain coming down.

BILL SERAFINI

What happened next?

MITCHELL CLARKE

I think I just lost it for a minute, to be honest. Next thing I knew there are two coppers coming at me from the house shouting and I just turned and ran.

Some of the others exchange glances.

I know, you'd all have stood your ground, right? Told them what you were doing there? But you weren't *me* - a poor black kid from Ladbroke Grove who'd had his fill of Stop and Search—

(stops himself and takes a deep breath)

Thirty seconds later *I'm* on my back in the mud, and they're arresting me for murder.

HUGO FRASER

They arrested you there and then?

MITCHELL CLARKE

Right. Then dragged me round the front and shoved me in a police car. Meanwhile the whole bloody circus is pitching up. Ambulance, forensics, three more cop cars, the works. They just left me there, stewing, while it all went down. I didn't get processed at Notting Hill nick until gone one.

CUT TO: Maura Howard, same set-up as Ep 1.

MAURA HOWARD

I do remember something happening outside. There was suddenly a lot of shouting, and the sound of some sort of scuffle in the garden and the policewoman who'd been left to look after us didn't want us going out to look. I don't remember seeing a man. Amelie may have done – she was at the window – but I can't remember that.

CUT TO: RECONSTRUCTION, video only, no audio. High-angle down on 'Mitchell' as he is led into a police interview room by two plain-clothes officers. They show him to a seat then sit down opposite, their backs to the camera. They start to question him and things clearly get heated very quickly. Footage continues under following.

MITCHELL CLARKE

They kept me there for six sodding hours. Asking the same questions over and over again. What was I doing there, how did I get in. I told them I was a hack, told them to check out my stuff, but they weren't buying it. And then *he* arrived. Peter Lascelles. *DI* Peter Lascelles.

On the screen the two officers get up and leave, and 'Mitchell' is left alone for a few moments. He sits unmoving then leans back in his chair and looks straight up into the camera. The door opens and another man comes in. He's tall, slightly balding on top. He sits down and the questioning begins again.

MITCHELL CLARKE

And we went over it all again. Same questions, same fucking answers. He seemed to have some sort of mental block that a black man could even *be* a journalist. Started asking if I had gear on me – if I *sold* gear, if I sold gear to Ryder, if *that* was what I was doing there—

CUT BACK TO: Team in garden.

LAILA FURNESS

I don't remember anything about drugs in relation to Ryder – there was definitely nothing in the post mortem.

JJ NORTON

No, there was no mention of drugs anywhere.

LAILA FURNESS

(to Mitchell)

So why did Lascelles focus so much on that, aside from the obvious racial bias?

MITCHELL CLARKE

Search me.

ALAN CANNING

Which I assume they did? Search you?

MITCHELL CLARKE

(shifting a little uneasily)

Yes, they did.

ALAN CANNING

And your car?

MITCHELL CLARKE

Look, it was just a bit of weed. For personal use.

HUGO FRASER

So *that's* why they latched onto the drugs angle.

MITCHELL CLARKE

Right. They seemed to think I'd gone there to meet Ryder - sell him some gear - that there'd been a row and things had turned nasty—

LAILA FURNESS

You didn't have an alibi for earlier in the evening?

MITCHELL CLARKE

Unfortunately not.

LAILA FURNESS

But if there had been a 'row' and he'd ended up dead, why on earth would you have hung round afterwards? It makes no sense.

JJ NORTON

And why was the marijuana in the car and not on you, if you were planning to sell it to him?

MITCHELL CLARKE

There you have it. In a nutshell.

ALAN CANNING

Just for the record, so we're all clear. You didn't know Luke Ryder?

MITCHELL CLARKE

(turning to look at him)

No, I didn't know him.

ALAN CANNING

You'd never met him before?

MITCHELL CLARKE

No.

ALAN CANNING

Never even seen him?

MITCHELL CLARKE

No.

ALAN CANNING

But the police didn't believe you, did they?

MITCHELL CLARKE

No. They did not.

ALAN CANNING

Do you know why?

MITCHELL CLARKE

No, I don't. You'd have to ask them.

BILL SERAFINI

(looking round at the team)

Well, I guess we're going to have to do just that.

CUT TO: Bill and Alan in a car, en route to see Peter Lascelles. Bill is driving, he's wearing sunglasses and has the driver's window wound down with his elbow resting on the ledge. Alan is in a heavy coat and scarf.

BILL SERAFINI

Did you know Peter Lascelles when you were on the job?

ALAN CANNING

We worked a couple of cases together, but they were major investigations involving a huge number of people. I didn't 'know' him. Not in that sense.

BILL SERAFINI

(glancing across)

He ever talk to you about this case?

ALAN CANNING

(looking out of the window)

I was never involved in this case.

BILL SERAFINI

But that's not what I asked, is it?

ALAN CANNING

I never spoke to him about it at the time.

BILL SERAFINI

And since then?

ALAN CANNING

(not looking at him)

We spoke a while back. When he heard I was doing this show.

BILL SERAFINI

(braking hard)

Doesn't matter how often I drive in this country I can never get the hang of these traffic circle things—

ALAN CANNING

Roundabouts.

BILL SERAFINI

Best bit of advice a Brit ever gave me – he said once you're on 'em, you own 'em. You just have to remember which way round to go.

(sound of horns)

CUT TO: Bill and Alan at the door of Peter Lascelles's house. A bungalow with a path across a neat paved garden. It's windy and there's the sound of gulls. The door opens and Lascelles appears on the step. He's recognizable from the press photos seen earlier, but stooping now, and wearing glasses.

BILL SERAFINI

(taking off his shades and holding out his hand)

Mr Lascelles, Bill Serafini, formerly one of New York's finest. It's an honour to meet you, sir.

PETER LASCELLES

(shaking his hand, looking somewhat dumbfounded)

Likewise, likewise.

(nodding to Canning)

Alan.

ALAN CANNING

Nice to see you, Peter.

PETER LASCELLES

(standing to one side)

Come in, come in.

CUT TO: Bill, Alan and Peter having tea in Peter's sitting room, overlooking the back garden. Most of it is patio. There's a slightly rusted barbecue in one corner and a child's swing. The tea is in cups, and on a tray with a jug and sugar bowl.

BILL SERAFINI

So we've been talking to Mitchell Clarke.

PETER LASCELLES

I rather thought you might.

BILL SERAFINI

And he's convinced that he was targeted for purely racial reasons.

(holding up his hands)

I don't mean to disrespect you or your procedures - we've had issues of our own in the NYPD, as I'm sure you know - but it's something we just have to cover off.

PETER LASCELLES

I'm well aware that's what he thinks, and I'm not going to sit here and claim that the Met had an impeccable record back then. But in Clarke's case, it's not quite as black and white as it might seem. In any sense of the word.

BILL SERAFINI

Explain that to me.

PETER LASCELLES

Clarke told us he was a journalist, and that's right, he was. But he had a finger in a whole lot of other pies too. If you look at the sort of stories he was writing most of them were all of a piece: crime, drugs, gangs. He knew that world and he had connections in it, and he didn't just use those connections to gather raw material.

We knew full well he was a small-time drug dealer, but at that point we never caught him with enough of the stuff on him to bring a prosecution.

BILL SERAFINI

He denies supplying Luke Ryder, and as far as we can determine Luke wasn't even a user.

PETER LASCELLES

Ryder didn't have a serious habit, no, but we did find evidence to suggest he'd dabble recreationally. Cocaine mostly.

BILL SERAFINI

So you thought Mitchell was there to sell Ryder some gear. Even though he wasn't carrying any coke at the time?

PETER LASCELLES

We did, yes.

BILL SERAFINI

But Ryder had no money on him when he was found, right?

PETER LASCELLES

No, he didn't. Our theory was Clarke took it, after the killing. He had £300 on him. In fifties. Not a common combination of notes.

BILL SERAFINI

Were Ryder's prints on those notes?

PETER LASCELLES

No, unfortunately, back in 2003 the banknotes over here were still made of paper. We were never going to get anything from them.

BILL SERAFINI

But even if you're right about the supposed drug deal, the sequence of events doesn't add up, does it? If they'd arranged to meet, but it ended up in some sort of disagreement that led to Ryder's death, why would Clarke stick around until the police got there?

PETER LASCELLES

Our working hypothesis was that Clarke was going through Ryder's pockets for the cash when he saw the Howard girls arrive – they'd have been clearly visible through the drawing-room windows. He hid in the bushes, then saw Maura Howard come out and discover the body, then run back inside. He'd know the first thing she'd do was call the police, and there was no way he could get off the property without going back down the drive and scaling the gate, and that'd be far too risky: he could easily have been seen.

We believe he decided to hide in the garden, hoping to slip out when the officers' attention was elsewhere.

BILL SERAFINI

But they found him right by the body, didn't they?

PETER LASCELLES

(giving him a wry look)

Is that what he told you?

BILL SERAFINI

He says the uniform officers saw him, he ran – out of instinct – and they caught up with him on the other side of the house.

PETER LASCELLES

(shaking his head)

Didn't happen. It was one of my DCs who saw him skulking in the bushes and gave chase.

BILL SERAFINI

So you're saying he's lying?

PETER LASCELLES

(smiles dryly)

Let's just say 'recollections may vary'. And when we did the house-to-house later that night one of the neighbours reported seeing a man matching Clarke's description in a car along the street around forty minutes *before* he says he got there. But it was dark, and she didn't get a good enough look at either Clarke or the vehicle to identify him in a line-up.

BILL SERAFINI

Did you find any proof that he and Luke knew each other? That Ryder was expecting him that night?

PETER LASCELLES

No. There were no phone records to link them, no emails, nothing.

BILL SERAFINI

But it could have been Clarke calling from that payphone at King's Cross?

PETER LASCELLES

Precisely. He was unable to prove where he was at the time that call was made.

ALAN CANNING

So that's why he only got a caution for being 'found on enclosed premises'?

PETER LASCELLES

Exactly. We never had enough evidence for anything else.

(looks from one to the other and picks up his tea)

But maybe you'll have more luck.

FREEZE FRAME, then the CAMERA PANS back and we see that the whole team has been watching this footage. They're now in a studio environment with the pinboard, whiteboard, and screen set up in a high-ceilinged room with big windows and exposed brickwork painted white. It looks like a Victorian school building.

BILL SERAFINI

(turns to Mitchell)

So what do you say to what we just heard?

MITCHELL CLARKE

(shrugs)

I stand by what I said before. Every word of it. I didn't know Ryder, I never called him from that payphone or at any other time, and I wasn't in the street an hour before he died. I just went there looking for a story. And I wasn't - for the record - dealing drugs.

The reason the police found no proof of anything else was because there *was* nothing else. Period. And that's the God's honest truth.

JJ NORTON

You got your own back, though, didn't you? I mean, you put the Met through the absolute wringer on that case.

CUT TO: MONTAGE of articles written by Mitchell, some locals, some nationals.

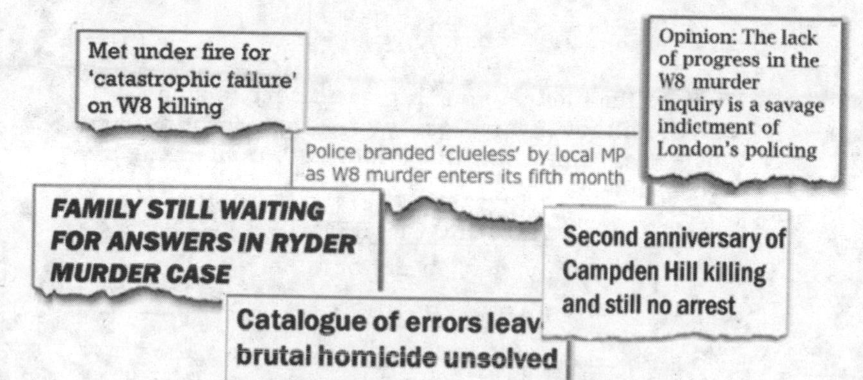
Met under fire for 'catastrophic failure' on W8 killing

Opinion: The lack of progress in the W8 murder inquiry is a savage indictment of London's policing

Police branded 'clueless' by local MP as W8 murder enters its fifth month

FAMILY STILL WAITING FOR ANSWERS IN RYDER MURDER CASE

Second anniversary of Campden Hill killing and still no arrest

Catalogue of errors leav[...] brutal homicide unsolved

JJ NORTON

(raising an eyebrow)

Best served cold, eh, Mitch?

MITCHELL CLARKE

(shrugs)

Someone has to hold the police to account.

LAILA FURNESS

So what do you think now, Mitch? After writing about this case for so long, you must have a theory about what happened.

MITCHELL CLARKE

I don't know who killed him, but I do know the police didn't look hard enough at why someone might have wanted to.

BILL SERAFINI

They didn't do enough on the victimology?

MITCHELL CLARKE

I doubt the Met even knew what that word meant back then.

LAILA FURNESS

I'm not sure that's fair—

JJ NORTON

(to Mitch)

Just so I'm clear - you think the perp is some as-yet-unknown third party? i.e., not Caroline, and not Rupert Howard? We're looking for the King's Cross Killer?

MITCHELL CLARKE

Almost certainly, yes. In my opinion.

LAILA FURNESS

(sceptically)

Really? Caroline was by far the most obvious suspect.

JJ NORTON

But there was never enough evidence to charge her, was there? Let alone convict. I'm not necessarily disagreeing with you, Laila, I'm just saying that Mitch could be right about the motive - that there was something going on in Luke's life the police never found.

LAILA FURNESS

I just think we have to eliminate Caroline - and, indeed, Rupert - before we go careering about looking for some mysterious 'UnSub' the police never identified at the time and will be even harder to track down now.

ALAN CANNING

My thoughts entirely.

BILL SERAFINI

Laila's right. That has to be where we go next.

(looking round the table)

Agreed?

(general nodding and murmurs of assent)

So, let's start with Caroline.

JJ – perhaps you could recap what we know?

JJ NORTON

With pleasure.

(opening his file)

Caroline was born Caroline Farrow in a suburb of Hull in 1963, the only child of Alan and Jane Farrow.

CUT TO: MONTAGE of photos of Caroline as a child, with her parents, on the beach, in school uniform, in a ballet class, with a group of friends at her birthday tea, wearing a party hat. She's a very pretty child, with brown hair and a bright confident smile. All her clothes are very girly.

The family was comfortably off and Caroline was sent to private school, but judging by her 'O' levels she wasn't an especially diligent student. And by the time she was 16 she'd started seeing an older man her parents didn't approve of, so they packed her off to spend the summer with her uncle in Edgbaston to get it out of her system.

She came back in September, refused to return to school, and enrolled on a course to train as a children's nanny. By the time she was 20 she was living and working in the Kensington area of London. This is the early '80s of course, and given the lapse of time we've struggled to track down anyone who knew her back then, apart from one woman she worked for briefly in 1984.

CUT TO: Ruth Cameron, sub-captioned 'Former Employer of Caroline Howard'. An elderly lady in a chintzy sitting room. Knick-knacks, potted plants, a brown Burmese cat blinking on the sofa. She has a slight American accent.

RUTH CAMERON

We always got on very well. Not the best nanny we ever had – she was too easily distracted, which is a problematic quality in a childminder. But I liked her. She was good company. Quite the talker.

We didn't keep in touch after she left but I remember the wedding being announced in the papers. I wasn't at all surprised she was getting married. I always assumed the nannying was just a stopgap until she found someone who'd provide for her.

CUT TO: Studio. JJ is at the whiteboard in front of an array of images.

JJ NORTON

It was when Caroline left the Camerons that she took the job at Dorney Place, working for Andrew Howard and his wife. This was 1985 and Rupert had just turned five.

CAMERA PANS over the pictures on the board: Dorney Place in the '80s: Andrew and Amanda with friends in the garden; Rupert as a toddler sitting on his mother's lap, and being carried on his father's shoulders, smiling and waving. Then police photos of the wreckage of Amanda Howard's Golf GTi, upside down on the hard shoulder of the A3, and finally several of Andrew with Caroline on the steps of Chelsea Town Hall on the day of their wedding. She's blonde now, in a pale blue two-piece with a Jackie O feel to it, he's rather dapper in a grey suit and silver tie. Rupert is in one shot, holding tight to his father's leg, as far away from Caroline as he can get. He's not smiling.

As we discussed before, it was only a few months after Caroline started working at Dorney Place that Amanda Howard died, and less than a year later Caroline and Andrew got married in a relatively low-key ceremony at their local registry office. If you can call Chelsea Old Town Hall 'low key'.

They always denied they'd been having an affair before Amanda's death, and clearly there's no way of proving it either way now.

LAILA FURNESS

What about Amanda's car crash – was there really any reason to think it was suspicious, or was that just more malicious gossip?

ALAN CANNING

I went through the accident report and there was nothing wrong with the car.

MITCHELL CLARKE

(looking through his papers)

Wasn't it put down to icy roads?

JJ NORTON

Yes it was, but according to the PM Amanda had a blood alcohol level only just below the legal limit.

Which surprised a lot of people, as it was only eleven o'clock in the morning. And the police never did establish what she was doing on that road in the first place. The A3 goes from London to Surrey and Hampshire and she didn't have any friends or family in that part of the country.

LAILA FURNESS

Did Amanda have a problem with alcohol?

JJ NORTON

No, she didn't. In fact, she rarely drank at all, which was another thing that fuelled the rumours.

LAILA FURNESS

(sighs)

Human nature. Don't you just love it.

MITCHELL CLARKE

So what exactly did people think had happened? That Caroline had spiked her cappuccino to get her out of the way?

ALAN CANNING

Pretty much.

LAILA FURNESS

But that's ludicrous—

ALAN CANNING

(shrugs)

I know, but that's what people thought.

LAILA FURNESS

I assume those allegations were investigated at the time?

ALAN CANNING

Yes, there was a full police inquiry. Amanda's family saw to that.

LAILA FURNESS

And?

ALAN CANNING

It was - almost inevitably - inconclusive. Andrew had left early for the office that day, Rupert was barely 6, and the only other person in the house was Caroline. She claimed she didn't know where Amanda was going, she hadn't seen her drinking that morning, and certainly hadn't given her anything. But how do you prove a negative?

LAILA FURNESS

Speaking of Rupert, much of what I said earlier about Luke would also apply to him: losing his mother so suddenly, and then seeing her replaced almost immediately by someone he clearly didn't like would have been profoundly unsettling for a child of 6. And while research suggests that very young children do often accept a new step-parent, this certainly doesn't seem to have been the case here.

BILL SERAFINI

If Andrew and Caroline *were* having an affair, maybe the kid picked up on it – wouldn't be the first time.

CUT TO: Felicity Grainger, sub-captioned 'Sister of Amanda Howard'. She's in a big kitchen with bifold doors onto a large garden; the kitchen has black units, a white tiled floor, and a large spiky modern chandelier.

FELICITY GRAINGER

It was patently obvious to me that Caroline set her sights on Andrew right from the start. You could tell the way she looked at him, the way she batted those eyelashes of hers.

I told Amanda – 'that one's trouble, get rid of her', but she just laughed it off. And I just *know* my sister wouldn't have driven that car if she'd been drinking, especially on icy roads. The whole thing stank to high heaven.

It was Rupert I felt most sorry for, of course – poor little mite, losing his mum at that age. And Caroline completely lost interest in him after she'd got a ring on her finger. Kept complaining that he was being 'difficult' and 'morose'. It was just as well he still had us he could turn to.

CUT TO: Studio.

HUGO FRASER

But where does this get us – apart from the inference that Caroline wasn't exactly on the sister-in-law's BFF list?

JJ NORTON

I think it indicates Caroline could be ruthless if there was something she wanted. Let's face it, even if she had absolutely nothing to do with

Amanda's death she moved in on Andrew pretty sharpish afterwards.

BILL SERAFINI

That doesn't give her a motive for murdering Luke, though, does it? It might explain why she went ahead and married him in the first place: she wanted him so she was damn well going to have him, whatever anyone else said.

But it doesn't explain why she'd want him dead.

MITCHELL CLARKE

Maybe he was having an affair. That's the oldest motive in the book.

Bill SERAFINI

Actually we raised that possibility with Peter Lascelles when we went to see him. Here's what he told us.

CUT TO: Peter Lascelles INTERVIEW with Bill and Alan.

PETER LASCELLES

We looked into that, naturally. Even the mere suggestion of infidelity can throw a bomb into a relationship, especially one where there is a significant age difference. And Caroline never struck me as the sort of woman who'd tolerate being scorned.

BILL SERAFINI

So you questioned her explicitly about it?

PETER LASCELLES

Absolutely. And she flat-out denied Luke was having an affair. She said she 'would have known'. That she 'could always tell when he wasn't telling the truth'.

And everyone else we spoke to said pretty much the same thing: they'd never seen anything to suggest Luke was playing away. If there was another relationship going on he was keeping it extraordinarily quiet.

BILL SERAFINI

And you believed Caroline?

PETER LASCELLES

I did. I don't think she was lying to me.

CUT TO: Studio. Guy is now sitting at the table with the team.

GUY HOWARD

I promised you all that you'd only see me in front of the camera in this series if there was a very good reason. This is one of those times. Because it turns out Peter Lascelles was wrong: my mother *was* lying to him. Though more by omission, than commission.

Have a look at this.

CUT TO: INTERVIEW with Maura Howard. This time she's sitting in the kitchen at Dorney Place, wearing an oversized cowl-neck jumper, pale blue jeans and a pair of Ugg boots. She's pulled the sleeves of the jumper down over her hands, as if she's cold. The room doesn't look very lived in.

GUY HOWARD - off

How were things between Luke and Mum that autumn - in the weeks before he died?

MAURA HOWARD

(shrugs)

You were there too - you'd have seen just as much as me.

GUY HOWARD - off

I don't think I would. I was only 10, and to be honest I don't think I was very observant.

MAURA HOWARD

(sighs and looks away)

Mum was – distracted. She was going out more during the day and getting back late. There were phone calls too – phone calls she'd take upstairs and close the door.

GUY HOWARD – off

Could she have been having an affair?

MAURA HOWARD

(looking back at him)

I never thought so at the time. I guess it wouldn't have occurred to me.

GUY HOWARD – off

Seriously? You were 15. You had a boyfriend yourself by the following summer.

MAURA HOWARD

Look, I told you, I didn't think about it.

GUY HOWARD – off

What about Amelie?

MAURA HOWARD

(starting to fiddle with her sleeves)

You'd have to ask her that, not me.

GUY HOWARD – off

She doesn't want to talk about it – you know that. She doesn't think we should be 'raking up the past'. That's why she's refusing to be interviewed on camera.

MAURA HOWARD

(takes a deep breath)

Look, if you're asking if Amelie thought something had been going on with Mum that summer then the answer is Yes.

She had to go home at lunchtime one day because she'd forgotten her swimming kit, and as soon as she opened the door she could hear people upstairs. Grunts, moans. Sex noises, basically. Which was, of course, excruciatingly embarrassing, so she just went and got her stuff as quickly as she could and tried to pretend she hadn't heard anything, but when she got back downstairs Mum was in the kitchen. Apparently she looked a bit flushed and her blouse was buttoned up all wrong.

GUY HOWARD – off

Am told you this at the time?

MAURA HOWARD

No, not till years later. She said she hadn't wanted to freak me out.

GUY HOWARD – off

How did she know it wasn't Luke?

MAURA HOWARD

He'd gone up north that day. And in any case Am heard the bloke's voice. It was too muffled to make out what he was saying but she said he sounded 'posh'. So *definitely* not Luke.

And there was an old MGB parked out on the road that day. A bright red one. She'd noticed it a few times before as well. Just hadn't put two and two together till then.

GUY HOWARD – off

But couldn't it just have been one of the neighbours' cars? Or a visitor?

MAURA HOWARD

That's what I said. All I know is that neither of us ever saw it again. Though apparently there was a gym bag on the passenger seat with some T-shirts and trainers in it. If you're 'looking for clues'.

(raises an eyebrow)

Good luck with that.

CUT TO: Studio.

GUY HOWARD

(looking round the table)

She's not wrong, of course. The research team have been looking into it but it's almost two decades ago and a gym bag and a red sports car isn't a lot to go on.

BILL SERAFINI

Just to be clear, Amelie never told the police any of this at the time?

GUY HOWARD

No. I guess she was trying to protect Mum - stop the family name being trashed in the papers. *Again.* We were having a bad enough time without that.

And remember, this incident would have been at least three months before the murder, so maybe Amelie didn't think it was relevant.

JJ NORTON

I'm not so sure about that. What if Caroline had decided to finish it with this man and he wasn't accepting it? Maybe he came round to confront her that night and found Luke. They could have argued.

ALAN CANNING

It's a plausible scenario. One I'd certainly have investigated. And I'm sure Peter and his team would have done the same if they'd been given the information. It could have been a very significant lead.

BILL SERAFINI

(turning to Mitchell)

Do you by any chance remember seeing an MGB outside Dorney Place the night of the murder? You were there.

MITCHELL CLARKE

No, but in that neck of the woods sports cars aren't exactly uncommon.

ALAN CANNING

Even a vintage one like that? In bright red?

MITCHELL CLARKE

Well, a) it was dark so it could have been sky-blue pink for all I'd have known, and b) it's twenty years ago, mate. Yes, it could have been there, but I don't remember seeing it, OK?

LAILA FURNESS

So what can we do about it now, all this time later?

GUY HOWARD

Like I said, Tarek and the research team are continuing to dig, so something may come up. And in the meantime—

BILL SERAFINI

—In the meantime, I suggest we focus on Caroline's alibi. If this man *did* go to the house to see her that night it had to have been a surprise - she wouldn't have gone out for a drink if she'd known he was coming.

JJ NORTON

On the other hand, he could have called her when she was at the party saying he was going round to the house, maybe even threatening to confront Luke? Maybe she panics, rushes back home, but it's too late—

LAILA FURNESS

(frowning)

—And faced with her husband's bloody corpse she just shrugs her shoulders and leaves it at that? Doesn't call the police, doesn't call an ambulance, just sashays on back for another strawberry daiquiri?

BILL SERAFINI

(nodding)

And no one at the party notices anything is wrong either. I'm not buying that.

ALAN CANNING

You're all forgetting one thing. If this mysterious lover had called her when she was at the party, there'd be something in her phone records.

(gestures at the file)

But there's nothing there. No calls made *or* received on her phone that night that weren't thoroughly checked and double-checked during the original investigation. Including the missed call from Maura at 10.52.

LAILA FURNESS

Texts?

ALAN CANNING

(shaking his head)

No. None.

LAILA FURNESS

She hit the delete key?

ALAN CANNING

Yes, clearly she could have done that, but digital forensics would have been able to retrieve them. It's got a lot more sophisticated since then, but they'd still have found a deleted text, even in 2003.

JJ NORTON

And no WhatsApp or Snapchat back then, of course. Just saying.

MITCHELL CLARKE

There is one obvious explanation.

(The team look at him.)

JJ NORTON

Go on.

MITCHELL CLARKE

This man was *at* the party.

LAILA FURNESS

So – what are you saying? They speak at the do, arrange to meet back at the house and he goes on ahead of her? That's pretty risky on her part, isn't it? Knowing Luke's there?

JJ NORTON

(goes over to the site plan and points)

But there's the apartment here, right? The one over the workshop, where Caroline lived when she was the au pair? Maybe they arranged to meet there?

LAILA FURNESS

But that was Maura's room by then.

JJ NORTON

Yes, but Maura was at the cinema that night, wasn't she – Caroline had dropped her off herself. The coast would have been clear. Or at least she'd have thought so.

MITCHELL CLARKE

(nodding)

Only they're not careful enough. Luke sees something – maybe lights going on. He goes over to investigate and all hell breaks loose.

LAILA FURNESS

That scenario would make Caroline much more complicit, though. If that's what really happened, she was there throughout.

MITCHELL CLARKE

(grimly)

And then promptly scarpered, leaving her teenage daughter to find that horror show.

JJ NORTON

(going back to the table and picking up the paperwork)

Do we know exactly who was at that drinks party she went to?

ALAN CANNING

The police compiled a list, but they suspected it wasn't complete. It was a bit of an 'open doors' thing, by all accounts.

BILL SERAFINI

Do we have that list? Guy?

GUY HOWARD

Not as such. But Tarek's fixed for one of the team to talk to Phyllis Franks. The party was for her husband's birthday, at a Spanish restaurant called Penedès, about half a mile from Dorney Place. It's long gone, before you ask.

BILL SERAFINI

So you knew this woman?

GUY HOWARD

Phyllis? Not really. Her husband was one of my dad's City contacts. Some big-shot banker or other. Jack and Phyllis used to come to my parents' dinner parties, but I don't think they socialized outside that.

And just to clarify, I've never spoken to Phyllis about this - obviously not back then, given I was only 10, but not since we started working on this show either. So I have no idea what she might tell us.

(looks round the table)

So who wants to take this one?

MITCHELL CLARKE

I vote Laila. Woman to woman.

LAILA FURNESS

Is there a whiff of everyday sexism in there by any chance, Mitch?

ALAN CANNING

Laila has no interrogation experience I'm aware of—

MITCHELL CLARKE

That's my whole point – we don't *want* this woman feeling like she's being cross-examined.

LAILA FURNESS

(to Alan)

I interview people all the time. I'm a *psychologist*. It's *what I do*.

ALAN CANNING

This isn't quite the same—

BILL SERAFINI

—Hugo, JJ – you have a view?

JJ NORTON

Maybe Laila goes with Hugo, to balance it out?

(turning to him)

You question people on the stand, right?

HUGO FRASER

(laughs)

Well, yes, but to Mitch's point, I find the letters 'KC' tend to turn the man in the street into a rabbit in the headlights.

(glancing at Laila)

Or woman in the street, in this case. Obviously.

BILL SERAFINI

(grinning)

No one was suggesting you show up in one of those crazy lawyer wigs, Hugo.

MITCHELL CLARKE

Well, I seem to spend most of my life interviewing people, one way or another - happy to tag along?

BILL SERAFINI

Great - Mitch and Laila it is.

Furness and Clarke - sounds like a cop show.

(Mitch smiles, Laila doesn't.)

CUT TO: The pavement outside the Franks's house in Belgravia. Four storeys, white stucco, with a large and very old wisteria covering the two lower floors. Sunlight and birdsong. Mitch and Laila stop at the wrought-iron gate.

LAILA FURNESS

Well, Phyllis Franks is hardly 'the woman in the street', is she? Whichever way you look at it.

MITCHELL CLARKE

They weren't living here in 2003, though.

LAILA FURNESS

(smiling dryly)

So this is the 'downsized' version. All right for some.

CAMERA FOLLOWS as they go up the path; the door is opened by an Asian woman in a dark grey dress. She shows them through to a front sitting room overlooking the square. Pale teal walls, heavy brocade curtains, a huge rococo mirror, Aubusson rugs. Phyllis Franks gets to her feet to welcome them. She's very petite and appears quite frail, but her manner is crisp and animated.

PHYLLIS FRANKS

(shaking their hands)

Dr Furness, Mr Clarke. Please, do sit down.

LAILA FURNESS

Thank you for agreeing to see us, Mrs Franks.

PHYLLIS FRANKS

Oh, Phil, please. Everyone calls me Phil. So, you want to talk to me about Caroline and Luke.

LAILA FURNESS

You must have been asked about that night many times.

PHYLLIS FRANKS

(shaking her head and sighing)

Many, many times.

MITCHELL CLARKE

Do you mind talking us through it? If that's OK?

PHYLLIS FRANKS

Of course. It was my husband's birthday. His sixtieth. But he didn't want a big sit-down thing – Jack was never one for fuss. Just drinks with friends. A 'come as you are' sort of thing. He liked that Penedès place and it was just down the road, so it made sense.

We hired the whole thing and we had canapés. They did the most wonderful seafood, it was such a shame when it closed. I remember one terribly nice young chap complimenting me on the cava.

(laughs)

It was actually Dom Pérignon.

LAILA FURNESS

I know there were a lot of people coming and going but you must have had some sort of guest list, mustn't you?

PHYLLIS FRANKS

Oh yes, at least to start with. The police had a copy of that right from the start. But I'd made a point of saying people could bring friends and colleagues. It was all very relaxed. And Jack had such a wide circle - business associates, people from the golf club, old school friends, his peers at Cambridge. So it was a very mixed bunch - a lot of the guests wouldn't have known that many people outside their own group.

MITCHELL CLARKE

But Caroline Howard was definitely there?

PHYLLIS FRANKS

Caroline Ryder, by then, of course. And yes, I definitely spoke to her at one point. She was very bubbly - very different from when she was married to Andrew. I remember saying to someone that if that was what a much younger husband did for you then I was going to put my name down for one.

(smiles)

I was only joking, of course.

MITCHELL CLARKE

Do you remember Caroline talking about anything in particular?

PHYLLIS FRANKS

Not really. It was just party chit-chat. I do recall her saying Luke was under the weather and that was why she was there alone, but I suspect the real reason was that he couldn't be bothered with a bunch of old fogeys like us. I can't say I blamed him—

(laughs)

—Jack was old enough to be his grandfather.

MITCHELL CLARKE

Do you have any idea at what stage of the evening that conversation took place?

PHYLLIS FRANKS

The police asked me the same thing. I told them at the time that I thought it was around nine thirty. I haven't remembered anything since then that would lead me to change that.

LAILA FURNESS

So that's relatively early on. Could she have slipped out and come back later without anyone noticing?

PHYLLIS FRANKS

Oh absolutely. There was a crowd in the pergola round the back smoking, for a start. People were going in and out all the time.

LAILA FURNESS

And she was definitely there at the end of the evening?

PHYLLIS FRANKS

Yes, I'm very sure about that, because the police came looking for her. It must have been around eleven thirty.

MITCHELL CLARKE

But you hadn't spoken to her yourself since nine thirty - you don't know if her mood had changed?

PHYLLIS FRANKS

No. Though I think someone told me later she'd been looking rather pale. Before the police arrived, I mean. Clearly she was looking very distressed when she left.

MITCHELL CLARKE

You don't know who it was who said that? About her looking pale?

PHYLLIS FRANKS

I'm afraid not. As I told the police.

LAILA FURNESS

And no one mentioned seeing her looking like she'd been out in the rain? It was raining by the end of the evening, wasn't it?

PHYLLIS FRANKS

God yes, absolutely pouring down. But no, I didn't. I did notice she had mud and little bits of grass on her shoes when she left. She was wearing very high heels – cream, they were, positively bridal, so I suppose the dirt stood out.

LAILA FURNESS

Wouldn't that suggest she'd been outside?

PHYLLIS FRANKS

Well, there was that grass area at the back I just mentioned, so if she'd gone out there for a ciggie that might account for it.

MITCHELL CLARKE

And we do know she smoked.

LAILA FURNESS

Thinking about it now, are there any names that have come back to you that weren't on the list the police worked from?

PHYLLIS FRANKS

I'm afraid not – I'd have told them if there were.

LAILA FURNESS

You said her shoes were cream – what else was she wearing, do you remember?

PHYLLIS FRANKS

The dress was navy, some sort of pleated thing. And before you ask, yes, it definitely *was* dark enough to conceal blood stains. At least to a degree. The police specifically asked me about that.

MITCHELL CLARKE

Does a red MGB mean anything to you?

PHYLLIS FRANKS

(looks a little taken aback)

Now why on earth should you mention that?

MITCHELL CLARKE

You know what type of car I mean?

PHYLLIS FRANKS

Of course I do - Jack had one when we first knew each other. British Racing Green. That was such a lovely little car—

LAILA FURNESS

Do you by any chance remember one being parked near the restaurant that night? I know it was a long time ago—

PHYLLIS FRANKS

Do you know, I think I do. I'm pretty sure Jack pointed it out to me. After all, you didn't see many of them around by then - even fewer now, of course—

MITCHELL CLARKE

Did Jack know whose it was?

PHYLLIS FRANKS

(shaking her head)

No, I'm sure he didn't. Or if he did, he didn't say. I'd have remembered that. If only he was still here - you could have asked him.

LAILA FURNESS

I'm so sorry, Mrs Fr- Phil- I didn't know your husband had died.

PHYLLIS FRANKS

(smiling sadly)

No need to apologize, my dear. Jack isn't dead, he's just gone. Alzheimer's. I'm afraid these days my husband doesn't even know who I am.

Now – tea?

CUT TO: Studio. Time has clearly passed, as the team are in different clothes. Guy is again at the table.

LAILA FURNESS

(looking round)

And that's as far as we got. Sorry.

BILL SERAFINI

Not your fault. You did what you could. But we hit a brick wall.

(turns to Guy)

I guess you've already spoken to your mother about all this?

GUY HOWARD

Yes, when the idea for this project first came up. But it wasn't much use. I'm afraid she's not in a good way – she's very confused a lot of the time and gets distressed very easily. And even if she appears to have remembered something I don't think it's necessarily reliable.

(looking round)

But whenever we've talked about this – I mean, in the past, before she was ill – she's always maintained exactly the same story. The same one she told the police. She was at the party all night, she had no reason to kill Luke or have him killed, and she didn't know anyone else who did either.

ALAN CANNING

(flicking through the papers)

There's no mention of the dirt on her shoes in the police file.

GUY HOWARD

I didn't know about that, not till I heard what Phyllis said. I guess her being out in the smoking area is the simplest explanation.

ALAN CANNING

But not the only one.

GUY HOWARD

All the same, Occam's razor and all that—

MITCHELL CLARKE

Occam's what?

HUGO FRASER

'The simplest explanation is nearly always right'.

ALAN CANNING

'*Nearly* always'. Not *always*. Let's wait and see, shall we?

BILL SERAFINI

(to Alan)

You think the police missed it - the shoes? Seems a pretty big thing to overlook. Under the circumstances.

ALAN CANNING

Clearly someone should have noted the state of her footwear when they went to inform her at the party.

But one thing we know they definitely *did* do was test the dress for blood, as well as the coat she took to the party. I've checked with Peter Lascelles and he confirmed there was nothing on either of them.

And I personally can't see anyone carrying out that sort of attack and not getting body matter all over them.

JJ NORTON

And all the more so because the initial blow to the back of the head wasn't fatal. Dead people don't bleed, but unconscious ones most certainly do. Those facial blows would have bled profusely.

MITCHELL CLARKE

OK, so where does all this leave us? Do we think this mystery man of hers exists or not?

LAILA FURNESS

If you ask me, yes. Amelie had no reason to make up a story like that about her own mother. But as to how we identify him, that's a different matter.

JJ NORTON

Seems to me we've reached the point where this enquiry can go in several different directions.

CAMERA FOLLOWS as he gets up, goes to the white-board, and starts to write.

Number one: Caroline's possible lover, who may or may not have been the owner of a red MGB and a gym bag.

Number two: Luke's background. I still think there's more to him than meets the eye. Maybe there's a person - or incident - in his past that came back to haunt him. Which could well explain that call from King's Cross, too.

MITCHELL CLARKE

If it *was* something from the past it would have to be something pretty big. An attack like that - that's a crime of rage.

LAILA FURNESS

I agree.

JJ NORTON

And then there's *number three*: Rupert. He's always claimed he was out of town that night, but I think that bears a closer look.

MITCHELL CLARKE

But where's the motive? He and Luke were mates – he was the one who introduced Luke to Caroline in the first place—

LAILA FURNESS

(dryly)

Quite.

MITCHELL CLARKE

You think that might have been enough?

LAILA FURNESS

Not on its own, no, of course not. But taking your mate to your stepmother's drinks do is one thing, having him actually *marry* her is quite another. And when you add in the cash factor—

HUGO FRASER

I agree – half my criminal work is down to precisely that. Trust me: you should *never* underestimate how quickly money can detonate even supposedly happy families. And as far as I can see, this one was hardly that.

(glances across at Guy)

No offence.

GUY HOWARD

(holding up his hands)

Not a problem.

LAILA FURNESS

Was there a financial angle, though, in Rupert's case? From memory, Andrew's will gave Caroline a life interest in Dorney Place, which she still has, even though she married again—

MITCHELL CLARKE

(drily)

Twice.

LAILA FURNESS

—but it's Rupert who inherits it when she dies. How did her marrying Luke change any of that? I can see it might give Rupert a motive to kill *her*, to get his hands on the house - but not Luke—

GUY HOWARD

(laughing sardonically)

And if Rupert dies before me I'm next in line for the house, which would give me a big fat motive to kill *him*.

LAILA FURNESS

(looking a little embarrassed)

Well, yes, I suppose so. But like I said, how did Luke's death benefit Rupert?

HUGO FRASER

I think we need to do a deep dive into the Howard family finances. There may be something buried in Andrew's will, for example, or in the wording of the trust funds - I think I'm right in saying he set up separate trusts for all his children. Assuming that's OK with you, of course, Guy?

GUY HOWARD

Absolutely. Like I said, I only want the truth. I can put you in touch with our lawyer.

JJ NORTON

So we're agreed? We take a closer look at Rupert?

There's general agreement around the table.

So shall we divvy up? Alan - could you pick up on the mystery lover? I reckon your Met connections might serve us well there, especially if we're trying to run down that car. No pun intended.

HUGO FRASER

I'd be happy to pitch in on that aspect too.

JJ NORTON

Which leaves Rupert, and Luke's possibly murky past. I'm happy to take Rupert - Bill, Laila, Mitch what about you?

BILL SERAFINI

I'll step up for Luke. Should be right up my alley.

MITCHELL CLARKE

Actually, I'd like to take a closer look at that too.

JJ NORTON

Looks like it's you and me then, Laila.

FADE OUT

- end credits -

Text messages between Maura and Amelie Howard, 18th April 2023, 2.35 p.m.

Hey Am

They interviewed me again

So...?

Look you're probably not going to be v happy about this but I mentioned about that incident that summer

That thing with Mum?

Yeah that

Like WTF?

Why?

What difference does it make now? No-one cares about that sort of shit any more

Well I do. I just hate the idea of Guy using what happened to make fucking *money*

You know that better than anyone

Look Mum's never going to see any of this so she won't be upset by it. And in any case isn't it better they all run around looking for this mystery bloke and leave us alone?

I suppose so

You know I'm right Am

I'll handle it. Just like I always have. That's what big sisters are for, right?

Love you x

Love you more

You know that

Date: Fri 21/04/2023, 16.35
From: Laila Furness
To: Mitch Clarke
Subject: Down Under

Hi Mitch,

I was just wondering if you'd like any help on the Aussie end of things – I have an old friend who's a journalist down there, and he might have some useful contacts. Entirely up to you of course.

Laila

Date: Sat 22/04/2023, 17.07
From: Mitch Clarke
To: Laila Furness
Subject: Re: Down Under

Sounds good.

M

Date: Sat 22/04/2023, 17.15
From: Laila Furness
To: Barry Bonnett
Subject: Favour?

Hi Barry,

Saw you came second in the national championships again 👏 Still impressed you can find the time for all that training when you have the job and everything else. But I guess cycling is no hardship in Sydney weather. Anyway, I'm sure you remember me mentioning I'd be doing this Showrunner thing. Turns out there's an Aussie angle and one of my colleagues would appreciate some help from someone on the ground. If you have time, I'd really appreciate it. I'm sure you know what I'm getting at.

Laila

Date: Sun 23/04/2023, 23.42

From: Barry Bonnett

To: Laila Furness

Subject: Re: Favour?

Hi Laila,

Yeah, pretty happy with coming second, I have to say – a podium placing's always good. Not bad for an old guy, eh? I've got the boys hooked as well now – Stephen's shaping up pretty well and yes, still breaking the hearts of half the female population of UNSW.

(I'm imagining you shaking your head at this point and saying something about chips and old blocks 😉)

He says hello btw and a belated thanks for his Chrimbo present.

And yes, no worries, send your mate my way. Happy to give him a hand, and don't worry, I'll make sure he doesn't go poking round where he isn't wanted.

I'll keep you posted.

Baz 🚴

Episode two

Broadcast

October 6

The Times, 7 October 2023

TELEVISION

The real housewives of W8

Angst, adultery and affluence make for a compelling cocktail

Infamous: Who Killed Luke Ryder?
Showrunner

Close to Home
Crimetime TV UK

I suspect last night's episode of **Infamous** would have made distinctly uncomfortable viewing in certain quarters of the Met. As far as I know this is the first time it's been made public that the police arrested a man at the crime scene that night. He was never charged, he was a local journalist, and he was black. And yes, he did have a small quantity of drugs in his car, but there was no forensic evidence linking him to the crime. Certainly nothing to justify six hours of hostile police interrogation. I'm sure we'd all like to think we've moved on, but you only have to read the news to know that good old-fashioned racial profiling is alive and well.

Aside from that, the chief pleasure on offer last night (though it was admittedly a guilty one) was the chance to eavesdrop on the everyday trials and treacheries of the well-heeled set who cluster round Campden Hill, where Luke Ryder was living at the time of his death. They say money doesn't buy happiness; they also say the rich are different. On this showing, they're right on both counts. Though whether any of this was relevant to what happened to Ryder remains to be seen. Watch this space.

Meanwhile, in drama-land, we're back in England's most murderous city with **Close to Home**, a new series set in Oxford. But we are very far from the golden quads and genteel crime-as-a-crossword world of Inspector Morse. In

← → ↻ ⌂ https://www.groopz.com/truecrimeaddiction

Infamous/LukeRyder Join

Warming up nicely, I think we'd all agree ☺

submitted 5 hours ago by Slooth
15 comments share hide report

I know the press are making a big deal about the race issue with Mitch and don't get me wrong, I reckon it was definitely a factor. But seriously – sneaking up the drive and looking in the windows. Who *does* that?

submitted 5 hours ago by BernietheBoltcutter
7 comments share hide report

> A hack, that's who, but I agree he was asking for trouble and he certainly got it
>
> submitted 4 hours ago by AngieFlynn77
> 2 comments share hide report
>
> You really think that's all it was? Sounds pretty fishy to me. I just don't reckon anyone would act that way, however desperate they were for a story.
>
> submitted 4 hours ago by Investig8er
> 4 comments share hide report
>
> > But what he said made sense – if he'd been there to sell Ryder drugs why would he leave the gear in the car?
> >
> > submitted 4 hours ago by AngieFlynn77
> > share hide report
> >
> > > All I'm saying is someone's lying – he said he was by the body, the police claim he was hiding in the bushes. They can't both be right
> > >
> > > submitted 3 hours ago by Investig8er
> > > 2 comments share hide report
> >
> > I've read some of his stuff – that guy has a chip on his shoulder the size of Mount Rushmore
> >
> > submitted 3 hours ago by FinnShaw1616
> > share hide report

I reckon that bloke Canning knows more than he's letting on. For a start, he'd deffo gone back and checked up on Clarke's involvement before all this started. He was just too well informed

submitted 4 hours ago by TruCrimr
comments share hide report

> I agree. Definitely has an agenda. The question is, what
>
> submitted 3 hours ago by RonJebus
> 8 comments share hide report
>
> Though him and Bill were just hilarious on that road trip. LMFAO – talk about The Odd Couple
>
> submitted 3 hours ago by JasonGlover45
> share hide report

And what about the wife? Caroline? No-one knew she was cheating did they? Not back then

submitted 3 hours ago by DilltheDog1962
8 comments share hide report

> Good point. Made me wonder if this 'dementia' of hers is just a bit *too* convenient
>
> submitted 3 hours ago by RonJebus
> 19 comments share hide report
>
> > Oh come on – who'd make up something like that?
> >
> > submitted 2 hours ago by AngieFlynn77
> > 11 comments share hide report
> >
> > > Someone with a lot to lose
> > >
> > > submitted 2 hours ago by TruCrimr
> > > 39 comments share hide report

Episode three

Filming

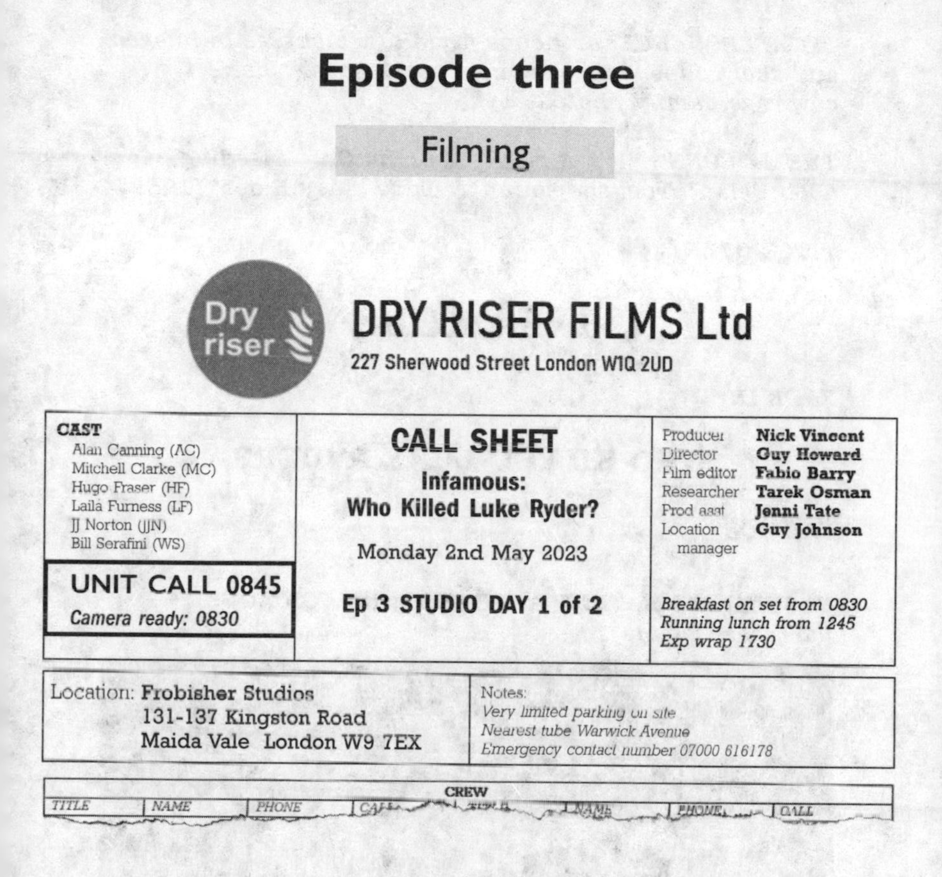

DRY RISER FILMS Ltd
227 Sherwood Street London W1Q 2UD

CAST	CALL SHEET	
Alan Canning (AC) Mitchell Clarke (MC) Hugo Fraser (HF) Laila Furness (LF) JJ Norton (JJN) Bill Serafini (WS)	**Infamous: Who Killed Luke Ryder?** Monday 2nd May 2023	Producer **Nick Vincent** Director **Guy Howard** Film editor **Fabio Barry** Researcher **Tarek Osman** Prod asst **Jenni Tate** Location manager **Guy Johnson**
UNIT CALL 0845 *Camera ready: 0830*	**Ep 3 STUDIO DAY 1 of 2**	*Breakfast on set from 0830* *Running lunch from 1245* *Exp wrap 1730*

Location:	Notes:
Frobisher Studios **131-137 Kingston Road** **Maida Vale London W9 7EX**	*Very limited parking on site* *Nearest tube Warwick Avenue* *Emergency contact number 07000 616178*

CREW

TITLE	NAME	PHONE	CALL	TITLE	NAME	PHONE	CALL

TITLE SEQUENCE: arthouse-style b/w montage of images and short clips: crime scene, contemporary news coverage, family photos

THEME SONG – 'It's Alright, Ma (I'm Only Bleeding)' [Bob Dylan] from the soundtrack to 'Easy Rider' [1969]

TITLE OVER

INFAMOUS

FADE IN

WHO KILLED LUKE RYDER?

FADE OUT

BLACK FRAME, TEXT APPEARS, with VOICEOVER – narrator (female)

Twenty years ago, on October 3, 2003, Luke Ryder was found savagely beaten in the garden of his wife's home.

They had only been married a year but it's possible that Caroline Ryder was already cheating on him.

Could that simple fact have triggered a fatal series of events, or could something in Luke's past have come back to haunt him?

Or maybe the answer – then as now – lies far closer to home …

FADE OUT

CUT TO: Team in studio. Even more pictures and diagrams on the boards now.

BILL SERAFINI

So, to update everyone, it's been two weeks since we last met and a lot of water under the bridge in that time. One or two of us have had a haircut, for a start—

Several of the team smile, Bill rubs his hand over the back of his head.

—and yes, that does include me.

Anyway, we're back together now, to debrief. To recap, we've been pursuing three lines of enquiry.

(gestures towards the whiteboard)

One, the man Caroline Howard Ryder may have been seeing at the time of the killing.

Two, Luke's own past.

And three, whether Rupert Howard, Caroline's stepson, had any motive - or opportunity - to kill Luke.

So, who wants to go first?

JJ NORTON

Happy to do that, Bill.

Bill takes his seat and JJ replaces him at the white-board.

I was looking into Rupert Howard, and any reason he might have had to kill Luke. So let's do this the old-fashioned way.

He picks up the marker pen and starts writing; some of the others exchange smiles: JJ does love his lists.

MEANS: That's the easy one. Anyone who got access to that garden could have picked up a rock or a slab of paving from the flowerbeds. *All* our potential perpetrators had the means.

He puts a tick against Means; the board wobbles a little and he moves it around until it's more stable.

OPPORTUNITY: Rupert is fairly unique among the suspect cohort in that he didn't need anyone to let him in: he had his own key. So in that respect he's right up there. The question, however, is whether he was actually in the vicinity at the time.

He moves over to the pinboard and gestures at a map of England and Wales. London and Cambridge are both marked.

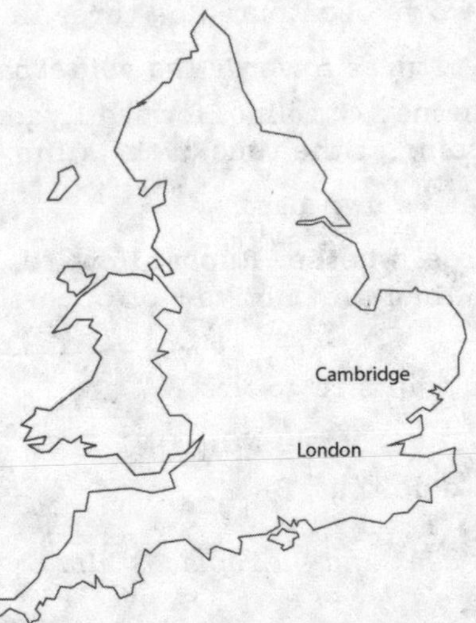

Rupert has always claimed that he was at his old college for a dinner that night. And as you can see from the map, we're talking about a distance of 60-odd miles. At least a couple of hours by car, not much less by train, if you factor in the time it would take to travel across London to Dorney Place as well. And that's just the time to get there – it'd be another two hours getting back.

So given the murder took place between around 9.30 and 10.20, Rupert would have had to leave Cambridge at eight at the absolute *latest*, which would have been right in the middle of the dinner.

And he wouldn't have got back to Cambridge till well after midnight.

(turning to face the team)

So was Rupert really in Cambridge that night, and if he was, was he there all night? The only way I was going to get answers to either of those questions was by talking to someone who was there.

Thankfully the college keeps pretty good records, and they put me on to Malcolm Severn, who was a friend and contemporary of Rupert's. And now - conveniently - a professor at the same college.

CUT TO: JJ and a middle-aged man sitting in a Cambridge college hall. Panelled walls, period portraits, long tables with silver candlesticks. Severn is heavily built, with thick white hair and a florid complexion.

JJ NORTON

Thank you for meeting me, Professor Severn.

MALCOLM SEVERN

No problem at all.

JJ NORTON

So, do you remember the dinner on October third, 2003?

MALCOLM SEVERN

I certainly do. Not least because I was questioned by the Metropolitan Police about it very shortly afterwards. I and most of the rest of my year group.

JJ NORTON

And do you remember Rupert being there that night?

MALCOLM SEVERN

I do. We were actually sitting fairly close together - we were all part of the same group of friends.

And hard as it might be to imagine looking at us now, we were a pretty fast lot back then.

(laughs)

I remember the Dean had to send a message from High Table asking us to pipe down.

JJ NORTON

So there's no way Rupert could have absented himself without you knowing?

MALCOLM SEVERN

Certainly not for the time it would have taken for him to get to London and back.

(hesitates)

Though I do remember him leaving the table at one stage—

JJ NORTON

Oh yes? When was that?

MALCOLM SEVERN

They'd just started serving the entrée so it must have been around 8.30. He was only gone about half an hour.

JJ NORTON

And when he got back where did he say he'd been?

MALCOLM SEVERN

(looking slightly flustered)

He said he had to make a call. Something about a minor emergency and needing something sorted out re DP.

JJ NORTON

DP?

MALCOLM SEVERN

Dorney Place. He'd always called it that, ever since I first knew him.

JJ NORTON

I'm confused – he said it was an emergency, which implies something that's suddenly happened, so how did he know about it? Had someone called or messaged him during the dinner to say there was a problem?

MALCOLM SEVERN

I think he may have got a text. You weren't supposed to have mobile phones in Hall, but Rupert never thought rules like that applied to him.

JJ NORTON

So he left the dinner to make a call?

MALCOLM SEVERN

Which was a big thing, by the way. He got a severe ticking-off for doing that – you're not supposed to leave until the Master gives permission.

JJ NORTON

And he never told you what the 'emergency' was?

MALCOLM SEVERN

No.

JJ NORTON

Wasn't that rather odd?

MALCOLM SEVERN

(hesitates)

I suppose so. I didn't think so at the time, but now you mention it, yes. It was a bit odd.

CUT TO: Studio, as before. JJ is still by the pinboard.

HUGO FRASER

Well, one thing we know is that whoever Rupert called that night it wasn't the landline at Dorney Place – there's no record of any such incoming call. And nothing on Caroline's mobile either.

JJ NORTON

Though the timing is interesting - barely an hour after Rupert makes that mystery call, Luke is dead. Rather a coincidence, wouldn't you say? Who knows, he could have been setting the whole thing up—

LAILA FURNESS

(sceptical)

Oh come on, you're not really suggesting Rupert put a hit out on Luke? It's Campden Hill we're talking about, not the *Cosa Nostra.*

JJ NORTON

I agree. But it's strange all the same.

BILL SERAFINI

Did you ask Rupert about it?

JJ NORTON

(giving him a dry look)

I most certainly did.

CUT TO: INTERVIEW with Rupert. He's at his flat this time. A leather armchair, piles of newspapers, a log burner. He's wearing a check shirt, a woollen waistcoat, and a knitted tie.

JJ NORTON - off

The night Luke died you were at a dinner in Cambridge, right?

RUPERT HOWARD

Correct. What our Oxford counterparts would call a 'gaudy'.

(rather condescendingly)

That's a reunion dinner. For my year.

JJ NORTON - off

I do know what a gaudy is. One of your fellow alumni says you went out to make a call during the dinner.

RUPERT HOWARD

I don't really recall.

JJ NORTON - off

This person also told us that you said there was an 'emergency' re DP that needed 'sorting out'.

RUPERT HOWARD

(frowning)

I have no recollection of that.

JJ NORTON - off

That's an odd form of words for him to use if it didn't happen. He says you always referred to home as 'DP'.

RUPERT HOWARD

(dismissive)

Look, Caroline was absolutely hopeless about the house. Things were always going wrong or needing to be fixed. Washing machines, plumbing, that sort of stuff. And the garden was in a complete state—

JJ NORTON - off

And she called *you* when things like that went wrong? Even though by all accounts you weren't that close?

RUPERT HOWARD

(his eyes narrowing)

On occasion.

JJ NORTON - off

You're a dab hand at plumbing, are you? Spot of decorating? DIY?

Rupert gives a withering look in his direction but says nothing.

JJ NORTON - off

In any case, we know you didn't call her that particular evening. There were no calls from your mobile to hers that night. And none to the house either. We checked.

RUPERT HOWARD

(getting tetchy)

I don't even remember making any damn call—

JJ NORTON - off

Your friend was pretty certain.

RUPERT HOWARD

Who is this 'friend'?

JJ NORTON - off

Malcolm Severn.

RUPERT HOWARD

(laughing out loud)

Christ almighty, Severn Bore? He was always tagging along where he wasn't wanted. Jesus, I haven't spoken to him in years.

JJ NORTON - off

His memory of that night seems pretty clear. You're sure you don't remember that call?

RUPERT HOWARD

I told you—

JJ NORTON - off

Because Malcolm seems to think you were told off for leaving the Hall during dinner without permission. That strikes me as something you wouldn't forget.

RUPERT HOWARD

Like I said—

JJ NORTON - off

And it is odd, when you think about it - I'd have thought everything about that night would be etched in your mind.

RUPERT HOWARD

Look, what are you getting at?

JJ NORTON - off

I'm trying to 'get at' the truth—

RUPERT HOWARD

The police weren't interested in my fucking phone calls at the time—

JJ NORTON - off

Maybe they should have been—

RUPERT HOWARD

(tearing off his mic and getting up)

I've had enough of this - we're done. I'd like you to leave.

Film cuts out to static.

CUT TO: Studio, as before.

JJ NORTON

That's not exactly the demeanour of an innocent man. Not in my book. But as at now, that's all we have on him.

LAILA FURNESS

Maybe 'DP' didn't mean Dorney Place. He just used it as an excuse. A smokescreen.

HUGO FRASER

He was only 23 - what does a kid that age need a smokescreen for? He was hardly some big-time crime boss—

LAILA FURNESS

No, but he could have been dabbling in drugs – something like that—

HUGO FRASER

(smiling)

I get it – 'DP' *really* stood for Drug Pusher—

LAILA FURNESS

Thanks for the man-descension, Hugo, but you know as well as I do that he could easily have been doing a bit of dealing on the side. It would account for why he's so touchy about it, not just then but especially now – it's hardly a good look for an aspiring Tory MP.

BILL SERAFINI

For what it's worth, I agree. But either way he does seem to have an alibi for that night. And to be honest, I still can't see what motive he could have had.

That said, there may be something in the family finances that could have given him one. JJ – what did you find out about that?

JJ NORTON

Laila's the one who's been on the case there.

LAILA FURNESS

(looking up)

Ah, yes. To recap, this was all about establishing whether Rupert had a reason to kill Luke, his one-time friend, let's not forget.

Given we've now confirmed that Rupert was definitely in Cambridge that night, it couldn't have been an argument-gone-bad murder: someone else must have carried it out on his behalf. If not a professional hitman then a friend or associate. In other words, it *had* to have been premeditated.

So did Rupert have a motive that was strong enough for him to *arrange* to have Luke Ryder killed?

The short answer is, I don't think so.

I took a look at Andrew Howard's will—

Cut to library FOOTAGE of documents headed 'Last Will and Testament', etc.

—and Caroline did pretty well out of it. Not just the life interest in the house but a rather handsome portfolio of cash and financial investments, which are hers to use during her lifetime.

Whatever remains at the time of her death is to be divided equally among the four children: Rupert, and Caroline's own three, Maura, Amelie and Guy. The house, as we know, passes to Rupert on her death, as Andrew Howard's eldest son.

BILL SERAFINI

So Caroline's kids are relying on her not burning through that entire stack of cash, because if she does they'll get nothing?

LAILA FURNESS

That was my reading of it too. Though of course, I'm not a lawyer—

HUGO FRASER

Well, I am, and I agree. The obvious next question being what was the legal position at the point of Luke's murder?

LAILA FURNESS

Ah, that's where it gets interesting – as far as I could make out Caroline definitely *was* burning through the cash, and at a rate of knots. It looks like the value of the portfolio dropped by about thirty per cent between Andrew's death in December 1999, and Luke's death in October 2003.

Some of that was down to market fluctuations, but even so she was clearly draining funds at quite a lick.

ALAN CANNING

And you think that level of expenditure was down to Luke?

LAILA FURNESS

Not directly - he had no access to the money, as it was all in her name. But it seems she was spending money both *on* him and *with* him. She bought him a Harley, for a start, and they went on several expensive holidays.

ALAN CANNING

So your theory is that Rupert might have had Luke killed to slow down her spending? Seems pretty tenuous to me.

MITCHELL CLARKE

(nodding)

If he was going to go to all that trouble - and take that big a risk - it would have been far more efficient to get rid of *her*.

That way he'd cash out straightaway. *And* get the house.

LAILA FURNESS

Which is precisely why I think this one's basically a non-starter. The phone call at Cambridge is odd, and Rupert is way too defensive, but that could be down to something completely unconnected.

And in any case, as Bill's already said, it makes no sense. Killing Luke wasn't going to solve Rupert's problems. In fact, it could even have made them worse: Caroline could have simply got married yet again - to someone even more unsuitable.

BILL SERAFINI

Which brings us to the mystery man she may or may not have been having an affair with.

Hugo, Alan - where did you get on that?

ALAN CANNING

Well, I called in a few favours and got access to the DVLA database.

(pulling a sheet of paper from his file)

There were just over thirty thousand MGBs listed as still being on the road in October 2003. If you refine that down just to red models then obviously it reduces fairly drastically, but you're still looking at several thousand. You *could* then refine it geographically, but we clearly have no way of knowing where this man was actually living—

MITCHELL CLARKE

Surely it's a reasonable assumption he was in London?

LAILA FURNESS

I'd agree with that.

ALAN CANNING

—which is exactly what I was about to say, if you'd allowed me to finish. I agree that someone Caroline was seeing regularly would probably have been living fairly close by. In London, at least, or maybe the Home Counties.

If you apply that filter to the DVLA list on top of the paint colour you end up with just under a hundred vehicles. Eighty-six, to be precise.

LAILA FURNESS

That's not too bad. Actually fewer than I'd have expected.

ALAN CANNING

If you then apply an age and gender filter on top of that and look only at male owners over 25, it comes down a bit more - to forty-two.

He goes to the pinboard and puts up a map of Greater London with a scatter of red dots across it.

And this is where those forty-two were.

BILL SERAFINI

That's still a big task. And the data's twenty years old. Half those guys could be dead by now.

LAILA FURNESS

(agreeing)

Or have moved away.

ALAN CANNING

(turning to face them)

Which is exactly what I'm finding. I started with those living closest to Dorney Place, on the assumption that Caroline's lover, if he did exist, was probably of a similar socio-economic class. And yes, I do know that may be a false assumption—

LAILA FURNESS

(in an undertone)

Then again, I can't see Caroline going for a Hackney plumber—

ALAN CANNING

(raising his voice slightly)

As at now I've spoken to sixteen people who owned a red MGB at that time, and lived in the same general area of London as Dorney Place. But thus far, there are no obvious hits.

BILL SERAFINI

I guess it always was a bit of a Hail Mary.

HUGO FRASER

(turning to him)

You know, I've never understood what Americans mean by that.

BILL SERAFINI

(grinning)

It's a long pass right at the end of a football game. Basically a last-ditch long shot.

Anyway, what have you been doing all this time while Alan's been racking up his phone bill?

HUGO FRASER

I, my good sir, have been talking to Caroline's friends, those of them we could find, to see whether they might have a clue who Mr X was.

BILL SERAFINI

Now *that* sounds like a plan.

CUT TO: Madeleine Downing, sub-captioned as before 'Friend of Caroline Howard'. In her sitting room this time.

MADELEINE DOWNING

You're asking the wrong person. I never saw the slightest suggestion she was having an affair.

(laughs)

Why would she need to, with a young fit husband on tap? What was that thing Paul Newman said? 'Why go out for a burger when you can have steak at home?'

CUT TO: JENNIFER DENNISON, sub-captioned 'Friend of Caroline Howard'. Dark hair in a French pleat, a patterned silk shirt. She's in a blue-and-white tiled kitchen with a view of a garden beyond.

JENNIFER DENNISON

She never said anything to me, and I'm pretty sure she would have, if something really was going on.

HUGO FRASER – off

So she would confide in you? You had that sort of relationship?

JENNIFER DENNISON

I certainly confided in her, if that's what you mean.

(flushes slightly)

Look, if you must know, I was going through something like that myself, back then, OK? I ended up leaving my husband. So I think she'd have said if she was in the same position.

HUGO FRASER – off

Were she and Luke happy?

JENNIFER DENNISON

As far as I know. She never said otherwise. Not to me, anyway.

CUT TO: CARMEL PIPER, sub-captioned 'Friend of Caroline Howard'. A well-built woman with a long ash-blonde bob and a quilted leather gilet. She's at a table in a café. There's abstract art in pastel colours on the walls, fresh flowers on the table, and the coffee is in a blue cup with a saucer; it's clearly an independent, not one of the big chains.

CARMEL PIPER

We weren't that close, to be honest. I was just one of her 'ladies who lunched'. We'd get together every six weeks or so – it was just light-hearted stuff. Gossip, one-upmanship about holidays, that sort of thing; you know what it's like round here. All very harmless, in the big scheme of things.

HUGO FRASER - off

Did you ever see her get a call or text that might have suggested she had a lover?

CARMEL PIPER

(laughing)

I'm not sure how you could tell! But the answer is no. I never saw her rush off to answer her phone, or suddenly say she had to be somewhere else, or anything like that.

To be honest, I got the impression she kept her life pretty compartmentalized. A place for everyone, and everyone in their place. If you know what I mean.

CUT TO: Studio, as before.

BILL SERAFINI

What about the sports bag angle? Any better luck with that? Though it's another long shot, I know.

HUGO FRASER

'Fraid not. There were and still are any number of gyms in that part of town, not to mention the tennis courts at Queen's, and three squash clubs to my certain knowledge.

JJ NORTON

Is it worth cross-referencing the members of those clubs with the owners of red MGBs?

ALAN CANNING

I doubt many of them still have their records for 2003. I mean, yes, clearly we can *ask*, but even if the information still exists they almost certainly won't give it to us.

MITCHELL CLARKE

Data Protection. Bane of my bloody life.

LAILA FURNESS

And this man may not have belonged to a club anyway. He could just have been, you know – a jogger. Does anyone still jog these days? Is it still a thing?

JJ NORTON

(laughing)

I think you have to 'run' to be taken seriously now.

ALAN CANNING

(not laughing)

So to summarize, based on Maura Howard's new evidence, I tend to agree that Caroline Ryder *did* have some sort of extra-marital relationship, but as at now, we don't have any live leads on who the man in question might have been.

LAILA FURNESS

But you'll keep looking? At the cars, I mean?

ALAN CANNING

(wearily)

Yes, I can keep looking.

HUGO FRASER

So all that leaves us with now is Bill and Mitch, and what they've managed to dig up about Luke.

MITCHELL CLARKE

(to Bill)

You OK if I start?

BILL SERAFINI

Knock yourself out.

Mitch gets up and goes to the pinboard, to the map of Australia.

MITCHELL CLARKE

So back to Kalgoorlie. Which is clearly something Luke himself never planned on doing.

I contacted the local primary school to see what records they had from back then, and to be honest there wasn't much. No photos, sadly, but they do have a Facebook group for old pupils, so the school posted something on that for me, and I got four or five messages back, and we did a group Zoom call.

CUT TO: VIDEO of Mitch at his desk, with six people on a Zoom screen.

So you were all in the same class as Luke Ryder back in the day?

CUT TO: Close-up of Tracy Ryan, sub-captioned 'Schoolmate of Luke Ryder'. Pretty, with red hair in a ponytail, and a striped top. She has Uluru as her screen background.

TRACY RYAN

God yeah, I remember Luke. Right geeky little kid. Always getting sand kicked in his face. Not literally, of course, but you know what I mean.

CUT TO: Scott Grant, sub-captioned as above. He's blond but thinning on top. A Motorhead T-shirt and an earring.

SCOTT GRANT

Shit you're right, that's exactly how I remember him. Could have knocked me down with a feather when it came out about him getting killed. I mean, him being in London at all, to be honest, never mind married to some foxy older woman with a ton of cash.

(laughs)

Never thought he had it in him.

CUT TO: Donna Gilchrist, sub-captioned as above. Dark hair in a pixie cut. The sound of children in the background.

DONNA GILCHRIST

Always struck me as a bit fishy, that whole thing. And they've never solved it, have they?

CAMERA PANS back to capture the whole group.

MITCHELL CLARKE

That's what we're trying to do now. But after all these years, it's not easy.

SCOTT GRANT

I don't envy you your job, mate.

TRACY RYAN

So what do you need from us? I mean, I never saw the guy again after he left for Sydney.

MITCHELL CLARKE

And why do you think he left?

TRACY RYAN

You are joking, right? I mean, his parents die, he inherits the cash, what else is he going to do? I'd have gone myself, given half a chance.

CUT TO: Studio, as before.

MITCHELL CLARKE

As you can see, I drew a pretty predictable blank there. So the next stop was Sydney. Unfortunately, the bar Luke worked in has long since gone, but thanks to an old friend of Laila's who now lives there I did manage to track down the man who owned it back then.

CUT TO: Mitch at his desk, this time on speakerphone.

MITCHELL CLARKE

(into phone)

Hello, is this Don?

DON WYNDHAM

Don Wyndham, that's right.

MITCHELL CLARKE

And you used to own the Board Room, is that right? The bar?

DON WYNDHAM

Sure did, mate. Owned it till I retired. Fifteen years ago now.

MITCHELL CLARKE

And I'm guessing from the name that it was popular with the surfing crowd?

DON WYNDHAM

(laughs)

Couldn't move for 'em. Specially on a Friday night.

MITCHELL CLARKE

And Luke Ryder worked for you? This would have been soon after he arrived in Sydney in 1994.

DON WYNDHAM

Young 'Easy' – absolutely, worked for me a couple years. Nice kid. A bit shy to start with, but he soon came out of his shell, especially once he got the surfing bug. And he got a serious case of it, too – first the board, then the birds.

Shit, sorry – probably shouldn't use that word, should I, not these days. #MeToo and all that malarkey—

MITCHELL CLARKE

So he was popular with the girls?

DON WYNDHAM

Not to start with. Like I said, he was shy and a bit weedy, if I'm honest, a bit on the small side. And there was one hell of a lot of competition, too, with all the other lads. But once he bulked up a bit it was all systems go. Though a year or so later he met this one girl and suddenly it was all about her. Didn't have eyes for anyone else.

MITCHELL CLARKE

Do you know her name?

DON WYNDHAM

Nah, sorry. It's a long time ago. I reckon she was sweet on him, though. You could tell the way they were together. It was soon after that he left.

MITCHELL CLARKE

He left? Do you know why?

DON WYNDHAM

To be honest, it was all a bit of a mystery. One minute he's trying to find a place for him and this girl to move in together, and then all of a sudden he's handing in his notice and gone within the week.

MITCHELL CLARKE

But he never gave you a reason?

DON WYNDHAM

No, he never said anything to me. He looked pretty bloody stressed about it, though, whatever it was. Some of the other guys thought he got that girl up the duff and was looking for the escape hatch.

MITCHELL CLARKE

Do you think that's what happened?

DON WYNDHAM

Search me. I do know she didn't go off with him, because I saw her once or twice a couple of weeks after that. Looked right upset, she did, poor little cow. But if you're about to ask me where Easy went off to, don't bother. I don't have a bloody clue.

MITCHELL CLARKE

And when was this?

DON WYNDHAM

Now you're asking. Summer '95, I think. Maybe late November?

MITCHELL CLARKE

Do you by any chance have any pictures of him back then?

DON WYNDHAM

(laughs)

I doubt it, mate! It's twenty bloody years ago! But I'll have a shuft around and see what I can find.

CUT TO: Studio, as before. Mitch is still by the pinboard.

MITCHELL CLARKE

Though as it turned out, we were in luck. Don did find a couple of old snaps, but as you can see—

(gesturing at the board)

—they don't exactly tell us much.

CAMERA ZOOMS in on PHOTOS. One shows a crowded bar - at least fifteen people in shot, mostly young men. They're all holding up beer bottles and smiling; they look quite drunk. There's a circle drawn in red marker pen around a figure in the back row, but he's more than half obscured by the person in front. In the second picture a bunch of young guys are running towards the waves carrying surfboards. The sun is only just coming up and slants low across the sand. Luke is again marked in red, but he's only visible from behind.

HUGO FRASER

Oh well, it was a good try—

MITCHELL CLARKE

Actually, I haven't quite finished. Don still had his tax records from the bar, so he was able to tell me exactly when it was that Luke left – it was the twenty-ninth of November 1995. So I did a web search for anything that happened in Sydney round then that might explain why he suddenly upped and left.

JJ NORTON

You don't buy that it was just about the girl?

MITCHELL CLARKE

I don't know, maybe it was, but I thought it was worth checking out other possibilities as well. Especially given that Don hadn't seen any evidence of a problem with the girlfriend.

JJ NORTON

And?

MITCHELL CLARKE

And I found something.

He turns to the board and pins up a printout of two cuttings from the Sydney press.

Drunk driver sought in Sydney hit-and-run

By Mickey Boone

Inspector Field confirmed that the NSW police believe the incident was a hit-and-run and … drinking

"Sadly, we've seen too many instances of drunk drivers causing serious accidents and then fleeing the scene," she said. "We urge the person concerned to come forward

The Australian
28th November 1995

Road accident in Waverley leaves man in coma

By Siobhan Burnham

Police were called to the scene of a serious road accident in Rosewood Road, Waverley, in the early hours of Saturday morning, after a passing motorist called to report a young man lying unconscious in the middle of the road.

The victim was immediately transferred to the Emergency

he is not believed to have regained consciousness.

Police are appealing for information from witnesses who saw or heard anything on Rosewood Road between 11.50pm Friday and 1.30 am Saturday to come forward. The police can be contacted on Crimestoppers or at the Waverley police station in Bronte Road.

Sydney Morning Herald
27th November 1995

The team exchange glances; the level of energy in the room has definitely gone up. Mitch puts up a map of central Sydney, picks up the marker pen and starts annotating the map.

The Board Room bar was *here*, the address Don has on file for Luke at the time was *here*, and the accident took place *here*.

JJ NORTON

(nodding)

So the accident was in a direct line between where he lived and where he worked.

MITCHELL CLARKE

Right. And five days after it happened, just as the police are turning up the heat, Luke resigns.

BILL SERAFINI

(letting out a long breath)

Jeez.

MITCHELL CLARKE

And that sort of time in the morning is precisely when Luke would have been on his way home from work. And it's a fair bet he could have been drinking.

JJ NORTON

Which as that article says, would have given him a very good reason not to have stopped.

MITCHELL CLARKE

Exactly.

JJ NORTON

Did you speak to the Sydney police?

MITCHELL CLARKE

I did. They told me the driver responsible was never found. And there was nothing at the scene to help ID the vehicle – no paint fragments or anything like that. But one local resident did hear a very loud engine noise at around that time.

ALAN CANNING

Did the police ever suspect it could have been a motorbike?

MITCHELL CLARKE

Apparently not. And it's too late to follow up on that now, of course. And no way of tracking down the bike either, to see if it had any damage—

JJ NORTON

That might not have been conclusive anyway. If it was just a glancing blow the bike might have come off completely unscathed.

MITCHELL CLARKE

So as at now this avenue looks like a dead end. But even so, it may offer us one possible - and I think compelling - explanation for why Luke Ryder suddenly decided to leave the country.

HUGO FRASER

And why someone might have wanted to kill him. One of the victim's relatives would be right up there as a potential suspect. Always assuming they knew where Luke had absconded to, of course.

ALAN CANNING

Yes, but that wouldn't have been easy. And they'd have to be carrying one hell of a grudge to still be on his case seven years later, on the opposite side of the world.

JJ NORTON

What do we know about the victim?

MITCHELL CLARKE

(sighs)

Not much, I'm afraid. The police were a bit cagey about the whole thing. I got the impression the family put a lot of pressure on them not to release the man's name. There were 'personal reasons' apparently.

BILL SERAFINI

(knowingly)

Someone who was where he wasn't supposed to be.

JJ NORTON

That would be my guess too - maybe a married man caught going over the side—

HUGO FRASER

Do we know what happened to him? Did he survive?

MITCHELL CLARKE

Right now, your guess is as good as mine. But I've started going through death records for the weeks after the accident, to see if I can find anything. Though we have no way of knowing whether any of this has anything to do with Luke Ryder, of course.

LAILA FURNESS

True. The hit-and-run might have been caused by someone else entirely. This could just be a total wild goose chase.

BILL SERAFINI

Good work, though, Mitch. Very good work.

JJ NORTON

Agreed. And it's also something the Met don't seem to have discovered at the time, so props for that.

ALAN CANNING

Only if it turns out to be relevant. As Laila says, it could have absolutely nothing to do with it.

HUGO FRASER

(ignoring him)

How do you top that, then, Bill?

BILL SERAFINI

(smiling and getting to his feet as Mitch sits down)

I'll do my best, Hugo. I'll do my best.

(turning to face them)

So, while Mitch's been chasing Luke across the Outback, I've been looking at where he pitched up next. Back in 2003, the UK police established that when he left Sydney he went first to Bali, and then to Cambodia.

He pins up maps of both countries with markers on Kuta and Kampot respectively.

In both places he just did casual work, or at least as far as I can determine. If there were other untoward 'incidents' I haven't found them. Though in the light of what Mitch has just told us, the fact that he doesn't seem to have gone in for bar work in either location may be significant. Along with the fact that he didn't stay long in either place. His next stop after Cambodia was Beirut—

(He pins up another map.)

-where he arrived in January 1997. We don't know quite what he was doing there or why he chose it, but Lebanon was hardly the obvious choice for a holiday in the sun. The country was still recovering from a savage civil war, the government was weak to non-existent in some parts of the country, and there were areas where terrorist groups like Hezbollah and HAMAS operated pretty much with impunity. As Luke was to find out.

He turns and puts up a press cutting from the New York Times.

BEIRUT BUS BOMB LEAVES 13 DEAD

Westerners Are Among The Casualties
White House Condemns 'Atrocious' Terrorist Attack

By KEN DAVEY

BEIRUT – At just after two PM local time yesterday the center of Lebanon's capital city was rocked by an explosion that shattered windows up to a mile away.

has yet claimed responsibility for what is one of the worst attacks in Beirut in recent memory. More than thirty people are being treated in hospital, and the 13 dead so far confirmed include three Westerners. One American

New York Times
August 5, 1997

CUT TO: CNN FOOTAGE of the aftermath of the attack. Bodies lying in the street, the tangled wreckage of the bus, debris and broken glass strewn across the ground, then a tracking shot in a crowded and chaotic hospital, people on makeshift beds, one missing a leg, several with bandages around their heads and faces.

LAILA FURNESS

(clearly shocked)

I remember that happening. Just dreadful. And you're saying *Ryder* was mixed up in it?

BILL SERAFINI

(nods)

He was one of the injured. He had superficial cuts and a broken arm, spent three days in a Beirut hospital, and then – not surprisingly – decided to leave the country.

The next time we catch up with him is in Assos, where, two years later, he would meet Rupert Howard and the last chapter of his life would start to play out. Not that he knew that then, of course.

HUGO FRASER

Horrible thing to happen, of course, but I can't see how Ryder being caught up in a bus bomb in Beirut could possibly lead to someone tracking him down and killing him in London six years later.

Mitch's lead, on the other hand—

There's a general agreement and nodding of heads.

BILL SERAFINI

Not so fast, folks. That wasn't the only thing I found out.

He turns and puts up a photo on the pinboard. It's a well-built young man with dark-blond hair and a confident smile.

HUGO FRASER

Who the hell's that?

BILL SERAFINI

It's Luke Ryder.

People stare at one another, and then at Bill, clearly confused.

HUGO FRASER

No it's not.

BILL SERAFINI

Yes it is. This is the man who left Sydney in November 1995, and was injured in a bus bombing in Beirut in August 1997.

Only he wasn't injured that day.

He was killed.

The man we've been chasing - the man who met Rupert Howard in Greece, the man who married Caroline Howard and ended up beaten to death in her garden - that wasn't Luke Ryder.

It was an imposter.

FADE OUT

- end credits -

Wrap-up email from Nick Vincent, 5th May 2023

Date: Fri 5/05/2023, 9.15 **Importance:** High

From: Nick Vincent

To: Guy Howard, Hugo Fraser, Alan Canning, Mitch Clarke, Laila Furness, Bill Serafini, JJ Norton

CC: Tarek Osman

Subject: HUM-dinger

I think we can all agree that was one hell of a showstopper! Massive massive creds to Bill for pulling that out of his hat and doing it with such aplomb. And apologies again for insisting on stopping filming at that point. I know you all have a ton of questions – I do too – but we need you to ask those on camera, to keep the energy and momentum of the investigation. And you don't have long to wait – next shoot day is the 16th, and Tarek will be getting in touch with logistics etc

Cheers,

Nick

Date: Sat 6/05/2023, 9.55

From: Alan Canning

To: Guy Howard

Subject: Bill

Guy,

Could I just confirm whether or not you were privy to Bill's revelation before it happened? I'm frankly astonished that he's managed to make such an extraordinary discovery in the short time he's been on the case: he only started investigating Luke's past less than a month ago.

Moreover, it's quite clear the Met had, and still have, no idea whatsoever about this alleged 'imposture'. But maybe you and Nick have been sitting on this from the start? It would be good to know, if so.

Best,

Alan

Date: Sat 6/05/2023, 10.03

From: Guy Howard

To: Alan Canning

Subject: Re: Bill

I had no fucking idea.

Text messages between Amelie and Maura Howard, 6th May 2023, 11.49 a.m.

Did you get my voicemail? About Luke, and him being a fucking *fake*

Like WTF?

That's pretty much what I said

What did Guy say? Did he know?

No I'm sure he didn't

He looked like crap tbh

Said Nick had gone behind his back

Yeah well what did he expect

I still can't believe that fucker Luke had us fooled and got away with it. And what about Mum? Do you think she knew?

To begin with I thought there's no fucking way she knew

And now?

I don't know, Am. I just don't know

It might explain a lot of things

A LOT of things

Oh fuck

Voicemail left for Guy Howard by Nick Vincent, 6th May 2023, 11.05 p.m.

Guy? It's me. Look, I know you're pissed off and in your position I would be too, but I think once you've calmed down and had a chance to think about it you'll see that it was absolutely the right thing to do for the show. That last freeze frame on your face was one of the best closing shots I've seen in I don't know how long. Pure telly gold, mate, pure telly gold.

Anyway, let's catch up on Monday. I've got the kids this weekend so it's like the End of Days round here.

0.46 -0.09

Speaker Call back Delete

Episode three

Broadcast

October 9

The Times, 10 October 2023

TELEVISION

The plot is thickening nicely

The new Infamous is far more than just a rehash of old material

ROSS LESLIE

Infamous: Who Killed Luke Ryder?
Showrunner

Red White on Blue: The Chelsea FC Story
ITV

True crime may be the genre *du jour* - and as regular readers will know, I am a self-confessed devotee - but it does have an Achilles heel: however detailed, insightful and well-produced such shows are, all too many merely warm over the old remains of a cold case, adding nothing new or significant to the mix. One could argue that the mere act of bringing such long-dormant cases back into the light of day can prompt new witnesses to come forward, or new evidence to be discovered, and there have, indeed, been several high-profile examples, most notably the case of Adnan Syed, following the worldwide success of the Serial podcast. Yet all too often the gruesome details of someone else's pain are offered up simply for the purposes of entertainment. The ethical issues this raises are, of course, self-evident.

But the same cannot be said of the new series of **Infamous**. Last night's episode closed with new evidence so genuinely jaw-dropping that one was left wondering how the Met failed to unearth it at the time. I will, needless to say, allow you to discover the exact nature of this revelation, but safe to say, you will not be disappointed.

Red White on Blue: The Chelsea FC Story charts the club's evolution from a struggling mid-table side to giddying success on the back of Roman Abramovich's inexhaustible pot of cash. Presenter Jim White (a lifelong Red, hence the title) is an entertaining front-man, bringing a lifetime of football knowledge to proceedings, as well as a keen eye for irony as the odd

https://www.groopz.com/truecrimeaddiction

Infamous/LukeRyder Join

HOLY SHIT! WTAF?

submitted 2 hours ago by Investig8er
29 comments share hide report

And we all thought the Mitch thing was a cliffhanger. This puts a bomb under the whole bloody case

submitted 2 hours ago by BerniethεBoltcutter
7 comments share hide report

> See what you did there, Bern 😊
>
> submitted 2 hours ago by Brian885643
> 2 comments share hide report
>
> Bit crass, don't you think? In the circs? People died
>
> submitted 2 hours ago by AngieFlynn77
> share hide report

That guy Serafini is either the luckiest effin' investigator in the history of crime or there's more to this than meets the eye. No way something like that just fell into his lap

submitted 2 hours ago by TruCrimr
48 comments share hide report

> Lucky, maybe. Insufferable, definitely. He's really starting to get on my tits
>
> submitted 1 hour ago by RonJebus
> 1 comment share hide report
>
> > Not as bad as that t*sser Rupert. What a self-important 🍆
> >
> > submitted 1 hour ago by Slooth
> > 11 comments share hide report
> >
> > > AND lying through his arse. Haven't heard so much bullsh*t in under five minutes since the last Tory party political broadcast #figures
> > >
> > > submitted 1 hour ago by JimBobWalton1978
> > > share hide report

I definitely think that hit and run in Sydney could have something to do with it. Yet *another* thing the Met don't seem to have found

submitted 2 hours ago by PaulWinship007
share hide report

> Don't get me started. That investigation had more holes than my grandad's old socks
>
> submitted 1 hour ago by TCFanatic88
> 1 comment share hide report
>
> > Im not so sure - I reckon conspiracy is way more likely than cockup on this one. All that 'old money'? The Met bigwigs are just looking after their own
> >
> > submitted 1 hour ago by Slooth
> > share hide report

That bloke Fraser seems to know a lot about Campden Hill btw – all that stuff about tennis and where the squash club is #justsaying

submitted 2 hours ago by ProDTecktiv
4 comments share hide report

> Maybe he's just into racquets?
>
> submitted 1 hour ago by TachtRocker1964
> 1 comment share hide report
>
> > Rackets more like. He's a bloody KC
> >
> > submitted 1 hour ago by Slooth
> > share hide report

Back to square one if you ask me – on the investigation I mean. This changes EVERYTHING

submitted 2 hours ago by ProDTecktiv
177 comments share hide report

Episode four

Filming

Dry riser

DRY RISER FILMS Ltd

227 Sherwood Street London W1Q 2UD

CAST
Alan Canning (AC)
Mitchell Clarke (MC)
Hugo Fraser (HF)
Laila Furness (LF)
JJ Norton (JJN)
Bill Serafini (WS)

UNIT CALL 0845
Camera ready: 0900

CALL SHEET
Infamous:
Who Killed Luke Ryder?

Tuesday 15th May 2023

Ep 4: STUDIO DAY 1 of 2

Producer	**Nick Vincent**
Director	**Guy Howard**
Film editor	**Fabio Barry**
Researcher	**Tarek Osman**
Prod asst	**Jenni Tate**
Location manager	**Guy Johnson**

Breakfast on set from 0830
Running lunch from 1245
Exp wrap 1730

Location: **Frobisher Studios**
131-137 Kingston Road
Maida Vale London W9 7EX

Notes:
Very limited parking on site
Nearest tube Warwick Avenue
Emergency contact number 07000 010170

CREW							
TITLE	*NAME*	*PHONE*	*CAL[illegible]*	[illegible]	*NAME*	*PHONE*	*CALL*

TITLE SEQUENCE: arthouse-style b/w montage of images and short clips: crime scene, contemporary news coverage, family photos

THEME SONG – 'It's Alright, Ma (I'm Only Bleeding)' [Bob Dylan] from the soundtrack to 'Easy Rider' [1969]

TITLE OVER

INFAMOUS

FADE IN

WHO KILLED LUKE RYDER?

FADE OUT

BLACK FRAME, TEXT APPEARS, with VOICEOVER – narrator (female)

On the night of October 3, 2003, the brutally beaten body of a young man was found in the garden of his wife's London townhouse.

For the past twenty years, everyone – including his family and law enforcement – thought the man's name was Luke Ryder.

But thanks to our investigations, we've now proved, conclusively, that this was not his real name.

'Luke Ryder' was living a lie.

FADE OUT

CUT TO: Studio. The team are sitting round the table. They're dressed differently from last time: time has passed.

HUGO FRASER

Well, I think we can all agree that was one hell of a revelation last time, Bill.

MITCHELL CLARKE

Yeah, you certainly kept *that* one under your hat.

BILL SERAFINI

(laughing)

Sorry, guys.

ALAN CANNING

So are you going to tell us who 'Luke Ryder' actually was?

BILL SERAFINI

(turning to the board and starting to pin up mug shots)

There were five Westerners on that bus that day, three of whom died. Those five people were the real Luke Ryder, a Brit called Joe McGrath, two Dutch girls called Famke Meijer and Marit Reitsema, and our guy—

(tapping the first photo)

An American, a man by the name of Eric Dwight Fulton. A native of North Birmingham, Alabama, born on 11th March 1966.

(It takes a moment for this to sink in.)

LAILA FURNESS

But that would have made him at least ten years older than the real Luke—

BILL SERAFINI

Eleven, actually, but yes.

JJ NORTON

Hang on, so you're saying the bloke who married Caroline Howard wasn't Luke Ryder at all, but someone *eleven years older*?

(sits back)

I'm amazed he could pull that off. And that no one around him ever suspected.

BILL SERAFINI

You and me both, JJ - and I don't think Guy will mind me saying that he was just as stunned as the rest of us.

CUT TO: Guy at Dorney Place, the chair is in the middle of the room, he's in shirtsleeves and jeans this time.

GUY HOWARD

To be honest I'm still trying to get my head round this. I had no idea - honestly. I know I was only a kid at the time, but children can be surprisingly good at sensing whether people aren't genuine. I never got that vibe off him. Not once.

CUT TO: Maura, sitting on the same chair. She's now wearing a black long-sleeved T-shirt with a scoop neck. Her nails are painted black too.

GUY HOWARD - off

You know I told you Luke wasn't who he said he was? Turns out he wasn't even Australian. He was from Alabama.

MAURA HOWARD

(staring)

Alabama? Seriously? What the fuck?

GUY HOWARD - off

Did you ever suspect anything?

MAURA HOWARD

Me? Of course not - why would I? I was, like, *thirteen* when Mum met him, how the fuck would I know? He didn't *sound* American.

GUY HOWARD - off

(with a quick laugh)

At least it explains why he was so crap at cricket.

But seriously, you don't remember Mum ever saying anything - about his accent or anything like that? Or how old he looked? Even as a joke?

MAURA HOWARD

(frowning)

I'm not with you—

GUY HOWARD - off

It wasn't just that his name was fake, Maurie - he was living on someone else's identity. Someone a whole lot younger than he was.

When they first met, he wasn't 23 like he told Mum. He was 34.

MAURA HOWARD

(her eyes widening)

You have *got* to be kidding me. Thirty-*four*? All the shit she went through about the age difference and all the time they're basically the same fucking age?

GUY HOWARD - off

Yup.

MAURA HOWARD

But how the fuck did he get away with it? How did nobody even *notice*? Not us - not the kids - but the adults? Like bloody Rupert, for a start?

CUT TO: Rupert Howard, in his study this time. He's in an open-necked shirt and a cable-knit cardigan.

RUPERT HOWARD

You're saying that when I met him in Assos he was really *32*? Trust me, there is no way *on earth* that that guy, whatever his name was, was as old as that.

No way.

No. Fucking. Way. There must have been some sort of mistake.

NICK VINCENT (Producer) – off

It doesn't look like it.

RUPERT HOWARD

Oh come on, he was behaving like a bloody *student* – getting pissed, sleeping on other people's floors, generally making an arse of himself. Why would anyone in their thirties even *want* to go through all that shit again? I bloody wouldn't.

NICK VINCENT (Producer) – off

He was living on someone else's passport – he didn't have a choice.

RUPERT HOWARD

Yeah, but trust me, he was *enjoying* it. If what you say is true, this bloke wasn't just faking it, he was bloody certifiable.

CUT TO: Diana Moran, sub-captioned 'Consultant psychiatrist'. She's pale-skinned, with dark shoulder-length hair and glasses that are slightly too heavy for her face. She's sitting in a low settee in what is clearly a clinic environment: muted colour schemes, functional furniture, banal inoffensive artwork. Camera pans back to show Guy sitting alongside her.

DIANA MORAN

What we could be talking about here is a condition known as 'Peter Pan Syndrome', but I need to stress that it's not a recognized mental disorder, though the term is in fairly wide use in therapeutic circles. As the name suggests, people who exhibit this pattern of behaviour basically don't want to grow up.

It's a much more common phenomenon in men, and shows itself in 'adolescent' characteristics such as a refusal to take on responsibility, a reluctance to be tied down to specific plans or goals, and the tendency to use drugs or alcohol as a means of escape. Such men are often hopeless with money and leave a string of bankruptcies in their wake, while blaming everyone but themselves for the fact that things have gone wrong.

The flipside of all this is that they are often very charming – their 'childishness' can come over as playfulness and emotional accessibility, which women can find very attractive. A breath of fresh air, you could say. Until, that is, it becomes obvious that these appealing qualities are almost always accompanied by an inability to commit in the long term. Like children, these men are very easily bored.

GUY HOWARD

Is this something you're born with, or is it the result of your upbringing or some sort of trauma or what?

DIANA MORAN

As I say, it is not a formally recognized condition, but some documented cases do seem to have sprung from a particularly strict childhood. A father with a military background, for example, may find it hard to express his feelings, making the child feel no one is 'looking after him', which leads him to seek that kind of attention and nurturing from other people later in life.

GUY HOWARD

So you think 'Luke Ryder' was suffering from this syndrome?

DIANA MORAN

I didn't say that – it's always very dangerous to offer a diagnosis without seeing the patient. But there are some characteristics you describe in him which I think could be suggestive.

But others you've mentioned seem to diverge quite markedly from typical Peter Pan behaviour. For example, from what you say, this man functioned perfectly adequately as an adult, at least after he began the relationship with your mother –

so much so that her friends commented on his apparent maturity. Likewise he had no problem making a long-term commitment to her, though again, as you yourself pointed out, there could have been a significant element of self-interest at play there.

It's also unusual for Peter Pans to go for women older or the same age as they are – they tend to target much younger women – in part to prove to themselves and others that they're still 'young'. So 'Luke' definitely did not fit that particular pattern.

On the other hand, in some of these cases the desire to be 'taken care of' is so strong it can lead men like this to gravitate towards older women, especially those with significant means or status. There's quite a famous case from the States where a prominent Nevada politician got involved with her husband's critical-care nurse, who was about ten years younger than her.

GUY HOWARD

What happened to her?

DIANA MORAN

I'm afraid she ended up dead. He killed her. But clearly we're not looking at anything like that here. Though it's interesting, in that context, to look not only at Luke but at your mother's personality type too: some psychologists believe that certain individuals – in this case, mostly women – will actively seek out partners who will be reliant on them, partners they can 'mother'.

It won't surprise you to learn that this is known as 'Wendy Syndrome': it's often found as a co-dependency with the 'Peter Pan' personality type.

Do you think that could have been relevant in your own mother's case?

GUY HOWARD

(shaking his head)

My immediate response would be no. Luke was the exception, not the rule, in my mother's life. Both before and after Luke she was in relationships with men considerably older than she was. Men who for the most part looked after *her*.

DIANA MORAN

Interesting.

GUY HOWARD

You said there were other aspects of Luke's behaviour that did appear to have followed the Peter Pan pattern. What sort of thing did you mean?

DIANA MORAN

The fact that he was easily bored, his lack of ambition, his reluctance to get a job–

GUY HOWARD

Though you could just put that down to laziness – because he didn't actually *need* to work–

DIANA MORAN

Absolutely. Which is why it's so perilous to draw conclusions from second-hand accounts.

I believe you said Luke was extremely interested in physical fitness?

GUY HOWARD

(with a wry smile)

Yeah, he got Mum to put a gym in the basement.

DIANA MORAN

Which is also interesting, because these 'Peter Pans' are often obsessed with their looks and physique: another way of proving that they're 'still young'. In some extreme cases these men even dress and behave like adolescents.

There are examples from the US of people in their thirties taking on fake identities and allowing themselves to be taken into foster care. Or enrolling in a series of different high schools using fake adolescent personae. Basically just about anything to avoid taking on the responsibilities of adulthood.

GUY HOWARD

But didn't 'Luke' do a version of exactly that, living off the passport of someone much younger than him?

DIANA MORAN

Yes, but he didn't actively *choose* to do that, did he? He acquired that passport by a freak accident. That said, he saw no problem in becoming that much younger person when fate thrust it upon him.

So I think the key question here is whether Luke was *forced* to play the role of a much younger man, simply because that was the only passport available to him, or whether that passport merely *allowed* him to live in a way that he was already naturally drawn to.

I'm not sure we'll ever know the real answer to that.

CUT TO: Studio.

JJ NORTON

I guess it does at least explain all that stuff Caroline's friends told us about her saying Luke was an 'old soul'—

ALAN CANNING

Hang on a minute - we're getting way ahead of ourselves. How come the Met never discovered all this back in 2003?

BILL SERAFINI

(*shrugs*)

Maybe they just didn't look. To be fair, on the face of it there was no reason to. As far as they were concerned a man called Luke Ryder had entered the UK on a valid Australian passport. It wouldn't have raised any red flags.

ALAN CANNING

Oh, I get why they didn't find it. What I don't get is how *you* did.

BILL SERAFINI

What does that mean?

ALAN CANNING

You said yourself, there was no reason for anyone to doubt 'Luke Ryder' wasn't exactly who he said he was.

But you did.

I just want to know why.

BILL SERAFINI

Easy.

He gives a wry smile when he realizes what he's said.

But you wanted to know how I worked it out?

He turns to the array of pictures on the pinboard and taps the one with the group of surfers on the beach in Australia.

It was this.

LAILA FURNESS

I'm still not with you.

BILL SERAFINI

Take a closer look.

She hesitates, then gets up and goes over to the board. Bill turns to the rest of the team.

As Laila's about to discover, the real Luke Ryder had a tatt on the back of his left shoulder. It's hard to make out exactly what it is, but my guess is a version of the Hokusai wave. It's pretty popular with surfers.

Laila turns to the rest of them.

LAILA FURNESS

He's right. Once you know what you're looking for you see it straightaway.

JJ NORTON

Don't tell me – the 'Luke Ryder' who married Caroline had no tattoos.

BILL SERAFINI

You got it.

He gestures to the body map that's been pinned on the board since the first Ep.

As confirmed by the autopsy: Eric Fulton, AKA 'Luke Ryder' had no tatts.

LAILA FURNESS

But he could easily have had one like that done if he wanted to pass himself off as Luke—

JJ NORTON

(shaking his head – he's already one step ahead)

He didn't get one done because he didn't know he needed to—

MITCHELL CLARKE

(nodding)

—because they didn't know each other. He had no idea the real Luke Ryder had that ink. On his shoulder or anywhere else for that matter.

BILL SERAFINI

Yup. It was just a random trick of fate that put the two of them on the same bus at exactly the wrong moment. They'd never met before.

HUGO FRASER

So what do you think happened? This Eric Fulton stole the real Luke Ryder's passport?

BILL SERAFINI

I think so. By all accounts the real Luke was right next to the bomb when it went off. There wouldn't have been much of him left to identify.

JJ NORTON

And in all the smoke and confusion immediately afterwards Fulton switches passports with a dead guy?

BILL SERAFINI

Right.

He turns and pins up a picture of the real Luke alongside the fake one.

LAILA FURNESS

There's a superficial resemblance, certainly, but enough to get away with using his passport?

BILL SERAFINI

Think about it – that passport must have been in quite a mess by the time Fulton got his hands on it. It may not even have been in one piece. All he had to do was send what was left to the Australian authorities and get them to issue him with a new one—

HUGO FRASER

—supplying a picture of him*self* this time. Hey presto, a spanking new identity, with an official passport attached. The only other thing he needed was a passable Aussie accent. Hardly insurmountable, as such challenges go.

BILL SERAFINI

Right. And it's quite possible he didn't only take the passport - maybe he stole the real Luke's bag as well. Who knows what else there was in there - photos, letters - enough to fake a whole new life.

ALAN CANNING

You're forgetting about Fulton's family - about *Ryder's* family.

BILL SERAFINI

Well, Fulton was listed as killed in the bombing, so no one was about to start looking for him. As for Ryder's family, I guess that must have been a risk worth taking.

JJ NORTON

(nods)

And he was probably right: people don't end up in war zones unless they're trying to get lost. Or on the run. Which, as we know from Mitch, the real Luke Ryder might well have been.

LAILA FURNESS

But Fulton couldn't have known that.

JJ NORTON

(shrugs)

Takes one to know one.

LAILA FURNESS

You think Fulton was on the run too?

JJ NORTON

Has to be a possibility.

MITCHELL CLARKE

(nodding)

I agree. A bomb's gone off, there's bodies and screaming and complete mayhem on all sides and what's the first thing this guy does? He goes ferreting about in a dead man's baggage to steal his passport. That's not 'normal' behaviour, not by any definition of the term.

But I'm not a psychologist. What do you think, Laila?

LAILA FURNESS

Well, I agree with Diana Moran that it's always perilous to attempt any sort of diagnosis at second or third hand. But with that proviso, the switching of the passports does suggest to me that changing his identity was an urgent, maybe even a desperate, priority for Fulton at that time.

So much so, that immediately the bomb went off, and even though he himself was injured, he saw it not as a disaster, but a golden opportunity.

JJ NORTON

Which makes it even *more* likely he was running from something.

MITCHELL CLARKE

(to Bill)

What do we know about this Fulton guy? Apart from the fact that he came from Alabama. Do we know why he was so keen to leave his real name behind?

BILL SERAFINI

I'm on it, but right now, we don't know much.

ALAN CANNING

On the contrary, you seem to have discovered a vast amount in a remarkably short space of time.

JJ NORTON

You certainly have. I, for one, am impressed.

They all agree.

HUGO FRASER

Of course, you know what this means, don't you?

There's a silence; they're all staring at him.

This man Fulton – he ended up being murdered, six years and three thousand miles from that bomb blast, because he was, or someone *thought* he was, 'Luke Ryder'.

Fulton went to all that trouble to lose what we can only assume was a dangerous real identity, only to find himself with an even more dangerous fake one.

Out of the frying pan, and all that.

MITCHELL CLARKE

Or maybe it was his own past that caught up with him? Someone worked out he wasn't 'Luke Ryder' at all, but Eric Fulton?

There's another silence, as they take in the full implications of this.

JJ NORTON

(taking a deep breath)

So where does that leave us? Where do we go now?

HUGO FRASER

(laughs)

It's like that old Irish joke: 'I wouldn't start from here'.

LAILA FURNESS

(turning to him)

But we have to go *some*where, don't we? Is it the real, pre-Beirut Luke Ryder we should be focusing on, or the fake one after it?

JJ NORTON

I don't think it's either/or. I think it's both.

BILL SERAFINI

Agreed.

LAILA FURNESS

But don't we have to re-evaluate all our previous lines of enquiry in the light of this? Reconsider all the existing suspects, even those we thought we'd eliminated?

ALAN CANNING

First and most notably, Caroline. Did she know about this bogus identity?

Maybe she found out - maybe that's what all this was about. Because if that isn't a motive, I don't know what is.

JJ NORTON

To divorce him, yes, but to have him murdered?

BILL SERAFINI

A deception like that? I've seen plenty of people killed for less.

HUGO FRASER

(shaking his head)

I'm not buying it. If you ask me, we should follow the money.

LAILA FURNESS

In the sense that—?

HUGO FRASER

In the sense that when Fulton stole the real Luke Ryder's passport he couldn't possibly have known there was a family fortune just waiting to be claimed.

There's a pause while they take this in.

MITCHELL CLARKE

Actually, I think you could be onto something there. For someone like him, that would have been like winning the bloody lottery. All he had to do was rock up and schmooze the old lady and bingo - ker-ching.

JJ NORTON

You really think he could have fooled Florence Ryder?

HUGO FRASER

Quite possibly, if you ask me. Remember, she'd never *met* him - never even seen a photo as far as I can work out. And if Fulton really had stolen the real Luke's personal effects I'm sure a practised conman like him could have pieced together more than enough to fool her.

But the point is, money is a zero-sum game, especially when it comes to inheritance: 'Luke's' gain would have been someone else's loss.

JJ NORTON

(nodding)

Whoever stood to get the old lady's cash *before* the long-lost grandson turned up.

ALAN CANNING

Could have been the cats' home.

BILL SERAFINI

Still–

LAILA FURNESS

So how do we find that out?

HUGO FRASER

Wills are public information. If we can find out where and when she died we can find out pretty easily who the money went to.

LAILA FURNESS

But by definition that will was made - or at least updated - *after* 'Luke' died. It won't tell us what the original one said.

HUGO FRASER

Clearly not, but it stands to reason that she probably reinstated the original recipients.

BILL SERAFINI

Can you pick up on that, Hugo? Track down the old lady's will? If anyone knows their way round the British legal system, you do.

ALAN CANNING

I find it hard to believe the police didn't establish that in 2003. Luke didn't need to be an imposter for the will to be a factor.

HUGO FRASER

True, but I don't remember anything in the paperwork we were given.

LAILA FURNESS

Neither do I.

BILL SERAFINI

Maybe you could talk to some of your old pals in the Met as well, Alan? See if anything comes up?

ALAN CANNING

I can try. Though I still have a pile of those old red MGBs to check.

BILL SERAFINI

That sort of work is tedious, but it can pay off in the end. So thank you – for what it's worth.

LAILA FURNESS

OK, so what about the other suspects – does the fact that 'Luke' was an imposter make any difference where they're concerned?

Rupert, for example – if he knew Caroline's new husband was a fake would that give him a motive?

HUGO FRASER

Judging by that video we just saw, all this came as a complete revelation as far as Rupert was concerned. If he knew all along, he's a far better actor than I'm inclined to give him credit for.

And even if he *had* found out, I reckon he'd have been far more likely to shop 'Luke' to Caroline and get rid of him that way, rather than resorting to a messy and high-risk murder.

And like we said before, whichever way you cut it, Rupert had a far more plausible motive for wanting *her* out of the way, rather than Luke.

JJ NORTON

I'd agree with that.

LAILA FURNESS

And the mystery lover, assuming he exists?

MITCHELL CLARKE

I think it's the same as with Rupert: surely he'd have just used the information to turn Caroline against 'Luke'. He didn't have to actually *kill* him to get him out of the way.

JJ NORTON

True, but in my book, he's still in the frame.

BILL SERAFINI

I agree.

HUGO FRASER

One thing that just occurred to me when we were talking about mobile phones. Even allowing for the state of technology at the time, might it be worth having another look at the online/social media side in the light of what we now know?

ALAN CANNING

But it's the same issue – Facebook only launched in 2003 – there won't be anything to find.

LAILA FURNESS

Twitter?

MITCHELL CLARKE

(shaking his head)

2006.

LAILA FURNESS

(sighing)

Back to square one.

JJ NORTON

It's a relevant point though, Hugo – it's not just web technology that's come a long way in the last twenty years. I'm now wondering if it's worth revisiting the forensics. There might be something from the scene that didn't yield results originally but could now. On the clothing say, or the shoes.

HUGO FRASER

Do we know if any of the evidence has been re-tested since 2003?

BILL SERAFINI

I've seen nothing along those lines.

LAILA FURNESS

In that case it's definitely something we should pursue.

JJ NORTON

I'm happy to pick up on that. Busman's holiday and all that.

MITCHELL CLARKE

I can carry on digging in Australia – see if I can find out any more about the hit-and-run victim.

LAILA FURNESS

I could help you there?

BILL SERAFINI

Actually, Laila, what if you pick up on Caroline's mystery man? You might have more luck with getting her friends to open up.

LAILA FURNESS

(slightly hesitating)

OK, if that's what you want.

BILL SERAFINI

Which leaves me with our friend Mr Fulton.

JJ NORTON

(laughing)

It's not all bad, Bill. You might get a jolly to Alabama out of it.

BILL SERAFINI

(laughing in turn)

You ever actually *been* to Birmingham, JJ?

JJ NORTON

(winking)

Not *that* one, no, but when it comes to its big UK brother I'm an expert - born and bred a Brummie.

(putting on an exaggerated Birmingham accent)

Seeing as you've got such a bob on y'self, big tyma, let's me and you hop on a buzz and find somewhere we can chobble some bostin fettle and a couple or three tots. What d'ya say?

Bill stares at him, evidently dumbfounded, then smiles and shakes his head and the two of them start laughing.

FADE OUT

FADE IN

TEAM IN STUDIO. Bill is now in shirt sleeves with an open collar. He has a tan. It's raining outside.

JJ NORTON

Bet you're thrilled to be back in London, Bill.

BILL SERAFINI

Just delighted, JJ, just delighted.

(shaking his head)

One thing I do know is I'm getting way too old for the red eye. Used to take bounce back quick enough back in the day, but not now. Not now. Anyway, enough about me—

(looking round the table)

How's it been here - much to report?

MITCHELL CLARKE

Oh, we've all been beavering away at our homework. Teacher will be impressed.

BILL SERAFINI

(laughing)

I'm sure you'll get a gold star, Mitch.

So who wants to kick off?

LAILA FURNESS

Well, since I'm pretty certain *I* won't be getting a gold star, I think I should start.

BILL SERAFINI

I think you're selling yourself short, Laila.

LAILA FURNESS

I doubt it. And I'm not sure any of us will be able to compete with your little showstopper about Eric Fulton.

(takes a deep breath)

But here goes anyway. Last time we met we heard from Jennifer Dennison and Carmel Piper, who were part of Caroline's 'ladies who lunch' set. Neither of them thought she was having an affair, but it wasn't clear whether they knew her well enough to really know. I wasn't convinced, anyway, I don't know about anyone else.

So, with Guy's help, I dug a little deeper, and we found Shirley Booker.

CUT TO: INTERVIEW. Hotel foyer. Plush carpet, a bar in the background, people milling about, most of them men in business suits. The woman seated in the armchair in the foreground is in her sixties, short grey curls, a dark jacket, a blouse with a tie neck, and a gold brooch in the shape of a clover leaf.

LAILA FURNESS - off

So just for the record, can you tell us who you are and how you knew Caroline?

SHIRLEY BOOKER

My name is Shirley Booker and I was Caroline Farrow's flatmate when she first came to London.

LAILA FURNESS - off

When she was first working as a nanny?

SHIRLEY BOOKER

That's right. I was at Law School and had a spare room. And like most students I needed the money.

LAILA FURNESS - off

Did you know her before or did you advertise, or what?

SHIRLEY BOOKER

A cousin of mine was at school with her. She told me she had a friend who was looking for somewhere in London so I suggested we meet. We hit it off straightaway.

(smiles)

I think it was our shared obsession with Bryan Ferry that sealed the deal. She moved in later that week.

LAILA FURNESS - off

What was she like as a flatmate?

SHIRLEY BOOKER

What everyone hopes for really. Tidy, always did her share of the cleaning, never stole my milk. I had a lot of exams that year and I needed peace and quiet to work and Caroline never gave me any trouble on that front. She didn't go out much, but she never made that much noise. Unlike next door and their bloody piano. You barely knew Caroline was there.

LAILA FURNESS - off

That doesn't sound like the person other people have described to us. One of her employers around the time you're talking about said she was chatty and 'easily distracted'.

SHIRLEY BOOKER

That was probably a bit later. She did seem to come out of her shell rather more towards the end of our time sharing.

LAILA FURNESS - off

How long did she stay with you?

SHIRLEY BOOKER

Just over a year, from memory.

LAILA FURNESS - off

But you kept in touch after that? Even after she got married?

SHIRLEY BOOKER

Oh, I went to all three of her weddings. They got glitzier every time. But to answer your question, yes, we kept in touch. Three or four times a year, something like that. I never met any of her other friends apart from at the weddings, but I think she liked it that way - our relationship was something 'apart' from the rest of her life. She could tell me things she would never tell other people.

I think the fact that I was a lawyer helped too - she knew she'd always get a straight answer, even if she didn't like what it was.

LAILA FURNESS - off

What did you think of her relationship with Luke Ryder?

SHIRLEY BOOKER

As a *relationship* I thought it was a terrific idea. He was fun, he took her out of herself, they did things together. Andrew had never been interested in doing that. Luke spoiled her, in emotional terms. And she made no bones about the fact that it was the best sex she'd ever had.

LAILA FURNESS - off

But? Because I think I can hear a but coming.

SHIRLEY BOOKER

But as a *marriage*? No, absolutely not. I thought it would be a complete disaster. He was too young, too erratic. She should have kept him separate - rather like she did with me, actually. I've never thought of it that way before.

But anyway, she should have just enjoyed it while it lasted and then moved on. No one would have blamed her for that. But *marrying* him - making it official - just about *everyone* blamed her for *that*.

The Howards, because of the money - especially Rupert, of course.

Her so-called 'friends', even if most of them were motivated by envy.

Her children—

LAILA FURNESS - off

Her children didn't like him?

SHIRLEY BOOKER

They couldn't stand him, none of them. Especially Amelie.

LAILA FURNESS - off

No one's raised that before. Guy certainly hasn't.

SHIRLEY BOOKER

Well, that's hardly surprising, is it? You're a psychologist - Guy is hardly going to come straight out and tell you the three of them loathed the sight of a man who ended up dead, now, is he?

LAILA FURNESS - off

But Guy was only a child at the time - barely 10—

SHIRLEY BOOKER

That's precisely my point. His mother was replacing the father he adored with some Johnny-come-lately with a funny accent who couldn't be bothered to play with him. There can't be many more unsettling experiences for a 10-year-old than that. But you're the psychologist, you tell me.

LAILA FURNESS - off

I tend to agree. Though it must have put some dampeners on the wedded bliss.

SHIRLEY BOOKER

The wedd*ing* bliss as well - Guy famously pushed the cake off its stand on the morning of the ceremony. It was a complete write-off - cream and sponge all over the floor. Caroline kept on and on insisting it was only an accident - that Guy was just 'overexcited'.

LAILA FURNESS - off

You obviously didn't agree.

SHIRLEY BOOKER

Let's just say that he certainly didn't look 'excited' to me. Just absolutely furious. And of course there was the most tremendous panic because they had to send out for another cake at the last minute.

(makes a wry face)

Thankfully Fortnum's were happy to oblige. Admittedly Guy had always been a difficult child but after Luke arrived he became almost unmanageable. And not just at home. The school really struggled with him - disruptive one minute, daydreaming the next. The sort of behaviour that would get you an assessment for ADHD these days.

And it actually got *worse* after Luke died. You might have thought it would have helped, having his mother all to himself again, but it was quite the opposite. I suspect Caroline was just too distracted to devote enough time to him.

CUT TO: MONTAGE of shots of Guy, Amelie, and Maura Howard in the mid 2000s. The girls are growing up fast - make-up, shorter skirts, higher heels. Guy, by contrast, still seems like a little boy. In one shot he's on the window seat in his bedroom with Amelie. She's reading him a story and he's clutching a teddy bear; a closer look reveals tears on his cheeks. The terrace and gardens can be seen through the window directly below; it's raining.

SHIRLEY BOOKER

As for the girls, they always were incredibly tight, and they just shut Luke out. As for their mother, they just went full-on passive-aggressive - stopped cooperating with anything she asked them to do. She said it was a complete nightmare.

And of course there was all that trouble with Maura that summer.

LAILA FURNESS - off

Maura? That's the first time anyone's mentioned any problems with her.

SHIRLEY BOOKER

Well, I doubt it was something Caroline wanted people to know. In the circumstances.

LAILA FURNESS - off

As in—?

SHIRLEY BOOKER

It doesn't take a lot of guessing. Maura was 15. A very precocious and *rebellious* 15. She knew exactly how to push Caroline's buttons, and what better way than to get involved with some completely inappropriate people.

LAILA FURNESS - off

Inappropriate in what way?

SHIRLEY BOOKER

People a lot older than her, for a start - much too old to be hanging around with someone Maura's age. And regardless of age, they were absolutely not the sort of people Caroline wanted her teenage daughter associating with.

LAILA FURNESS - off

I'm surprised Maura came into contact with anyone like that in the first place. I got the impression the Howard children lived rather a sheltered life. And it's not as if they could have met anyone online. Not back then.

SHIRLEY BOOKER

I think she met one of them at a charity event at her school. Rather an unfortunate case of the law of unintended consequences. And by the time Caroline found out what was going on it was, of course, far too late. I think there was some suspicion of drug use as well. Nothing hard-core, but we all know how easily things can escalate where drugs are concerned.

LAILA FURNESS - off

I can see why Caroline would have been anxious.

SHIRLEY BOOKER

She was out of her mind with worry that whole summer before Luke died. Nothing she did had any effect - she tried talking to Maura, grounding her, stopping her allowance, but it made no difference.

LAILA FURNESS - off

Yet to the outside world everything seemed fine.

SHIRLEY BOOKER

Of course it did. That's how people like Caroline deal with situations like that. What goes on behind closed doors is one thing; letting the world and his wife find out is quite another.

It was the same after the murder – she just battened down the hatches, shut the world out. Even to the extent of not acting quickly enough to get her children counselling, even though it was obvious to anyone with eyes in their head that they were struggling. These days all three would probably have been diagnosed with some form of PTSD.

LAILA FURNESS – off

I wasn't aware any of the kids had had therapy.

SHIRLEY BOOKER

All of them, in fact. But like I said, Caroline kept that sort of thing very private. I seem to remember there was an incident at the girls' school – some sort of damage, I don't think I ever knew what, exactly. I do know Caroline had to pull a lot of strings to keep it out of the press. I can't remember which of the girls was involved, but I'm pretty sure it was that incident which forced Caroline's hand on the therapy issue: it was made clear to her that she no longer had a choice.

LAILA FURNESS – off

By whom? The police?

SHIRLEY BOOKER

The school, as a condition of further attendance.

LAILA FURNESS – off

I see.

There's a pause; if Laila was hoping Booker might say more, she's disappointed.

LAILA FURNESS – off

So, going back to the summer before the murder, what effect did the antipathy of the children towards Luke have on the domestic dynamic?

SHIRLEY BOOKER

Well, it can hardly have helped. I know Luke did offer to try talking to Maura about her behaviour, but Caroline thought it would only make matters worse. Maura disliked him so much she'd have positively *enjoyed* sticking two fingers up at him.

LAILA FURNESS - off

And the other children? How were things on that score?

SHIRLEY BOOKER

According to Caroline, Luke was absolutely convinced it was only a matter of time before all three of them came round. Apparently he was always like that - you know, the 'something will turn up' type. Very easy-going.

The girls took advantage of that, of course. Treated him like their personal chauffeur. But if it kept the peace I suspect that was all Caroline cared about.

LAILA FURNESS - off

That summer - there have been suggestions she might have started an affair

SHIRLEY BOOKER

Oh yes, she definitely had. There's no question about that.

LAILA FURNESS - off

(evidently surprised)

She told you about it?

SHIRLEY BOOKER

Not *who* it was, no, but that she was seeing someone, yes, absolutely.

LAILA FURNESS - off

What did she say about him?

SHIRLEY BOOKER

That she hadn't gone looking for it – it had just happened. An 'instant attraction', and something about 'forbidden fruit'. I definitely remember that because it sounded so corny, even back then. And I know she felt bad about Luke, but she said no one would get hurt if they never found out.

LAILA FURNESS - off

That suggests two things to me. One, that in her eyes, just a fling; and two, that this other man was married as well. It's the use of the word 'they' I'm referring to there. The plural. Implying Luke wasn't the only person who'd get hurt if it all came out.

SHIRLEY BOOKER

Is that a psychological analysis?

LAILA FURNESS - off

If you like.

SHIRLEY BOOKER

Actually, I think you're right on both counts. I do know she had no intention of divorcing Luke – not at that stage, at any rate.

In fact, I'm pretty sure she was on the point of finishing it with this other man at the time Luke died.

LAILA FURNESS - off

Do you think she might already have done so – or tried to?

SHIRLEY BOOKER

Quite possibly. We had a lunch booked for the following week – which of course never happened – so I wasn't absolutely up to speed as to whether she'd spoken to him. I do know she was apprehensive about it. About how he might react.

LAILA FURNESS - off

To the point of being actually afraid of him?

SHIRLEY BOOKER

(*considers for a moment*)

Not actively *afraid*, no. But definitely uneasy. I remember her saying she'd 'done it again' - got involved with someone completely unsuitable.

LAILA FURNESS - off

A reference to Luke?

SHIRLEY BOOKER

No, I'm pretty sure not. I think she was talking about the man she got mixed up with when she was still at school.

LAILA FURNESS - off

I remember now - the man her parents disapproved of? The reason they sent her off to her uncle's in Edgbaston?

SHIRLEY BOOKER

That's right. I think it took her quite a while to get over it - I suspect that's why she was so subdued when she first moved in with me.

And of course, it made her doubly concerned about Maura - she didn't want her making the same mistakes.

LAILA FURNESS - off

One last question. What would you say if I told you that we've uncovered evidence that Luke wasn't who he said he was.

That he was, in fact, an American of 37, not an Australian of 26.

Shirley looks staggered and then starts laughing.

LAILA FURNESS - off

What's so funny? It's a serious matter, surely.

SHIRLEY BOOKER

Of course it is. It's just that I said pretty much exactly that to Caroline myself.

My son was just getting into surfing back then - we have a place in Cornwall - and *he* said it was clear as day from what I'd told him that Luke didn't know the first thing about it.

And on top of that his Aussie accent was *execrable.* I told Caroline she should check his passport. I mean, it was a *joke*, of course, but after all these years you're now telling me—

<u>LAILA FURNESS - off</u>

When was this - when did you have that conversation?

<u>SHIRLEY BOOKER</u>

It must have been a few weeks after the wedding. I only met him for the first time at the ceremony—

<u>LAILA FURNESS - off</u>

And how did she react when you said that? I mean, she'd already married him by then—

<u>SHIRLEY BOOKER</u>

She laughed. Said she'd seen his passport, thank you very much, when they went on honeymoon, and in any case she didn't care. She didn't give a fig where he came from or who he was. It didn't matter.

<u>LAILA FURNESS - off</u>

So if she'd found out he actually *was* an imposter, it wouldn't have particularly upset her?

<u>SHIRLEY BOOKER</u>

(raises an eyebrow)

If what you're really getting at is whether she'd have been affronted enough to *kill* him, then no. Absolutely not.

I'm sorry, Dr Furness, but I'm afraid you'll need to find another tree to bark up on that one.

CUT TO: Studio.

LAILA FURNESS

So as you can see, my week ended up being rather a case of two steps forward, three steps back.

On the positive side there definitely *was* a mystery man, even if we still don't know his name.

But on the other hand, it looks like Caroline would have been supremely *un*bothered to discover that her husband wasn't quite who he said he was.

JJ NORTON

Those were quite some revelations about the girls, though - the therapy, the incident at the school. What did you make of it? With your professional hat on?

LAILA FURNESS

Well, as I've said before, one has to be very cautious about attempting any sort of analysis at third-hand, especially when we don't even know exactly what occurred. I mean, obviously *something* happened and it was serious enough for the school to insist on counselling, but it could have been a genuine accident, or just a silly prank that got out of hand.

Let's face it we've all found ourselves in situations like that when we were that age, it's part of growing up—

BILL SERAFINI

(smiling)

I can attest to that—

LAILA FURNESS

So in the absence of any other information, I'd be wary of making too much of it.

JJ NORTON

I guess we could ask Maura?

LAILA FURNESS

We could, though I gather she's not very keen to talk to us again. But yes, we could certainly try.

BILL SERAFINI

And in the meantime our quest for the mystery lover goes on. Alan, what've you got on that?

(smiling)

How many MGBs were you down to last time, remind me?

ALAN CANNING

(not smiling)

There were forty-two owners in the London area and I'd spoken to sixteen of them. As at now, I've spoken to another fifteen.

(gets up and puts a list on the pinboard)

I also started contacting some of the women listed as owners, as I figured this man could have been driving someone else's car. A sister, a wife—

JJ NORTON

Pretty brutal, using your wife's car for leg-overs with your bit on the side—

ALAN CANNING

Maybe his own car would have stood out too much.

JJ NORTON

A bright red MGB is hardly shy and retiring.

LAILA FURNESS

But a Bentley would have been worse - or, I don't know, a Lamborghini—

MITCHELL CLARKE

Not round there! You can't move for them—

ALAN CANNING

(ignoring them)

And there are still a lot more male owners I haven't yet spoken to.

BILL SERAFINI

But no one's stood out so far?

ALAN CANNING

Not so far.

BILL SERAFINI

OK. What about you, Hugo, what did you find out about old Mrs Ryder's will?

Hugo gets to his feet and goes over to a table at the side where there are stacks of paper and files. As he passes the pinboard he stops briefly and takes a look, then turns to the team.

HUGO FRASER

Well, I've been able to establish that Florence Ryder was living in a care home in Ambleside when she died, which was in May 2005. The will went through probate early the following year.

(passing round sheets of paper)

As you can see, it's pretty straightforward as these documents go. There are several relatively small bequests to charities - the usual stuff, Marie Curie, the RSPCA, that sort of thing - and a specific gift of jewellery to a woman called Sylvia Carroll. She took a bit of finding, but it turns out she was one of the staff at the care home. I'll come back to her in a moment.

The remainder of the estate - which amounted to over four million pounds, by the way - went to a cousin of her late husband. A woman by the name of Margaret Wilson.

LAILA FURNESS

And what do we know about her?

HUGO FRASER

When Florence died Margaret was living in Cornwall, at a little place called Poltreath, about ten miles from St Ives. She died eighteen months later, but by that time she was living *in* St Ives, in a house overlooking the harbour—

JJ NORTON

Amazing what four million quid can do—

MITCHELL CLARKE

Quite.

HUGO FRASER

She'd been a widow since 1998 and had one child, Ian, born in 1977. We're trying to track him down but Wilson is a tiresomely common name.

LAILA FURNESS

And at the risk of stating the obvious, back in October 2003 both mother and son had four million fabulous reasons for wanting Luke Ryder out of the way.

HUGO FRASER

I don't disagree. Though there are a couple of important caveats.

Firstly we don't know for certain whether the *original* will - the one that was changed in favour of Luke - had the same terms as the one in force at the time Florence Ryder died.

The one person who could tell us that would be Florence's lawyer, but of course he'd be bound by client confidentiality.

LAILA FURNESS

Is he even still around?

HUGO FRASER

Yes. Long retired, but yes.

The second caveat - assuming the original will *was* indeed the same - is whether Margaret Wilson and/or her son actually *knew* how much they stood to gain from Florence's death. And by extension how much they lost at the stroke of a pen when the long-lost 'grandson' appeared on the scene.

LAILA FURNESS

That's going to be hard to prove.

HUGO FRASER

Without the lawyer's cooperation, yes. But there are some things we may be able to ascertain without needing his intervention.

One of those being whether or not Florence was in regular touch with the Wilsons while she was still alive, which would increase the likelihood of them knowing about the contents of the will.

And that's where Sylvia Carroll comes in.

CUT TO: INTERVIEW. Sylvia Carroll is seated in the lounge area of a care home. There are chairs with plastic seat covers arranged around the edge of a large open space, and a TV on in the corner showing a cooking programme. Sylvia is a large middle-aged woman with dyed auburn hair in a ponytail and a turquoise overall. She has a nose ring and several piercings in both ears.

SYLVIA CARROLL

Flo was one of the nicest residents I've ever had to look after. Always easy to get on with, never made a fuss. Not like some of 'em.

HUGO FRASER - off

How long did you know her?

SYLVIA CARROLL

Must have been about seven years. Yeah, from when I started at Lakeside to when she died in 2006.

CUT TO: MONTAGE of photos of Florence Ryder taking part in activities at the care home. Bingo, seated keep-fit, a Christmas party with paper hats and crackers. There are several images of her with a younger and thinner Sylvia. They're both smiling, and Sylvia has her arm round her.

HUGO FRASER – off

She left you a very nice gift in her will. That jewellery? The brooches and bracelets?

SYLVIA CARROLL

Yeah, that's what I mean – she was such a lovely lady. She wanted me to have them.

HUGO FRASER – off

Quite valuable, too. Diamonds – emeralds—

SYLVIA CARROLL

(flushing slightly)

Like I said, she wanted me to have them. She said she didn't have any daughters or granddaughters and I was the nearest thing. It was all above board. The lawyer did it in the will. Look, I hope you're not suggesting—

HUGO FRASER – off

No, no, I'm not suggesting anything. I'm sure you *were* like a granddaughter to her.

SYLVIA CARROLL

(still looking wary)

I was, actually. I looked out for her. No one else was, that's for sure.

HUGO FRASER – off

So no one else visited, then? No one else in the family?

SYLVIA CARROLL

When I first started at Lakeside she told me that she didn't have any family. That was why it was such a big surprise when that Luke turned up.

HUGO FRASER – off

Luke?

SYLVIA CARROLL

You know, the grandson. The one that got killed. You must remember him. It was in all the papers.

HUGO FRASER - off

You met him?

SYLVIA CARROLL

(smiling)

Of course I met him. I was there the first time he came. He'd written beforehand saying he wanted to come and was that OK, but the manager was deffo a bit wary at first. You know, people turning up out of the blue and claiming to be long-lost rellies, it isn't always legit. But he was. The lawyer checked him out.

HUGO FRASER - off

Mrs Ryder's lawyer?

SYLVIA CARROLL

Mr Hepworth, yes. He wanted her to make Luke take a DNA test as well but she refused. Said the passport and stuff was enough. That demanding a DNA test would make Luke think she didn't believe him. That he'd be insulted.

HUGO FRASER - off

Interesting. And I'm guessing it came as quite a shock. For Mrs Ryder, I mean - him turning up like that after all those years.

SYLVIA CARROLL

I know. I remember overhearing him saying as much to the manager. How he'd wondered initially whether it was the right thing to do, and the last thing he wanted was to cause Flo any distress. That was so like him - always worrying about other people.

HUGO FRASER - off

So you liked him?

SYLVIA CARROLL

(smiling again)

He was a right little charmer.

(quickly)

Oh, not in a bad way, I didn't mean that. I just meant he was really nice. All the old ladies fell in love with him. He knew exactly how to talk to them. Flattered them, teased them a bit, you know. He had them eating out of his hand. And of course he was very good-looking. Made a nice change round here, I can tell you. We all looked forward to him coming.

HUGO FRASER - off

And Mrs Ryder liked him too?

SYLVIA CARROLL

She *adored* him. He was her blue-eyed boy. She was always teasing him about his accent. I remember her telling him once that she couldn't believe her Brian could have produced a gorgeous boy like him.

HUGO FRASER - off

That makes it sound like she saw him a lot.

SYLVIA CARROLL

Oh yes, he used to come up a couple of times a month. On that flashy motorbike of his.

HUGO FRASER - off

Really? I mean, even with a motorbike it's a long way - London to Ambleside.

SYLVIA CARROLL

I know. But he didn't seem to mind. I think he genuinely enjoyed her company. They made each other laugh.

HUGO FRASER - off

Did he ever bring his wife?

SYLVIA CARROLL

No, never saw her once. He never talked much about her, not that I heard, anyway. Or about his parents.

HUGO FRASER – off

Didn't that strike you as strange?

SYLVIA CARROLL

(shrugs)

Not really. I know there'd been some sort of family tiff before his parents left for Australia, though I don't know what it was about, because Flo never talked about it. And after Luke reappeared she just wanted to move on, let bygones be bygones.

And it wasn't anything to do with Luke, anyway, was it – that row? He wasn't even born. She was just pleased he'd plucked up the courage to try and contact her. You know, before it was too late. She was in her eighties, remember. She knew she didn't have that long left.

HUGO FRASER – off

But given that, do you know if she'd ever tried to contact her son herself, before Luke turned up? Try to bury the hatchet?

SYLVIA CARROLL

I don't know. If she had, it hadn't worked. But I reckon she wouldn't have known where to start to find them. Not with them being so far away.

HUGO FRASER – off

In fact Brian had died in 1993.

SYLVIA CARROLL

There you are then.

HUGO FRASER – off

How did she react when Luke was killed?

SYLVIA CARROLL

Devastated. Inconsolable. She wanted to go to the funeral but it was too far. She sent the most beautiful wreath. Dahlias. I sorted it out for her.

HUGO FRASER - off

Did the police come and see her?

SYLVIA CARROLL

Oh yes. More than once. That tall bloke, Peter something—

HUGO FRASER - off

Peter Lascelles.

SYLVIA CARROLL

That's it. Quite a nice bloke. He did his best but the poor old girl was in such a state I don't think he got much out of her. And what could she tell him, anyway? Like I said, she didn't know anything about Luke's life in London.

HUGO FRASER - off

I imagine he was asking her about her will. Who would get the money now that Luke was dead.

SYLVIA CARROLL

Maybe.

HUGO FRASER - off

You never met Margaret Wilson? Or her son?

SYLVIA CARROLL

(her face hardening)

No, but I knew all about them.

HUGO FRASER - off

And?

SYLVIA CARROLL

They turned up at the home after Flo's funeral. With a bloody lawyer, would you believe. Wanted to go through her stuff. Make an 'inventory'. Accused me of exerting 'undue influence' on a 'vulnerable elderly person' because of me getting the jewellery. They obviously thought that should have gone to them as well, the greedy bastards. Throwing round accusations like that, I could have *lost* my *job*—

HUGO FRASER - off

That must have been very upsetting. I'm guessing, though, from what you just said, that you hadn't come across them while Mrs Ryder was still alive? They never visited?

SYLVIA CARROLL

Never saw hide nor hair of either of 'em. And thankfully I wasn't on duty when they came poking around or there'd have been ructions—

HUGO FRASER - off

Did she ever talk to you about her will? About who she'd planned to give her money to before Luke got in touch?

SYLVIA CARROLL

Not really. But she never mentioned the bloody Wilsons, that I do know. Not once.

CUT TO: Studio.

JJ NORTON

Round of applause for Hugo, I think. That was an impressive piece of interviewing.

MITCHELL CLARKE

(laughing)

Yeah - anyone would think he'd done this sort of thing before.

LAILA FURNESS

It certainly put paid to any doubts we might have had about whether 'Luke' could fool Florence. She was obviously deeply regretting the breach with her son, but all those years later she had no way of doing anything about it.

So when someone turns up saying he's her grandson, she accepts him at once. Psychologically speaking, she was primed to believe. No wonder she refused a DNA test.

BILL SERAFINI

I agree, Laila. Though my principal take-out was Ian Wilson. He clearly had one hell of a motive and definitely doesn't sound like someone who'd have taken the loss of that sort of cash lying down.

General agreement round the table.

HUGO FRASER

Speaking of which, I had that chat with Peter Lascelles about how far the Wilsons were in the frame at the time.

CUT TO: Hugo at a desk, with a phone on speaker in front of him.

HUGO FRASER

(into phone)

Peter? It's Hugo Fraser. I'm working on the Showrunner series with Alan Canning and Bill Serafini.

PETER LASCELLES

Yes, they mentioned you were on the team. And I'm aware of you, of course.

HUGO FRASER

We've been looking at the issue of Florence Ryder's will, and whether that gave rise to any viable lines of enquiry.

PETER LASCELLES

Ah, the Wilsons.

HUGO FRASER

The Wilsons, exactly.

PETER LASCELLES

Well, as you will appreciate more than most, the investigation remains open - officially, at any rate - so I'm limited as to what I can say publicly.

HUGO FRASER

Understood.

PETER LASCELLES

But speaking hypothetically, in a case where certain parties could have a substantial financial interest in the death of a victim, we would always carry out a thorough investigation as to whether a) they were aware of this financial interest, and b) if they were indeed aware, whether they also had the means and opportunity to carry out the crime.

HUGO FRASER

Our working assumption on a) is yes.

PETER LASCELLES

You may think so, I couldn't possibly comment. As the saying goes.

HUGO FRASER

Did you establish if the Wilsons had solid alibis for the night of the third of October 2003?

PETER LASCELLES

Let's just say that neither Mrs Wilson nor her son were ever charged. That is, of course, a matter of public knowledge as no charges have yet been brought against anyone in this case.

HUGO FRASER

Do you know where Ian Wilson's now living?

PETER LASCELLES

He moved abroad, I believe, in fairly short order after the murder. But as to where, I'm afraid I have no idea.

(pause)

Sorry, I haven't been much help, have I?

CUT TO: Studio.

HUGO FRASER

So that's where we are. If we take Lascelles's word for it, neither of the Wilsons were in the frame for the murder back then. And to be honest, I'm not sure a woman could even carry out an attack like that, especially one as old as Margaret would have been by then.

ALAN CANNING

I've seen cases where women were capable of that degree of violence, though they were almost always under acute mental or emotional pressure at the time.

JJ NORTON

Domestic abuse victims, you mean?

ALAN CANNING

Primarily, yes. But *none* of those crimes came out of a blue sky. They were the last act in a long drama.

LAILA FURNESS

I agree. For a woman to attack someone she'd never met, and do it that savagely, just for money, without any personal grievance at all, you'd be looking at someone on the psychopathy spectrum.

Which, of course, is not impossible, but the odds are very much against.

JJ NORTON

That still leaves Ian. How old was he then - 28? He'd have been more than capable—

LAILA FURNESS

And he's someone Luke might have opened the door to, even if they'd never met: 'Luke' would have known about the Wilsons from Florence, so he wouldn't see them as a threat. Ian could have spun a line about her being unwell, then as soon as he gets inside—

ALAN CANNING

(nodding)

We definitely need to try and find him. And investigate that alibi of his too.

BILL SERAFINI

Agreed.

(turning to Hugo)

Why don't I have a word with Peter Lascelles, off the record. Cop to cop. See if he might be prepared to give me more of a steer.

HUGO FRASER

(rather acidly)

Be my guest.

BILL SERAFINI

So, next up is the hit-and-run the real Luke Ryder may have been involved in before he left Australia. Any news on that, Mitch?

MITCHELL CLARKE

(looks up)

Actually, yes, something that could be quite significant, I think.

As we discussed last time, the press coverage said the victim was in a coma immediately after the accident, so we had no way of knowing when - or even *whether* - he actually died.

So I started by doing a trawl of death records for the Sydney area for the two months after the date of the accident, to see if anything stood out. That gave me five fatalities where the cause of death was listed as multiple blunt-force trauma injuries resulting from a road traffic accident, but obviously no details of where and when those accidents happened.

So I then cross-referenced those names with the listings for the coroner's court of New South Wales. But again, I'm afraid, no luck. Nothing at all referencing an incident for that day, in that area. Which suggests to me that either the victim didn't actually die from his injuries, or if he *did* it was somewhere else, or some considerable time later.

JJ NORTON

Well, well done for persevering – I'm getting a headache just listening to it.

MITCHELL CLARKE

It was erring on the thankless side by then, I'll admit, which may be why my helpful police contact decided to take pity on me. He wouldn't give me any actual details, but he did drop a fairly heavy hint that the victim was a student, and maybe that could be a useful angle to pursue.

To be honest, when he said that my first thought was 'bloody hell, how many students are there in Sydney?', but then I thought, with an accident that serious, maybe there'd be something about it in a student newspaper. My journo contact thought I was wasting my time but I've always been a belligerent sod—

BILL SERAFINI

Well, it clearly paid dividends this time.

MITCHELL CLARKE

(smiling)

Certainly did. Though it still took bloody ages because there was nothing online back then. But I did eventually dig up something on the Sydney Technology College website – their alumni section has PDFs of the student rag going back to the 1980s.

He taps his keyboard. An image appears on the screen.

And this is what I found.

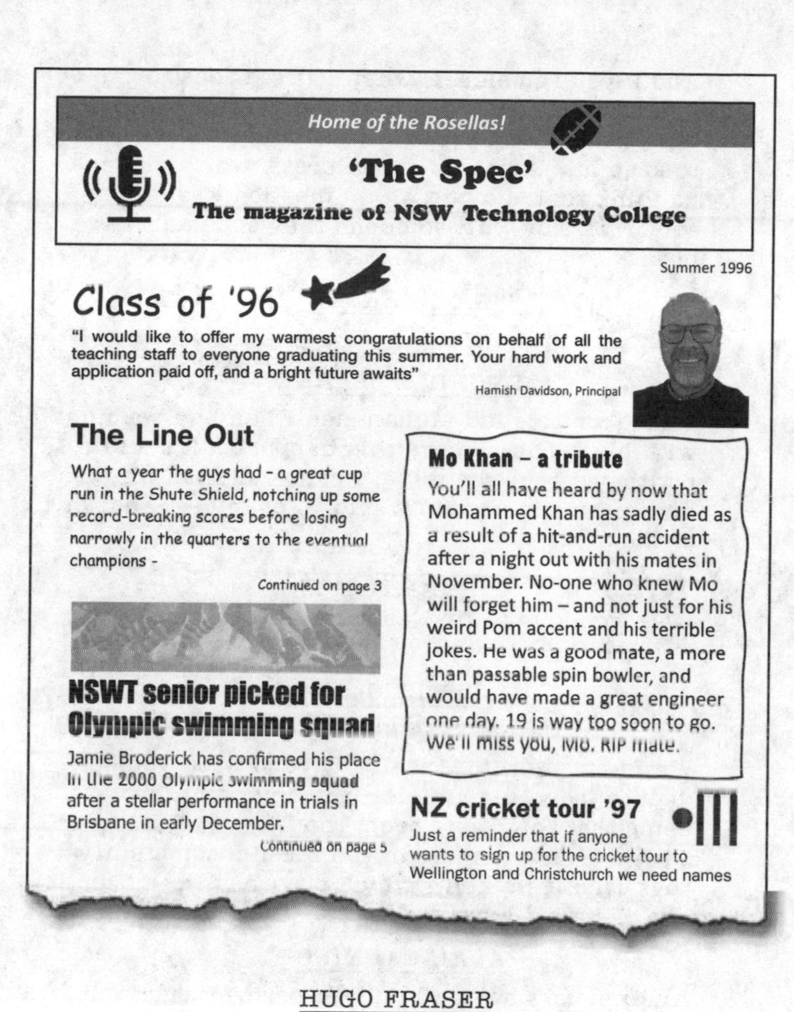

Home of the Rosellas!

'The Spec'

The magazine of NSW Technology College

Summer 1996

Class of '96

"I would like to offer my warmest congratulations on behalf of all the teaching staff to everyone graduating this summer. Your hard work and application paid off, and a bright future awaits"

Hamish Davidson, Principal

The Line Out

What a year the guys had - a great cup run in the Shute Shield, notching up some record-breaking scores before losing narrowly in the quarters to the eventual champions -

Continued on page 3

NSWT senior picked for Olympic swimming squad

Jamie Broderick has confirmed his place in the 2000 Olympic swimming squad after a stellar performance in trials in Brisbane in early December.

Continued on page 5

Mo Khan – a tribute

You'll all have heard by now that Mohammed Khan has sadly died as a result of a hit-and-run accident after a night out with his mates in November. No-one who knew Mo will forget him – and not just for his weird Pom accent and his terrible jokes. He was a good mate, a more than passable spin bowler, and would have made a great engineer one day. 19 is way too soon to go. We'll miss you, Mo. RIP mate.

NZ cricket tour '97

Just a reminder that if anyone wants to sign up for the cricket tour to Wellington and Christchurch we need names

HUGO FRASER

(under his breath)

Jesus Christ, death by Comic Sans.

MITCHELL CLARKE

(going over to the screen and pointing to the 'Tribute' article)

As you can see the date's about right, and the details of the accident tally as far as they go.

And if you remember, when I first spoke to the Sydney police they made it pretty clear that the victim's family had moved heaven and earth to keep his name out of the press, which made us think that the person in question was either some*where* or with some*one* they shouldn't have been.

BILL SERAFINI

Right.

MITCHELL CLARKE

And given this lad Mohammed Khan had been out with his friends before this happened, it's a fair bet they'd been drinking. I can easily see why a devout Muslim family would want to keep that out of the press.

BILL SERAFINI

Were you able to find out anything about the family?

MITCHELL CLARKE

(shaking his head)

'Fraid not. Nothing, really, beyond what you can deduce from this article – the key point for us being that they were from the UK. But Khan is such a common name in the Muslim community that even if we knew which city they were from it wouldn't be a lot of help.

ALAN CANNING

And we can't be one hundred per cent sure this is the right guy, either – I mean, I assume your police officer contact wasn't prepared to go as far as to confirm it?

MITCHELL CLARKE

No, he wasn't, so you're right, we can't be absolutely sure. This is just an informed guess.

LAILA FURNESS

And as we've said before, Luke may have had nothing to do with any of it. It could all just be a coincidence.

MITCHELL CLARKE

Right. All we have is the proximity of the accident to where Luke was working, and the fact that he upped and left the country less than a week later.

ALAN CANNING

Police officers don't like coincidences. If it was my case, I'd still want to investigate.

BILL SERAFINI

Likewise.

MITCHELL CLARKE

Well, I'm not sure how much more we'll be able to find, but Tarek is on the case now. Let's see what he and the team can find.

JJ NORTON

(looks round the table)

I think I'm up next?

(clears his throat and opens his file)

As we agreed last time, I took another look at the forensic evidence, to see if there was any chance further testing might yield any results, specifically on the clothing. And guess what. They never actually tested it.

LAILA FURNESS

They never tested the clothes at all? *Seriously?*

JJ NORTON

I know it sounds like someone dropped the ball, but you need to remember this was 2003. DNA testing was much more rudimentary back then and it was also way more expensive and took weeks to do. And let's not forget the body had been in a downpour, so all things considered, I guess the SIO didn't think it was worth his budget on the off-chance something survived the rain.

BILL SERAFINI

SIO?

JJ NORTON

Sorry - Senior Investigating Officer.

But on the positive side, what it *does* mean is that we can now get the clothing tested ourselves, and who knows what we might find.

LAILA FURNESS

So how do we go about doing that?

ALAN CANNING

I'll call the officer who's handling the file. It'll be someone in the cold case unit.

LAILA FURNESS

Not so much cold as permafrost, if you ask me. At least as far as active enquiries are concerned.

BILL SERAFINI

Well, that's why we're here, isn't it, Laila?

(looking round)

Do we need next-of-kin permission or something like that? I'm not up to speed on all your British procedures.

ALAN CANNING

The police can apply for further testing, they don't need agreement from the family. Let's just hope the Met play ball.

JJ NORTON

They might - given what else I found. As we know from the file, three hairs were found caught in the zip of Ryder's jacket during the original investigation, but they weren't tested in 2003 because none of them had roots.

But as some of you may be aware, we can now extract DNA from hair samples like that. It's fiddly and pricey, but it can be done.

LAILA FURNESS

Remind me, what colour were the hairs?

JJ NORTON

Mid brown, and undyed. Which ruled out Luke himself, as he was blond, and also Caroline, because her hair was bleached. But that's as far as they could get at the time.

BILL SERAFINI

All the same it presumably reinforced the Met's working hypothesis that Caroline was not the perp. But from what you say, JJ, I think we should definitely put pressure on the police to go for testing now.

ALAN CANNING

I can pick up on that. Though we need to remember that even if they do get something they're not going to give us full access. The most we could hope for would be a steer.

LAILA FURNESS

Well, a 'steer' is a lot more than nothing at all, which is all we have right now.

BILL SERAFINI

Thanks, Alan. Appreciate it.

And in the meantime, this sounds like my cue.

He gets to his feet, goes up to the board, and starts pinning up photos: abandoned industrial sites behind wire fencing, derelict one-storey homes, wide roads, telegraph poles.

This, my friends, is North Birmingham, Alabama. Population 1,273, a high proportion of whom are African American. Once a thriving industrial district it's now a rust-belt town - drugs, street crime, and prostitution are rife, and household incomes are well below the national average.

So it's hardly at the top of a tourist's bucket list. Though there is one thing that's on our side: even if it's a suburb of a big city, in other respects it's just like a small town, meaning that everyone knows everyone else's business, and people like to talk.

JJ NORTON

Which definitely makes your job easier.

BILL SERAFINI

Right. Though this one took some diplomatic handling, I can tell you. Remember, as far as everyone in North Birmingham was concerned, 'Eric Fulton' died in a bus bomb in Beirut more than two decades ago.

And here I come, parachuting in out of nowhere, telling them that not only did he *not* die then, he actually stole the identity of a guy who did.

MITCHELL CLARKE

I see what you mean.

JJ NORTON

So how did you play it?

BILL SERAFINI

(smiles)

Very, very carefully.

CUT TO: Bill, in short-sleeved shirt and sunglasses, by a high chicken-wire fence. The building behind looks like a school, with a concrete basketball court and a stars-and-stripes flag hanging limply from a pole. The light is very bright. Bill's standing with a man in his seventies, who's wearing a check shirt and baseball cap. Sub-captioned 'Frank Tappin, Former Little League coach'.

FRANK TAPPIN

Jeez, I haven't heard the name Eric Fulton in over twenty years.

BILL SERAFINI

You taught him ball, back in the day?

FRANK TAPPIN

Yes, sir. Eric was a good kid. Quiet. Never gave me any trouble. Even though it was obvious he hated every goddamn minute. Mainly because he was no good at it. It was his dad made him play.

BILL SERAFINI

What did you know about the family?

FRANK TAPPIN

Not so much, to tell you the truth. There were three brothers. Eric was the youngest. His mom worked in a supermarket and his dad worked two jobs. Eric was always in hand-me-downs that were too big for him. Both his brothers were way taller than he was.

BILL SERAFINI

Do you remember the brothers' names?

FRANK TAPPIN

Can't say I do. I never had no dealings with 'em. Just with Eric.

BILL SERAFINI

Does the family still live around here?

FRANK TAPPIN

No, sir, not for a while. Mr and Mrs Fulton both passed away and I don't know what happened to the other boys. Though they're not living here, that I do know.

BILL SERAFINI

Did it surprise people when they found out that Eric had been in Beirut?

FRANK TAPPIN

Could'a knocked me down with a feather, to tell you the truth. Eric had never seemed like the adventurous type. I was surprised he even had a passport. Most folks here don't.

BILL SERAFINI

Was Eric living here before he left for Lebanon or had he already moved away?

FRANK TAPPIN

Nah, he hadn't lived here for a few years. Too small, I reckon. And not just the town.

BILL SERAFINI

How do you mean?

FRANK TAPPIN

Small town, small minds. I think Eric had gotten tired of that. Moved to New York I believe. I can't vouch for the truth of that, but that's what people said.

CUT TO: Bar, interior. Wood-panelled walls, beer posters and printed mirrors, a couple of good old boys at the counter. The woman at the table with Bill has white hair, deeply wrinkled tanned skin and withered hands, but she has a twinkle in her eye, all the same. Sub-captioned 'Nancy Kozlowski, Former teacher, North Birmingham High'.

BILL SERAFINI

So, Nancy, why don't you tell us how you fit into this story?

NANCY KOZLOWSKI

I was Eric's 11th Grade teacher. Class of '82.

BILL SERAFINI

But you took more than just a teacher's interest in him, right?

NANCY KOZLOWSKI

I was fond of him, if that's what you mean. Poor boy needed some motherin'. Don't get me wrong, his mom was a real nice lady but she was a little ditsy. Sorta *absent*, shall we say. And as for his daddy, well, Jim was a hard nut. A decent, hard-working man, yes - no arguin' with that, but he hated weakness, especially in his boys. The other two, he approved of, but Eric was different.

BILL SERAFINI

How so?

NANCY KOZLOWSKI

You have to remember this was the 1980s, and it was - and *is* - the South. Attitudes take their time to change here, and some never do. Eric wasn't like the other kids, and I can tell you now, it frightened him. Children hate to stand out, whether it's red hair, or being the tallest, or the only one with no dad. And this was a-ways more than that.

BILL SERAFINI

By which you mean—?

NANCY KOZLOWSKI

Eric knew from a young age that he didn't like girls. But he also knew, without needin' no tellin', that this was not somethin' he could go round talkin' about. And *especially* not to his father.

BILL SERAFINI

So he confided in you?

NANCY KOZLOWSKI

Well, he didn't come right out and say it, no, it wasn't nothin' like that. I could just sense, that last year, that somethin' was eatin' away at him and I could make a pretty good guess at what it might be. But he had to come to it in his own good time. But then one day I found him cryin' out back. Some of the other boys had been callin' him a faggot and I don't know what else. Kids can be so cruel.

BILL SERAFINI

What did you say to him?

NANCY KOZLOWSKI

Like I said before, I told him maybe North Birmingham wasn't the best place for him. That he couldn't change what he was and shouldn't try, even though some folks round here might-a disagreed with me. That he didn't have to be ashamed of who he was because God made him that way and loved him regardless. He just needed to surround himself with other folks who would think the way I did.

He dropped out the end of that year and left town soon after. If his mother had known it was my doin' she'd never have forgiven me. But I don't regret it, Bill, I don't regret it at all.

BILL SERAFINI

When I spoke to Frank Tappin, he said he was surprised Eric ended up in Beirut. What did you think when you heard about that?

NANCY KOZLOWSKI

I didn't believe it at first, I don't mind tellin' you. I'd had a card or two from him in New York and he seemed real happy. Real at ease with himself. I just don't see what could-a made him decide to leave. Especially for someplace like that.

BILL SERAFINI

Do you still have any of the cards he sent?

NANCY KOZLOWSKI

No, they're long gone. I do have those photos we talked about, though.

CUT TO: MONTAGE of pictures of Eric Fulton at school: in various class line-ups, receiving a prize, attempting to play baseball. He's clearly small for his age, with soft blond hair and a shy, timid smile.

NANCY KOZLOWSKI

That prize was for best handwritin' in the class. Kinda fits, somehow. He was such a nice, polite little kid.

CUT TO: Studio, Bill is on his feet at the board. The photos we just saw are now pinned up alongside the rest.

BILL SERAFINI

(looking round at the team)

This feels like one of those 'are you thinking what I'm thinking' moments.

LAILA FURNESS

Well, what *I'm* thinking is that this Eric Fulton doesn't sound anything like the Eric Fulton who impersonated Luke.

BILL SERAFINI

That's what I'm thinking too.

HUGO FRASER

(dryly)

The homosexuality is a bit of a giveaway.

LAILA FURNESS

It's not just that, though, is it? There are some similarities, yes: hair colour, eyes, that sort of thing. But this Eric is small for his age, whereas 'Luke' was tall. 'Luke' was athletic, this Eric wasn't; 'Luke' was outgoing, Eric was shy.

Taking it all together I think we have to conclude that—

JJ NORTON

—the Eric Fulton who died in the bus bomb was not the Eric Fulton from North Birmingham, but someone else entirely.

MITCHELL CLARKE

You think we have the wrong Eric Fulton? Well, I suppose it's not that unusual a name—

BILL SERAFINI

(shaking his head)

No - I've checked and double-checked. This is the right guy. Or rather, this is the right *passport.*

There's a silence; they're all processing.

JJ NORTON

Shit, are you saying—?

BILL SERAFINI

(nodding)

That the guy who married Caroline Howard wasn't 'Eric Fulton' any more than he was 'Luke Ryder'?

That's exactly what I'm saying.

We're dealing with a serial imposter.

ALAN CANNING

Hold on, hold on, one step at a time. The real Eric Fulton, from Alabama - the one you were just talking to those people about - he moved to New York when?

BILL SERAFINI

1982. He was 17.

ALAN CANNING

So he starts a brand-new life out and proud in the Big Apple, until at some point, years later, the future 'Luke Ryder' steals his passport?

BILL SERAFINI

No, I don't reckon it happened quite that way. Remember what Frank just said about Eric being a homebody? No, I don't reckon it was Eric's passport that was stolen, for the simple reason that I doubt he ever had one. Just like ninety-six per cent of my fellow Americans.

ALAN CANNING

So you're saying our man used Eric's name and details to get a passport issued in that name? Without the real Eric knowing?

BILL SERAFINI

Right.

ALAN CANNING

(sits back and folds his arms)

Bit risky, wasn't it? What if the real Eric had suddenly decided to take a holiday to Torremolinos?

BILL SERAFINI

I don't think that was very likely. Dead men don't go on vacation.

ALAN CANNING

You think he was already dead? You sure about that?

BILL SERAFINI

As sure as I can be.

ALAN CANNING

Do you have any evidence?

BILL SERAFINI

Not actual evidence, no—

HUGO FRASER

Then how can you be so certain?

BILL SERAFINI

Instinct. Plus thirty years' experience. And the fact that it's the only workable theory.

LAILA FURNESS

So what do you think happened?

BILL SERAFINI

I think the real Eric Fulton died in New York. Died, or maybe got killed. Remember, the city was still dealing with the AIDS crisis as late as the mid '90s, and he would definitely have been in a high-risk group.

Add to that the fact that NYC was in the middle of a crack epidemic and fatal shootings were a daily occurrence. Trust me, you didn't have to be a drug dealer to get caught up in that, just in the wrong place at the wrong time.

JJ NORTON

It could have been a hate crime. If Eric was openly gay.

BILL SERAFINI

'Fraid so. Sadly.

LAILA FURNESS

So our serial imposter finds out some way or other that the real Eric Fulton has died, and knows enough basic info about him to apply for a passport in his name?

BILL SERAFINI

That's my assumption, yes. And our thief was in luck – no one back in North Birmingham knew for certain where Eric was. There was no Facebook to fall back on, as we've said before, and they'd have found it damn hard tracking him down any other way. As far as the folks back home were concerned Eric had gone completely off grid.

HUGO FRASER

And the next they hear is 1997, when he turns up dead in a Beirut bus bombing.

Only little do they know but the dead man isn't him at all, it's some surfer dude from Kalgoorlie called Luke Ryder, and our mystery man has now walked off with *his* identity instead. What the hell was this guy up to that he had to keep changing his name?

BILL SERAFINI

That, Hugo, is what we need to find out.

LAILA FURNESS

Do you have a theory, Bill?

BILL SERAFINI

Well, yes, I do, as a matter of fact.

ALAN CANNING

(under his breath)

Why am I not surprised.

BILL SERAFINI

(ignoring him)

I think we're dealing with a conman. A very clever conman, who always managed to stay one step ahead of law enforcement.

LAILA FURNESS

What sort of cons are we talking about?

BILL SERAFINI

The worst kind, at least in my book, i.e., up close and *very* personal.

I think he chose people who'd be either too ashamed or too humiliated to come forward to the police. People who would blame themselves for being duped.

JJ NORTON

But even so, they'd still have friends and family who'd want the perp caught. Caught and locked up.

BILL SERAFINI

Precisely. Which is exactly why I think our man kept having to disappear. And what better way to disappear than faking your own death?

ALAN CANNING

Just about plausible, I suppose. The whole idea is rather too Sunday-night-drama if you ask me, but I suppose stranger things have happened.

LAILA FURNESS

(to Bill)

I'm guessing you think most of his victims were women?

BILL SERAFINI

Yes, I do. And I suspect they were older than him, too, maybe even significantly older. Remember what Sylvia Carroll said about him being a charmer? That he knew just how to sweet-talk the old ladies in the care home?

Don't get me wrong - I'm not saying all his victims were quite *that* elderly, but all the same it speaks to a talent for gaining trust, for breaking down reserve.

MITCHELL CLARKE

Topped off with a truck-load of good old-fashioned laying it on thick. That famous 'charm' of his.

BILL SERAFINI

(smiling dryly)

Yes, that too.

HUGO FRASER

I buy it that someone could *in theory* have been so pissed off with this guy that they pursued him all the way to London—

ALAN CANNING

(turning to him)

But how do you think your average Joe would have managed that? In practice, I mean. Tracked him from New York to Campden Hill, via Greece, Bali and who knows where else including bloody Beirut?

MITCHELL CLARKE

(shrugs)

Any journo worth the name could have had a go. And Bill managed it in a couple of days.

ALAN CANNING

Bill has access to a team of professional researchers, not to mention contacts in law enforcement—

BILL SERAFINI

(with a self-deprecating smile)

Well, that sure helps.

LAILA FURNESS

So you think this conman was active in New York in the mid '90s? Weren't you in NYPD yourself then?

BILL SERAFINI

I was.

LAILA FURNESS

But you don't remember anything like this at the time?

BILL SERAFINI

(smiling)

It's a lot of years ago, Laila, and it's a big city. But let's see what the guys back home come up with.

JJ NORTON

So no cliff-hanger to end with, Bill? You're losing your touch.

BILL SERAFINI

(breaks into a laugh)

Well, I'll try harder next time, JJ.

FADE OUT

- end credits -

Text messages between Amelie and Maura Howard, 18th May 2023, 8.49 a.m.

I'm sorry Am. I just had a call from Guy. Something's come up

I fucking KNEW this would happen

So what is it

They're going to bring up the therapy thing

Like WTF?

That stuff is *private*

He said to say sorry. Says he tried to call you but you didn't pick up

Sorry Am

He has NO RIGHT to put private stuff like that on fucking Showrunner

There's something else

It's going to come out

About that fire. At school

FFS it's like a million years ago

And it was a fucking ACCIDENT

I know. I'm sorry Am

Stop apologising. None of this is down to you.

It's Guy I'm pissed off with, not you

I know what you mean

How about we start airing *his* shit in public - how would he like that?

Best not go there

Date: Sat 20/05/2023, 10.54

From: Alan Canning

To: Gordon.Evans@Met.Police.uk

Subject: Hello

Gordon,

I can't remember if I replied about the Sports & Social do but I think I should definitely be able to make it. Not sure about the golf day yet, as it will depend on my filming commitments.

On which subject, the show is proving interesting and – as you rightly suspected – not as straightforward as it initially appeared. On which subject, I seem to remember you used to have a contact at NYPD? Am I remembering that right? If so, I'd appreciate a discreet word.

Kath sends her regards,

All best,

Alan

Date: Sat 20/05/2023, 15.30

From: Hugo Fraser

To: serena.f.hamilton@hhllp.com

Subject: Dad's birthday

Have you given any more thought to where you'd like to go for lunch? I was wondering about Ozymandias – you know, that place by Holland Park tube? He's always loved it there.

And thanks for your understanding about the other thing. Like I said, it's no big deal. I just want to keep things simple.

H

Voicemail left for Bill Serafini by David Shulman, 20th May 2023, 3.41 p.m.

Bill, it's David. I got your message and thanks for keeping us in the loop. Clearly we will be very interested if there are any further developments. Either way, let's catch up when you're back in New York.

0.26 -0.34

Speaker Call back Delete

Date: Sun 21/05/2023, 16.50

From: Mitchell Clarke

To: Laila Furness

Subject: Just checking

Hi Laila,

Sorry to bother you at the weekend but there was just something I wanted to check with you. It's about Mohammed Khan, that student in Sydney. I just stumbled over a paper you gave at a conference back in 2002, before you got married. Your maiden name was Khan, right?

I realize it's a common name so I assume it's just a coincidence? Hope you don't mind me asking.

M

Date: Sun 21/05/2023, 16.58

From: Laila Furness

To: Mitch Clarke

Subject: Re: Just checking

Ha – well spotted! And yes, it's just a coincidence. Khans are almost as common as Smiths.

By the way, I think you're handling this whole thing really well – you're the only one of us outside the family who's been touched by this personally and I know it can't be easy having to rake it all up again after such a long time. Let's just hope we can give both you and the Howards some closure.

See you next week,

L

Voicemail left by Laila Furness for her mother, 21st May 2023, 5.23 p.m.

Hi Mum, hope you're OK. I forgot you were in Karachi this week. Can you give me a call when you get back?

Love you. Bye

0.26 -0.34

Speaker **Call back** **Delete**

Episode four

Broadcast

October 12

The Times, 13 October 2023

TELEVISION

Home is where the hurt is

The real insight of Infamous is what it tells us about family relationships

ROSS LESLIE

Infamous: Who Killed Luke Ryder?
Showrunner

Keep it in the Family
Netflix

Tolstoy was wrong. If this series of **Infamous** proves anything, it's that all unhappy families fall apart in similar ways, however wealthy or advantaged they may appear to be.

You only had to look at images of the haunted faces of Caroline Howard Ryder's children in the years following their stepfather's murder to know that money just serves to paper over the cracks. Behind the anonymous walls of that huge Campden Hill house, children were acting out to the point of petty criminality, and being sent for professional therapy. Some of these revelations were distinctly uncomfortable to watch, and at the same time the whole thing was, of course, utterly compelling. The unfolding psychological drama continues to be underpinned by a succession of new discoveries about the dead man at the heart of the case, a man - as we discovered last night – whose true identity still eludes us.

To continue the domestic dysfunction theme, the latest offering from Netflix is **Keep it in the Family**, adapted from a 2022 novel by John Marrs. Newly-weds Finn and Mia have taken the perhaps unwise decision to buy an almost derelict house

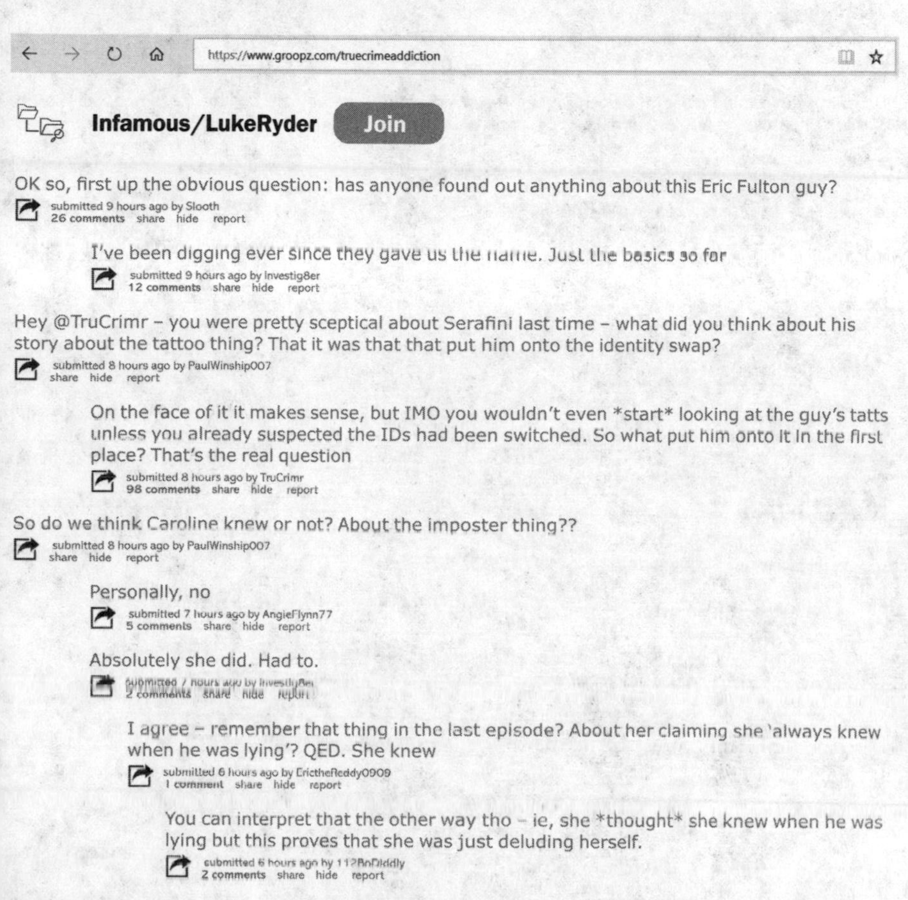

https://www.groopz.com/truecrimeaddiction

Infamous/LukeRyder Join

OK so, first up the obvious question: has anyone found out anything about this Eric Fulton guy?
submitted 9 hours ago by Slooth
26 comments share hide report

> I've been digging ever since they gave us the name. Just the basics so far
> submitted 9 hours ago by Investig8er
> 12 comments share hide report

Hey @TruCrimr – you were pretty sceptical about Serafini last time – what did you think about his story about the tattoo thing? That it was that that put him onto the identity swap?
submitted 8 hours ago by PaulWinship007
share hide report

> On the face of it it makes sense, but IMO you wouldn't even *start* looking at the guy's tatts unless you already suspected the IDs had been switched. So what put him onto it in the first place? That's the real question
> submitted 8 hours ago by TruCrimr
> 98 comments share hide report

So do we think Caroline knew or not? About the imposter thing??
submitted 8 hours ago by PaulWinship007
share hide report

> Personally, no
> submitted 7 hours ago by AngieFlynn77
> 5 comments share hide report

> Absolutely she did. Had to.
> submitted 7 hours ago by Investig8er
> 2 comments share hide report

>> I agree – remember that thing in the last episode? About her claiming she 'always knew when he was lying'? QED. She knew
>> submitted 6 hours ago by EricTheReddy0909
>> 1 comment share hide report

>>> You can interpret that the other way tho – ie, she *thought* she knew when he was lying but this proves that she was just deluding herself.
>>> submitted 6 hours ago by 112BnDiddly
>>> 2 comments share hide report

You have to feel sorry for that bloke Canning, don't you? There's Big Bill strutting about creaming the whole thing while poor ol' Al's left trying to chase down secondhand cars... What a bummer
 #teamCanning
submitted 5 hours ago by Edison5.0
6 comments share hide report

Good call for them get the forensics run again. In fact, I can't believe the Met haven't done that already. On second thoughts, of course they haven't. It's the Met. Duh

submitted 5 hours ago by ForensicsGeek
26 comments share hide report

Incidentally I'm feeling pretty damn smug that Hugo Boss obviously agrees with me about follow the money. Keep an eye on old Mrs Ryder's cash. We haven't heard the last of that, you mark my words
submitted 4 hours ago by TruCrimr
78 comments share hide report

> Agreed. Keep an eye on that guy Ian Wilson, that'd be my take
> submitted 4 hours ago by Investig8er
> 12 comments share hide report

That Sylvia from the care home was a right grasping sneaky cow too #justsaying

submitted 4 hours ago by RonJebus
12 comments share hide report

The thing I'm finding most interesting is the team's reactions as they discuss the new material. Some of them seem way more emotional about some of it than you'd have expected. Or is it just me?

submitted 3 hours ago by KatMcAlisterOIB
3 comments share hide report

No, I agree.

submitted 3 hours ago by MaryMary51523x
9 comments share hide report

I wish we had some footage of Luke/Eric/whatever his name is. Wouldn't you just love that bloke off Faking It to have a go at him?

submitted 3 hours ago by LemonandCrime
6 comments share hide report

Cliff Lansley? Hell yes. Talk about clash of the titans...

submitted 2 hours ago by Starsky6145
3 comments share hide report

👉👉👉 Heads-up here guys, Major Discovery klaxon 📢 Someone got in touch with me via email last night after the show. She didn't want to come on here but what she told me was pretty f**king big. She says she *met* Amelie Howard. In 2012, in REHAB. She was calling herself Emma not Amelie but apparently it was deffo the same person

submitted 2 hours ago by Slooth
314 comments share hide report

Shit, really? Rehab as in drugs?

submitted 2 hours ago by Investig8er
2 comments share hide report

Right. Full on opioid detox apparently

submitted 2 hours ago by Slooth
15 comments share hide report

Oh crap. That poor kid

submitted 2 hours ago by AngieFlynn77
5 comments share hide report

But thats 10 yrs after the murder. Not sure how thats relevant tbh

submitted 2 hours ago by PaulWinship007
12 comments share hide report

I think the relevance wd depend on how early the drug use started. Tho the thing about the damage at the school was interesting/possibly significant in this context

submitted 2 hours ago by ForensicsGeek
32 comments share hide report

Nah – those posh private schools, spilling your teacher's G&T wd probably be classified as 'damage' ☹

submitted 1 hour ago by 112BoDiddly
2 comments share hide report

Not as bad as trashing your ma's wedding cake 🎂😂

submitted 1 hour ago by SemSaida88
share hide report

All the same, drugs *could* be more important than we've previously thought – what I mean is, this is the first time anyone's mentioned that Maura had friends with drug connections at the time of the murder. Maybe that's what's at the heart of this? ie not Amelie but Maura's dodgy mates, maybe even a drug deal gone bad? Not sure how it wd have gone down in practice but has to be worth considering?

submitted 1 hour ago by ErictheReddy0909
11 comments share hide report

Yes but even tho *we* didn't know Maura had those connections the police must have? Surely they'd have checked that out at the time?

submitted 1 hour ago by PocusHous1978
7 comments share hide report

I thought the psych stuff was really interesting this time – the Peter Pan thing

submitted 1 hour ago by AngieFlynn77
32 comments share hide report

I agree. I looked up that Nevada woman they mentioned too, Kathy Augustine. Bloody awful case. The husband injected her with a paralytic called succinylcholine – took her ten minutes to die and she was conscious the whole time, the bastard.

submitted 1 hour ago by JimBobWalton1978
9 comments share hide report

Ive been googling that succinylcholine stuff – never heard of it b4. Apparently its only used in hospital settings so hard to get hold of but he was a nurse so wd have known all about it.

submitted 45 minutes ago by ForensicsGeek
5 comments share hide report

Yeah, and if you don't know what to look for it can look just like a heart attack. It also metabolises really quickly after death so it's almost impossible to trace at autopsy. Basically if a couple of nurses hadn't smelt a rat and taken samples from Augustine while she was still alive the cops wd never have nailed him

submitted 30 minutes ago by PerfectMurder616
15 comments share hide report

Episode five

Filming

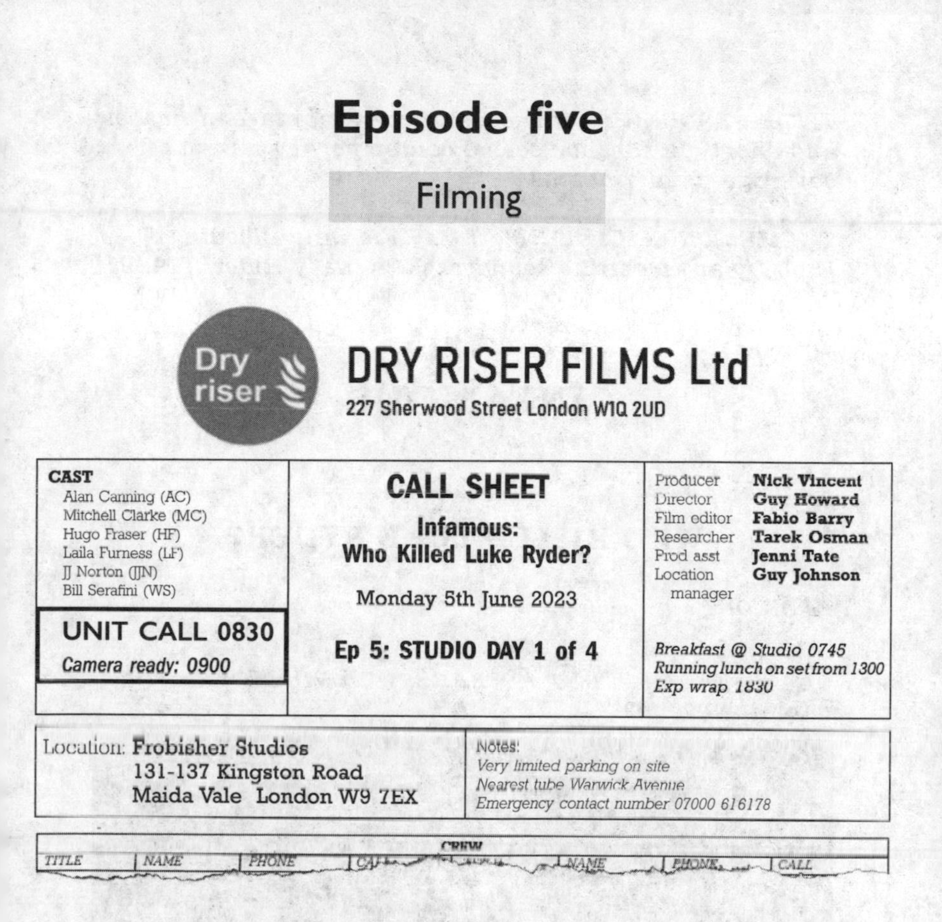

DRY RISER FILMS Ltd
227 Sherwood Street London W1Q 2UD

CAST
Alan Canning (AC)
Mitchell Clarke (MC)
Hugo Fraser (HF)
Laila Furness (LF)
JJ Norton (JJN)
Bill Serafini (WS)

UNIT CALL 0830
Camera ready: 0900

CALL SHEET
Infamous: Who Killed Luke Ryder?
Monday 5th June 2023
Ep 5: STUDIO DAY 1 of 4

Producer	**Nick Vincent**
Director	**Guy Howard**
Film editor	**Fabio Barry**
Researcher	**Tarek Osman**
Prod asst	**Jenni Tate**
Location manager	**Guy Johnson**

Breakfast @ Studio 0745
Running lunch on set from 1300
Exp wrap 1830

Location: **Frobisher Studios**
131-137 Kingston Road
Maida Vale London W9 7EX

Notes:
Very limited parking on site
Nearest tube Warwick Avenue
Emergency contact number 07000 616178

CREW

TITLE	NAME	PHONE	CALL	TITLE	NAME	PHONE	CALL

TITLE SEQUENCE: arthouse-style b/w montage of images and short clips: crime scene, contemporary news coverage, family photos

THEME SONG – 'It's Alright, Ma (I'm Only Bleeding)' [Bob Dylan] from the soundtrack to 'Easy Rider' [1969]

title over

INFAMOUS

FADE IN

WHO KILLED LUKE RYDER?

FADE OUT

BLACK FRAME, TEXT APPEARS, with VOICEOVER – narrator (female)

On the night of October 3, 2003, Luke Ryder's body was found in a garden in the upscale district of London West-8.

He was 26, and a native of Kalgoorlie, Western Australia.

Or at least that's who he said he was.

But we now know that the man passing himself off as 'Luke' had used at least one other identity, and may have been a serial conman.

Did something in the real Luke Ryder's past come back to haunt the man who stole his name?

Or did someone he had wronged track this imposter down, intent on exacting a terrible revenge?

FADE OUT

CUT TO: Guy, in the studio, sitting with Nick.

NICK VINCENT (Producer)

You said at the beginning that you didn't want to play an active role in this film – that even though you're the director, you wanted the team to be free to follow the investigation wherever it led.

Why have you decided to go in front of the camera again now?

GUY HOWARD

So much has come out since we started this process – and even since I last said anything myself on screen – that it's probably time that viewers heard the family take on all this.

In particular how far the Luke we knew tallies with – or is changed by – what the team's now discovered.

NICK VINCENT (Producer)

And where do you all stand?

GUY HOWARD

Well, as you heard in an earlier episode, I was finding it hard to believe that 'Luke' was actually a man called Eric Fulton who was eleven years older than he claimed.

But if the team's right, 'Eric Fulton' was just one more in what could be any number of stolen identities. I guess we may never know who he really was, or how old he was for that matter.

Though I won't deny it's unsettling, even all these years later, to find we had a complete stranger in the house all that time, someone we now discover we knew absolutely nothing about, not even his name.

NICK VINCENT (Producer)

The picture that seems to be emerging is of someone who may have defrauded a whole series of women.

Clearly we have yet to gather any actual evidence to back that up, but it seems a reasonable hypothesis. What's your reaction to that - do you think your mother was going to be his next victim?

GUY HOWARD

I have to admit I'm struggling with that one too. Right up until she got ill Mum was always a really strong character. I just don't see her as a victim.

And 'Luke' didn't *behave* like that sort of predator - not that I can remember. I mean, yes, she did buy him things, most notably that Harley, but she never gave him large sums of money. And as her friends have told the team, as far as Mum knew, he stood to inherit a pile of cash of his own. He didn't *need* her money.

NICK VINCENT (Producer)

Though that sort of set-up is a standard MO for certain types of fraudster - look at that whole Anna Delvey story a few years back, or those supposedly rich men who've tricked women on dating apps like Tinder.

The fraudster poses as filthy rich but claims they're temporarily unable to access any of the money. So it's the old 'I just need your help with this minor cash-flow issue' story.

GUY HOWARD

True, but like I said, I don't think Luke ever asked my mother for money in that sort of way - I'm pretty sure there were no big payments to him at all while they were married. She gave him *stuff*, not cash.

NICK VINCENT (Producer)

The other issue I wanted to raise with you is what Shirley Booker said, especially about how you three children felt about Luke. She said you 'loathed' him.

GUY HOWARD

She was talking about Amelie—

NICK VINCENT (Producer)

Yes, you're right, she said Amelie disliked him the most, but she said you loathed him too. You even wrecked the wedding cake—

GUY HOWARD

(roaring with laughter)

I have absolutely *no* memory of doing that—

NICK VINCENT (Producer)

All the same, I have to ask you - why haven't you said any of this before?

GUY HOWARD

To be fair, I think I have. I said I didn't like him. I don't think it was ever *loathing*, as such—

NICK VINCENT (Producer)

Shirley said that according to Caroline you became 'unmanageable'. So disruptive that these days you would be diagnosed with ADHD.

GUY HOWARD

(laughs again)

Mum always was a bit of a drama queen. See above under Cake.

NICK VINCENT (Producer)

Shirley also told us all three of you kids went into therapy. Is that true?

GUY HOWARD

(his face closing)

That's not something I'm prepared to talk about on screen.

NICK VINCENT (Producer)

OK, fair enough. So what about your sisters' relationships with Luke? We still haven't been able to talk to Amelie directly - did she really hate him as much as Shirley Booker claimed?

GUY HOWARD

(after a pause)

I suppose of the three of us she disliked him the most. I guess that much is accurate.

NICK VINCENT (Producer)

Do you know why?

GUY HOWARD

(shrugs)

Search me. As far as I remember she took an instant dislike to him and it only got worse. But don't forget, I was only 10 at the time. There could have been subtleties I was missing.

NICK VINCENT (Producer)

What about Maura?

GUY HOWARD

I think she mainly just stayed out of his way. She was at that age - all adults were a pain in the arse, whoever they were. But why don't you ask her?

NICK VINCENT (Producer)

In fact we did. She wasn't that keen to talk to us again, but she did eventually agree.

CUT TO: Maura, in her room in the old stable block at Dorney Place. We can see the garden and the main house through the window behind her. Her hair is up in a messy bun; she's wearing a navy long-sleeved top under a navy gilet, with a wool scarf around her neck. She's sitting slightly turned away, both arms wrapped around her.

NICK VINCENT (Producer) - off

Since we last spoke we've interviewed Shirley Booker—

MAURA HOWARD

(flashing him a look)

Not that old bag.

NICK VINCENT (Producer) - off

—and she says that of the three of you, Amelie hated Luke the most. Do you remember it that way?

MAURA HOWARD

(looks dismissive)

She never came to the house so I don't know how come she's so fucking knowledgeable all of a sudden.

NICK VINCENT (Producer) - off

She got it from your mother.

MAURA HOWARD

So she says. Mum's not exactly in any state to contradict her, now, is she?

NICK VINCENT (Producer) - off

You're saying she's wrong? Amelie *didn't* hate him?

MAURA HOWARD

(shrugs)

I'm not saying she *liked* him, but we were just kids, none of it really meant anything. And we all really loved Dad. We were broken up when he died, so to be honest we'd probably have hated anyone Mum married. Especially so soon after.

NICK VINCENT (Producer) - off

The team now think 'Luke' may have been a conman. That he may have defrauded several other women.

MAURA HOWARD

If you say so.

NICK VINCENT (Producer) - off

You seem surprisingly unfazed about it.

MAURA HOWARD

(shrugs)

I didn't like him, but he probably didn't deserve the shit he got from us kids. He was always really nice to Mum—

(she catches her breath, suddenly emotional)

OK so back then I didn't want him around, but looking back at it now, it would have been so much better if he hadn't died. Mum was never really happy again after that.

(looks away, her eyes filling with tears)

NICK VINCENT (Producer) - off

I also wanted to ask you about the therapy—

MAURA HOWARD

(getting to her feet and pulling off the mic)

I am absolutely *not* going to talk to you people about that.

She throws down the mic and walks away.

CUT TO: Studio, team now around the table.

LAILA FURNESS

I find the Howard family dynamics endlessly fascinating.

(looking slightly embarrassed)

Sorry, I know that sounds rather insensitive. And rather off the point.

BILL SERAFINI

I think it's the *whole* point.

HUGO FRASER

Stating the obvious, I know, but it doesn't look like we're going to get anywhere pushing the family on the therapy issue.

LAILA FURNESS

Which is only to be expected.

(giving an arch look at Nick beyond the camera)

Though it might have helped if Mr Vincent had been a *tad* more sensitive.

JJ NORTON

The thing that fascinates *me* is the psychology of this 'Luke' person, whatever his real name was.

Is it just me or is anyone else wondering whether the relationship with Caroline might have been rather different from previous ones?

ALAN CANNING

In the sense that—?

JJ NORTON

In the sense that he wasn't just 'really nice' to her, he actually married her.

Conmen like that tend to fleece women and move on, don't they? You don't need to bother with the legals to achieve that. Indeed, I'd argue it just makes things a whole lot more complicated. *And* far more likely to attract unwelcome attention from the powers that be.

MITCHELL CLARKE

We don't *know* he didn't marry any of the others.

BILL SERAFINI

JJ's right, though: marriage leaves a paper trail. He'd be much easier to track down.

ALAN CANNING

Only if you knew the name he was going under at the time.

BILL SERAFINI

True.

HUGO FRASER

In my experience, swindlers who actually marry the women they're conning do it precisely *because* of 'the legals'. I.e., to put themselves in line to inherit their property, including any life insurance. Which they've often taken out without the wife's knowledge. I prosecuted a case exactly like that only last year.

JJ NORTON

You're talking about a different sort of conman there, though, are you? A conman who wants to inherit is a conman who intends to kill. Like the man who murdered that novelist - Helen something–

MITCHELL CLARKE

Helen Bailey. Now he *was* a nasty piece of work–

LAILA FURNESS

Just to interject - psychologically speaking, a conman of that kind would be a very different personality type.

And like Mitch just said, we don't *know* 'Luke' didn't marry other women. In fact, how do we know he didn't murder them?

I mean, he could have, right? He could even have been planning to kill Caroline, for all we know.

HUGO FRASER

(looks round the table)

Do we know if Caroline - or indeed Luke - took out any new life insurance policies after the marriage?

NICK VINCENT (Producer) - off

I've already asked Guy that and he says not.

HUGO FRASER

In that case I think it's unlikely he was planning to murder her. They'd been married more than a year. He'd have had plenty of time to get the financial side of things in place, if he really did intend to kill her.

MITCHELL CLARKE

Perhaps he had a change of heart. He may have conned women in the past but this time it was The Real Thing. He married her because he actually loved her.

LAILA FURNESS

(smiling at him)

You old romantic, you.

BILL SERAFINI

(shaking his head)

Nice try, Mitch, but I don't buy it.

HUGO FRASER

There is one other possibility: maybe he realized he stood to gain more by playing a long game? I mean, all he had to do was sit on his hands and wait for Florence Ryder to die and he'd be quids in.

MITCHELL CLARKE

I think you could be onto something there. Maybe that's what made it different this time.

LAILA FURNESS

But we're just spinning on nothing without some actual *facts* about this man.

ALAN CANNING

Precisely. So, Bill - have you discovered anything more since we last got together? Did New York's finest come up with the goods?

BILL SERAFINI

I was just coming to that.

(gets up and goes to the board)

I got lucky. One of the detectives in Manhattan PD is a guy I trained back when he was just a rookie, so I called in a favour.

(turns and pins up a photo)

Given that our current theory is that the real Eric Fulton died some time in the mid to late '90s in New York, I got my guy to run Fulton's picture against deceased John Does in the city for that period. And we hit pay dirt.

He gestures to the picture; it's an autopsy shot, the eyes are closed and the face is badly bruised on one side.

Remember I said I thought the real Eric Fulton might have been the victim of some sort of violence? Well, this man died as a result of a street mugging in Brooklyn in December 1994. There were no witnesses - at least none who were prepared to make a formal statement - but there was definitely some suggestion that it could have been a hate crime. The attack took place in the early hours of the morning only a few hundred yards from a known gay bar.

The vic had no ID or wallet on him when he was found a couple of hours later, and despite repeated police appeals no one came forward. As of now, he remains officially unidentified.

JJ NORTON

You think it could be the real Eric Fulton? And our mystery man stole the ID off the body?

BILL SERAFINI

Has to be possible. There was more than enough time for someone to find him and go through his pockets before the cops showed up. And we know our man was nothing if not opportunistic. Look at what happened in Beirut.

JJ NORTON

Did you ask NYPD to run this John Doe's DNA against Fulton's family?

BILL SERAFINI

I did. No news as yet though.

LAILA FURNESS

(*still staring at the photo*)

He'd been living in New York for years and yet no one appears to have noticed he was missing?

BILL SERAFINI

Evidently not.

LAILA FURNESS

That strikes me as very sad.

BILL SERAFINI

They may have had their reasons. But I guess we'll never know.

HUGO FRASER

So you think that as at December 1994 our mystery man started a whole new life as 'Eric Fulton'?

BILL SERAFINI

I don't think; I *know*. Because within six months of that John Doe's death, the hitherto gay Eric Fulton began a sexual relationship with a woman.

This woman.

He puts up another picture – it's a clipping from a glossy magazine. The woman is late middle-aged, in a floor-length gold sequinned gown, smiling and holding a glass of champagne.

BILL SERAFINI

This is Rose Shulman at the Met Gala in May 1994. She was 56 at the time.

And by the time the gala came round again, she had an escort.

He pins up another photo; Shulman again, in another long gown, accompanied this time by a tall and much younger man in evening clothes. He's turned away from the camera.

LAILA FURNESS

Well, based purely on height and physique that definitely isn't Eric Fulton of North Birmingham, Alabama.

JJ NORTON

But you can't really see his face, can you? Is that deliberate, do you think?

BILL SERAFINI

Well observed, JJ. And yes, I think it is. I did a trawl of other images of Rose at around this time and 'Eric' is notable by his absence. And when he *is* pictured he's clearly doing his best not to be in shot.

And as we've discussed many times before, there was no social media back then, so if you were careful you had a pretty good chance of keeping your face out of the public eye.

(raises an eyebrow)

Always assuming you had good reason to want to.

ALAN CANNING

I agree he's about the same height and build as 'Luke', but the hair is definitely darker. And shorter.

LAILA FURNESS

But those things are easy to change, aren't they. Like wearing glasses. Or not.

ALAN CANNING

I suppose so.

HUGO FRASER

So what happened with Rose? I assume something did or you wouldn't be telling us all this.

BILL SERAFINI

(looks grim)

In the space of five months he relieved her of something in the neighbourhood of eight hundred thousand dollars. Along with several pieces of heirloom jewellery she never saw again.

JJ NORTON

(sardonically)

Nice guy.

Do we know how they met? Might give us a clue about how he operated.

BILL SERAFINI

He seems to have weaselled his way into some gallery opening she was at. Told her he was an artist—

MITCHELL CLARKE

Well, that's actually true - he was a bloody *con* artist.

BILL SERAFINI

—and he'd clearly done his research, because the Shulman family are noted patrons of the arts, and support a number of charities benefiting young painters.

HUGO FRASER

You just said 'she never *saw* her jewellery again'. Past tense.

BILL SERAFINI

(takes a deep breath)

Rose was diagnosed with breast cancer in 1996 and died nine months later. Her family firmly believe that the stress of losing the money was a major contributing factor. She felt humiliated. Not least because she thought Fulton actually cared about her.

MITCHELL CLARKE

I don't suppose any of the Shulman family were in London on October third 2003 by any chance?

BILL SERAFINI

(laughs dryly)

No, sadly not. And yes, we have checked.

LAILA FURNESS

(sighs)

Another dead end.

HUGO FRASER

Did your colleague at NYPD have any idea which name our man might have been going under before he became Eric Fulton?

BILL SERAFINI

Afraid not. But safe to say they're on the case.

Talking of being on the case, did you speak to the Met about getting those hairs tested, Alan?

ALAN CANNING

I had a word with the cold case unit and they've agreed to do testing on the hair and a full DNA analysis of the clothes.

But don't hold your breath: we'll be at the back of the queue compared to live investigations.

BILL SERAFINI

(looking round)

What else did we have outstanding from last time?

He gets up and goes over to the whiteboard, which we now see has a list in Bill's handwriting.

Camera ZOOMS in.

IAN WILSON
AUSTRALIAN INCIDENT/HIT-AND-RUN
CAROLINE'S MYSTERY LOVER

BILL SERAFINI

So, first up, our current name in the frame: Ian Wilson. And the news here is that Tarek has tracked down some footage of him. It's from the '90s so not directly relevant, but it might help give us a picture of the guy.

He nods towards the camera and the screen on the wall comes to life. It's a clip from BBC South News. A solidly built young man with blond hair and braces, wearing a green and navy-striped rugby shirt is being interviewed by a journalist holding a huge grey microphone. There are two older people standing at his side, and behind them another group of adults. The colours are faded and yellowish and there are a few jumps on the film.

JOURNALIST

(to camera)

I'm here with Ian Wilson, of Sir William Penrose School in Guildford, who's just been selected to play for the England Under-16s rugby side.

(turning to Ian)

Quite a day, Ian. You must be very excited.

IAN WILSON

(grinning)

Yeah, I'm pretty chuffed.

JOURNALIST

I believe you've been playing rugby ever since you were at primary school?

IAN WILSON

(running a hand through his hair)

Yeah, I used to play with my dad in the garden and I suppose it just went from there.

JOURNALIST

This is your mum and dad with you here, am I right? They must be very proud.

MR WILSON

Very proud, very proud. Ian's done terrifically well.

Wilson smiles indulgently. He's an older, more florid version of his son; his wife is a much less substantial figure, clutching her handbag and smiling nervously. Ian pulls his hand through his hair again; he's starting to look rather like Boris Johnson.

JOURNALIST

And I think you have your special new shirt with you too?

Ian grins and holds up a white England shirt with a red rose on the chest. It clearly hasn't been worn yet.

JOURNALIST

And your first game is later this month I believe?

IAN WILSON

(grinning again)

Yeah, we're playing Scotland on the twenty-first.

(he leans forward into the camera lens, holds up a fist and roars)

Stuff the Jocks - YEAH!

JOURNALIST

(looking alarmed and turning quickly away to camera)

Well, I'm sure we all wish the team every success. Back to you in the studio.

FREEZE FRAME.

LAILA FURNESS

For such a short clip, that was extraordinarily revealing.

HUGO FRASER

Ian Wilson is a boorish overprivileged little tosser, for a start.

Alan shoots him a quick glance and seems about to say something, but changes his mind.

MITCHELL CLARKE

Oh come on, he was only a kid back then—

HUGO FRASER

He was 16. People don't change much after that. Aren't I right, Laila?

LAILA FURNESS

Well, I would agree that you rarely see profound personality shifts after that age - not without some significant triggering event—

HUGO FRASER

There you are then.

JJ NORTON

Either way, based on what we just saw, I reckon the grown-up Ian would've been more than capable of doing Luke some serious damage. He was a *rugby player*, for Christ's sake.

LAILA FURNESS

I tend to agree. And if this is anything to go by, I can also see why he made such a poor impression when he turned up at that care home—

HUGO FRASER

(nodding)

And then tried to bully Sylvia Carroll.

ALAN CANNING

(rather impatiently)

None of that makes any difference: Peter Lascelles specifically told us that Wilson had an *alibi*. He's *out of the picture*. This is a dead horse and I can't for the life of me understand why we're still flogging it.

MITCHELL CLARKE

We were *told* he had an alibi, but we still don't know what it was, do we? Maybe Lascelles didn't check it out that hard—

LAILA FURNESS

What did Peter say about that, Bill? You were going to speak to him, weren't you?

BILL SERAFINI

I was, and I did.

MITCHELL CLARKE

And what did he say?

BILL SERAFINI

Let's take a look, shall we.

CUT TO: INTERVIEW sequence. Bill is sitting in a pub with Peter Lascelles. He has a pint of bitter in a jug glass, Bill has a bourbon on the rocks.

BILL SERAFINI

I still don't get the Brit thing with warm beer.

PETER LASCELLES

(smiling)

It's all part of the package: goes along with the stiff upper lip and the bad teeth.

(Bill laughs)

So, you wanted to ask me about Ian Wilson's alibi. Of course there's only so much I'm at liberty to say, given it's still an open case—

BILL SERAFINI

Understood.

PETER LASCELLES

—but this much I *can* tell you. As we discussed before, we did investigate Margaret and Ian Wilson in 2003, as both clearly had a prima facie motive for wanting Luke Ryder dead. The real Luke Ryder, needless to say.

(takes a deep breath)

Taking them in turn, I'm sure you'll understand me if I say that – theoretically speaking, of course – a middle-aged woman who was suffering from severe arthritis would be an unlikely suspect for the murder of a very fit 26-year-old male.

BILL SERAFINI

We don't know how old he *actually* was, of course, but point taken.

However – and likewise, purely hypothetically – there'd be nothing to stop someone in that state of health from getting another person to commit the crime on her behalf. Especially someone close to her, who also stood to gain financially. Like her own kid.

PETER LASCELLES

Of course. And any competent police officer would conduct their enquiries accordingly. Such a child would be investigated and his – or her – alibi verified.

BILL SERAFINI

And?

PETER LASCELLES

Well, as you well know, Bill, some alibis are harder to verify than others. Especially if by the time you speak to the person in question they're no longer in the country.

BILL SERAFINI

And I guess in those circumstances you'd want to establish exactly when they left. As in, did they leave before or *after* the date of the crime.

PETER LASCELLES

Precisely. And in our hypothetical case it was three days after the murder.

BILL SERAFINI

And wouldn't that timing strike you as suspicious? Might it make you think they were fleeing the jurisdiction?

PETER LASCELLES

Clearly that would have been an important consideration. And even if the person concerned had insisted that they'd been planning that particular trip for some time, that would have been hard to verify. Twenty years ago, travel documentation wasn't digitized like it is now.

BILL SERAFINI

And in any case he'd still need an alibi for the night in question.

PETER LASCELLES

Right. But again, there was a lot less technical evidence to draw on back in the day - there weren't many CCTV cameras, even in city centres, and only a very few mobile phones had GPS tracking. So almost all alibis relied on human beings, not digital data.

BILL SERAFINI

(nodding)

And unlike machines, people can lie. And even if they *think* they're telling the truth their memories can still deceive them. Eyewitness testimony is notoriously unreliable.

PETER LASCELLES

I agree, though when a suspect offers an alibi witness who allegedly spent several hours with them on the evening of the crime, then the evidence provided should in theory be a lot more solid.

Always assuming, of course, that the witness hasn't mistaken the day. Either accidentally or, of course, deliberately.

BILL SERAFINI

So are we talking a one-off encounter on that particular day, or an ongoing relationship of some kind?

PETER LASCELLES

For the purposes of our hypothetical case, let's assume it was a woman the person in question met in a bar, and then spent the night with.

BILL SERAFINI

(nodding)

OK. And I see why that might be hard to substantiate in terms of an exact date. Unless they paid by credit card, or went to a hotel—

PETER LASCELLES

I think you should assume they didn't.

BILL SERAFINI

Can I ask how old this hypothetical woman was?

PETER LASCELLES

Let's say in her forties.

BILL SERAFINI

Right. OK, let's park our hypothetical case for a moment and focus on the real one. Wilson's in his twenties, right? Good-looking guy, too. So if he'd got hot and heavy with a lady of a certain age I can easily see him charming her into slipping him a fake alibi.

He continues to speak over RECONSTRUCTION. Video only, no audio: 'Ian' is in bed with an older woman. They talk, she smiles, then nods her head.

He asks her, casually, while they're still in the sack, if she can do him a favour - it's no biggie, just a spot of bother he can't be bothered dealing with, so if anyone comes asking can she tell them their night of passion was actually the day before. She's just had the best bang she can remember since way back when, so maybe she thinks, 'Why the hell not?'

And by the time she realizes she's gone and got herself tangled up in a murder inquiry Mr Smooth is long gone and she's way too terrified to change her story and tell the truth.

PETER LASCELLES

(reaches for his beer)

You certainly tell a good tale, Bill. Ever thought of writing a novel? You could give that Ian Rankin bloke a run for his money.

BILL SERAFINI

(smiling)

Thanks. But do you think it's plausible, as a scenario?

PETER LASCELLES

Only too plausible. And - hypothetically speaking - we would certainly have put exactly that version of events to the witness.

BILL SERAFINI

But she wouldn't budge. And never has since, or we wouldn't be having this conversation.

PETER LASCELLES

You might think so; I couldn't possibly comment.

BILL SERAFINI

And I'm guessing this night of passion was too far from London for our man to be in two places at the same time?

PETER LASCELLES

Far enough, I imagine.

BILL SERAFINI

And I'm likewise guessing you never had probable cause to compel him to supply DNA or prints?

PETER LASCELLES

Again, you might very well think so.

(pause)

You planning on doing any sightseeing while you're over here, Bill?

BILL SERAFINI

Well—

PETER LASCELLES

There are some great places to visit. And not too far from London. Far enough, though, if you catch my drift. Like Salisbury, for example.

BILL SERAFINI

(frowns a moment then realization dawns)

Oh, you mean that place where those two Russkies tried to off that defector - Sergei something?

PETER LASCELLES

Skripal. And then claimed they were only there to 'look at the cathedral'. Yeah, right, as my grandchildren would say

BILL SERAFINI

I'm still not sure why—

PETER LASCELLES

There's a nice little B&B I would definitely recommend you try. The woman who owns it - I met her, oh, it must be very nearly twenty years ago now.

BILL SERAFINI

(slowly)

Right.

I get you.

Sounds like it's definitely worth my time.

PETER LASCELLES

I'm sure you won't regret it.

(smiling)

And the cathedral really is quite something.

CUT TO: Studio.

HUGO FRASER

I assume you took the hint, Bill? I mean, he was clearly marking your card.

BILL SERAFINI

I certainly did, Hugo, and he certainly was.

(grins)

And he was right about that old church, too.

CUT TO: FOOTAGE of Bill sitting at a café table with a view across an expanse of grass to Salisbury cathedral. The sun is shining but it's obviously cold as he's wearing a leather coat as well as the trademark sunglasses. There's a woman sitting opposite him who has her back to the camera. We can see she's slim, with well-cut short hair which has been professionally highlighted. She's wearing a chocolate-coloured faux-fur jacket. Sub-caption: 'Christine'.

BILL SERAFINI

I guess I should start out by saying that you've agreed to speak to us as long as we protect your identity, which is why we're calling you Christine.

And the reason why we want to talk to you is because you were the woman who gave an alibi for the night of October third, 2003, to Ian Wilson.

'CHRISTINE'

Yes, I did.

BILL SERAFINI

Can you take us through that evening?

'CHRISTINE'

(laughing - a husky smoker's laugh)

Well, I'm not sure *quite* how much detail you want me to go into—

BILL SERAFINI

(with a wry smile)

Let's keep it family-friendly.

'CHRISTINE'

OK. So, I was working in a bar in town back then. It's long gone now but it was quite a hip place back in the day. I was the manager so I wasn't front of house the whole time, but I was obviously in and out throughout the evening.

BILL SERAFINI

And that's how you met Ian?

'CHRISTINE'

Right. He stood out, to be honest. You don't get many guys turning up alone. They're mostly with girlfriends or with mates, not alone. A couple of girls had a go at getting his attention, as the evening wore on, but he didn't seem interested.

(laughs)

In fact, I was beginning to wonder if he was gay. Though I didn't know what he was doing in our gaff if he was, not with a gay bar only fifty yards down the street.

BILL SERAFINI

So what happened?

'CHRISTINE'

Around midnight I went outside for a fag. It was bloody freezing but we didn't allow smoking inside so I didn't have a choice. A couple of minutes later, there he was.

BILL SERAFINI

He was having a smoke too?

'CHRISTINE'

No. I offered him one but he said he didn't. Said he just wanted some fresh air.

BILL SERAFINI

What name did he give you?

'CHRISTINE'

Ian.

BILL SERAFINI

That's all?

'CHRISTINE'

Just Ian. I never knew his surname.

BILL SERAFINI

So what happened next?

'CHRISTINE'

We got talking, and I let slip it was a bit of a bummer working on my birthday and he insisted on buying me a glass of champagne. We weren't supposed to drink when we were working but what the hell, I reckon I deserved it.

BILL SERAFINI

So you go back inside?

'CHRISTINE'

Right. And he gets the fizz—

BILL SERAFINI

Don't tell me - paying cash?

'CHRISTINE'

Yup. And then we sit down at the bar and all of a sudden this hen party arrives. Whole bunch of girls with flicky hair and tiaras and skirts up over their knickers and I thought, oh well, it was nice while it lasted.

But it did. Last, I mean. He didn't seem interested in them. We moved over to a table, and one thing led to another and we ended up back in my flat.

BILL SERAFINI

And you're sure he was with you all night?

'CHRISTINE'

(laughs again)

Oh yes. I don't think either of us got much sleep.

BILL SERAFINI

And I guess the fact that it was your birthday meant you were pretty certain of the date, when the police came calling?

'CHRISTINE'

Do you remember *your* fortieth?

BILL SERAFINI

Certainly do—

'CHRISTINE'

Right. And I bet mine was way more memorable than yours. No offence.

BILL SERAFINI

(shaking his head and grinning)

None taken.

'CHRISTINE'

So yeah, I didn't have any problem remembering. And don't forget – it was only a couple of weeks later that the coppers came calling.

BILL SERAFINI

Wouldn't other bar staff have remembered him as well?

'CHRISTINE'

They definitely recognized him but they couldn't be sure if it was the Friday or the Saturday, just that it was that weekend.

BILL SERAFINI

I see. So when you spoke to the police, how was the identity confirmed?

'CHRISTINE'

Peter showed me a photo. Looked like something off a passport.

BILL SERAFINI

Peter Lascelles - the Senior Investigating Officer?

'CHRISTINE'

Right.

BILL SERAFINI

And you were one hundred per cent sure it was the same man you spent that evening with?

'CHRISTINE'

Absolutely.

CUT TO: Studio. Bill is still at the whiteboard.

JJ NORTON

So if we believe this 'Christine', Ian Wilson couldn't have been the killer.

BILL SERAFINI

Right.

LAILA FURNESS

And did you? Believe her?

BILL SERAFINI

Actually, I did. She kept eye contact with me the whole time, no rapid blinking - none of the usual bodily indicators for lying.

So to sum up, I think we need to park the Ian thing for now. Pending any further evidence, at any rate.

ALAN CANNING

(under his breath)

Thank Christ for that.

BILL SERAFINI

So next up, Down Under. Mitch? Anything more on the Sydney angle?

MITCHELL CLARKE

Nothing new, I'm afraid. Though what I did do was do a trawl of the UK press from around the time Caroline and 'Luke' got married. Basically to see how easy it might have been for the family of the hit-and-run victim to track him down. And this is what I found.

CUT TO: MONTAGE of press coverage.

CAROLINE HOWARD AND LUKE RYDER

PLANNING AN INTIMATE ROMANTIC WEDDING AT HOME

Forthcoming Marriages

MR L. RYDER AND MRS C. J. HOWARD

The engagement is announced between Luke, son of the late Brian and Maureen Ryder of Kalgoorlie, Western Australia, and Caroline, widow of Andr

JOY AS RYDER WEDS HIS SWEET CAROLINE

MITCHELL CLARKE

There was also coverage when they attended a charity gala at Holland Park which was only six weeks before the murder. Though I couldn't find very much by way of pictures, either of the wedding or later, and what I did find were mostly of her, not him.

LAILA FURNESS

Our man avoiding being photographed again?

MITCHELL CLARKE

Could be. But it does show us that as long as you had a name, there were enough mentions of Ryder in the press for someone to track him down. There are even references to him being an Australian.

BILL SERAFINI

OK, noted. Thank you. So next up, Caroline's not-so-mystery lover. Alan?

ALAN CANNING

Actually, I think I've finally made some progress. I've tracked down the owner of a red MGB which might fit the bill - I've only spoken to them on the phone but it sounds promising.

BILL SERAFINI

I'm impressed! So who is this guy?

ALAN CANNING

It's not a man, it's a woman. She was living in the W8 area at the time and often lent her car to her brother.

HUGO FRASER

What's her name?

ALAN CANNING

(without looking at him)

I'd rather not say right now - not till I've done some more legwork.

HUGO FRASER

(frowning)

Sounds a bit flaky to me.

MITCHELL CLARKE

(laughing)

Easy, tiger, anyone would think you had something to hide—

HUGO FRASER

(quickly)

Well, you should know—

MITCHELL CLARKE

What the hell's that supposed to mean?

BILL SERAFINI

(intervening)

Hey, I'm sure Hugo was just referring to the fact that you were in the cross hairs yourself on this case, for a while, weren't you, Mitch. Right, Hugo?

Neither man says anything; there's an awkward pause. Then suddenly, the sound of movement from behind the camera.

NICK VINCENT APPEARS IN SHOT. He's tanned and wearing an open-neck white shirt. A moment later he's followed by someone else. A newcomer. He's slight, with longish dark hair, glasses, and a grey marl T-shirt with a UCLA logo on the front. He's clutching a laptop and a pile of papers. He looks a little uncomfortable.

NICK VINCENT (Producer)

OK, guys, I think this might be a good time to bring you all up to speed on something Tarek's been working on. We've heard his name mentioned more than once over the course of the series but up till now he's always been on the other side of the camera. But this time he gets to be on screen, because he's come up with some pretty exciting stuff.

TAREK OSMAN

(pushing his glasses up his nose)

No pressure, eh, Nick.

NICK VINCENT (Producer)

Don't do yourself down, kid. Anyway, I'll leave it to you to explain.

Nick goes round the table to perch against the windowsill, tapping Tarek lightly on the arm as he passes.

CLOSE-UP on Tarek as he pulls out a chair and sits down.

TAREK OSMAN

(fiddling with the laptop and papers)

OK, so me and the team have done some more digging on 'Luke Ryder' to see whether we could find out anything more about his past. And we managed to turn up something - about when he was on Assos.

FOOTAGE of Tarek on location in Greece. Panorama across the harbour: fishing boats, quayside tavernas, brightly coloured houses and blue hills beyond.

CUT TO: Tarek walking up a street - flowering creeper up the walls, a cat blinking in the sun, tables and chairs outside a bar. He stops outside and turns to camera. He's not wearing sunglasses and is squinting slightly.

TAREK OSMAN

You probably remember that Rupert Howard didn't have any pictures of himself and Luke from the summer they met here, and we weren't able to find anything useful online either. So we decided it might be worth coming over and actually talking to people.

CUT TO: Interior of bar. Tarek is with a man in his forties. The walls are painted teal blue, with a whitewashed floor and white wooden furniture.

TAREK OSMAN

I'm here with George Nicolaides, who took over the bar from his father ten years ago. I think I'm right in saying you weren't in Assos the summer Luke Ryder was working here?

GEORGE NICOLAIDES

(speaking perfect English with a slight American accent)

No, I was at university then and took the summer off to go travelling.

TAREK OSMAN

And looking round you've clearly had the bar refurbed since 1998?

GEORGE NICOLAIDES

Right. We completely remodelled it when I took over. It had a much more traditional look under my paps.

TAREK OSMAN

Almost unrecognizable from what it is now, right?

GEORGE NICOLAIDES

(laughing)

You could say that. Paps was a terrible hoarder – he wouldn't throw anything away until it fell apart. By the end none of the furniture matched and he had posters up that were older than me. But that turned out to be helpful in the end. For you, I mean.

TAREK OSMAN

Yes, talk us through that.

GEORGE NICOLAIDES

This is what the place looked like before we started the refurbishments.

He passes over a photo. CAMERA ZOOMS in to show the bar with a corkboard behind it, pinned with layers of beermats, taxi flyers, Post-its and photos, many of them curling at the edges.

As you can see a lot of that stuff was years old.

TAREK OSMAN

But you didn't throw it away? When you did the refurb, I mean?

GEORGE NICOLAIDES

No, we boxed it all up and gave it to Paps. He'd never have forgiven me if I'd dumped it.

TAREK OSMAN

Which is why we have him to thank for these—

CUT TO: Sequence of three stills. The first is of 'Luke' and Rupert Howard, their arms around each other's shoulders, clearly quite drunk. Someone has scrawled 'Assos Amigos' in biro across the bottom. The second photo is of the bar. It's late in the evening and the lighting is low. Rupert can be seen at one of the tables with a group of lads his age, glass in hand, slightly red-faced. Further back, and not so visible, 'Luke' is sitting at a table with a woman; she's in her forties with short dark hair. Only part of her face is visible.

In the third picture she and 'Luke' are standing in sunlight in the street outside the bar; she's wearing sunglasses and a hat, he has his arm round her, pulling her quite close. She's smiling up at him, one hand touching his hair. The picture appears to have been taken from inside the bar, without either of them being aware of it. There's no one else visible in the picture.

CAMERA PANS out to the two men looking at the photos on the table.

TAREK OSMAN

Do you have any idea who this woman is?

GEORGE NICOLAIDES

I'm afraid not. Like I said, I was away that summer. I did speak to Paps about it and he remembered her face but not her name. He said he was pretty sure she was English and was renting a flat in the town somewhere, but that's all I've managed to find out.

CUT TO: Studio. The team shift slightly in their seats. This is a lot of new information to digest on the fly.

TARAEK OSMAN

We also spoke to some of the older residents while we were in Assos, and one old lady thought the woman might have been called Irene. But someone else came up with Carrie, so your guess is as good as mine.

LAILA FURNESS

But if she was renting a place there must have been some sort of paperwork—

TAREK OSMAN

Probably, but it's so long ago it'd be a miracle if anyone still had it. And in any case rentals like that can be pretty informal in Greece.

HUGO FRASER

For which read 'to avoid tax'.

BILL SERAFINI

But it does give us another potential victim of 'Luke's' scams, and another set of suspects who might have wanted to track him down.

LAILA FURNESS

(to Tarek)

What about Rupert - did he remember this woman?

TAREK OSMAN

(sighs and shakes his head)

You'd have thought he might, wouldn't you? Or that the photo might have triggered something, but sadly not. He said he had a vague memory of seeing her around but absolutely no sense there was anything going on between her and Luke.

LAILA FURNESS

Though like you said, it's a very long time ago. If she was in her forties then she'd be over sixty now.

ALAN CANNING

And near nigh impossible to track down. It'd be yet another complete waste of bloody time. And that's assuming there *was* some sort of relationship between them, which I'm *very* far from convinced was actually the case. Not on the basis of one bloody photo.

BILL SERAFINI

I'm not so sure - I mean, I don't know about you, Alan—

He gestures at the third photo where it's pinned on the board.

—but I don't behave like that with random women I meet in bars.

ALAN CANNING

(getting tetchy)

Maybe you don't, but some men do - especially selfish bastards like this 'Luke' bloke clearly was.

LAILA FURNESS

(under her breath)

Wow, that escalated quickly—

NICK VINCENT (Producer)

OK guys, let's not get too hung up on it at this stage - there's plenty of other leads we still haven't fully run down.

BILL SERAFINI

Fair enough. You're in charge.

NICK VINCENT (Producer)

In fact there's one more thing we need to share with you.

The team exchange glances: now what?

MITCHELL CLARKE

(with rather forced jocularity)

So what else have you been holding out on?

NICK VINCENT (Producer)

Not 'holding out', exactly, Mitch. It's something Fabio found.

JJ NORTON

(frowning)

Fabio as in the film editor?

NICK VINCENT (Producer)

Exactly.

Tarek opens his laptop. The screen on the far wall pings into life.

TAREK OSMAN

OK, so, a while back Guy gave us some old family cine films to use for fillers. We digitized them all but to be honest we didn't think they'd tell us much - useful background footage, obviously, but it was more a production job than a research one, hence it being Fabio who found it rather than me.

He taps the keyboard, and as he does so Nick comes forward and stands to the right of the screen.

The FOOTAGE starts to play. It's of Caroline and Andrew Howard's wedding. Slightly jumpy, the colour faded, and there's no sound. They're pictured on the steps of Chelsea Old Town Hall, then sitting together at the reception, drinking a toast and cutting the cake. They look self-conscious and it feels a little staged.

Then the scene shifts to the honeymoon. White sand and palm trees. The camera pans across, a little unsteadily, to show couples on the beach and in the sea, and then Caroline, sitting on a towel, applying sun lotion. She's wearing large mirrored sunglasses and a rather old-fashioned-looking one-piece swimsuit.

GUY HOWARD (off)

(laughing)

As usual Mum's the only one not in a bikini. She hated the things – the girls bought one for her birthday once but she refused to wear it.

TAREK OSMAN

(pushing his glasses up his nose)

Actually, I think we may be about to find out why.

The screen now shows Caroline in a hotel bedroom. The mood is very different – more intimate, more playful. She's sitting on the bed with her back to us, drying her hair, dressed only in her underwear, but she's holding a mirror and we can see Andrew's reflection as he films her. After a moment or two she turns laughing and puts her hand out and pushes the camera away; the lens dips, turns upside down and then the screen goes blank. The whole sequence takes only a few seconds. Tarek presses Pause, then looks round the table.

MITCHELL CLARKE

Is there supposed to be something there, because I can't see it.

Tarek rewinds and plays the last scene again, freezing it a few frames before the end, then zooming in on Caroline.

LAILA FURNESS

(starting)

Oh my God – is that what I think it is?

JJ NORTON

(nodding slowly)

It most certainly is.

MITCHELL CLARKE

Care to share? Because I'm still blanking.

JJ NORTON

(getting up and going over to the screen)

To be fair, it's not that easy to see, not unless you know what you're looking for. This line here, just above her knicker line? That's a postoperative scar.

MITCHELL CLARKE

What, she had an appendectomy, something like that?

ALAN CANNING

(shaking his head)

No, it's not that. I've seen those before in PMs. It's from a Caesarean.

MITCHELL CLARKE

(as realization dawns)

Shit - she had a *baby*. And *before* she married Andrew Howard.

TAREK OSMAN

That's the obvious conclusion, yes. Of course, we haven't had access to her medical records and we're not likely to get it—

There's a sudden commotion, the camera swings round and there's a brief slightly out-of-focus image of Guy. He looks horror-struck. Then he turns away and the camera loses sight of him. There's the sound of footsteps and a door slamming.

NICK VINCENT (Producer)

Sorry, everyone, I think this has come as rather a bolt from the blue for Guy.

LAILA FURNESS

(looking at Nick, clearly shocked)

Oh my God, he didn't *know*?

HUGO FRASER

(sardonically, under his breath)

Evidently not.

LAILA FURNESS

(to Nick)

And you didn't think you should have *talked* to him? Warn him what you'd found and what it implied? I mean, leaving aside the small fact that he's supposed to be the *director* of this thing, to spring something like that on him, *on camera*—

HUGO FRASER

Exactly.

(staring at Nick)

How would *you* like to be ambushed like that? The guy has a brother or sister he never even knew he had.

BILL SERAFINI

OK, I think we can all agree the reveal was a touch crass, but the info's still a game-changer, right?

NICK VINCENT (Producer)

(smiling, not very pleasantly)

Certainly is, Bill. Certainly is.

FADE OUT

- end credits -

Date: Fri 9/06/2023, 9.14 **Importance:** High

From: Alan Canning

To: Nick Vincent

CC: Guy Howard, Hugo Fraser, Mitch Clarke, Laila Furness, Bill Serafini, JJ Norton

Subject: Your approach

Nick,

I'm writing to express my frustration and – frankly – irritation – at the way the last episode was handled.

I'm sure we all understand the need to create 'cliff-hangers' for the audience, and I accept that you did raise this explicitly at the outset, but you don't have to keep us all completely in the dark in order to achieve that. It makes us feel – and probably look – like idiots. I can't believe anyone would find it acceptable to be ambushed like that on TV. Especially in a context where they're being presented as an 'expert witness'. We are entitled to a degree of respect.

I hope I speak for all of us when I say that I would like your assurance that this will not happen again.

Alan

Date: Sat 10/06/2023, 11.17 **Importance:** High

From: Laila Furness

To: Bill Serafini

Subject: Alan's email

Hi Bill,

What are your thoughts on this? Alan clearly has a point even if he expresses it rather ponderously (now there's a surprise). I do agree Nick is pushing it now, but not having done any TV work before I'm reluctant to weigh in if this is just par for the course.

Any thoughts?

L

Date: Sun 11/06/2023, 12.45

From: Bill Serafini

To: Laila Furness

Subject: Re: Alan's email

Laila,

IMO Alan's just doing his usual blowhard shtick. I'm staying well out of it.

B

Date: Sun 11/06/2023, 16.39 **Importance:** High

From: Alan Canning

To: Nick Vincent

CC: Guy Howard, Hugo Fraser, Mitch Clarke, Laila Furness, Bill Serafini, JJ Norton

Subject: Fwd: Your approach

Just checking you got this?

Text messages between Maura and Amelie Howard, 7th June 2023, 5.49 p.m.

Well that was shit

What happened

Fucking Shirley Booker, that's what happened

That old cow - what's she got to do with anything?

She told them that we hated Luke. Or whatever the fuck his real name was

Oh

I'm afraid I got a bit teary

Hey, you OK?

I guess it was the first time I'd really thought about him and how he was with mum

I know how you felt about him back then but he did make her happy Am

I know

And when you look at her now

😢

I'm so sorry Maurie

I wish there was something I could do

No you're best out of it

I just hope Guy knows what he's putting us through for the sake of his bloody 'career'

Yeah right

Voicemail left for Tarek Osman by Bill Serafini, 8th June 2023, 9.45 a.m.

Hi Tarek, It's Bill. Can you give me a call when you get this? There's something I need your help with.

-0.34

Speaker   Call back   Delete

Voicemail left for Tarek Osman by Nick Vincent, 9th June 2023, 8.03 p.m.

Hi Tarek, it's Nick. Just to say I've seen the new stuff and it's dynamite. Brilliant work, as always.

Just make sure you keep it to yourself - this is absolutely Need to Fucking Know. So just the camera crew, OK? No-one else.

See you Monday.

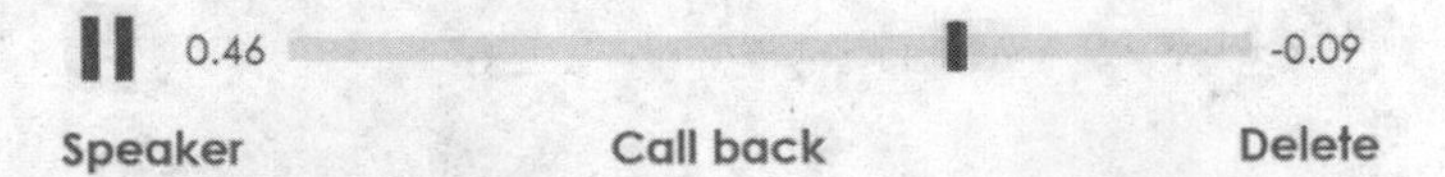

Episode five

Broadcast

October 15

TELEVISION

What price truth?

Infamous may be a new kind of reality TV but the cost is only too real

ROSS LESLIE

Infamous: Who Killed Luke Ryder?
Showrunner

It's taken us from Ambleside to Alabama, and now to Assos, as the **Infamous** team of experts continue to pursue the elusive 'Luke Ryder', a man whose ability to morph seamlessly through a whole sequence of different identities must surely put him high on the list to become the next Dr Who.

I've talked before about the psychological resonance of this case, and how compelling its exploration of complex family relationships has been. Last night's episode added a new layer of complexity and genuine poignancy, as Nick Vincent, the producer of Infamous, revealed 'live' on screen that Caroline Howard Ryder had had a baby when she was still a teenager. This clearly came as a complete shock to her son Guy, the show's director, which certainly made for can't-tear-your-eyes-away TV, even if it left me, for one, wondering if we had finally crossed the notoriously blurry line between viewing and voyeurism.

It's not the first time I've been prompted to reflect on the ethical issues raised by this genre; a few weeks ago I referred to Infamous as the ultimate true-crime reality TV. But seeing even a brief glimpse of Guy Howard's hurt and bewildered face last night was a powerful reminder of the human cost of this type of television. In TS Eliot's memorable phrase, surely no-one caught up in these crimes should be asked to bear quite as much 'reality' as that.

https://www.groopz.com/truecrimeaddiction

Infamous/LukeRyder Join

Bloody hell that Nick Vincent knows how to light a blue touchpaper and withdraw KABOOM!

submitted 5 hours ago by Slooth
6 comments share hide report

> Sneaky bastard. And did you see Guy? Talk about ambushed, poor sod. Would love to be a fly on the wall at *their* next 'meeting'....
>
> submitted 4 hours ago by MsMarple99
> 2 comments share hide report

I have to say I think they went too far last night. It wasn't just the Guy thing they're talking about in the papers – it was the violation of Caroline's privacy. She may have Alzheimers but she's not *dead*. She deserves the same consideration as anyone else.

submitted 5 hours ago by AngieFlynn77
28 comments share hide report

> With you on that one Ange. It was a definite bum note
>
> submitted 5 hours ago by MsMarple99
> 2 comments share hide report
>
> But in terms of the investigation it was a pretty big deal? Don't get me wrong, I found it uncomfortable too, but it is after all what the show's supposed to be doing – finding out as much new info as poss that might be relevant. That's bound to be problematic at times
>
> submitted 4 hours ago by Investig8er
> 2 comments share hide report
>
>> Sorry but you still need to treat people with dignity
>>
>> submitted 4 hours ago by AngieFlynn77
>> share hide report

That scene with Wild Bill and that woman 'Christine' was just bloody hilarious #letskeepitfamilyfriendly #sweatingupthesheets 😂

submitted 3 hours ago by RonJebus
5 comments share hide report

> And Sherlock Serafini did it yet *again*. That whole Rose Shulman thing. I mean, who gets that lucky that often? Just remind me never to play poker with that guy... 😲 😄
>
> submitted 3 hours ago by PaulWinship007
> share hide report

Anyone else playing red MGB bingo? Big cheer here every time it gets a mensh

submitted 3 hours ago by Brian885643
7 comments share hide report

> It's doing my head in – I see the bloody things everywhere now 😵
>
> submitted 2 hours ago by 123JackofAllTrades
> 2 comments share hide report

What the hell was that thing with Hugo F and Mitch? Like there was some sort of other agenda going on we don't know about?

submitted 2 hours ago by TCFanatic88
12 comments share hide report

> I wondered about that too – do you think it's possible they actually *know* each other? I mean vastly different jobs etc etc but like everyone keeps saying Ladbroke Grove is only a stone's throw from Campden Hill, and HF deffo knows his way round *that* part of town (that tennis /squash club thing for starters)
>
> 
> submitted 2 hours ago by NoddyHolder1977
> 27 comments share hide report
>
>> I agree – definitely one to keep an eye on
>>
>> submitted 2 hours ago by TruCrimr
>> 31 comments share hide report

Episode six

Filming

DRY RISER FILMS Ltd
227 Sherwood Street London W1Q 2UD

CAST Alan Canning (AC) Mitchell Clarke (MC) Hugo Fraser (HF) Laila Furness (LF) JJ Norton (JJN) Bill Serafini (WS) **UNIT CALL 0815** ***Camera ready: 0830***	**CALL SHEET** **Infamous:** **Who Killed Luke Ryder?** Tuesday 11th July 2023 **Ep 6: STUDIO DAY 1 of 4**	Producer **Nick Vincent** Director **Guy Howard** Film editor **Fabio Barry** Researcher **Tarek Osman** Prod asst **Jenni Tate** Location manager **Guy Johnson** *Breakfast @ Studio 0745* *Running lunch on set from 1230* *Exp wrap 1830*

Location: **Frobisher Studios** **131-137 Kingston Road** **Maida Vale London W9 7EX**	Notes: *Very limited parking on site* *Nearest tube Warwick Avenue* *Emergency contact number 07000 616178*

CREW							
TITLE	*NAME*	*PHONE*	*CALL*	*TITLE*	*NAME*	*PHONE*	*CALL*

TITLE SEQUENCE: arthouse-style b/w montage of images and short clips: crime scene, contemporary news coverage, family photos

THEME SONG – 'It's Alright, Ma (I'm Only Bleeding)' [Bob Dylan] from the soundtrack to 'Easy Rider' [1969]

TITLE OVER

INFAMOUS

FADE IN

WHO KILLED LUKE RYDER?

FADE OUT

BLACK FRAME, TEXT APPEARS, with VOICEOVER – narrator (female)

October 3, 2003: the husband of a British socialite is found beaten to death in an upscale district of the British capital.

Twenty years on and the killer has still not been brought to justice.

But thanks to the work of the Infamous team, new light has now been shone on this baffling case.

In 2003, the London police did not even know who the victim really was. He was not Australian, or 26, as he claimed, and 'Luke Ryder ' was not his real name.

Was that the reason he had to die?

FADE OUT

CUT TO: Studio. The atmosphere appears to have changed; more uneasy, more uncertain. The team are round the table, along with Tarek. Nick is standing at the window. Sunlight is streaming in, and they're all in summer clothes.

MITCHELL CLARKE

Well, Nick, you did it again. Led us all to water and then tipped us straight in.

NICK VINCENT (Producer)

(smiling)

Well, everyone loves a cliff-hanger, don't they.

ALAN CANNING

(sarcastically)

And here's all of us thinking bolts from the blue were exclusively Bill's department.

(Bill grins but doesn't rise to it.)

LAILA FURNESS

(to Tarek)

What more can you tell us about Caroline's baby? Do we know when it was born?

TAREK OSMAN

Well, none of her friends that we've spoken to seems to have known anything about it – no one brought it up, that's for sure.

And in terms of a date of birth, there's really only one period before she married Andrew Howard where Caroline goes off the radar for any length of time.

ALAN CANNING

(nodding slowly)

That summer after she left school – when she was at the uncle's in Birmingham.

TAREK OSMAN

Edgbaston, right—

MITCHELL CLARKE

So *that's* why she was 'sent away'. It wasn't to get over an unsuitable bloke, it was to get rid of his even more unsuitable baby—

BILL SERAFINI

It certainly looks that way.

LAILA FURNESS

But she was only 16 at the end of that summer, which means she must have been underage when the child was conceived.

BILL SERAFINI

All the more reason for the family to want to cover it up.

ALAN CANNING

Have you been able to find any record of the birth?

TAREK OSMAN

I'm afraid not. It's a reasonable bet it was at a Birmingham hospital, but we don't have any way of narrowing down the date, and if she had the baby adopted we won't be able to access the original birth certificate anyway - only the kid themselves could do that. The original would have been replaced by a new one after the adoption was finalized.

MITCHELL CLARKE

We don't *know* she had it adopted—

JJ NORTON

Well, she certainly didn't keep it, did she—

TAREK OSMAN

(pushing his glasses up his nose)

No, obviously not. But as I'm sure you know, adoption records are sealed, so it's basically impossible to find out where the child ended up. Though it would probably have been placed with a local Midlands family, given that it would have been a Birmingham local authority dealing with it.

MITCHELL CLARKE

And as far as we know she never told anyone?

NICK VINCENT (Producer)

Well, Andrew Howard must have known: he'd have seen the scar just like we just did. But he's the only one, as far as we can tell.

LAILA FURNESS

I haven't seen Guy today - is he OK?

NICK VINCENT (Producer)

(shrugs)

As far as I know.

LAILA FURNESS

(evidently not impressed by this as an answer)

I'm not surprised he's distraught - everything he thought he knew has been thrown into doubt—

JJ NORTON

I know what that's like. And the older you are the more traumatic that is.

HUGO FRASER

I'm sure we're all extremely sympathetic. But what I'm less sure about is whether this gives us a viable new line of enquiry in the murder investigation.

MITCHELL CLARKE

True. I mean, however resentful the abandoned child might have been, he or she would have no beef with anyone but Caroline. And certainly not with a husband she didn't meet till more than twenty years later.

BILL SERAFINI

But we know *someone* came to the house that night - it has to be possible it was Caroline's long-lost kid.

MITCHELL CLARKE

(doing the math)

If the kid was born in 1979 it'd be 44 now.

LAILA FURNESS

More to the point, he or she would have been 18 in 1997 and entitled to see their records at that stage, but there's no suggestion they made contact with Caroline then. Why leave it till 2003?

JJ NORTON

Not all adopted kids want to. Some never do. And 18 is just the earliest you can do it - lots of people leave it a lot later than that. Just saying.

MITCHELL CLARKE

But if they did track Caroline down it might have been a pretty difficult encounter. What if the kid had quite a disadvantaged upbringing - it has to be possible if it was inner-city Birmingham, right?

Then all those years later they suddenly find out their real mother and her other kids have been sitting pretty on a pile like Dorney Place, while they were unceremoniously dumped and left out in the cold—

JJ NORTON

Quite.

LAILA FURNESS

I think that's a little unfair - for all we know Caroline may have wanted to keep the baby, but her parents put a stop to it. And remember, she was incredibly young - still a child herself—

MITCHELL CLARKE

I'm just saying the kid may well not have seen it that way. What if they turned up that night, looking for Caroline? No Google Earth back then - they'd have just had an address. They probably had absolutely no idea quite what a fuck-off house it was. They get angry, demand to be let in, 'Luke' tries to calm them down but things take a nasty turn - and if the kid was a *boy*—

HUGO FRASER

Actually, that's not such a ludicrous scenario, Mitch.

LAILA FURNESS

And of course the police never track him down because they don't even know he exists.

HUGO FRASER

(to Tarek)

We know that for certain, do we?

TAREK OSMAN

Well, there's nothing anywhere in the case files to suggest they knew.

LAILA FURNESS

But if the adoption records are sealed there's nothing we can do, apart from yet more speculation.

NICK VINCENT (Producer)

Nothing *we* can do, no, but we've passed everything we've found to the Met. It's up to them now.

MITCHELL CLARKE

But where does that leave us? What have we got left?

(telling them off on his fingers)

Rupert's out, Caroline's out, we can't pursue the adopted child, Ian Wilson has an alibi. We've basically run out of road.

JJ is about to say something but Alan cuts across him.

ALAN CANNING

Oh, I'm not so sure about that.

LAILA FURNESS

(with a smile)

Don't tell me we've finally found the owner of the infamous red MGB—

ALAN CANNING

Funny you should mention that. As it happens the woman I was following up with has suddenly got cold feet. Completely refuses to speak to me.

JJ NORTON

You think someone got to her? Told her to keep shtum?

HUGO FRASER

Oh for God's sake, it's not the bloody *Sopranos*—

LAILA FURNESS

Could just be a coincidence?

MITCHELL CLARKE

(with a knowing nod to her)

But Alan doesn't believe in coincidences, does he?

ALAN CANNING

(steadily)

No, I don't.

LAILA FURNESS

(to Nick)

Do you know about this?

NICK VINCENT (Producer)

(not answering her)

What is it you have, Alan?

ALAN CANNING

(sitting back)

It struck me for the first time when Bill was interviewing the people in Alabama who knew the real Eric Fulton as a child.

CUT TO: CLIP previously shown of Bill interviewing Nancy Kozlowski (edited):

NANCY KOZLOWSKI

I could just sense, that last year, that somethin' was eatin' away at him and I could make a pretty good guess at what it might be. But then one day I found him cryin' out back. Some of the other boys had been callin' him a faggot and I don't know what else. Kids can be so cruel.

BILL SERAFINI

What did you say to him?

NANCY KOZLOWSKI

Like I said before, I told him maybe North Birmingham wasn't the best place for him. That he couldn't change what he was and shouldn't try. He just needed to surround himself with other folks who would think the way I did.

He dropped out the end of that year and left town soon after. If his mother had known it was my doin' she'd never have forgiven me. But I don't regret it, Bill, I don't regret it at all.

BILL SERAFINI

When I spoke to Frank Tappin, he said he was surprised Eric ended up in Beirut. What did you think when you heard about that?

NANCY KOZLOWSKI

I didn't believe it at first, I don't mind tellin' you. I'd had a card or two from him in New York and he seemed real happy. Real at ease with himself. I just don't see what could-a made him decide to leave. Especially for someplace like that.

BILL SERAFINI

Do you still have any of the cards he sent?

NANCY KOZLOWSKI

No, they're long gone. I do have those photos we talked about, though.

CUT TO: Studio. People are looking confused.

LAILA FURNESS

I'm not sure what you're getting at, Alan—

ALAN CANNING

It's only when you've seen it a few times that it jumps out at you.

MITCHELL CLARKE

I'll have to take your word for it, because, trust me, nothing's jumping out at me *at all*—

ALAN CANNING

It was still just a hunch at that point, so I gave Tarek a call and asked if I could speak to one of the film crew.

LAILA FURNESS

(frowning)

The film crew for the Alabama shoot? But what on earth could they possibly—

ALAN CANNING

And he put me through to one of the women on the camera team. She's asked me not to give her name, but she confirmed exactly what I'd suspected: this was very far from being the first time Bill and Nancy Kozlowski had met.

Silence; Bill shifts a little in his chair but says nothing.

JJ NORTON

I'm not sure where you're going with this, but the first question that comes to mind is how could she be so sure?

ALAN CANNING

For starters, their body language, also the fact that they arrived at the shoot together—

HUGO FRASER

I'd hardly call *that* conclusive.

ALAN CANNING

And on top of that, what Nancy says in that clip: 'Like I said before', 'those photos we talked about', the fact she calls him Bill—

HUGO FRASER

At the risk of repeating myself, I don't think that proves anything.

ALAN CANNING

(glancing at him)

No? OK, then try this for size.

He opens his laptop and connects it to the main screen. A scan of a document appears, headed 'Detective Bureau, Investigation Card'.

MITCHELL CLARKE

What am I looking at?

ALAN CANNING

This is an NYPD I-Card. It is, in effect, a request to patrol officers to apprehend a named individual, either because they're believed to be a witness to a crime, because there are grounds for arrest, or because in some other way they're a Person of Interest.

This—

(gesturing)

—is the I-Card for Eric Dwight Fulton.

DETECTIVE BUREAU
INVESTIGATION CARD

Date prepared: 9/08/97	Control No: 774/813
Last Name: FULTON	First Name(s): Eric Dwight
Last Known Address (Street, Apt, State, Zip) Apt 6,8495 West Green Hill St.Brooklyn, NY 11229	

Sex:	Race:	Date of Birth:	Social Security No:	Height:	Weight:	Hair Color:	Eve Color:
M	White	11/03/1966	[redacted]	6'2"	170	Blonde	Blue

Aliases/Nicknames: Not Known/Possible	Complaint No: 88565/090/G
Sought As: X Perpetrator - Probable Cause to Arrest Suspect Only - No Probable Cause to Arrest Witness	**Precautions to be Observed** Armed and Dangerous / Resists Arrest X Flight Risk / Other
Crime/Charge: Theft/Fraud	Domestic Violence? No

JJ NORTON

(scanning it)

OK, so this was obviously issued after he made off with Rose Shulman's stack of cash—

ALAN CANNING

In fact, after her death. It was only then that the official complaint was made.

JJ NORTON

—either way I'm not sure where it gets us, given we already knew about that.

ALAN CANNING

You're right. We did.

(taps his keyboard)

But we didn't know about *this*.

DETECTIVE BUREAU
INVESTIGATION CARD

Assigned Investigator: Yes	Rank: DT3	Name: William R. Serafini	Command:	Command Code:

JJ NORTON

(turns to Bill, clearly shocked)

It was *your case*? Why didn't you say anything?

BILL SERAFINI

(shifting slightly)

I don't think I ever explicitly denied it.

LAILA FURNESS

Oh come on, Bill, I'm sure you never said anything about being the - what does it say there? - 'Assigned Investigator'.

BILL SERAFINI

Look, if I omitted to mention—

ALAN CANNING

(quietly)

It was rather more than an 'omission'.

He taps his keyboard again; the screen changes to FOOTAGE from the previous episode.

LAILA FURNESS

So you think this conman was active in New York in the mid '90s? Weren't you in NYPD yourself then?

BILL SERAFINI

I was.

LAILA FURNESS

But you don't remember anything like this at the time?

BILL SERAFINI

It's a lot of years ago, Laila, and it's a big city. But let's see what the guys back home come up with.

CUT TO: Wide shot of whole team; no one is making eye contact.

HUGO FRASER

With the benefit of hindsight, that last response was a classic lawyer's answer – not strictly speaking a lie, but not the whole truth either. Not by a *very* long way.

LAILA FURNESS

(staring at Bill)

So you've known about Eric Fulton all along.

BILL SERAFINI

It's not as simple as that—

MITCHELL CLARKE

Why the hell didn't you say? OK, maybe at the beginning of all this you didn't know he and Luke Ryder were one and the same person, but as soon as that was obvious—

ALAN CANNING

I think you'll find that only *became* obvious in the first place because Bill was already three steps ahead of the rest of us.

LAILA FURNESS

(to Nick, who's still standing by the window)

Did you know?

JJ NORTON

(to Bill)

You've been on Fulton's trail right from the start, haven't you? I'm right, aren't I?

You knew about Rose Shulman. You knew 'Eric Fulton' had stolen at least one identity already, and you knew the real Eric Fulton was in all probability dead—

BILL SERAFINI

Whoa - hold on a minute there—

JJ NORTON

(gesturing at the screen)

That thing's dated September 1997. You've been on this case *twenty-five years.*

ALAN CANNING

I spoke to that colleague of yours - the one you trained up. He said you were *obsessed* with Fulton - you just wouldn't let it go, even when your captain told you to drop it. He said you worked evenings, weekends—

BILL SERAFINI

(dismissively)

He's exaggerating—

ALAN CANNING

He also told me you've been working for the Shulmans ever since you retired - you went to Alabama, you even went to bloody *Beirut*—

CAMERA PANS round table; they are literally open-mouthed.

JJ NORTON

(looking at Bill and then at Alan)

Fuck me - seriously?

ALAN CANNING

Seriously.

That's how he knew it was Luke Ryder who really died in that bombing. And that's how he knew 'Eric Fulton' was in the wind.

(turning to Bill)

You going to tell me I'm wrong?

BILL SERAFINI

No. But like I said, it's not that simple—

JJ NORTON

(slowly, as if putting it all together)

So that's really what's been going on here: you've been using *our* investigation to solve *yours*.

You knew we'd work out eventually that Ryder wasn't who he said he was, and if we were too thick to manage that on our own, you were right there, ready to give us a nudge in the right direction—

ALAN CANNING

(pointing at him)

That's absolutely it, JJ. Spot on.

Canning taps his keyboard again; more previous FOOTAGE appears on the screen, this time an edited version of Bill putting a photo of 'Eric Fulton' on the pinboard.

BILL SERAFINI

Yes it is. This is the man who left Sydney in November 1995, and was injured in a bus bombing in Beirut in August 1997.

Only he wasn't injured that day.

He was killed.

The man we've been chasing - the man who met Rupert Howard in Greece, the man who married Caroline Howard and ended up beaten to death in her garden - that wasn't Luke Ryder.

It was an imposter.

CUT TO: Team.

HUGO FRASER

(dryly)

Looks like he wasn't the only one. You're not exactly who you said you were either, Bill.

BILL SERAFINI

Oh come on—

MITCHELL CLARKE

Now we know where all those cliff-hangers of yours came from. Not hard to drop a bombshell if you've a whole arsenal of them primed and ready to go.

LAILA FURNESS

(turns back to Nick, her eyes narrowing)

You didn't answer my question: did *you* know? You didn't pick him for this series precisely because he was already halfway there?

Because it strikes me as a pretty damn big coincidence that you alighted on the one ex-cop from the whole of the NYPD who was already on the case—

NICK VINCENT (Producer)

(holding up his hands)

Laila, -I-

HUGO FRASER

(sarcastically)

And of course it would make such *great* TV, wouldn't it, Nick? You could choreograph the whole damn thing, all those so-called discoveries, the big reveals—

MITCHELL CLARKE

(nodding)

The perfect story arc.

NICK VINCENT (Producer)

Bill - come on, help me out here.

There's a silence; they're all now looking at Bill.

HUGO FRASER

Well? We're waiting.

BILL SERAFINI

(takes a deep breath)

Look, I heard about the series through the grapevine - that some British TV company was looking at making a series about the Luke Ryder case. And yes, of course I was interested, I'm not going to apologize for that.

JJ NORTON

So you're admitting you knew that Eric Fulton and Luke Ryder were one and the same, even back then.

BILL SERAFINI

Yes, I did.

The team react with varying degrees of anger and indignation. Bill holds up his hands.

And yes, for that I apologize. But I'm not apologizing for wanting to be involved. I knew it might be my best chance to get some closure for the Shulmans once and for all.

LAILA FURNESS

But you said you've known about Eric for years. Isn't that enough 'closure'? Why are the Shulmans still paying you after all this time? What can they possibly hope to find?

BILL SERAFINI

Simple. Their money. If we can nail this man's real identity then there's a chance we can find the missing cash too.

There could be bank accounts out there in his real name. Not to mention Rose Shulman's Cartier diamonds—

HUGO FRASER

And no doubt you're on a percentage of value recovered. Nice work if you can get it—

BILL SERAFINI

(ignoring him)

That's why the family are paying me, and that's why I got in touch with Nick when I heard about the show.

HUGO FRASER

And did you tell him what you just told us?

BILL SERAFINI

Some of it. I told him that I'd established - to my own satisfaction at least - that 'Eric Fulton' had stolen the identity of Luke Ryder in Beirut.

When I first got the case, on the job back in '97, Fulton was long gone and no one knew where. And for a long time, that's how it stayed.

But after I retired the Shulmans asked me to take another look at the case, and that's when I made the link to Lebanon. And when I saw that old CNN footage of the blast there was one face that suddenly looked very familiar...

The reel of Beirut news FOOTAGE is played again: the carnage on the street, the injured in hospital. FREEZE FRAME on a man in a bed with a bandage across one eye. It's 'Eric Fulton'.

MITCHELL CLARKE

Shit – he's been right under our noses the whole bloody time.

BILL SERAFINI

Right. So the next thing I did was go to Beirut myself to try to find out which name he'd given when they took him to the hospital.

JJ NORTON

Don't tell me: Luke Ryder.

BILL SERAFINI

Right. So I started looking for a man with that name. And I found him. First in Assos, and after that – finally – in London. The rest you know.

ALAN CANNING

That's not the whole story, though, is it? Not by a long way.

You didn't just fail to tell *us* any of this, you didn't tell the Met team either.

You kept everything you knew about 'Luke' to yourself, even though the fact that he was an imposter would have been significant new evidence in the murder investigation—

BILL SERAFINI

(interrupting)

I was on the verge of doing that when I heard about the series. And I figured a few weeks' delay wouldn't make that much difference - not after twenty years.

JJ NORTON

You wanted a chance to work it out yourself before you handed it over to them. *You* wanted to be the hero who solved the case—

BILL SERAFINI

(shaking his head)

It wasn't like that, honestly—

HUGO FRASER

You are - or *were* - a law enforcement officer, for God's sake. You had a *duty* to inform the Met.

BILL SERAFINI

(shrugs)

Fair enough. My bad. But they sure as hell know now, don't they?

LAILA FURNESS

Is there anything else you haven't told us? Any other unexploded bombs?

BILL SERAFINI

Absolutely not.

LAILA FURNESS

Are you sure?

BILL SERAFINI

Scout's honour.

He smiles; no one else does.

ALAN CANNING

(quietly)

Where were you on the night of October third, 2003?

BILL SERAFINI

(stares at him)

Seriously?

ALAN CANNING

Seriously.

Bill is clearly about to say something he might regret but restrains himself just in time.

HUGO FRASER

To be fair, it's not an unreasonable question.

ALAN CANNING

It's the *obvious* question.

(turning to Bill)

You, of all people, could have tracked Ryder down. You demand the money, the jewellery - he refuses, it gets ugly—

BILL SERAFINI

(shaking his head)

Didn't happen. Back in '03 I didn't even know that 'Eric Fulton' and 'Luke Ryder' were the same person. That came much later - after I left the job.

ALAN CANNING

So you say—

BILL SERAFINI

And if that's not enough for you, I was in the US the whole of that October.

ALAN CANNING

How convenient. I'm assuming you can prove that?

BILL SERAFINI

(staring him out)

If I have to.

ALAN CANNING

That's very interesting. Because something's been bugging me ever since I saw you listed on Nick's kick-off email.

'Serafini'. It's a pretty distinctive name, isn't it? I knew I'd heard it somewhere before. And then I remembered. It was on a delegate list for a joint Met/NYPD conference I went to, years back.

(holds up a sheet of A4)

'Urban Policing in the 21st Century', The Eden Park Hotel, Windsor, 1st-4th October—

(he pauses)

2003.

BILL SERAFINI

I never made it.

ALAN CANNING

Oh, really?

BILL SERAFINI

(visibly struggling to keep his temper)

Really. There was a last-minute crisis at work. I had to pull out. Feel free to check if you want.

ALAN CANNING

I think I'll do that.

They're staring at each other, openly hostile. There's an awkward silence, then Laila clears her throat and looks round the table.

LAILA FURNESS

So in the meantime, where does that leave the rest of us, apart from majorly pissed off at Bill?

JJ NORTON

(looking up)

Actually, I might have something to add.

He gets up, goes over to the pinboard and points to one of the photos.

Remember this? The picture 'Luke' had in his wallet that we all thought was taken in Australia?

Camera zooms in on the PHOTO of a woman and a small blond boy standing stiffly outside a one-storey house with a concrete water tower in the background.

I've been wondering about this for a while. Obviously in theory this picture could be exactly what we assumed it was to start with: i.e., an image of the real Luke Ryder, which he had in his backpack when that bus bomb went off.

HUGO FRASER

Which 'Eric' found and kept because he knew it might help corroborate his identity? With Florence Ryder, for example.

JJ NORTON

Precisely. And I can see why he'd keep it, on that basis - it could be damn useful. But keeping it is one thing; keeping it in his *wallet* is quite another.

Remember, it was the only photo he had in there. To my mind, that argues something much more personal.

LAILA FURNESS

I agree. That's about 'identity' in a much more intimate sense.

MITCHELL CLARKE

Sorry - I'm not with you - are you saying this is actually a picture of Eric Fulton, so not taken in Kalgoorlie, like we thought, but in Alabama?

HUGO FRASER

(shaking his head)

No, JJ's logic would still apply. We know this man wasn't really Eric Fulton, any more than he was really Luke Ryder. An image of the real Eric would have no personal significance for him, so he'd have no reason to carry it around.

JJ NORTON

(nodding)

Exactly. I don't think this photo is of *any* of this man's aliases. I think it's actually *him*. The one thing from his real past that he allowed himself to keep. For whatever reason. In which case—

HUGO FRASER

—if we can work out *where* this was taken, we might just be able to work out *who* he was.

JJ NORTON

(pointing towards him)

In one.

BILL SERAFINI

(under his breath, frowning)

Why the hell didn't I think of that?

ALAN CANNING

I agree with the logic, though actually *doing* that will be much easier said than done.

(gesturing at the picture)

I mean look at it - it could be anywhere.

HUGO FRASER

(to JJ)

You're thinking that the water tower could be identifiable?

JJ NORTON

(smiling)

Not could be.

Is.

He goes back to his seat and taps his keyboard; a close-up of the water tower appears on the screen. The image has been digitally enhanced, and as a result it's now possible to see a fragment of lettering on the left-hand side: the end of a word.

MITCHELL CLARKE

(sitting forward)

What is that? GH?

JJ NORTON

UGH.

LAILA FURNESS

So the name of the town ends in UGH? Like something-borough?

JJ NORTON

That was our working assumption, yes.

ALAN CANNING

Good luck narrowing that down. Must be hundreds of places with names like that.

JJ NORTON

(evenly)

If you're thinking of the UK, then yes, obviously. But there are very few water towers over here, so a UK location is pretty unlikely. Towers like that are far more common in the US – you only need to watch a few old movies to know that. On the other hand, the vast majority of American towns with that sort of name actually end 'B-O-R-O' not 'B-O-R-O-*U-G-H*'.

BILL SERAFINI

I can attest to that.

No one acknowledges him.

JJ NORTON

Though there is one other country where that suffix is fairly common, for obvious historical reasons.

Canada.

LAILA FURNESS

Canada?

JJ NORTON

Absolutely. And if you cross-reference towns with a name ending in -UGH with those with water towers, and then do an image search of those towers, this is what you find.

He taps his keyboard and a MONTAGE of Google images appears. It only takes the team a few seconds to recognize a photo on the second row.

LAILA FURNESS

(pointing)

Where is that?

JJ NORTON

That, Laila, is Flamborough, New Brunswick.

LAILA FURNESS

I confess my Canadian geography is a wee bit sketchy—

JJ NORTON

(smiling)

Don't worry, so was mine.

He taps his keyboard and a MAP of Canada appears with Flamborough marked.

This is followed by a MONTAGE of images of Flamborough in the '70s and '80s. It's clearly the same place as in the original photo.

MITCHELL CLARKE

That looks to me like a classic one-horse town

HUGO FRASER

(*under his breath*)

One-moose town, more like.

JJ NORTON

(*smiling*)

Not far off, certainly. Even now the population is barely more than a thousand.

LAILA FURNESS

So we should be able to track down our man pretty easily?

JJ NORTON

Well, in theory, yes, but don't get too excited: we don't know his age, so we can't narrow it down that way, and there isn't much online from the local high school.

LAILA FURNESS

But you must be able to work out which house it was – Google Maps, maybe?

JJ NORTON

We did try that but it didn't get us anywhere – there's no StreetView in that location. But clearly there's nothing to stop us going over and having a look for ourselves.

Which is why Tarek and I are booked on a flight out to New Brunswick this time tomorrow.

LAILA FURNESS

At last, some progress.

MITCHELL CLARKE

Certainly looks that way. Well done, JJ. Chapeau.

JJ NORTON

(grinning)

Put it down to my not-too-deeply-buried inner geek. And a bout of vindaloo-induced insomnia last weekend that left me googling 'water towers' most of Saturday night.

BILL SERAFINI

I've lost count of the number of times cases of mine turned on something just like that – some tiny detail that seemed insignificant but ended up breaking the whole thing wide open.

But yes, I agree with Mitch: darn good work, JJ.

The others exchange glances; no one responds to Bill.

FADE OUT

CUT TO: Dorney Place. Time has clearly passed. The team are back in the drawing-room, which has been set up with the whiteboard, photos, and a screen. The room is dark – it's raining heavily outside.

BILL SERAFINI

(with slightly false cheeriness)

Great to see the British summer living up to expectations.

MITCHELL CLARKE

You get used to it. Eventually.

HUGO FRASER

(impatiently)

So, what news, JJ? Did you, like the Mounties, 'get your man'?

JJ NORTON

(grinning)

Saw what you did there, Hugo. And yes, I'm pleased to say that Tarek and I have not returned from the frozen north empty-handed.

CUT TO: FOOTAGE. JJ and Tarek are standing in the main street of Flamborough, New Brunswick. There's a soft furnishings store on one side of the street, a Subway and a real estate agency visible on the other. Cars are parked and people are on the sidewalks and sitting outside a café in the sunshine; everywhere looks a lot more prosperous than it did in the historical photos shown previously. In the foreground, Tarek is looking at his phone, and JJ has a map folded open on the bonnet of a car.

JJ NORTON

The water tower is north-east of here, so I reckon the house must be—

(looking up and pointing)

—in that direction.

TAREK OSMAN

(staring at his phone)

Yup, that looks about right.

CUT TO: JJ and Tarek outside what is clearly the house shown in the original photograph: the camera angle has been exactly replicated to allow the present-day image to morph slowly into the photo and then back again to the present.

The building has been extended and the front yard concreted over to give more space for cars. A large SUV has been reversed onto the drive. The water tower is barely visible through much heavier tree growth. JJ turns to camera.

JJ NORTON

As you can see, we're pretty sure we have the right house and thanks to Tarek, we've established who lives here now. But obviously we have no way of knowing whether they're related to the man we're looking for.

On that basis we need to be careful how we play this one, so I'm going to go over there on my own first, without the cameras, to get the lie of the land.

The CAMERA TRACKS him as he goes up to the house, rings the bell and waits for an answer. The door is opened by a woman holding a baby on her hip. Both her face and the baby's have been blurred out. JJ introduces himself, and shows her a copy of the photo. She points at it, nods, and they talk for a few moments. He then thanks her and comes back briskly towards Tarek and the film crew.

JJ NORTON

(brandishing the picture)

We're in luck. She knows who the woman in the photo is. None of the family live round here any more, but there's a retired minister who knew them well and he's still in town.

CUT TO: INTERVIEW, indoors in a clean but slightly shabby and old-fashioned house. A thin elderly man in a plaid shirt and slacks is sitting in a wooden armchair. He has reading glasses on a leather cord round his neck. There's a pastel picture of a smiling Jesus surrounded by angels and little children on the wall behind. The man must be well into his eighties but he still has considerable presence, he must have been a charismatic figure in his youth. Sub-captioned 'Paul Cormier, Minister, St Laurence Church, Flamborough (Retd)'.

JJ NORTON

So, Reverend Cormier, we've been told you knew the family who lived in the house on Greenall Road in the 1960s. I believe they were in your congregation, is that right?

REVEREND CORMIER

Certainly is. The McKenna family. Lawrence and his wife Marie. Very nice people. Very observant. In the religious sense, I mean.

JJ NORTON

And they had children?

REVEREND CORMIER

Two. Rebecca and Jonah. Rebecca was their first and it was a good number of years after that before Jonah came along. I reckon the McKennas had all but given up. Marie called him their miracle baby.

JJ NORTON

He was a bit spoilt then, maybe?

REVEREND CORMIER

I'm afraid there was very little money around for spoiling either of the children. Larry didn't bring in much of a wage and it must have been tough for the kids, not having all the material things their friends and schoolmates did.

JJ NORTON

Well, I know what that's like. But what about 'spoiling' them in other ways – were they an affectionate family?

REVEREND CORMIER

I wouldn't exactly say that. Larry was a pretty strict father, if you want an honest opinion. But I guess Marie did cosset Jonah a little. Tended to overreact if he had a sniffle or a grazed knee. I suppose she'd waited so long to have him she was terrified he'd be taken away.

JJ NORTON

(sitting forward)

I think you said you have some pictures you could show us?

Cormier reaches to a side table and hauls an old-fashioned photo album onto his lap. He reaches for his glasses and opens the pages. They're so dry the paper crackles.

REVEREND CORMIER

My wife used to run Junior Church on Sunday mornings. Both Rebecca and Jonah would come. Though by the time Jonah was old enough Rebecca had graduated to organizing a lot of the activities. She always did love kids.

He gestures to JJ, who pulls his chair a bit closer. Camera angle over Cormier's shoulder zooms into CLOSE-UP, tracking across a series of images: kids of six or seven sitting demurely listening to a woman with grey hair reading from a book of Bible stories; a sports day; a Nativity play with a dark-haired girl as Mary and a little blond boy in a bushy ginger beard as Joseph.

The camera comes to rest on a group photo with all the children lined up in rows, the older woman is standing on one side of the group and a tall red-haired young woman in glasses is on the other. Someone has written all the names neatly along the bottom of the page. The red-haired young woman is 'Rebecca', Mary from the Nativity is 'Julie-Ann', and Joseph is 'Jonah'. He's wearing a T-shirt with a whale on the front and is standing next to Rebecca; she has one hand on his shoulder.

REVEREND CORMIER

(gesturing)

That's Rebecca's handwriting.

JJ NORTON

I assume the whale thing on the T-shirt was deliberate?

REVEREND CORMIER

(smiling)

It was his favourite Bible story. For obvious reasons.

JJ NORTON

Looks like Rebecca was quite protective of him.

REVEREND CORMIER

Oh yes, most definitely. There was this one time – Jonah was around nine – when one of his classmates stole something from another boy and claimed it was Jonah who'd done it.

It was Rebecca, not Larry or Marie, who went round to the guilty boy's parents and insisted he confess his lie. It was in her nature: she couldn't rest until the situation had been set to rights and the boy responsible was punished.

JJ NORTON

Where is she now?

REVEREND CORMIER

Moved away. Went into nursing. Last I heard she was working for one of those charities who help people in need overseas. MSF, I think.

(sighs and shakes his head)

She took Jonah's death very hard. They all did. Marie was never the same after that.

JJ NORTON

(clearly taken aback)

Jonah *died*?

REVEREND CORMIER

When he was 17. He'd gotten a summer job over in Nova Scotia, just up from Halifax. One of his teachers put in a good word for him - she knew someone at one of those high-end marinas. You know the sort of thing - all shiny gin-palaces and New Yorkers up for the summer.

Jonah knew nothing about boats, of course - there's no water to speak of round here. But he was charming and happy to pitch in and he got hired on the spot.

JJ NORTON

So what happened?

REVEREND CORMIER

(sighing)

Maybe he was a bit *too* charming, if you catch my meaning. There was talk afterwards that he'd gotten tangled up with the wife of one of the yacht people. That she'd lent him money, or he'd wheedled it out of her, and the husband found out—

JJ NORTON

Something tells me this isn't going to end well—

REVEREND CORMIER

(shaking his head)

No indeed. There was a bad altercation between this man and Jonah and the man ended up in hospital.

When the police went looking for Jonah a few hours later he was nowhere to be found. They thought initially that he'd just skipped town and would be back as soon as things died down. But then they discovered that he'd left his possessions behind. Wallet, passport, everything.

About a week later some clothes washed up along the coast, and the police identified them as Jonah's. But that's all they ever found. Made it doubly hard for the family, with no body to lay to rest. Marie arranged for a memorial in the churchyard. It's still there. Just Jonah's name and the dates and a carving of a whale. She got a local stonemason to make it for her.

(shaking his head)

Very sad.

(silence)

JJ NORTON

Without wishing to sound insensitive, was there any possibility that Jonah could have staged the drowning? Did the police look into that, do you know? I mean, if he was in trouble—

REVEREND CORMIER

I think the police did look into it but never came up with anything. There was never any trace of him anywhere else. Though Rebecca clung to that for years - she always insisted she'd find him one day.

(shrugs)

I'm not a fool, Mr Norton - I know there *are* people who've walked away from their lives and started over, but it takes a powerful lot of planning to get away with it. Jonah was only 17 at the time, and frankly, even if he'd been older he never struck me as resourceful enough to pull something like that off.

And I find it very hard to believe he would have walked out on his family and never looked back. He'd have known the pain it would cause, especially to his mother and sister.

JJ NORTON

You said before that both his parents are dead. Is Rebecca still in touch with anyone round here, do you know?

REVEREND CORMIER

(shaking his head)

Not that I'm aware. There aren't many of her generation left around here. Most of the young people move away the first chance they have.

JJ NORTON

(reaching to shake his hand)

Thank you, Reverend, you've been very helpful.

CUT TO: Studio. Team are sitting round the table.

BILL SERAFINI

Hats off to you, JJ. In less than a week you achieved something I haven't managed in over twenty years.

HUGO FRASER

And we're certain this Jonah McKenna is the man we're looking for, are we?

JJ NORTON

Well, we'd need DNA from a family member to be sure, so as it stands everything hinges on finding Rebecca. We could then do a comparison with what the Met have on file for 'Luke'.

MITCHELL CLARKE

Did you try MSF?

JJ NORTON

We did, but we haven't turned up anything so far. Tarek's also getting in touch with the Red Cross and Médecins du Monde, and some of the religious organizations like Christian Aid. But thus far, no luck.

(looking round the table)

But we do still have the photo of the house 'Luke' had in his wallet, and as far as I can see, the only way he could have even *got hold* of that, never mind kept it, was because he was, in fact, Jonah McKenna—

ALAN CANNING

(dismissively)

That would never stand up in court—

JJ NORTON

(ignoring him)

—and we also have *this.*

He nods to Tarek who taps his keyboard. Two IMAGES appear side by side on the main screen. On the left, a close-up of Jonah from the Junior Church photo of him with the other children. On the right, one of the wedding pictures taken of 'Luke' at Dorney Place. The faces have been lined up to be exactly level. Tarek taps the keyboard again and the left-hand image of the boy begins to change.

JJ NORTON

As you can see, Tarek managed to get hold of some rather cool age-progression software.

Jonah's face gradually evolves from child, to youth, to young man. The final image is annotated as 'Age 25'. The resemblance to 'Luke' is startling.

And in case anyone's wondering, we didn't rig this process in any way. We simply put Jonah's photo through the programme, and this is what came out.

MITCHELL CLARKE

That's incredible.

LAILA FURNESS

I agree – it looks like you really did 'get your man', JJ.

HUGO FRASER

So what happens next?

JJ NORTON

Well, I've reached out to the Canadian police and they're going to liaise with NYPD to see if we can link the Jonah McKenna who went missing in Nova Scotia in 1991 to the 'Eric Fulton' who stole Rose Shulman's money in 1995.

BILL SERAFINI

(frowning)

You looped in NYPD and you didn't tell me?

JJ NORTON

Nick said not to. Sorry.

MITCHELL CLARKE

(under his breath, to Laila)

Sounds like a bit of a SorryNotSorry to me...

Laila tries and fails to suppress a smile.

HUGO FRASER

(waspishly)

Pot or kettle, Bill?

Bill opens his mouth to say something, then clearly thinks better of it.

HUGO FRASER

(looking round the table)

So unless someone else has something, I think that's it?

BILL SERAFINI

(turning to him)

Oh, I don't think we're quite done yet.

The others exchange slightly weary – and in some cases wary – glances: judging from his face, Bill evidently has something juicy up his sleeve.

HUGO FRASER

OK, Bill, I'll bite. What have you got?

Bill smiles and nods to Nick behind the camera. The screen changes to a STILL of Bill, once again in his trademark shades and short-sleeved shirt, sitting at a table in the sun with a beer in front of him.

MITCHELL CLARKE

(shaking his head)

How come I never get any of the good gigs?

LAILA FURNESS

(waspishly, under her breath)

I *thought* he was looking suspiciously tanned—

HUGO FRASER

Hold on – I recognize that bar. Isn't that the place Tarek went to—

BILL SERAFINI

(smiling)

In Assos. Right.

LAILA FURNESS

You went to *Assos*? But I thought—

BILL SERAFINI

—that we'd run into a dead end on that one? That even if 'Luke' did con another older woman over there we'd never be able to track her down?

Yeah, that's what we all thought, Laila. But I took a page out of Alan's book and decided to go back myself and take a closer look.

Alan flashes him a glance but says nothing. The still on the screen changes to FOOTAGE showing Bill talking to a series of elderly Greek ladies. Most shake their heads and look blank, but one nods and starts talking animatedly in Greek.

LAILA FURNESS

Don't tell me - someone remembered that woman after all?

BILL SERAFINI

Ah, it's not that straightforward.

HUGO FRASER

You've lost me.

LAILA FURNESS

Ditto.

BILL SERAFINI

Sorry, guys. Rewind. So like I said, I started wondering whether we might have missed a trick on the whole Assos thing. That maybe we needed to approach it from a different angle.

LAILA FURNESS

In the sense that—?

BILL SERAFINI

In the sense that if our theory was right and 'Luke' really *did* swindle another woman over there - and swindled her so bad it might have given someone a motive to track him down and kill him - then where would that 'someone' have started to look for him?

LAILA FURNESS

Ah, I think I see what you're getting at. You'd start in Assos, of course. Then Sydney, maybe, given 'Luke' was supposed to be Australian.

Certainly not London.

MITCHELL CLARKE

(nodding)

Makes sense. And I agree - Assos would have to be the first place you'd go.

HUGO FRASER

(frowning)

But without knowing this woman's name I don't see how that helps—

BILL SERAFINI

Bear with. So the first thing I did was contact George Nicolaides to check if anyone came looking for 'Luke' after he left the island.

LAILA FURNESS

I'm surprised Tarek hadn't asked him that already.

BILL SERAFINI

He had - but neither George or his father remembered anything. But when I caught up with George this time I tried a different tack: I asked if he could think of anyone else who was working at the bar around that time. And he put me onto this guy—

A STILL appears on the screen; a man in his forties, heavy stubble, salt-and-pepper hair; a very Mediterranean face.

This is Vasilis Mourelatos. He lives in Athens now but worked at George's bar for several months the year after 'Luke' left. He told me he was pretty sure a man came looking for him that summer. Which was what the old lady also told me.

CUT TO: INTERVIEW. Bill and Vasilis Mourelatos talking on Zoom. Bill's at an outdoor restaurant table, clearly still on Assos.

BILL SERAFINI

So what do you remember about this guy, Vasilis?

VASILIS MOURELATOS

I'm afraid I wasn't there the day he came, he spoke to one of the other barmen. But I remember them mentioning about it to me. It was a British guy. He was looking for Luke Ryder and wanted to know if any of us had information about him. He told my colleague it was important – that we should call him if we knew where Luke was.

BILL SERAFINI

But he didn't say why he wanted to know?

VASILIS MOURELATOS

(shrugging)

I never knew. Sorry.

BILL SERAFINI

But if he wanted you to call him he must have left a number, right?

VASILIS MOURELATOS

Yes, there was a piece of paper. Someone pinned it up on the board. I don't know what happened to it.

CUT TO: Studio. Bill looks round at the team.

BILL SERAFINI

But I think we do, don't we? It ended up in that crate of stuff George boxed up for his paps, just like all the rest of the junk.

LAILA FURNESS

(clearly impressed)

You actually *found* it?

BILL SERAFINI

Well, I can't be one hundred per cent sure because there was a hell of a lot of bits of paper with nothing but a name and a number, and no way of telling how long most of them had been there.

But I reckon these four are the most likely – mainly because they're all UK numbers, and the one thing old Mr Nicolaides remembered about that woman in the photo with Luke was that she was a Brit.

Taps his laptop and the screen shows an image of four crumpled bits of paper.

LUKE
44 –07001 900539

Mick
0121 496 0372

STEVE
0117 496 0917

tony
0118 496 0140

HUGO FRASER

I'm assuming you tried all these numbers?

BILL SERAFINI

Sure did.

LAILA FURNESS

'Luke' looks like the most promising – assuming that's a reference to the person this man was looking for, rather than his own name.

BILL SERAFINI

That was my assumption, too. The bad news is that the Luke number is out of service. As is the Tony one. Steve is just ringing out, and as for Mick, he turned out to be a guy who was trying to start a boat-rental business in Assos that summer. Seemed legit.

MITCHELL CLARKE

So are you going to try to run down who owned the other three numbers back in 1998?

BILL SERAFINI

Safe to say I'm on it.

ALAN CANNING

(shaking his head)

The phone companies will *never* give out that sort of information. And the Luke number is clearly a mobile. What if it was a burner phone? There wouldn't even be a record.

BILL SERAFINI

In my experience, regular people don't use burner phones, Alan. Only people who don't want to leave a trail.

LAILA FURNESS

But if someone did want to track Luke Ryder down to exact revenge, wouldn't they do everything they could to remain anonymous? That sounds like a very good reason to use a burner phone.

BILL SERAFINI

Agreed.

MITCHELL CLARKE

OK, but on that basis what can you do? It's just another dead end.

BILL SERAFINI

Not *quite* dead, Mitch. Because my professional instincts tell me that someone who's prepared to go all the way to Assos to find Luke would almost certainly try other methods too.

LAILA FURNESS

As in—?

BILL SERAFINI

As in personal ads, for example.

MITCHELL CLARKE

(dryly)

That long ago? Good luck with that—

BILL SERAFINI

Actually it's not as impossible as it seems. We have those phone numbers, remember, which means we can do a digital search for a match. And that's exactly what Tarek and the team have been doing.

(taps his laptop again)

And this is what they found.

IEDS

a Van'
ul driver
ansit van.
Call Jim

Blue. 12
000 miles.
ce history.
enings on

fered
(grade 8).
ginners.
provided

APPEAL

Do you know a man called LUKE RYDER? Thought to be from the Sydney area and may now be residing in London. Blonde, medium build, approx. 6'. Last known sighting, Delphi Bar Assos, Greece, late summer of 1998. Information in confidence to P.O. Box 7675

Reward Offered

FOR RENT

Double room in attractive house with en-suite shower room. Fully furnished. Recently redecorated. No pets. Non-smokers only. Rent per

LAILA FURNESS

OK, so this proves *someone* was definitely trying to track Luke down, and well done, that's a pretty big step forward.

But all the same, there's nothing here—

(gesturing at the screen)

—that will help us identify *who* was looking for him, is there? Apart from a PO box number that's over twenty years old?

BILL SERAFINI

Not so fast, Laila. If you've been in this trade as long as I have, you get to recognize a certain way of doing things. Or, in this case, a certain way of *saying* things. The use of certain terms, for example, or particular forms of words.

There's a brief silence as they all read the ad again.

HUGO FRASER

(taking a deep breath)

OK, so I suspect that you're going to say that this is exactly the sort of language police officers tend to use. Anyone who works with law enforcement on a regular basis would recognize that.

So is that what you're getting at? You think this ad was posted by someone with a background in policing?

BILL SERAFINI

Not acting in their official capacity, of course. But someone with that training, yes, I think *that's* a distinct possibility.

ALAN CANNING

(shaking his head despairingly)

Once again, you're building a massive number of - frankly - tenuous assumptions on absolutely no actual *evidence*—

BILL SERAFINI

Hear me out, please. As I said before, it's little things like this, that are easy to overlook that often break a case.

LAILA FURNESS

OK, but—

BILL SERAFINI

(*cutting across her*)

Remember how Alan went poking about in my Alabama interviews? I thought, hell, maybe I should take a leaf out of his book.

He nods to the cameraman; the screen changes to edited FOOTAGE from Ep 5.

TAREK OSMAN

We also spoke to some of the older residents while we were in Assos, and one old lady thought the woman might have been called Irene. But someone else came up with Carrie, so your guess is as good as mine.

LAILA FURNESS

And what about Rupert – did he remember this woman?

TAREK OSMAN

You'd have thought he might, wouldn't you, or that the photo might have triggered something, but sadly not.

LAILA FURNESS

Though like you said, it's a very long time ago. If she was in her forties then she'd be over 60 now—

ALAN CANNING

And near nigh impossible to track down. It'd be yet another complete waste of bloody time. And that's assuming there *was* some sort of relationship between them which I'm *very* far from convinced was actually the case. Not on the basis of one bloody photo.

BILL SERAFINI

I'm not so sure – I mean, I don't know about you, Alan, but I don't behave like that with random women I meet in bars—

ALAN CANNING

Maybe you don't, but some men do – especially selfish bastards like this 'Luke' bloke clearly was.

LAILA FURNESS

Wow, that escalated quickly—

FREEZE FRAME on Alan. His face is thunderous.

CUT TO: Studio.

BILL SERAFINI

(turning to the team)

I'm with Laila – that *did* escalate quickly. Too darn quickly, in fact. Which made me wonder, what could possibly have got Alan so exercised? I mean, he has no dog in this fight, right?

He turns to Alan, but he says nothing.

Cat got your tongue, buddy? Oh well, I think I can do the next part on my own.

He taps his keyboard again. MONTAGE of photos appears on the screen. A school photo of small boys sat in rows; a family snap of two parents, a girl, a boy and a younger boy; a much later picture of a family gathering, clearly screen-grabbed from Facebook.

ALAN CANNING

Where the hell did you get all that?

BILL SERAFINI

(smiling and shrugging)

All on the web, my friend, if you know where – and how – to look. As my friend Tarek most certainly does.

He turns to the team again; some of them are looking distinctly uneasy.

So, to resume, our friend Alan here was born in Croydon in 1967. He had an older brother, Graham, born in 1962, and a sister, Eileen, born in 1958. I'll save you the trouble of doing the math: Eileen's 65 now. And she would have been 40 in 1998.

LAILA FURNESS

Don't tell me you think Eileen was the woman Luke met in Assos?

BILL SERAFINI

Irene would be an easy mistake for Eileen, wouldn't it? And someone else thought she was called Carrie.

He gives them a meaningful look.

MITCHELL CLARKE

OK - so you think Carr*ie* could be an equally easy mistake for Cann*ing*.

BILL SERAFINI

Right—

ALAN CANNING

(pointing at Bill)

How dare you - how fucking *dare* you go poking about in my family's business—

BILL SERAFINI

You're saying I'm wrong? That this woman *wasn't* your sister?—

LAILA FURNESS

(intervening)

Hold on a minute, before we all get carried away. Bill, when you and Tarek were poking about in the wilder reaches of the internet did you happen to find a picture of Eileen in the late '90s? Maybe that would help establish if she's the woman in the photo with 'Luke' in 1998.

BILL SERAFINI

Great minds, Laila. And yes, we did.

The screen changes to a PHOTO. It's an office environment: desks and computers, people wearing lanyards; several are holding files. There's a red circle around Eileen Canning. The image is lined up next to the two photos previously shown of Luke and the mystery woman on Assos.

JJ NORTON

Well, the hair is similar, but hundreds of women that age wear their hair like that.

LAILA FURNESS

(frowning)

There's a degree of resemblance, but that's as far as I'd be prepared to go.

HUGO FRASER

I agree. You can't see nearly enough of the Assos woman's face to make any sort of definitive identification.

MITCHELL CLARKE

But like Laila says, there *is* a resemblance. And I can see how the name thing might back that up.

He catches Alan looking daggers at him and holds up his hands.

Hey, man, just saying.

LAILA FURNESS

Is this all you have, Bill? Because I don't see how you can make a connection back to Alan based solely on this. Is there anything else?

BILL SERAFINI

There sure is. In November 1997, Eileen Canning divorced her husband - the owner of a successful construction company, by the way - and resumed using her maiden name. Six months later a woman of about the same age was pictured with 'Luke' on Assos.

I can't *prove* that was Eileen, or that she ever even vacationed there, but the logic would make sense. She's just gotten divorced, she's hit forty - why wouldn't she want to enjoy her freedom - find a last chance at love?

HUGO FRASER

(dryly)

Based on his previous track record, I doubt *lurve* was what 'Luke' had in mind.

BILL SERAFINI

(nodding)

Right. And Eileen Canning was declared bankrupt in 1999. She must have gotten a decent settlement from the husband, but she managed to run through the whole lot in two years. That's some going, under any normal circumstances.

LAILA FURNESS

But on the other hand, if she was being scammed by someone like 'Luke'–

BILL SERAFINI

(nodding)

And I think we'd all agree that anyone who loved her might well want to find the person responsible for that scam and make him pay - in every sense of the word.

A brother, for instance. Especially a brother with access to all the resources of the Metropolitan Police.

LAILA FURNESS

(to Alan)

Is this true? Was it you who went looking for Luke in Assos in 1999?

HUGO FRASER

(dryly)

More to the point, did you track him down to Dorney Place four years later?

Alan gets up, goes over to the window, and stares out.

BILL SERAFINI

We're waiting.

ALAN CANNING

(turns to face them)

You're asking if I had a reason to hunt that man down? If I had a reason to loathe the very sight of him?

The answer is Yes.

I did.

FADE OUT

- end credits -

Date: Mon 17/07/2023, 11.09 **Importance:** High

From: Tarek Osman

To: Nick Vincent

Subject: [empty]

Just to confirm I've sent the stills to the lab. They think it's a long shot but I'll let you know as soon as I hear.

T

Episode six

Broadcast

October 18

TELEVISION

Moving fast and breaking things

As Infamous takes a savage turn, which little Piggy fits the bill?

ROSS LESLIE

Infamous: Who Killed Luke Ryder?
Showrunner

Who Do You Think You Are?
BBC1

OK, hands up who saw that one coming, because I certainly didn't. Just when you think you've got the measure of **Infamous**, they flip you another whiplash twist. I was tempted to describe last night's episode as up-ending the jigsaw (much like what Guy Howard did to his mother's ill-fated wedding cake) but it was actually rather more fundamental than that: by the final credits I wasn't even sure I had the right picture on the box: we may be getting closer to establishing who 'Luke Ryder' really was, but the basic premise of this entire series is now in play. The show's producer, Nick Vincent, has never been averse to puppet-mastering some fireworks, but hitherto he has, at least, played within the rules - rules, incidentally, of his own making. But as this episode unravelled it became painfully obvious that none of the people sitting round the table had the first idea what they had really signed up for, or the true reason he'd chosen them to take part. We were left open-mouthed with horrified schadenfreude as the expert team started to turn on each other. And how. Think Lord of the Flies on steroids. I'm studiously avoiding pronouns here so as not to give too much away, but if you're fond of a slow-motion train wreck in Ultra HD then this one's for you. In Golding's novel, Ralph (in)famously asks Piggy and the other boys, "Which is better, law and rescue, or hunting and breaking things up?" Judging by this episode, Nick Vincent has definitely opted for the latter.

From Who Do You Think It Was? to a new series of **Who Do You Think You Are?** This opened with the actor Greta Scacchi, who turned out to have the most fascinating

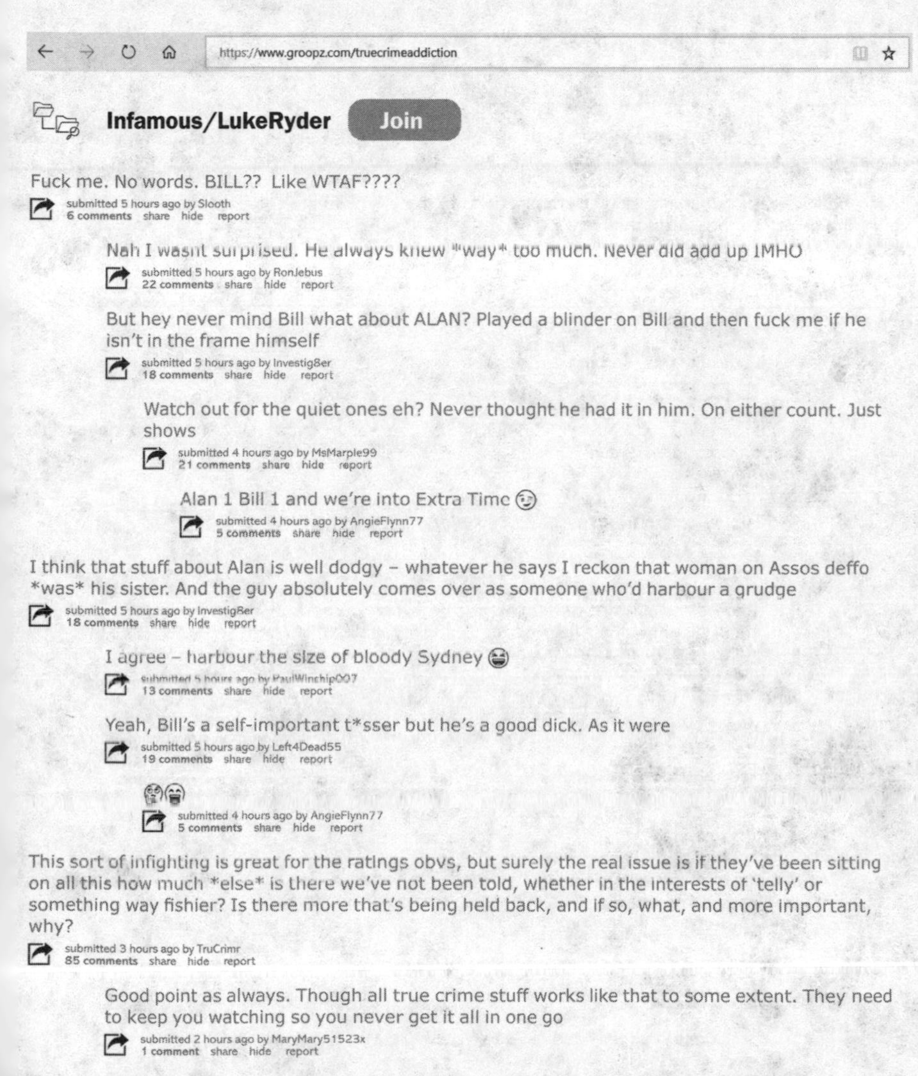

https://www.groopz.com/truecrimeaddiction

Infamous/LukeRyder Join

Fuck me. No words. BILL?? Like WTAF????

submitted 5 hours ago by Slooth
6 comments share hide report

> Nah I wasnt surprised. He always knew *way* too much. Never did add up IMHO
>
> submitted 5 hours ago by RonJebus
> 22 comments share hide report
>
> But hey never mind Bill what about ALAN? Played a blinder on Bill and then fuck me if he isn't in the frame himself
>
> submitted 5 hours ago by Investig8er
> 18 comments share hide report
>
> > Watch out for the quiet ones eh? Never thought he had it in him. On either count. Just shows
> >
> > submitted 4 hours ago by MsMarple99
> > 21 comments share hide report
> >
> > > Alan 1 Bill 1 and we're into Extra Time 😉
> > >
> > > submitted 4 hours ago by AngieFlynn77
> > > 5 comments share hide report

I think that stuff about Alan is well dodgy – whatever he says I reckon that woman on Assos deffo *was* his sister. And the guy absolutely comes over as someone who'd harbour a grudge

submitted 5 hours ago by Investig8er
18 comments share hide report

> I agree – harbour the size of bloody Sydney 😆
>
> submitted 5 hours ago by PaulWinchip007
> 13 comments share hide report
>
> Yeah, Bill's a self-important t*sser but he's a good dick. As it were
>
> submitted 5 hours ago by Left4Dead55
> 19 comments share hide report
>
> > 😱😱
> >
> > submitted 4 hours ago by AngieFlynn77
> > 5 comments share hide report

This sort of infighting is great for the ratings obvs, but surely the real issue is if they've been sitting on all this how much *else* is there we've not been told, whether in the interests of 'telly' or something way fishier? Is there more that's being held back, and if so, what, and more important, why?

submitted 3 hours ago by TruCrimr
85 comments share hide report

> Good point as always. Though all true crime stuff works like that to some extent. They need to keep you watching so you never get it all in one go
>
> submitted 2 hours ago by MaryMary51523x
> 1 comment share hide report
>
> I agree – all too easy to get sidetracked by all the Bill/Alan hoo-hah but let's pay due deference to that helluva cool piece of deduction work by JJ. Hell, he actually *found* this Jonah guy. After 20 frickin' years 🎩
>
> submitted 2 hours ago by Slooth
> 23 comments share hide report
>
> > That bloke Jonah faked his own death how many times? Is it three now? Three that we know of? Fuck me he's like sodding Lord Lucan
> >
> > submitted 3 hours ago by JimBobWalton1978
> > 17 comments share hide report

It was John Stonehouse who left his clothes on the beach 😂

But I know what you mean

submitted 2 hours ago by MsMarple99
1 comment share hide report

Hey heads up guys THIS IS BIG. My S-I-L is a retired Met DS. She's not been watching the show but I asked her, just on the off-chance, if she was at that conference in 2003. And fuck me, she WAS. Not just that, she actually REMEMBERED BILL. Straight up. Recognised him as soon as I sent over a pic. Apparently he was in a panel sesh on terrorism or something – he made some crap joke about his name and being 'on the side of the angels' 🤮 But the point is BILL *WAS* THERE

submitted 1 hour ago by Brian885643
113 comments share hide report

Holy fuck has she told the police?

submitted 1 hour ago by LemonandCrime
4 comments share hide report

Yeah but only this morning so I don't know any more yet. I'll keep you posted

submitted 50 minutes ago by Brian885643
11 comments share hide report

Does she remember which day and time the session was that she saw? Stating the obvious I know but it could give him an alibi

submitted 34 minutes ago by Edison5.0
17 comments share hide report

Only if it was a very late evening session. And on the right day. Just saying

submitted 30 minutes ago by PaulWinship007
10 comments share hide report

But the point is that Bill insisted he never made it to the conference *at all*. Regardless of which session he was on, we now know he was in the country. So he's been caught out in a lie. And we all know you don't lie about something like that unless you have a very good reason

submitted 25 minutes ago by TruCrimr
133 comments share hide report

Heads-up guys – has anyone else noticed Showrunner have put back the release of the final episode? It was supposed to be next week but it's been postponed till 7th Nov. That's news right?

submitted 34 minutes ago by RonJebus
7 comments share hide report

We have to wait till NOVEMBER???? Does it say why?

submitted 34 minutes ago by MisMarple99
2 comments

No just that it's being put back. Hang on – oh wow – it also says that Ep 7 will be 'released simultaneously with a Special Bonus Episode 8'. WTF?

submitted 34 minutes ago by RonJebus
10 comments share hide report

Holy shit

submitted 34 minutes ago by MisMarple99
2 comments

You know what that means, don't you? They've got something

submitted 32 minutes ago by TruCrimr
133 comments

Episode seven

Filming

DRY RISER FILMS Ltd
227 Sherwood Street London W1Q 2UD

CAST	CALL SHEET	
Alan Canning (AC) Mitchell Clarke (MC) Hugo Fraser (HF) Laila Furness (LF) JJ Norton (JJN) Bill Serafini (WS)	**Infamous: Who Killed Luke Ryder?** Thursday 13th July 2023 **Ep 7: ON-SITE DAY 1 of 2**	Producer **Nick Vincent** Director **Guy Howard** Film editor **Fabio Barry** Researcher **Tarek Osman** Prod asst **Jenni Tate** Location manager **Guy Johnson**
UNIT CALL 0815 *Camera ready: 0830*		*Breakfast on set from 0730* *Running lunch from 1230* *Exp wrap 1750*
Sunrise 0438 *Sunset 2114* *Weather forecast 24°, sunny*		

Location:	Notes:
Dorney Place **2 Larbert Road** **Campden Hill London W8 0TF**	*Some parking on site – must be reserved in advance* *Nearest tube Holland Park* *Emergency contact number 07000 616178*

CREW							
TITLE	NAME	PHONE	CALL	TITLE	NAME	PHONE	CALL

TITLE SEQUENCE: arthouse-style b/w montage of images and short clips: crime scene, contemporary news coverage, family photos

THEME SONG – 'It's Alright, Ma (I'm Only Bleeding)' [Bob Dylan] from the soundtrack to 'Easy Rider' [1969]

TITLE OVER

INFAMOUS

FADE IN

WHO KILLED LUKE RYDER?

FADE OUT

BLACK FRAME, TEXT APPEARS, with VOICEOVER – narrator (female)

For twenty years the death of Luke Ryder has been an unsolved mystery. The truth has eluded not only the Metropolitan Police, but the thousands of amateur sleuths who've pored over the case online.

But now everything we thought we knew about the case has been called into question.

Not only who the victim really was, but why someone might have wanted him dead. And who his killer could have been.

But is the real truth about to be revealed?

FADE OUT

CUT TO: Dorney Place. The team are around the table, alongside Guy and Tarek. Sunlight is streaming in through the French windows, they're all in summer clothes, but the atmosphere is ugly. Dark and ugly.

BILL SERAFINI

So, Alan. Now we're all here, I think you owe us an explanation.

ALAN CANNING

I don't think I owe *you* anything, mate. You've hardly been playing it exactly straight, now have you—

LAILA FURNESS

The rest of us, then. I think we deserve to know, don't you? Why didn't you tell anyone about this before?

ALAN CANNING

I did.

LAILA FURNESS

No, you absolutely did not.

The others start chipping in to agree, but then there's the sound of Nick's voice.

NICK VINCENT (Producer) – off

Actually, he did.

There's a silence as the others watch Nick walk round into shot, and take up his favourite position by the window.

He told me.

GUY HOWARD

(gaping at him)

He *told you*? Why the hell didn't you say something? I'm the bloody *director*—

NICK VINCENT (Producer)

(shrugs, evidently unabashed)

This makes better TV.

BILL SERAFINI

When, exactly? When *exactly* did he tell you?

NICK VINCENT (Producer)

(holding his gaze)

Well, that must have been right about the time *you* emailed me asking to be on the show.

GUY HOWARD

What - they *both* contacted you?

NICK VINCENT (Producer)

Absolutely. And that's when I realized we could *really* be onto something.

There's a stunned silence.

LAILA FURNESS

I don't believe it - both Alan *and* Bill have been one step ahead of us, the whole time?

JJ NORTON

(dryly)

Not just one step, I'd say. More like six or seven.

GUY HOWARD

You played us all for bloody fools—

NICK VINCENT (Producer)

Oh, come on, Guy. You know as well as I do what people want from these shows. They want *answers* - they want the damn thing *solved* - not just yet more pissing about churning over old ground—

HUGO FRASER

(coolly)

So you thought you'd stack the cards in your favour, is that it? Bring in a couple of people who appeared to be objective experts like the rest of us, but in reality not only had a *great* deal of prior knowledge, but actual skin in the game.

NICK VINCENT (Producer)

If you like. To be fair it didn't start out that way - it was only after word got out that we were taking another look at this case that Bill and Alan got in touch.

GUY HOWARD

But rather than tell us - tell *me* - you asked them to keep quiet. To keep it from the rest of the team.

NICK VINCENT (Producer)

Right. To spice things up. Add some drama to proceedings.

(looking round the table)

And it worked, didn't it? I mean, look where we are now.

LAILA FURNESS

It's underhand, and you know it.

HUGO FRASER

I agree. You should have been completely open with us, right from the start.

NICK VINCENT (Producer)

(raising an eyebrow)

Oh really? 'Completely open'? Just like the rest of you have been?

HUGO FRASER

Precisely.

NICK VINCENT (Producer)

Oh, I don't think it's quite as simple as that, is it, Hugo?

You see, while I'm sure you expected us to check out your professional credentials, I doubt you realized *quite* how much research we were going to do on you—

LAILA FURNESS

(realizing what he's saying)

You dug about in our *personal* lives? Without asking, or even telling us? That's completely unethical.

JJ NORTON

This is starting to sound way too Big Brotherish for my liking.

NICK VINCENT (Producer)

(spreading his hands)

We only found what was out there to *be* found.

GUY HOWARD

Hang on a minute - are you actually saying that *all* the people you slated for this team turned out to have a link to this case? That's an *insane* coincidence—

NICK VINCENT (Producer)

(shaking his head)

No, it wasn't like that. It was only after both Bill and Alan came forward that we thought, hang on a minute, maybe we should look at this in a different way?

Maybe, instead of choosing a team on the basis of their expertise, we flip it the other way round: do our own research on the case and see if we come across anyone who might have a possible connection to either Luke Ryder or the Howards—

GUY HOWARD

That's my *family* - you had no right - it's exploitation—

NICK VINCENT (Producer)

Oh really? May I remind you that if you weren't a Howard you'd never have been asked to do this show *at all*? Barely out of some also-ran college with not a single bloody cred to your name? Small wonder you absolutely bloody jumped at the chance when it came your way. You practically bit my arm off.

So don't come the outraged virgin with me, matey. You're absolutely fine with 'exploiting your family', just as long as you're the one who's doing it.

Guy opens his mouth to say something, then changes his mind and turns away. He's breathing heavily and biting his lip. The others are trying not to notice.

HUGO FRASER

(sitting back and looking Nick up and down)

Very adroit.

NICK VINCENT (Producer)

Why thank you. Though something tells me that wasn't exactly meant as a compliment.

HUGO FRASER

And having got that far, you must have realized that if you approached someone for the show who really *was* implicated in the case they'd be bound to accept. Guilty or not. If only to find out what you'd uncovered.

MITCHELL CLARK

No wonder you found it so easy to get this thing financed. It must have looked like a proper little gold mine.

NICK VINCENT (Producer)

(smiling)

Let's just say that our backers were quick to see the potential of this genuinely unique and innovative approach.

JJ NORTON

(under his breath)

I bet that's straight out of the pitch deck. Word for bloody word.

NICK VINCENT (Producer)

(turning to JJ)

Actually, when we started out, all we were hoping for was to find something new to say about the case – that's the whole point of doing this sort of show, after all.

But as soon as we changed the approach we realized that if we *did* manage to do that – if we did actually identify the real killer—

BILL SERAFINI

(nodding)

—that person could be sitting there right in front of you. Actually at this fucking table. It'd be frigging priceless.

NICK VINCENT (Producer)

(laughs)

No flies on you, Bill.

JJ NORTON

(sardonically)

And you'd get to out the guilty party, live on camera, like some sort of smug hipster Hercule Poirot.

NICK VINCENT (Producer)

I think 'smug' is a bit harsh, JJ, but in principle, yes.

Though Guy was right about one thing – the idea that we could find four more experts in criminal investigation *all* of whom had a connection to this case was more than even we could dare to hope.

He laughs again – he's clearly enjoying himself hugely.

But hell, we'd already found two without even trying, so what did we have to lose?

LAILA FURNESS

Let me get this straight – you're saying you chose some of us precisely *because* you thought we had some link to the Ryder case?

NICK VINCENT (Producer)

Had, or *could have*, yes.

LAILA FURNESS

So all of those 'discoveries' Tarek here has supposedly been making, that was all a sham? You knew all that already, before we even started? The Wilsons, Alan's sister in Assos, Caroline's baby?

NICK VINCENT (Producer)

Again, some of it, but not all of it—

GUY HOWARD

(gaping at him)

You knew about that? All this time? You are *unbelievable*.

NICK VINCENT (Producer)

Oh come on – you gave me that fucking honeymoon footage your*self*. It's not my fault if you can't see what's right in front of your bloody face. Some fucking film-maker you make—

Guy pushes his chair back with deliberate violence, gets up and walks away out of shot. Nick can be heard to mutter 'oh dear, tears before bedtime'.

HUGO FRASER

You just wound us up and watched us go – like a bunch of sodding woodentops. This whole bloody thing has been bogus right from the start.

NICK VINCENT (Producer)

In my world that's called 'dramatic licence', Hugo. Maybe you've heard of it?

HUGO FRASER

In *my* world it's called fraud, Nick, maybe you've heard of *that*?

BILL SERAFINI

(interrupting)

You said 'some' of us have connections to the case. So, just to be absolutely clear, you're not *just* talking me and Alan?

NICK VINCENT (Producer)

No, definitely not. But I did only say *possible* connections.

BILL SERAFINI

Nothing you can actually prove?

NICK VINCENT (Producer)

Let's just say some of what we've found out has definitely been verified, but a good part is still either supposition or educated guesswork.

And I should also add that some of what we thought we'd found turned out to be mere coincidence.

(he raises an eyebrow as he glances at Alan)

Despite what some round this table might think about that.

BILL SERAFINI

(refusing to take the bait)

So some of us are definitely off the hook?

NICK VINCENT (Producer)

Oh yes, absolutely.

BILL SERAFINI

Who, exactly?

NICK VINCENT (Producer)

(smiling)

Ah, that's for me to know, and you to find out.

HUGO FRASER

You bastard—

LAILA FURNESS

You're setting us up. Pitching us one against the other.

NICK VINCENT (Producer)

If you like.

But I don't see why you're so far up yourself all of a sudden, Laila. You haven't exactly been 'completely open', have you, for all your bloody sanctimony.

LAILA FURNESS

(suddenly defensive)

I don't know what you mean—

NICK VINCENT (Producer)

Oh, I think you do.

JJ NORTON

Laila? What's he getting at?

MITCHELL CLARKE

(slowly)

Actually, I think I know—

LAILA FURNESS

Mitch - we discussed this - I *told* you—

JJ NORTON

Can someone please tell me what the hell's going on?

MITCHELL CLARKE

(turning slightly from Laila and looking round at the others)

It was a while back, when I was researching that hit-and-run in Sydney. I came up with a name for the victim, remember? In that student magazine?

JJ NORTON

Mohammed Khan, right?

MITCHELL CLARKE

Right. Well, a couple of days later I stumbled over an article by Laila from years ago - something about coping strategies for sudden bereavement.

JJ NORTON

(frowning)

So?

MITCHELL CLARKE

The point is, that article was written before Laila got married. She wrote it in her maiden name.

Laila Khan.

HUGO FRASER

Oh fuck.

MITCHELL CLARKE

So I emailed her about it - just to make sure, you know? Because like I said when we were filming, Khan is a really *really* common Muslim name—

JJ NORTON

And what did she say?

LAILA FURNESS

(intervening)

I said that it was a coincidence—

(rounding on Alan)

And don't even *think* about coming out with your usual mealy-mouthed crap about not believing in coincidences—

ALAN CANNING

(holding up his hands)

Hey, I'm saying nothing.

BILL SERAFINI

To be fair, Nick did just say that some of what they dug up turned out to be just a coincidence. And like you say, it's a pretty common name—

MITCHELL CLARKE

It's not just that, Bill. The article I found - it drew on her own experience of losing a close family member. In her case, a brother.

(turning to her)

You talked about him, remember? About how he died when he was only nineteen. And how much harder it was because he was on the other side of the world and you couldn't be with him—

LAILA FURNESS

(absolutely furious with him)

What on *earth* gives you the right to poke about in my private life?

BILL SERAFINI

(steadily)

It's hardly that 'private', Laila, not if you wrote about it in a professional journal.

HUGO FRASER

(to Laila)

And if it really is just a coincidence, why don't you just clear it up for us, here and now?

Silence.

BILL SERAFINI

Laila?

LAILA FURNESS

(icily)

OK.

Fine. If that's the way you want it.

Yes, I did have a brother, and yes, he was called Mohammed. He did go to uni in Sydney, and he did die as a result of a hit-and-run in 1995—

JJ NORTON

Holy shit—

LAILA FURNESS

—but it was not, repeat *not*, Luke Ryder who was responsible. Consequently I had no reason to bear a grudge against him, far less track him down and bludgeon him to death.

ALAN CANNING

(quietly)

How do you know it wasn't Ryder? No one else was ever prosecuted.

LAILA FURNESS

No, nobody was charged, but we ended up being fairly sure who the driver was.

ALAN CANNING

'Ended up'? What does that mean?

LAILA FURNESS

(a little stiffly)

The man concerned made a deathbed confession, apparently. Wanted to get it off his chest. His widow got in touch with my father to let him know.

ALAN CANNING

The Sydney police don't seem to be aware of that.

LAILA FURNESS

(reddening a little)

I didn't know that until Mitch started looking at what happened. I thought my father had told the police years ago, but when I checked with my mother she said he never did. He tried calling them a few times but they never rang back and it just fell through the cracks.

ALAN CANNING

So when exactly was this 'confession'?

LAILA FURNESS

(hesitates a moment)

I think it was 2006.

They all realize at once what this means.

ALAN CANNING

Ten years *after* your brother died? And all that time, you could well have thought it really *was* Ryder. Including in *October 2003*—

JJ NORTON

How many times have I sat here and heard you insist that a woman couldn't commit an attack like that? Was that the objective psych talking, or a *very* interested party?

LAILA FURNESS

(exasperated now)

That's utterly ridiculous, and you know it.

(turning to Canning)

And as for you, Alan, in *theory*, I suppose I *could* have thought the culprit was Luke Ryder in 2003, but in *fact* I didn't - I didn't even know he existed—

JJ NORTON

Can you prove that?

LAILA FURNESS

Of course I can't prove it - how do you prove a negative?

ALAN CANNING

You were living in London by 2003—

LAILA FURNESS

(quickly)

So were a lot of us round this table - so were *you*, for that matter. And we've already established that you had one *hell* of a motive of your own for wanting Ryder dead.

(leaning towards him and pointing)

So why don't you tell us, *Detective Inspector* Canning? Where were *you* on the night of October third, 2003?

ALAN CANNING

You are joking, right? You can't seriously think—

BILL SERAFINI

Actually, I agree with Laila. After all, 'It's the obvious question'.

(raising an eyebrow)

Isn't that what *you* said when *I* was asked that exact same thing?

ALAN CANNING

Indeed it was. And I also remember that you never gave us an answer.

BILL SERAFINI

I was in New York that night - I *told* you that.

ALAN CANNING

And I told *you* that you were listed as a delegate at the same conference I was at in Berkshire. You could easily have got into London—

BILL SERAFINI

Not from Brooklyn, I couldn't.

But I agree with you about one thing: anyone who was at that conference could quite easily have made it to Dorney Place and back to the hotel that night.

(giving him a heavy look)

So is that what you did? Drive up there after the last session was finished and everyone was in the bar? Flash your badge at Ryder, telling him some cock-and-bull story to persuade him to let you in? And once you *are* in, *bam*—

ALAN CANNING

That's complete bollocks - you're just trying to distract us from focusing on *you*—

JJ NORTON

(to Alan)

Actually, speaking as a dispassionate observer, I have to say your motive does seem rather more compelling than Bill's.

ALAN CANNING

(turning on him)

Oh, you're *dispassionate* now, are you? And what about *you*, eh, JJ? What have *you* been hiding, because there has to be something.

JJ NORTON

Just because *you* didn't tell the whole truth, doesn't mean the rest of us were doing the same—

ALAN CANNING

Why don't we ask Nick about that? Because I bet he has something *really* juicy on you.

Let's face it, he could've had his pick of CSI experts for this show, couldn't he - Henry Lee, Werner Spitz, anyone. And yet he chooses you? Some washed-up loser with tatts from fucking *South Wales*?

(brutally sarcastic)

Oh, sorry, I forgot about you being a *genius* - Mensa, my arse.

HUGO FRASER

Ouch.

BILL SERAFINI

I have to admit, I have wondered about that myself. JJ's credentials, I mean.

JJ NORTON

Fuck you, Bill. *Fuck you.*

LAILA FURNESS

Nick? Is this true? Is JJ another suspect?

NICK VINCENT (Producer)

(clearly amused his little ploy is working so well)

Like I said, I'm saying nothing.

BILL SERAFINI

But speaking as a detective, JJ doesn't have any connection to London that I'm aware of, so I'm struggling to see how he could have even met the Howards or Luke Ryder, much less have a motive—

JJ NORTON

I've never lived in London, never studied there, I bloody hate the place—

LAILA FURNESS

(realization dawning)

It's not London, it's *Birmingham. That's* the link. That's where you were brought up.

JJ NORTON

(flushing slightly)

Yeah, so?

HUGO FRASER

I remember now - didn't you boast about being 'born and bred a Brummie'?

JJ NORTON

I'm not so sure it was boasting, more like joking—

HUGO FRASER

No, the point is, you said you didn't just live there, you were *born* there.

LAILA FURNESS

Exactly. Just like the baby Caroline Howard had when she was 16. The one that was adopted by another family, and in all likelihood in the Midlands area.

JJ NORTON

Oh come *on*–

BILL SERAFINI

Actually, I think you may have something there, Laila. And didn't JJ talk a while back about how adopted kids feel about going looking for their birth parents? Wasn't it when we first found out about Caroline's baby? I seem to recall it sounded pretty personal.

(turning to Nick)

Am I remembering that right?

NICK VINCENT (Producer)

(nodding)

I even have the clip to prove it.

(Nods to the cameraman.)

FOOTAGE appears on the screen.

MITCHELL CLARKE

If the kid was born in 1979 it'd be 44 now.

LAILA FURNESS

More to the point, he or she would have been 18 in 1997 and entitled to see their records at that stage, but there's no suggestion they made contact with Caroline then. Why leave it till 2003?

JJ NORTON

Not all adopted kids want to. Some never do. And 18 is just the earliest you can do it - lots of people leave it a lot later than that. Just saying.

MITCHELL CLARKE

But if they did track Caroline down it might have been a pretty difficult encounter. What if the kid had quite a disadvantaged upbringing – it has to be possible if it was inner-city Birmingham, right?

Then all those years later they suddenly find out their real mother and her other kids have been sitting pretty on a pile like Dorney Place, while they were unceremoniously dumped and left out in the cold—

JJ NORTON

Quite.

CUT TO: Studio.

ALAN CANNING

Sounds even more personal now, JJ.

It's you, isn't it? The long-lost kid? So how did it go down? You found out Caroline was your mother and came looking for her—

(gesturing round at the room)

—only to find out that all this time she'd been living in a house like this? Because I'm sure now that you also said something pretty bitter to that vicar in New Brunswick about being brought up on the poverty line.

JJ NORTON

You're delusional, the lot of you – Nick's got us all completely paranoid. *I had nothing to do with it.*

ALAN CANNING

That's not what I asked, though, is it?

Where were you on the night of October third, 2003?

JJ NORTON

(sarcastic)

No bloody idea, ask me another.

HUGO FRASER

You were born in 1979, though - that part's correct?

JJ NORTON

(turning to him)

Yes. Like hundreds of thousands of other people.

BILL SERAFINI

And adopted?

JJ NORTON

(after a pause)

Yes. Not that it's any of your business. Or anyone else's, frankly.

BILL SERAFINI

I agree. Unless, of course, you really are Caroline Howard's long-lost son. Then it most certainly *is* our business.

JJ NORTON

Well, I'm not. Happy now?

ALAN CANNING

Can you prove it?

JJ NORTON

If necessary. But frankly I don't see why the hell I should have to—

LAILA FURNESS

(intervening)

I'm sorry, but I'm very uncomfortable with this - it's getting perilously close to bullying. Nick did say some of us *appeared* to have connections to the case only it turned out to be pure coincidence. Maybe that applies to JJ—

ALAN CANNING

I just don't know why he's so reluctant to prove it.

LAILA FURNESS

But it might not be that easy.

He'd need to show us his original birth certificate with his biological mother's name, which is a document he may not even *have*, and certainly may not want to share in public. It's such a private thing.

ALAN CANNING

(tetchily)

I'm not asking to see any of that: all he needs to do is provide a DNA sample, which we can run against Guy's. If they're related, we'll find out soon enough.

JJ NORTON

For fuck's sake – you're wasting your bloody time. It's *not me*. And, no, I am fucking well *not* giving you a bloody sample – it's a gross invasion of privacy and you know it.

As he speaks he sits back and pulls down his sleeves. Alan watches him for a moment.

ALAN CANNING

(thoughtfully)

I'd forgotten about that tattoo. That's your DNA profile, isn't it?

JJ flushes but says nothing.

Maybe we can use that. I mean, you don't exactly treat that thing as 'private', do you? It's right there for any Tom, Dick or Harry to see.

(turns to Nick)

You must have footage you could lift an image from.

NICK VINCENT (Producer)

(giving a quick laugh)

Great minds, Alan. And you're right, we do. Trouble is the results were inconclusive - none of the images were quite good enough.

JJ NORTON

(gaping at him, furious)

You've already *done* it? You ran my fucking *DNA*? Without even *telling* me?

NICK VINCENT (Producer)

(shrugging, clearly unfazed)

Like Alan said, if you thought it was that bloody private you wouldn't have put it on your sodding arm.

There's an awkward silence; JJ is seething.

BILL SERAFINI

(with a slightly forced laugh, trying to lighten the atmosphere)

Hell I'm beginning to think we should put the whole team through a polygraph - that'd tell us once and for all what's genuine and what's just 'coincidence'.

NICK VINCENT (Producer)

(with a wry smile)

Funny you should mention that.

LAILA FURNESS

A *polygraph*? You're not serious.

NICK VINCENT (Producer)

Why not? Bill has a point. And let's face it, it would make—

HUGO FRASER

(darkly)

—don't tell me, '*great TV*'.

NICK VINCENT (Producer)

(laughing)

You're finally getting the hang of this, Hugo.

But seriously, why not? If you're all so sure you have nothing to hide.

LAILA FURNESS

(firmly)

There's a reason polygraphs aren't admissible in court, Nick. And not just here, in the US as well. The science simply isn't robust enough - some people find it relatively easy to beat the machine, while others react so badly to the stress it can lead to dangerous false positives.

TAREK OSMAN

(a little hesitantly)

Though they're used on sex offenders here, aren't they? If they've been let out on licence - to check if they're complying with their release conditions?

HUGO FRASER

Yes, that's true, but it's a very limited and strictly controlled exception to the rule. The Offender Management Act 2007 explicitly prohibits the use of any such polygraph test results in criminal proceedings. For all the reasons Laila mentions.

BILL SERAFINI

Understood. Though I've seen innocent people eliminated from enquiries thanks to polygraphs. But you're right: they do have to be administered by a trained practitioner, not some TV bum.

No offence, Nick.

NICK VINCENT (Producer)

(smiling)

I'm not that easily offended, Bill. Probably just as well.

And I agree with you, by the way – I definitely think polygraphs have a role to play.

JJ NORTON

(still clearly furious)

No one's treating me like a bloody lab rat, and that's final.

HUGO FRASER

I agree. Nick just wants to try and catch us out – go around grubbing under stones just to see what's underneath.

MITCHELL CLARKE

(raising an eyebrow)

'The lady doth protest too much'?

HUGO FRASER

(turning to him)

What the hell does that mean?

MITCHELL CLARKE

Oh come on, you haven't exactly been 'completely open' either, have you?

LAILA FURNESS

What are you talking about, Mitch?

MITCHELL CLARKE

(pointing at Hugo)

He knew her – back in the day.

Caroline Howard.

He never thought to mention that, did he?

LAILA FURNESS

(her eyes widening)

Hugo *knew* her? Are you sure?

MITCHELL CLARKE

Certainly am. They were all part of the same tight little W8 coterie. Same clubs, same dinner parties, kids at the same schools. All *very* cosy.

HUGO FRASER

(looking uncomfortable)

It wasn't like that—

JJ NORTON

Really? Then what was it 'like'?

HUGO FRASER

OK, yes, we did move in some of the same circles, but that's not that uncommon in that part of town.

BILL SERAFINI

So how close were you, exactly? Passing acquaintances? Friends? *Close* friends?

JJ NORTON

(grimly)

Maybe even friends with benefits? That 'unsuitable' man she was seeing - was that you?

LAILA FURNESS

(looking from one to the other)

You mean, he wasn't unsuitable because he was married, but because he was *black*? Oh my God—

There's a silence; Hugo isn't meeting anyone's eye.

ALAN CANNING

(clearing his throat)

I think this may be the moment to mention the car—

LAILA FURNESS

Oh shit.

ALAN CANNING

That woman I told you about who owned a red MGB back in 2003? The one I couldn't persuade to talk to me on camera? Her name's Serena Hamilton. But back then, before she got married, she was Serena *Fraser*. Hugo is her brother.

And for the avoidance of doubt, he used to borrow her car. Apparently he did it *all the time*.

LAILA FURNESS

(staring at Hugo)

My God, it was *you*. *You're* the one she was having an affair with.

HUGO FRASER

(shaking his head)

It's not what it looks like.

JJ NORTON

What it *looks like* is that you had a slam-dunk motive to kill Luke Ryder. Caroline wanted to finish it with you and you weren't taking no for an answer—

HUGO FRASER

That would be laughable if this whole thing wasn't such a bloody shit-show—

JJ NORTON

You decided to have it out with her - make her change her mind - only when you went over there she was out at that party, and the only person in the house was Luke—

HUGO FRASER

(shaking his head)

No, absolutely not - that did *not* happen - and in any case it was just a casual thing - a fling.

MITCHELL CLARKE

As JJ would say, 'yeah, right'.

HUGO FRASER

(rounding on him)

And what about you? Why don't you tell us what *you* were really doing there that night? Because it sure as fuck wasn't that crap you came out with about 'hearing a report on the police radio'—

MITCHELL CLARKE

And how the hell would you know?

HUGO FRASER

Because Caroline and I were *friends* - because she *talked* to me.

He takes a breath; the others are staring at him, and he holds up his hands.

Look, I couldn't say anything before because I knew how it would look—

A ripple round the table, someone mutters 'yeah, right'.

—but remember those 'inappropriate' friends Maura Howard was seeing that summer? One of them wasn't just a mate, she was *sleeping with him*. That was why Caroline was so worried—

MITCHELL CLARKE

(icily)

She called him 'inappropriate', did she? And why exactly *was* that? Because he was black, like you? No, *you* got a free pass because you're a fucking coconut and a rich bastard, but Maura's bloke, he was just poor black trash? The shit under your fucking Prada shoes? Is *that* what you're saying?

HUGO FRASER

You know that's not what I mean. Maura was *15*, for God's sake. It was statutory *rape*—

MITCHELL CLARKE

(shaking his head)

You have no way to prove it was me—

HUGO FRASER

(holding his gaze)

She met him at an event at her school. He was a journalist - *you* were a journalist, and you covered events in that area, *including* at that school.

(takes a deep breath)

And yes, the man in question was black. It narrows the field pretty fast—

MITCHELL CLARKE

(still shaking his head)

That's not proof.

HUGO FRASER

And it would explain why you were there that night. Sneaking in to see her when you knew her mother would be out? That apartment over the garage, wasn't that why Maura was so keen to move over there? So the two of you could fuck in peace? That's certainly what Caroline thought.

You didn't know Luke was going to bail on that drinks party, did you? As far as you knew, it was Beatriz who'd be babysitting that night - Beatriz who was in her seventies and deaf as a post. But Luke wasn't - his hearing was just fine. He heard something, he came out and he caught you at it—

MITCHELL CLARKE

You are *not* pinning this on me. No fucking way. If I'd killed him there'd be *evidence*, there'd be DNA, and let me remind you they found *nothing* linking me to *any of it.*

(pointing at Hugo)

Can you say the same? How about *you* give us a DNA sample and we'll see if the Met can find a match on that jacket?

HUGO FRASER

Bring it on - I have nothing to hide. Because I *wasn't there.*

Unlike *you.*

LAILA FURNESS

But you *were* at the party, right? That car - it was outside, Phyllis Franks saw it—

HUGO FRASER

(hesitates)

OK, yes, you're right, I was there - but—

JJ NORTON

(intervening)

Hang on, hang on. Hugo - what you just said about Mitch, it doesn't tally with the timeline.

Mitch couldn't have been sneaking in to see Maura that night because the girls were at the cinema the whole evening. Caroline bought their tickets, remember, and the film didn't finish till 10.15—

HUGO FRASER

Just because she saw the girls go in, doesn't mean they actually *stayed.*

BILL SERAFINI

You think they slipped out early?

HUGO FRASER

I think Maura may well have done - I know for a fact she'd done that before. And it was only a twenty-minute walk back to the house.

BILL SERAFINI

So your theory is she and Mitch had already arranged to meet in her room over the workshop? Only neither of them realized that Luke would be in the house because he only decided to bail on the party *after* Caroline had dropped the girls off?

HUGO FRASER

Precisely.

MITCHELL CLARKE

For fuck's sake, this is all *bollocks*—

ALAN CANNING

(quietly)

So why don't you tell us what really happened? Were you in a relationship with Maura Howard or not?

Or would you prefer we get her in here and ask her? Maybe we should ask Guy what he thinks of that?

He turns and looks towards the other side of the room. The CAMERA FOLLOWS his gaze, swinging round slowly to a wide-angle shot and we see not just the team but Guy, where he's been sitting this whole time. He's on a chair on the far side, his head in his hands. After a moment he looks up. He looks angry.

GUY HOWARD

You leave Maura out of this, you hear me?

NICK VINCENT (Producer)

Bit late to be coming the Big Man, mate—

GUY HOWARD

(getting up and coming towards him)

Fuck off, Nick - just fuck *right off*—

BILL SERAFINI

(holding up his hands)

OK, OK, let's take a time-out here, shall we?

Mitch - I think you really need to level with us. For Maura's sake, if no one else's.

MITCHELL CLARKE

(taking a deep breath)

OK, OK.

Yes.

ALAN CANNING

Yes, as in you *were* seeing her?

MITCHELL CLARKE

(swallows, then nods)

Yes. I was seeing her.

The camera is still on wide angle. Guy stares at him then drops his head and turns away. Mitch looks round at the rest of the team.

Look, I'm not proud of it, but you have to remember I was barely 21 myself back then. And she was a lot more sophisticated than I was—

(seeing their faces)

I didn't mean by that - shit, this is coming out all wrong - I'm not blaming her, seriously - it's all on me, I *know* that. I just meant she came from a completely different background - *I* was the kid by the side of her.

But yes, I did know she was underage and I'm not trying to excuse that, but as for *rape*—

(turning to Hugo)

—that's *not* what happened. I loved her. I'd never have forced her to do anything she didn't want to do. If anything, she was the one that pushed that side of it.

Hugo doesn't look convinced; the others clearly don't know what to believe. Guy goes over to the window, one hand on the glass, his back to the rest of the room.

LAILA FURNESS

(gently)

Did she love you?

MITCHELL CLARKE

(shrugs)

I thought so.

HUGO FRASER

Just used you to get back at her mother, more like.

MITCHELL CLARKE

(turning to him, angry now)

Look, she *said* she loved me, OK? And I don't know what gives you the right to get on your fucking high horse – you were banging her mother and cheating on your wife—

HUGO FRASER

(getting angry himself)

Her *mother* was an *adult*, not an underage *child*—

BILL SERAFINI

Whoa, guys. Like I said, time out—

There's an awkward silence; Hugo gets up and goes to pour himself a glass of water. Camera remains on wide angle.

BILL SERAFINI

Mitch, much as I hate to agree with Alan on anything, I think you do need to tell us what really went down that night.

Because Hugo's right – it clearly didn't happen the way you said it did back when we started all this.

MITCHELL CLARKE

I didn't kill him – I had *nothing* to do with it—

<u>BILL SERAFINI</u>

(placatory)

I'm not saying you did. But we do want the truth.

<u>MITCHELL CLARKE</u>

OK, OK.

(takes a deep breath)

You're right about the film - Maura'd fixed it with Amelie that she'd leave early and Amelie would cover for her. I picked her up on Notting Hill Gate and we went back to my flat.

<u>JJ NORTON</u>

Must have been a bit of a come down after Dorney Place—

<u>HUGO FRASER</u>

(sardonically)

Well, we already know she liked roughing it—

<u>MITCHELL CLARKE</u>

Piss off, Hugo.

<u>BILL SERAFINI</u>

Ignore him. What happened next?

<u>MITCHELL CLARKE</u>

I dropped Maura off on the corner of their road at around ten. She was supposed to meet Amelie there at ten fifteen so they could walk home together.

<u>ALAN CANNING</u>

(nodding)

Which accounts for a man answering your description being seen in the street—

<u>MITCHELL CLARKE</u>

Right. Anyway, I stopped for petrol on the way back and I was at the till when I got this weird call from Maura's mobile. I couldn't make it out -

it took me a few minutes to realize she'd called me by mistake. A butt-dial, basically.

BILL SERAFINI

So what time was that?

MITCHELL CLARKE

I didn't look at my watch, but I'm guessing about 10.35.

BILL SERAFINI

Could you hear what was going on? Anything she was saying?

MITCHELL CLARKE

(sighing and shaking his head)

Not really, to be honest. It was more like heavy breathing, moaning almost - I tried to talk to her but she obviously couldn't hear me—

BILL SERAFINI

So you turned round and went back?

MITCHELL CLARKE

Of course I did - wouldn't you?

BILL SERAFINI

Then what happened?

MITCHELL CLARKE

After that it was pretty much like I told you - by the time I got there the cops had already arrived.

BILL SERAFINI

You followed the police car down the drive and went round to the back of the house?

MITCHELL CLARKE

Right. I was looking for Maura.

ALAN CANNING

But what you found was a corpse.

MITCHELL CLARKE

(swallows)

Right.

BILL SERAFINI

Had you met Luke before?

MITCHELL CLARKE

(shaking his head)

No. I'd seen him, at a distance, but that's all.

HUGO FRASER

When you were skulking about shagging Maura in that stable block, no doubt.

MITCHELL CLARKE

(ignoring him)

I'd never spoken to him. And in any case, the state of the body - you wouldn't have recognized who it was - no one would—

BILL SERAFINI

So then what?

MITCHELL CLARKE

(shrugs)

It was like I said before. I saw the cops coming for me and I just ran.

LAILA FURNESS

Why didn't you tell the police you knew Maura?

MITCHELL CLARKE

You really need to ask?

HUGO FRASER

Because he didn't want to get slapped with a bloody rape charge, that's why.

MITCHELL CLARKE

I was just a *kid* - a *black* kid who'd grown up on a council estate in Ladbroke Grove. I didn't need any more trouble from the law. And I didn't want to cause a shitload of hassle for Maura either.

LAILA FURNESS

(sighing)

I suppose I can understand that.

ALAN CANNING

And that's it? There's nothing more you're not telling us?

MITCHELL CLARKE

That's it. Like I said, I had nothing to do with it. By the time I got there he was already dead. That's the God's honest truth.

JJ NORTON

(under his breath)

That's what you said the first time. Word for word.

There's a brief silence.

ALAN CANNING

So what about Maura?

They stare at him. Guy turns from the window and stands there, his eyes fixed on Alan.

LAILA FURNESS

What do you mean – what about Maura?

ALAN CANNING

The police were told the girls got home at 10.30, and no one's ever questioned that. It's right there on our timeline.

But if Mitch is telling the truth, Maura could have got back as early as just after *ten*, assuming she went straight home and didn't bother waiting for Amelie. And that would have been slap-bang in the middle of the window during which we know Luke was killed.

And if that butt-call really was at 10.35, it's a good ten minutes before Maura claimed to have found the body.

And there's something else too: she has brown hair.

People start to look uneasy: it's obvious where this is going. Alan sits back and looks round.

So.

What if it was Maura? What if *she* killed him?

Silence. At the window, Guy has gone very pale, his fists are clenched so hard the knuckles are white.

BILL SERAFINI

(shifting slightly in his seat)

Well, uncomfortable though it undoubtedly is to talk about this - for all of us - we do have to try to look at this whole thing objectively—

LAILA FURNESS

(glancing uneasily at Guy)

That's easy to say when it's not one of your own family in the frame—

BILL SERAFINI

I know, believe me, I know - but what's the point of doing this at all if we aren't going to look at *all* the possible suspects?

ALAN CANNING

Exactly.

So. Maura.

(gesturing again at the timeline)

Because, according to that, if she was home by ten, there was definitely enough time—

MITCHELL CLARKE

You *seriously* think a 15-year-old girl could have done that – that – *bloodbath*? Not to mention the small matter of motive – why on earth would she do it?

ALAN CANNING

(giving him a heavy look)

I can't believe you, of all people, need to ask that. 'Luke' was about to expose your little lovefest to her mother, wasn't he? Which would have put paid to your shag shenanigans once and for all. Motive enough, if you ask me, for an impetuous teenager. And we already know she hated him.

BILL SERAFINI

(agreeing)

Speaking professionally, I never cease to be staggered at what teens are capable of – and especially girls.

ALAN CANNING

(looking round at the team, though not at Guy)

And the timeline works: Mitch drops her off and she realizes it's about to rain so instead of waiting for Amelie she decides to go straight home.

As he speaks, cut to RECONSTRUCTION. 'Maura' gets out of a pale Ford car which immediately pulls away. We can see the man inside is black. Camera follows 'Maura' as she walks along the well-lit street to Dorney Place. There's no one else about. At the gate, she taps in the entry code and starts down the drive. The girl playing the part looks very like the photos of Maura at that age.

ALAN CANNING

She goes round the side of the house towards her room, but doesn't make any effort to stay out of sight because she assumes it's Beatriz who's babysitting and she won't even notice.

Only it's not Beatriz in the house, it's Luke.

As 'Maura' reaches the terrace 'Luke' appears at the French windows. He throws open the door, clearly furious. 'Maura' turns and tries to get away but he follows her, grabbing her by the arm. There's a tussle, and the camera zooms in to show her hair catching in his jacket zip. She pushes him away and he slips, falling heavily on the stone steps and then lies there unmoving.

Maybe she thinks she's killed him; maybe she's actually glad he's dead.

And maybe – just *maybe* – she doesn't know either way and decides she'd better make sure.

The FOOTAGE starts to slow down as she's standing over him, a rock in her hand, slowly lifting it above her head.

FREEZE FRAME.

CUT TO: Team. Alan sits back and looks around.

Either way, she beats his face to obliteration.

Silence. At the window, Guy has turned away.

MITCHELL CLARKE

(shaking his head)

I'm still not buying it. Even if her mother *had* found out, what's the worst that would have happened? She'd have been grounded or had her allowance docked or some shit like that. Come on, that is *not* a reason to kill the guy—

BILL SERAFINI

Laila – you're very quiet. As a psychologist, what's your read?

LAILA FURNESS

(looking concerned)

I'm just hoping this isn't going to be yet another instance of an all-too horribly familiar pattern.

A brief silence; JJ gets there first.

JJ NORTON

Shit, you think he may have been abusing her? That that was why she reacted the way she did?

LAILA FURNESS

(with a sigh)

I hope not, I really do. But it might explain why they both disliked him so much–

The CAMERA SWINGS round quickly to capture Guy as he pushes through the furniture and disappears behind the camera. Laila looks distraught.

Oh God, Guy, I'm so sorry - I shouldn't have raised this–

ALAN CANNING

(quietly)

We're here to establish the *truth*, Laila, 'whatever that truth turns out to be'. It was Guy *himself* who said that.

(spreads his hands)

If that's what he claims to be doing, he can't pick and choose which 'truth' we find, just because he doesn't like it.

BILL SERAFINI

(to Laila)

Could it have gone down that way? *Could* Maura have killed him?

LAILA FURNESS

(her face set)

Maybe. If he really was abusing her.

(taking a deep breath)

They'd been living in the same house for months - if it had been going on for that long, I can easily see how the pressure might have become intolerable.

And we do need to remember that the prefrontal cortex isn't yet fully developed in the teenage brain, which means they have significantly poorer impulse control than mature adults.

So yes, *maybe*, if she was already under that degree of mental pressure and then suddenly found herself in an angry confrontation with him, I suppose it's possible. She *might* have lashed out in the way Alan just described.

HUGO FRASER

Or *maybe* she was a lot cannier than you give her credit for. Maybe the real reason she caved his face in was to make it look like the work of some random psycho. To put the police off the scent.

BILL SERAFINI

Mitch, you were seeing her at the time – did she ever say anything to you about what really happened that night? I'm assuming she never said anything about abuse or you'd already have told us.

MITCHELL CLARKE

(shaking his head)

That night was the last time I ever spoke to her. She sent me a text breaking up with me the following morning. I tried to talk to her for weeks after but she refused to take my calls.

HUGO FRASER

Which to my mind is revealing in and of itself.

BILL SERAFINI

(to Mitch)

You didn't think that was odd?

MITCHELL CLARKE

(shrugging)

Not at the time. Not with all the crap that was going down. And let's face it, 21-year-old blokes aren't exactly renowned for their emotional intelligence. I just thought she had enough shit without me being in the mix.

And yeah, maybe, being totally honest, I thought I was well out of it. I'd already dodged one bullet that night.

(looking towards Bill)

And for the record, you're right: she never said a word to me about anything inappropriate going on with Luke. Not one word.

ALAN CANNING

(sitting back)

So if it *was* Maura, do we think Caroline knew?

It takes a moment to sink in. Bill gives a low whistle.

BILL SERAFINI

Jooz

ALAN CANNING

It has to be the obvious conclusion, doesn't it? Maybe not that night, but soon after.

Remember what Shirley Booker said about the kids having therapy? If Maura really did kill 'Luke' I can easily see why she'd have needed a shrink. She'd have been a psychological basket case.

LAILA FURNESS

(clearly annoyed at his choice of language)

She *found* him. Do you not think *that* alone—

(gesturing at the crime scene photos)

—would be enough to mess with your typical 15-year-old psyche?

ALAN CANNING

Of course. But there is another explanation, and like I said before, we can't just ignore it because we don't happen to like it.

BILL SERAFINI

(also looking at the boards)

But what about her clothes? If Maura had beaten Luke to death she'd have been covered with blood, not to mention body matter. There's no way the cops would have missed that.

HUGO FRASER

The simplest explanation would be that she got changed. She was at home - she'd have had access to plenty of clean clothes.

LAILA FURNESS

(glancing at the timeline)

But was there enough time to do that?

HUGO FRASER

(considering)

Just about, I think - assuming she was home by just gone ten. The 999 call wasn't until 10.47.

JJ gets up and walks over to the board and stops in front of a group of stills taken from videos shown earlier.

Camera zooms in.

JJ NORTON

(gesturing at one image)

Well, we know what she had on earlier that evening, at their mate's party. The question is whether she was still wearing the same stuff when the police arrived at the house after the 999 call.

TAREK OSMAN

(looking up)

I don't have any film, I'm afraid - the media weren't allowed to show any footage of the kids that night.

HUGO FRASER

(to Alan)

Surely the Met would have bagged up Maura's clothes if she was the one who found the body? In which case, there must be something in the file to say what she was wearing.

They start to go back through the paperwork. Bill finds it first.

BILL SERAFINI

Here we are - grey hoodie, white T-shirt, jeans.

(looks up at JJ, still by the board)

Does that stack up?

JJ NORTON

(looking back at him)

Yup, as far as it goes. But how many white T-shirts and pairs of jeans does your average teenager have? I'm not sure it's what you could call conclusive. She could easily have changed before the police got there.

LAILA FURNESS

What about the hoodie?

JJ NORTON

She's not wearing that in these earlier shots. But to be fair, that could be because she's indoors and didn't need it.

HUGO FRASER

Hang on a minute - this new version of events of yours, Alan: explain how '*Luke*' ends up wearing a jacket?

A couple of people look at him blankly, but Bill's quicker.

BILL SERAFINI

I see where you're going. If he's supposed to have been watching TV when he saw Maura out the window, why does he take the time to put on a jacket before going out to confront her? You just wouldn't, would you? Even if it was raining, which we know it wasn't – not by then.

ALAN CANNING

(shrugs)

It's no big deal. Maybe he wasn't watching TV. Maybe he was about to go out and work on the motorbike.

Cut again to RECONSTRUCTION. Camera 'rewinds' to the point where 'Maura' appears on the terrace and starts again. This time 'Luke' is standing in the drawing-room in his black denim jacket when he sees her. The rest of the sequence plays as before.

CUT TO: Team.

LAILA FURNESS

Though he didn't have the workshop keys on him when he died, did he? We talked about that already.

ALAN CANNING

(unperturbed)

Perhaps Maura turned up at the very moment he was looking for them.

HUGO FRASER

I'm not convinced. I think the *known* facts fit another scenario much better: i.e., that someone else turned up that night, unexpectedly or otherwise, and Luke decided to talk to them outside the house. Hence the jacket.

If you ask me, Maura didn't have anything to do with it.

(a pause)

Though I do accept that what Mitch told us raises some significant questions, most notably the fact that it's possible she got home early enough either to commit the murder herself, as Alan's suggesting, *or* to know rather more about it than she's ever admitted.

The trouble is, that's a question only she can answer.

There's a sudden noise and the camera pans round to see the doors to the adjoining room swinging open. Everyone turns to see Maura standing there, a hand on each door.

MAURA HOWARD

You want to know what happened?

Fine.

Just ask me.

I'll tell you what fucking happened.

Slow FADE OUT

CUT TO: Nick Vincent, plain black background, close-up and direct to camera.

NICK VINCENT (Producer)

By this point in the series, you've heard a lot about the rather controversial way we've gone about making it. We've been accused of underhandedness, exploitation, even fraud.

But I make no apology for any of it.

Why?

Because in a few short months we've managed to crack a case that had defeated the Metropolitan Police for two decades.

That's right, after all these years, we finally know the truth. We know who killed Luke Ryder.

Hold on to your hats - I can promise you, this is going to be one *hell* of a ride.

FADE OUT

CUT TO: DORNEY PLACE. Maura is still at the interconnecting doors and Guy is now standing a few feet away. The team are in the foreground round the table, all turned towards Maura.

GUY HOWARD

(taking a step towards his sister)

Maurie - you don't have to do this—

MAURA HOWARD

Oh, you think? I heard every bloody word they said. And *that* bastard—

(pointing at Alan, her hand shaking)

—just accused me of murder.

GUY HOWARD

(moving closer)

He didn't - not really. They're just trying to eliminate possibilities. No one really believes you did anything.

MAURA HOWARD

Really? Well, that's not how I heard it.

She pushes past him into the room and comes to a stop in front of Alan.

You want to know what happened? Then ask me to my fucking face, why don't you.

She drags out a chair with deliberate vehemence and slams it down a few feet from him, then sits back, openly hostile.

ALAN CANNING

(calmly)

OK if that's the way you want it, let's hear it. Tell us your version of what happened that night.

MAURA HOWARD

It's not a *version*—

ALAN CANNING

(shrugs)

Version, account, 'your truth', whatever. No need to get hung up on semantics.

Let's start with the film. Your mother took you and Amelie to the Gate in Notting Hill and bought you your tickets. It was *Intolerable Cruelty*, right?

MAURA HOWARD

(muttering under her breath)

How fucking apt was that.

ALAN CANNING

(evidently intrigued but not allowing himself to get side-tracked)

The programme began at eight and was due to finish around 10.15, so allowing for the time to walk back you and Amelie should have been home by 10.30.

(waits for her to reply but she doesn't bother)

Though evidently you had other ideas. You left the cinema almost immediately, and were picked up by Mitch.

Alan gestures at Mitch and, almost despite herself, Maura looks across at him. The two lock eyes just for a moment; there's been a lot of water under the bridge since they were last in the same room. Maura looks away again. Her lip is trembling slightly. Mitch has his back to the camera, but we see Laila give him an anxious glance.

MAURA HOWARD

Right.

ALAN CANNING

You spent the next two hours at his place, after which he dropped you back on Larbert Road at just before ten. You'd arranged to meet Amelie there so you could walk back together?

Maura nods; she's still not making eye contact.

But Amelie wasn't there when Mitch dropped you off, was she?

Maura hesitates for a tiny moment then shakes her head.

When did she get there?

MAURA HOWARD

About five minutes later. She was pissed off with me. She'd wanted to go to her mate's rather than the film but I needed her to be there to cover for me.

ALAN CANNING

What time did the two of you get back to Dorney Place?

MAURA HOWARD

About 10.30. You *know* that.

ALAN CANNING

But you didn't call 999 till 10.47. Why the delay?

MAURA HOWARD

(rolling her eyes)

How many more times? We went to the kitchen to get a Coke and something to eat. There was no sign of Luke—

ALAN CANNING

Don't you mean Beatriz? Surely you were expecting her to be babysitting, not Luke?

MAURA HOWARD

(flushing slightly)

Of course - what I meant was there was no one around.

ALAN CANNING

Didn't that worry you? I mean, Beatriz was supposed to be there, wasn't she? Your mother wouldn't have left your brother alone.

MAURA HOWARD

(staring at him for the first time)

When Beatriz babysat she usually spent the whole time ironing. I suppose I assumed that's where she was.

ALAN CANNING

She didn't iron in the kitchen?

MAURA HOWARD

(sarcastically)

We have a *laundry room*. The clue's in the name, genius.

ALAN CANNING

(refusing to be patronized)

OK. So what about the doors to the terrace - were they open or shut?

MAURA HOWARD

Look, you know all this—

ALAN CANNING

(with a dry smile)

Humour me.

MAURA HOWARD

They were closed, OK?

ALAN CANNING

And what happened next?

MAURA HOWARD

Me and Amelie talked for a bit, had our Coke, then she went upstairs and I headed out to my room.

(a pause)

That's when I found him.

And no, I am *not* going to go through all that again.

ALAN CANNING

So to recap: you didn't go straight home after Mitch dropped you off, you waited for your sister.

MAURA HOWARD

Right.

He moves into quick-fire questioning now.

ALAN CANNING

You didn't see anyone leaving the house when you got home.

MAURA HOWARD

No.

ALAN CANNING

You didn't argue with Luke, because he accused you of being with Mitch, rather than at the cinema.

MAURA HOWARD

No.

ALAN CANNING

It wasn't your hair caught in his jacket zip.

MAURA HOWARD

(her eyes widening)

No—

ALAN CANNING

Was he abusing you?

She gasps a little; there's a heartbeat's pause before she answers.

MAURA HOWARD

No.

ALAN CANNING

What about Amelie? She was younger - more easily manipulated. Was she the one he targeted? Was *that* why you both hated him so much?

MAURA HOWARD

(acidly)

Look, we just didn't like him, OK? End of. Not *everything* is sodding child abuse, you know. Not that you'd know it from all the TV crime shit.

ALAN CANNING

What did you wear to the cinema?

MAURA HOWARD

(slightly struggling to keep up with all his changes of direction)

The same as at the party - jeans, a T-shirt, trainers—

ALAN CANNING

And a jacket, surely? I mean, it was cold, it'd rained earlier in the day and was forecast to do so again—

MAURA HOWARD

Right, sorry, I had that hoodie thing Mum got me as well.

ALAN CANNING

Just that? I can't see that being much use in a downpour.

MAURA HOWARD

(smiling despite herself)

Yeah, that's exactly what Mum said. But I didn't have a coat I liked. Just my school thing which I wouldn't have been seen *dead* in on a Friday night.

ALAN CANNING

And that hoodie was the same one the police collected later that night? Along with the rest of your clothes?

MAURA HOWARD

Right.

ALAN CANNING

All of which tested negative for blood.

MAURA HOWARD

(frowning again)

Yeah, so? Why wouldn't they?

ALAN CANNING

You found the body - it wouldn't be so very odd for there to be at least *some* blood on you. Especially the hoodie.

MAURA HOWARD

(shaking her head)

I never got that close - I told you - I *ran*, as soon as I saw what it was—

ALAN CANNING

So you didn't swap the hoodie for another one? A clean one?

MAURA HOWARD

What would I do that for?

ALAN CANNING

Maybe it *did* have blood on it. *Too much* blood to be explained by you merely finding the body.

MAURA HOWARD

In case you've forgotten, Inspector sodding Canning, your lot searched the whole bloody house.

I mean, I know they're all fucking incompetent, but even that bunch of Keystone Cops would probably have managed to find a hoodie with a bucketload of blood all over it.

ALAN CANNING

Not if you'd stuck it in the washing machine before you called them—

MAURA HOWARD

(sarcastic)

Oh yeah? And how *exactly* was I supposed to do that, Einstein? The bloody machine was *already on*—

She stops - suddenly and horribly aware of what she's just said. Her cheeks burn red and she turns away.

ALAN CANNING

So somebody else had put the washing machine on. *Before* you got home.

Who?

MAURA HOWARD

(not meeting his gaze)

Don't ask me—

ALAN CANNING

I *am* asking you.

MAURA HOWARD

How am I supposed to fucking know? Mum, I suppose—

ALAN CANNING

But didn't you tell us, right at the start of all this, that your mother never did the laundry - that she hated doing it? Isn't that why she hired Beatriz in the first place?

MAURA HOWARD

(shrugging)

So it must've been Beatriz who put on the machine - what's the big deal, for fuck's sake—

She stops and bites her lip.

ALAN CANNING

(quietly)

It's a big deal because Beatriz wasn't there that evening. She'd left the house by 2 p.m. There isn't a washing machine on the planet that has a cycle lasting *eight hours.*

(There's a silence.)

It was Amelie, wasn't it?

It isn't a question. She doesn't reply.

Do you know what I think happened?

She turns away; she seems on the verge of tears.

I don't think you walked home with Amelie after Mitch dropped you off at all. I think you stood around waiting for her for quite a while before you realized she must have left the film early, just like you did. So you headed home, assuming she'd already be there, and you were right, she was.

But nothing could have prepared you for what you found.

CUT TO: RECONSTRUCTION. As previously shown, 'Maura' gets out of the Ford, but this time she waits there on the street, checking her watch. She hangs around for a while then starts towards Dorney Place, where she taps in the entry code at the gate and goes down the drive.

She lets herself into the house but there's no one around. Looking slightly confused she goes into the kitchen. She can hear a noise, and when she opens the door to the utility room, she sees that the washing machine is on. She looks perplexed, but then something makes her turn round: it's Amelie, blood on her face, as white as a sheet. Something terrible has happened.

ALAN CANNING

She was desperate – panicking – half out of her mind. She says she didn't realize it would be Luke babysitting or she'd never have come home early. She says they had a godawful row – maybe she'd threatened to tell her mother what he'd been doing to her, who knows.

He continues to speak over RECONSTRUCTION.

Whatever the trigger, there was a struggle and at some point her hair got caught in the zip of his jacket.

She managed to get away and tried to escape across the garden. But he followed her, ran her down at the steps, they struggled again, maybe she pushed him, maybe he slipped—

CUT BACK TO: Dorney Place. Maura has her hand to her mouth, sobbing noiselessly. Guy steps forward and puts his hand on her shoulder.

ALAN CANNING

She doesn't know what to do. She begs you to help her, and you say you will.

She's your sister and you love her, and you agree to help her cover it up—

MAURA HOWARD

(shaking her head)

No - it wasn't like that—

LAILA FURNESS

(gently)

What was it like then, Maura?

MAURA HOWARD

(her voice breaking)

She never asked me to help her. She didn't even know I was there—

BILL SERAFINI

Hold on - what did you just say?

MAURA HOWARD

(taking a deep breath; Guy tightens his grip on her shoulder)

When I got back, I went into the kitchen and saw her in the utility room - she looked like she was rinsing something. I couldn't see what it was, but it looked like there was blood on it. Then she opened the machine and put whatever it was inside and turned it on. It was a bit weird because I knew there were already clean clothes in there from earlier and she didn't bother taking them out, just put it on again.

BILL SERAFINI

You didn't ask her about it?

MAURA HOWARD

(shaking her head)

No. I didn't want to embarrass her. Look, I thought she must have had an accident with her period. She'd only just started back then and I just assumed it was that.

BILL SERAFINI

So you just backed off? Didn't let on you were there?

Maura hesitates then nods.

Then what happened?

MAURA HOWARD

I went straight out towards my room—

She falters, and puts her hand to her mouth again.

BILL SERAFINI

At which point you realized where the blood had really come from.

She glances up at him, then nods again.

And you decide that you're going to protect her. You're not going to let your 13-year-old sister spend the rest of her life in jail. Whatever it takes

Maura reaches up blindly and grasps Guy's hand.

So then what?

MAURA HOWARD

I went back inside and she was there, in the kitchen - she looked awful but she didn't say anything. I told her Luke was dead and she tried to look surprised but I knew she wasn't. Not really.

I told her I was going to call the police and that when they got there we should say we'd been at the cinema all night and had only just got back. That otherwise people might think we had something to do with it.

LAILA FURNESS

And what did she say to that?

MAURA HOWARD

She didn't really say anything. Just that she was going to go up and check on Guy.

She looks up; there are tears running down her face.

That's when I knew.

I knew she'd done it.

FREEZE FRAME and slow fade.

- end credits -

Voicemails left for Amelie Howard by Maura Howard between 5.40 and 11.05 p.m., 14th July 2023

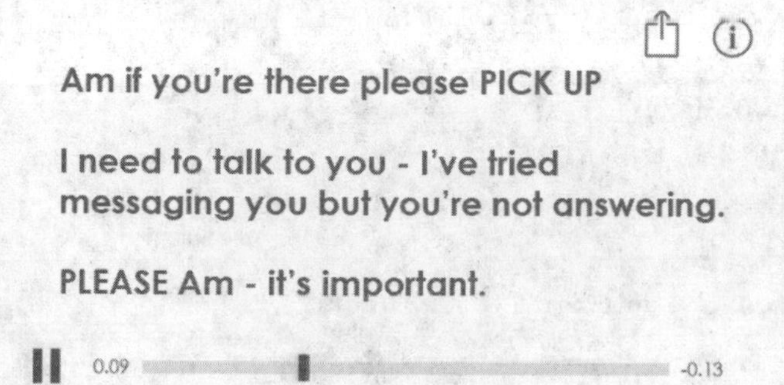

Am if you're there please PICK UP
I need to talk to you - I've tried messaging you but you're not answering.
PLEASE Am - it's important.
0.09
-0.13

Speaker Call back Delete

Amelie - I've tried to call you five times
CALL ME

It's URGENT

0.10 -0.13

Speaker Call back Delete

Am - I'm outside your flat but you're not answering the door

You're frightening me now

WHERE ARE YOU?

0.09 -0.13

Speaker Call back Delete

Episode eight

Filming

DRY RISER FILMS Ltd
227 Sherwood Street London W1Q 2UD

CAST	CALL SHEET	
Alan Canning (AC) Mitchell Clarke (MC) Hugo Fraser (HF) Laila Furness (LF) JJ Norton (JJN) Bill Serafini (WS)	**Infamous: Who Killed Luke Ryder?** Thursday 2nd November 2023	Producer **Nick Vincent** Director **Guy Howard** Film editor **Fabio Barry** Researcher **Tarek Osman** Prod asst **Jenni Tate** Location manager **Guy Johnson**
UNIT CALL 0815 *Camera ready: 0830*	**Ep 8: ON-SITE DAY 1 of 2**	*Breakfast on set from 0730* *Running lunch from 1230* *Exp wrap 1750*
Sunrise 0702 *Sunset 1637* *Weather forecast 14°, rain*		

Location:	Notes:
Dorney Place **2 Larbert Road** **Campden Hill London W8 0TF**	*Some parking on site – must be reserved in advance* *Nearest tube Holland Park* *Emergency contact number 07000 616178*

CREW							
TITLE	NAME	PHONE	CALL	TITLE	NAME	PHONE	CALL

TITLE SEQUENCE: arthouse-style b/w montage of images and short clips: crime scene, contemporary news coverage, family photos

THEME SONG – 'It's Alright, Ma (I'm Only Bleeding)' [Bob Dylan] from the soundtrack to 'Easy Rider' [1969]

TITLE OVER

INFAMOUS

FADE IN

WHO KILLED LUKE RYDER?

FADE OUT

Cut to: Nick Vincent, black background, direct to camera.

NICK VINCENT (Producer)

We ended the last episode with a truly astonishing moment of television.

A twenty-year-old case, solved, live on camera.

A murderer no one had ever even *suspected*.

For a film-maker, it was like *The Jinx* all over again. Remember that? Robert Durst, a serial killer who'd managed to evade justice for decades, finally agreeing to speak on the record?

And if that wasn't coup enough, that incredible last scene, when he retreated to the bathroom, thinking he was home and dry.

Only there was one thing he'd forgotten: his mic was still on.

'What the hell did I do?' he says quietly, staring into the mirror.

'Killed them all, of course.'

Boom.

No one thought that would ever be bettered, not in our industry.

And in the eight years since *The Jinx* was made, it never has been.

Never, that is, until now.

The makers of *The Jinx* naturally passed what they'd discovered to the authorities, and the night before the final episode aired, Robert Durst was arrested for first-degree murder.

An incredible climax, but it came too late to feature in the series.

We passed what *we'd* found out to the authorities too, and over the course of this summer the Met conducted their own investigation, including cutting-edge DNA testing on the hair found on the jacket.

By October they had enough evidence to make an arrest, and we had enough time to press Pause on the series.

Which means we're now able to show you this.

He continues to talk over FOOTAGE of Amelie Howard coming out of a block of flats, wearing handcuffs. She's followed by two uniformed police officers; the camera tracks them as they walk her to a police car, open the back door and put her inside. She makes no eye contact with anyone.

We thought we'd broken the case - we thought that, thanks to us, a line could be drawn under this case once and for all.

Only we were wrong. That wasn't the end of it.

Not by a long way.

CUT TO: MONTAGE of news coverage of the arrest.

Cutting-edge DNA technique identifies Luke Ryder killer

New evidence establishes Campden Hill killer 'beyond reasonable doubt'

New suspect in Luke Ryder case 'may have been abused by him'

SHOCK ARREST IN 20-YEAR-OLD MURDER CASE

Stepdaughter questioned over 2003 'Cougar Killing'

With an abuse victim outed on camera, has the True Crime craze finally gone too far?

CUT TO: FOOTAGE of Guy, crowded by cameras and microphones. He's unshaven and looks pale but he's calm, and in control.

REPORTER #1

What's your reaction to this news, Guy? It must have come as quite a shock.

GUY HOWARD

Well, yes, I mean - none of us expected this. It's the worst news we could possibly have—

REPORTER #1

Though it's down to you, isn't it - if you hadn't elected to make that documentary none of this would have come out. Your sister would have got away with it—

GUY HOWARD

It's not a question of 'getting away with it' - she was a *child*, a child under intolerable emotional pressure—

REPORTER #1

So you can confirm, can you, that she was being abused by the man you knew as Luke Ryder? You have actual evidence of that?

GUY HOWARD

No, but—

REPORTER #1

This new evidence the police have - those new DNA tests they ran - it proved the hair caught in the dead man's jacket was from your sister, right?

GUY HOWARD

So I've been told—

REPORTER #2

And his real name was Jonah McKenna? A Canadian who faked his own death in 1991?

GUY HOWARD

Apparently so—

REPORTER #2

What can you tell us about him?

GUY HOWARD

Nothing - I don't know any more than you do. I think the police are trying to track down his family—

REPORTER #3

What about *your* family? What do they think about all this? Do they blame you for your sister being arrested?

GUY HOWARD

(bridling slightly)

It's *not my fault* - how was I to know what we would find?

REPORTER #4

What about your mother? Maura? How do they feel about this?

GUY HOWARD

My mother has been diagnosed with Alzheimer's - she's not really in any state to—

REPORTER #4

She must have known, though, surely? I can't see two teenage girls keeping a secret like that.

GUY HOWARD

There is *no* suggestion my mother knew *any*thing.

REPORTER #4

Maybe not that night, but what about later? Didn't your sisters go into therapy? Didn't *you*? How could any mother *not* have known?

GUY HOWARD

That's *private*—

REPORTER #4

It's in your series, mate. That makes it public in my book. You can't have it both ways—

GUY HOWARD

(starting to back away)

I don't have anything more to say. If you have any further questions, you can direct them to my lawyer. In the meantime I'd be grateful if you could give me and my family some privacy—

REPORTER #4

—'at this difficult time'. Yeah, right.

(under his breath)

And meanwhile you milk it for all it's bloody worth.

REPORTER #3

(quietly agreeing)

Ratings up by twenty per cent. At a conservative estimate.

CUT TO: Studio. There are dark clouds outside and rain spattering against the windows. Nick is at the table, as is Tarek. There are now two TV screens on the wall.

NICK VINCENT (Producer)

So, I thought that with so much having happened we should all get round the table one last time.

And I'm pleased to say Guy is joining us by Zoom from Somerset, where he's been staying with his mother.

One of the TV screens comes to life. Guy is in a sitting room with a large garden visible beyond. The trees are bare and there's mist clinging to the hollows. Guy looks thinner than last time, subdued, untidy. He needs a haircut and his clothes have not been ironed. He's on Mute.

LAILA FURNESS

Can I just say, Guy, on behalf of all of us, how sorry we are about how everything's turned out. It must be a terrible time for you and your family. I hope you're getting the help you need.

And Amelie too – so much of what we've learned of her history makes sense now. If only someone could have seen that and intervened at the time. It's tragic, Guy, truly tragic.

Guy raises a hand in brief acknowledgement, but he doesn't Unmute.

JJ NORTON

(looking round at the rest of the team)

I don't know about anyone else but it seems like years since we started all this. Or maybe I've just aged that much as a result—

BILL SERAFINI

(dryly, to Nick)

Well, you must be pleased with how it's gone – you're all over the press. I've had calls from people I haven't spoken to in thirty years.

NICK VINCENT (Producer)

We are all over the press, Bill. It was a team effort.

HUGO FRASER

It didn't always feel that way, Nick. Not to us.

JJ NORTON

Though I'm still struggling to see how the police didn't solve this case at the time. It seems so obvious now. Didn't they notice the washing machine was on that night, for a start?

LAILA FURNESS

(shrugs)

It's a big house. If Amelie put the machine on a short programme it could easily have ended by the time the police got round to looking in the laundry room.

JJ NORTON

And in any case, hindsight is a wonderful thing, blah, blah. None of us saw it coming either, did we? And we went over this case with a fine-tooth comb for weeks. It's a bit rich to blame the Met on that basis.

(glancing towards Guy)

Let's face it, those girls did one hell of a good cover-up job.

HUGO FRASER

(under his breath)

Maybe a bit *too* good—

JJ NORTON

(apparently not hearing him)

Well, at least we're all off the hook now. All those 'coincidences' that Nick kept wanting people to believe weren't coincidences at all.

Hey, guess what, Nick? They really are a Thing.

Nick laughs but says nothing.

LAILA FURNESS

(looking towards Guy and then at Nick)

How's Maura doing, do we know? This must have come as an awful shock to her.

On the TV screen, Guy is looking off left. He doesn't appear to have heard.

NICK VINCENT (Producer)

OK, I think.

LAILA FURNESS

And Amelie?

NICK VINCENT (Producer)

As far as I know. The police aren't saying much.

JJ NORTON

(sardonically)

Well, they must be absolutely *delighted* with you, Nick: solving their case for them without it costing them a penny, all the loose ends tied up with a nice big shiny bow—

HUGO FRASER

Though that's not quite true, is it?

Several people turn towards him with questioning looks. On the screen, Guy glances up and frowns.

MITCHELL CLARKE

(frowning)

What are you getting at, Hugo?

HUGO FRASER

(sitting back)

Well, there are still some loose ends, aren't there? What about the jacket - the black denim jacket 'Luke' was wearing?

A brief silence.

LAILA FURNESS

(making an effort to remember)

Yes, we did discuss that, didn't we – you mean, as in, why did he have the jacket on when he died?

HUGO FRASER

Right. According to Nick's latest reconstruction – which I assume the police must think is a pretty fair approximation of what actually happened – Amelie got home, found 'Luke' there, the two of them got into a violent row and she tried to get away across the garden—

BILL SERAFINI

(nodding)

In which case, why was he wearing a jacket? He was indoors when she got back.

HUGO FRASER

Precisely.

LAILA FURNESS

Hang on, didn't we talk about exactly that point when we were wondering whether it could have been Maura?

MITCHELL CLARKE

We did, and we concluded he could have been on the point of going over to the workshop—

HUGO FRASER

And *I* observed that a far simpler explanation would be that he'd either just met, or was *about* to meet, someone else, who he was planning to talk to out in the garden.

His mystery caller from King's Cross, for example.

JJ NORTON

(half in jest, but only half)

Oh Christ, don't start all that up again - it'll just give Nick another excuse to start pointing fingers at all of us—

HUGO FRASER

(cutting across him)

And what about Amelie's injuries? As in, the lack thereof?

If the struggle with 'Luke' was so violent her hair got caught in his zip, how come there wasn't a mark on her? There wasn't even a scratch.

LAILA FURNESS

(frowning)

We know that for certain, do we?

ALAN CANNING

There's nothing about any injuries in the file. And I can't see the police missing that.

JJ NORTON

Actually, Hugo's just made a very good point. What do you think, Nick? Can we find out if anyone's ever asked Amelie about that?

NICK VINCENT (Producer)

(smiling)

Oh, I think we can do a bit better than that, JJ.

He nods toward Tarek, who taps his keyboard and we begin to hear an AUDIO recording.

The sound quality isn't very good - it's slightly muffled and it takes the team a few minutes to recognize the voices. It's two women - young women. One is asking the other how she is - if they're treating her OK.

HUGO FRASER

Hold on - that's *Maura*—

NICK VINCENT (Producer)

(quietly)

And Amelie. Right.

HUGO FRASER

(turning to him)

How the *fuck* did you get hold of this?

NICK VINCENT (Producer)

Just listen, Hugo. Just listen.

AUDIO continues.

MAURA HOWARD

There was something else - don't jump down my throat, OK, but Nick - the producer - he wanted me to ask you something—

AMELIE HOWARD

That wanker - if it hadn't been for him none of this would have happened. Guy was such a twat, agreeing to do that shit—

MAURA HOWARD

Look, I know, but Nick was really bloody insistent, so I said I'd ask, OK?

You can tell him to fuck off if you like but he wanted to know why you didn't have any scratches or anything. That night, I mean. If you'd had a fight with Luke.

AMELIE HOWARD

Right. Yeah, tell him to fuck off.

MAURA HOWARD

Come on, Am—

a silence

The hair in the zip was definitely yours - they proved that - the lawyer told me—

AMELIE HOWARD

Yeah, but that didn't happen then, did it. Look, I tried the bloody thing on, OK? The jacket. A couple of days before. I always liked it and I tried it on. That must have been when it happened. End of.

MAURA HOWARD

So you didn't have a fight with him that night?

AMELIE HOWARD

(lowering her voice)

Come on - you know I didn't.

MAURA HOWARD

No, I don't - I don't know anything—

AMELIE HOWARD

Oh for fuck's sake—

MAURA HOWARD

(quietly)

Was he abusing you? You can tell me - if he was—

AMELIE HOWARD

Of course he wasn't.

MAURA HOWARD

But you're letting everyone believe that - the police, the lawyer—

AMELIE HOWARD

Like, duh? Of course I am. It's what they all want to hear - they're practically gagging for it—

MAURA HOWARD

But if Luke wasn't abusing you then why? Why did you - you know—

AMELIE HOWARD

Bludgeon him to death? Beat his face till his brain exploded?

MAURA HOWARD

Shit, Am - really?

AMELIE HOWARD

Oh come on - you know as well as I do I had nothing to do with it—

MAURA HOWARD

I don't know that - I don't know that at all—

AMELIE HOWARD

You're shitting me, right?

MAURA HOWARD

Of course I'm not - all these years - I thought - I thought I was protecting you.

AMELIE HOWARD

(barely audible now)

You thought you were protecting me?

MAURA HOWARD

(whispering, almost hissing)

What the fuck else did you think I was doing? I saw you - the blood in the sink, that thing with the washing machine. And then when I went out and found him I just - I just - assumed—

AMELIE HOWARD

Jesus, Maurie, why the hell didn't you say something?

MAURA HOWARD

What the fuck was I supposed to say? When I told you Luke was dead you didn't look surprised at all, and when I said we had to tell the police we'd been at the cinema all night you just bloody agreed. You didn't even ask why.

Why the fuck would you do that if it wasn't you?

AMELIE HOWARD

Oh fuck.

Fuck fuck fuck fuck—

Nick nods to Tarek, who pauses the AUDIO. Nick looks round at the team, most of whom are in various stages of shock and disbelief.

HUGO FRASER

So everyone got it wrong. The police, us - everybody.

It wasn't Amelie.

NICK VINCENT (Producer)

So it would seem.

LAILA FURNESS

(to Nick)

Maura recorded this for you?

NICK VINCENT (Producer)

(nods)

At HMP Heathside, where Amelie's on remand.

JJ NORTON

So Maura thought Amelie'd done it, and Amelie thought Maura had, but neither of them said anything so they never found out they'd both got it wrong. It's like something out of bloody Thomas Hardy—

ALAN CANNING

(turning to him)

That's not quite what they said though, is it?

You're right, Maura definitely thought Amelie was the killer, but Amelie didn't say that about Maura, did she?

LAILA FURNESS

Are you sure? I'm not sure that's how I heard it.

BILL SERAFINI

Actually, I agree with Alan on this one—

MITCHELL CLARKE

(looking confused)

But if not Amelie, then who?

NICK VINCENT (Producer)

(with a wry smile)

It seems Hugo was right about what he said earlier: there *was* someone else there that night.

He looks around the table and raises an eyebrow. The full implications of what he's just said gradually sink in.

LAILA FURNESS

Oh shit, here we go again—

NICK VINCENT (Producer)

Well?

HUGO FRASER

Seriously? You *still* think it could have been one of us? Even after everything we've said to prove otherwise?

NICK VINCENT (Producer)

(shrugs)

If the cap fits, Hugo.

And in any case, I'm not sure how much actual 'proof' any of you have offered. A shedload of outraged protestations of innocence, yes, but that's not 'proof'. Not in my book.

MITCHELL CLARKE

Oh come on - that was all just for effect, right? To get the viewing figures up? You never *actually* thought it was one of us—

BILL SERAFINI

(agreeing)

It was all bullshit and he knows it.

NICK VINCENT (Producer)

Do I? Our viewers don't appear to agree with you. And I know that for a fact because we actually asked them.

After episode six aired, before either of the girls were in the frame, we ran a poll on Twitter asking our audience who they thought was most likely to be involved in the murder, and this is what they said.

And as you can see, pretty much none of you have been *entirely* convincing.

The screen shows the poll results.

Dry Riser Films Ltd ...

@dryriserfilms

Who do you think was most likely to have committed the crime? #Infamous #WhoKilledLukeRyder

Alan Canning	15 %
Mitch Clarke	14 %
Hugo Fraser	13 %
Lalla Furness	9 %
JJ Norton	11 %
Bill Serafini	9%

LAILA FURNESS

Oh well, I guess it could be worse—

HUGO FRASER

(mock-disappointed)

But as for Alan, oh dear oh dear—

ALAN CANNING

To use your own phrase, pot or kettle, Hugo?

JJ NORTON

(staring at the screen then turning to Nick)

These are percentages, right? In which case you're missing someone – this only gets us to seventy-one.

NICK VINCENT (Producer)

Well spotted. Always *so* useful to have a scientist in the room.

You're right. We *are* missing someone.

The screen updates to the full list.

Dry Riser Films Ltd
@dryriserfilms

Who do you think was most likely to have committed the crime? #Infamous #WhoKilledLukeRyder

Alan Canning	15 %
Mitch Clarke	14 %
Hugo Fraser	13 %
Laila Furness	9 %
JJ Norton	11 %
Bill Serafini	9%
Ian Wilson	29 %

16,845 votes Final result

HUGO FRASER

Ah, the elusive Mr Wilson. I suppose that was only to be expected.

JJ NORTON

Though I'm not sure where it gets us, given he's still doing a very passable impersonation of the bloody Scarlet Pimpernel—

NICK VINCENT (Producer)

Not so fast there, JJ. Turns out our viewers aren't the *only* people who've been in touch since the last time we were all round this table.

They stare at him.

LAILA FURNESS

(looking from Nick to Tarek)

You found *Wilson*?

NICK VINCENT (Producer)

Much as I'd love to take the credit, he found *us*.

He's been watching the series - with immense interest, may I say—

ALAN CANNING

(under his breath)

I bet he has.

NICK VINCENT (Producer)

And given *what* he saw, he felt honour-bound to come forward.

HUGO FRASER

(sardonically)

Oh really? After all this time he suddenly gets a bad case of late-onset moral responsibility?

NICK VINCENT (Producer)

Bear with, Hugo, bear with—

LAILA FURNESS

(impatiently)

For heaven's sake, what did he say?

NICK VINCENT (Producer)

Let's take a look, shall we?

Screen changes to INTERVIEW with Ian Wilson. He's sitting at a marble-topped table in a beachside bar. There are palm trees, low-rise houses with a gabled

Dutch feel, and in the distance shimmering orange dunes. He's tanned, in a cream linen shirt, with sunglasses propped on his head, a negroni on the table and a cigarette smoking in an ashtray. His blond hair is thinning and he's got even heavier, but the confidence and self-assurance remain.

MITCHELL CLARKE

Where is that?

NICK VINCENT (Producer)

(glancing across)

Swakopmund. On the coast of Namibia. That's where he's been living. I'd never been before but I can see why he chose it - great climate, nice people—

HUGO FRASER

(caustically)

I'm sure. And the absence of an extradition treaty with the UK no doubt only added to the attraction.

CUT TO: INTERVIEW, shown on the screen in the room, so we see the reaction of the team throughout.

NICK VINCENT (Producer)

So, Ian, why are you breaking your silence now, after all these years? You must have known the police have been wanting to talk to you for nigh-on two decades.

IAN WILSON

Of course - but 'on the advice of my lawyers I declined to comply'. As they say in American cop shows.

NICK VINCENT (Producer)

Until now.

IAN WILSON

Right.

NICK VINCENT (Producer)

So what changed your mind?

IAN WILSON

I've been watching your series, just like everyone else. Seeing all your little theories about how it went down. And then when you announced there was going to be some sort of shit-hot big reveal and the finale was delayed I put out some feelers and found out the Met were on the point of arresting that girl. Amelie.

NICK VINCENT (Producer)

And you think they've got the wrong person, is that it?

IAN WILSON

I bloody *know* they have.

NICK VINCENT (Producer)

OK then, let's hear it – what really happened that night?

IAN WILSON

(picking up his drink)

You were right about one thing. I was there. I did call Ryder from King's Cross that day.

There are a few gasps round the table; Hugo mutters 'I bloody knew it'. Nick surveys them with a smug smile, clearly enjoying their reaction.

NICK VINCENT (Producer)

You arranged to go round there? To talk to him?

IAN WILSON

Right. I wanted to discuss the will. Florence's will. Ryder was going to get the whole shit-show, and I didn't think that was fair. Mum was getting on, for a start. She wasn't well, couldn't get about like she used to. That money would have made a massive difference.

NICK VINCENT (Producer)

But you weren't exactly close to Florence, were you? Nor was your mother.

IAN WILSON

No, but my dad *was* close to her husband - he and Victor Ryder were massive mates, back in the day. And I know Vic would deffo have wanted us to get *some*thing, at least. He never even *met* bloody Luke.

(knocks back a swig of his drink)

Of course, I didn't know then that 'Luke' wasn't even Luke at all, so had fuck all claim to any of it, the self-righteous bastard.

(makes a face)

Probably just as well I didn't know, all things considered.

NICK VINCENT (Producer)

So you went to Dorney Place to talk about the will.

But before we go any further, since I know people are going to ask, you're admitting, are you, that your alibi was a fabrication?

IAN WILSON

(leaning forward for his cigarette)

Of course it was.

NICK VINCENT (Producer)

You got 'Christine' to lie for you?

IAN WILSON

(smiling rather unpleasantly)

Actually, she offered. I needed a favour and she was only too happy to help. We'd been friends for years. As the Met would have discovered if they'd actually bothered looking.

(blowing smoke in Nick's direction)

In fact, she was the one who tipped me off about all this in the first place.

NICK VINCENT (Producer)

She was taking quite a risk, giving you that alibi. She could have been prosecuted.

IAN WILSON

(gives a short dry snort)

Don't make me fucking laugh – back then the Met couldn't find their arses with both hands and a map. She ran rings round those stupid tossers.

And in any case, later on, after Mum died, I made it 'worth her while'.

NICK VINCENT (Producer)

(nodding slowly)

I did wonder how she managed to afford that B&B...

Wilson raises an eyebrow and takes another drag but says nothing.

NICK VINCENT (Producer)

So, let's get back to what actually happened that night.

You arrange to go round there. But he didn't let you in, did he?

IAN WILSON

(picking up his cigarette and taking a long drag)

He said he wanted to talk in the garden. It was just a fucking power play, of course. Treating me like some hairy-arsed prole.

NICK VINCENT (Producer)

What happened then?

IAN WILSON

I tried to make him see reason. Obviously.

(pause)

NICK VINCENT (Producer)

And?

IAN WILSON

Evidently he wasn't 'in the mood' for discussion.

(he leans forward and flicks ash into the dish)

Things got a little heated. There was some rather undignified pushing and shoving and, well, he sort of slipped.

NICK VINCENT (Producer)

Slipped?

IAN WILSON

(inhaling again)

Right. On those steps. Bloody death trap they were, if you ask me. Frankly, I was surprised no one had broken their neck long before.

NICK VINCENT (Producer)

You didn't push him, by any chance?

IAN WILSON

No, I didn't.

NICK VINCENT (Producer)

Not even a tiny little nudge?

IAN WILSON

Nope. Sorry to spoil your big TV climax, mate, but he managed it all on his little lonesome.

OK, yes, he might have been slightly off balance, but that's because *he* was pushing *me*. That's his fault, not mine.

NICK VINCENT (Producer)

But we know from the post mortem that the blow he sustained to the back of his head was pretty serious - certainly enough to knock him out. You didn't try to help him?

IAN WILSON

I'm not a bloody medic—

NICK VINCENT (Producer)

But you could have called 999—

IAN WILSON

(takes another drag, clearly buying time)

I suppose I could. But by that time I was more intent on getting the hell out of there. Mainly because I didn't want to be dragged into all the attendant shit.

NICK VINCENT (Producer)

'Mainly'? So that wasn't the only reason?

IAN WILSON

(hesitates)

If you really want to know, I saw a light go on in the house—

NICK VINCENT (Producer)

A light? Where?

IAN WILSON

Upstairs – above the terrace. Must have been one of the bedrooms. I thought I saw someone at the window—

NICK VINCENT (Producer)

So you legged it?

IAN WILSON

(his eyes narrowing)

I made myself scarce, yes. Tripped over and nearly broke my own bloody neck in the process, but yes, I removed myself from the premises forthwith.

NICK VINCENT (Producer)

So for the avoidance of doubt, the last time you saw 'Luke' he was unconscious, but broadly unharmed.

IAN WILSON

(reaching for his glass)

Right.

NICK VINCENT (Producer)

You didn't beat him up – didn't harm him in any way.

IAN WILSON

Nope. Never touched the bloke.

NICK VINCENT (Producer)

Well, we know someone did. Did you see who?

IAN WILSON

(slowly)

Not as such, no.

NICK VINCENT (Producer)

What does that mean?

IAN WILSON

Look, I didn't see anything actually *happen* – it wasn't till the next day that I knew the bloke was even dead, never mind what'd been done to him.

(he reaches to flick ash again)

The whole thing was completely screwed up. The police would never have believed me. They'd have thought *I'd* done it and frankly I would have too, in their position – if someone told me a mind-fucked story like that.

I wasn't prepared to take that risk. Not with a murder charge at stake. Nobody would have.

NICK VINCENT (Producer)

So what *exactly* did you see?

IAN WILSON

(taking another drag)

I legged it like you said, but when I got to the corner of the house I turned and looked back, just for a sec.

It was just starting to rain, but there was light streaming out from the house. The door to the terrace was open—

NICK VINCENT (Producer)

It hadn't been before?

IAN WILSON

(shaking his head)

Definitely not. Remember, he never let me in. We went round the side of the house and the back door was definitely closed then.

NICK VINCENT (Producer)

So what did you see when you looked back?

IAN WILSON

Like I said, it was a complete fucking freak-show.

There was someone there, standing over him - just, like, *staring* at him.

NICK VINCENT (Producer)

You didn't see this person actually hit him?

IAN WILSON

No. But I saw what they had in their hand.

NICK VINCENT (Producer)

You could see what it was, even in the dark?

IAN WILSON

I'd just tripped over the fucking thing not five minutes before. Of course I knew what it was.

NICK VINCENT (Producer)

And you saw *who* it was?

IAN WILSON

Yes, I saw who it was.

(takes another drag)

But like I said, no one would have believed me.

NICK VINCENT (Producer)

Because—?

IAN WILSON

Because it was a fucking *kid*.

He couldn't have been more than 10. Just standing there like a fucking zombie or something, with that bloody thing in his hand.

It was like something out of the fucking *Omen* – scared the living crap out of me if you really want to know.

NICK VINCENT (Producer)

You didn't go back – didn't try to talk to him?

IAN WILSON

Are you fucking kidding me?

I got the hell out of there, and I never looked back.

FREEZE FRAME.

In the silence that follows Nick reaches down beside his chair, and puts something in a plastic evidence bag on the table. It's a child's cricket bat. The camera swings slowly round so that we can see the stricken faces of each of the team. We cannot see Guy.

LAILA FURNESS

(her hand to her mouth)

Oh my God—

MITCHELL CLARKE

Where the hell did you find that?

NICK VINCENT (Producer)

Upstairs. Two days ago, when we were setting up for filming. Of course, we knew by then what we were looking for.

ALAN CANNING

I assume you don't need me to tell you that was an illegal search – I can't believe anyone gave you permission.

NICK VINCENT (Producer)

(evenly)

No, they didn't.

HUGO FRASER

(gesturing at the evidence bag)

You've had it tested?

NICK VINCENT (Producer)

By a private lab, yes.

JJ NORTON

And?

NICK VINCENT (Producer)

Someone's clearly wiped it down, but there are still minute traces of blood embedded in the wood. Clearly we haven't yet been able to establish whose—

LAILA FURNESS

(quietly)

Amelie – it was *Amelie* who cleaned it. The blood Maura saw, in the utility room. It was from *this*—

She must have seen what happened—

She's known the truth this whole time—

Her cheeks are flushed. Some of them are glancing towards Guy, but the screen is off-camera. We can't see him.

BILL SERAFINI

(shaking his head)

No wonder she needed therapy – Jeez – that poor kid—

MITCHELL CLARKE

(frowning)

So what was in the washing machine?

JJ NORTON

(turning to him)

My guess would be his pyjamas - they'd have been soaked in it—

LAILA FURNESS

Oh my God, she must have washed him, changed him, put him back to bed—

JJ NORTON

(nodding)

And then let Maura think that she was responsible - that *she* was the killer. She's been protecting her little brother for nigh-on twenty years—

MITCHELL CLARKE

But she couldn't really have thought he'd be locked up, surely? He was only 10 years old, for Christ's sake—

HUGO FRASER

(quietly)

So were the boys who killed Jamie Bulger. They *were* sent to prison, and they were still there, ten years later, when 'Luke' was killed. It was all over the papers. And Amelie was 13 - easily old enough to have known all about the case.

MITCHELL CLARKE

But the Bulger killers were psychopaths - we're talking about *Guy*. What the fuck could lead a normal 10-year-old kid to do something like that?

LAILA FURNESS

But 10-year-olds aren't 'normal', Mitch - at least not in the way adults are.

Like I've said before, children don't think like adults - you can't talk about motive with a child that age, just impulse.

And that 'impulse' could have been everything from a visceral dislike of the man who took his father's place, to being angry about missing a TV programme or not getting to play cricket—

JJ NORTON

(to Laila)

Do you think Guy even remembers what happened? He doesn't seem to - in fact, the way Wilson described it he could even have been sleepwalking.

LAILA FURNESS

I don't think he has any recollection at all - he can't do - he wouldn't be involved in this if he did—

HUGO FRASER

(intervening)

But we are talking about someone with a chronic case of selective memory. What about that bloody wedding cake? He claims he doesn't remember doing that either—

LAILA FURNESS

No, I don't think it's selective memory - or at least not in the way you mean.

Remember back at the start, when he said he was the only one present when his father collapsed and died? He was *6 years old*. Imagine the impact of something as sudden and violent as that on a child that age—

MITCHELL CLARKE

(nodding)

And yet he seems to have blocked it out entirely.

LAILA FURNESS

That's precisely my point. Children who experience serious trauma that young can't process it properly, so the memory is, in effect, jammed. I've seen it again and again in children who've experienced abuse. They retreat into dissociation as a survival mechanism.

MITCHELL CLARKE

I'm not sure I know what you mean by dissociation. What sort of behaviour are we talking about?

LAILA FURNESS

The child can go into a fugue state, 'zone out'—

(she takes a deep breath)

They can also exhibit violent and apparently random fits of anger. Fits they almost never remember anything about afterwards.

The following dialogue continues over RECONSTRUCTION. A high camera angle above the garden of Dorney Place. It's dark, raining, light streaming from the wide-open back door of the house. The camera gradually drops to ground level; 'Luke' is lying face up on the steps. 'Guy' is standing over him, a cricket bat in his hand. 'Luke' appears to be coming to, but as he starts to move 'Guy' raises the bat above his head and lets it fall, heavily, once, twice. The body jerks then lies still but the blows still rain down. The camera closes in slowly on the face of the little boy. Blood is running down his forehead, his cheeks, his hair. The close-up continues until all we can see are the child's eyes. They are completely blank.

MITCHELL CLARKE

So what might induce a violent reaction like that?

LAILA FURNESS

It varies. A particular noise or smell might be enough to evoke the original trauma, but there can be visual triggers too—

HUGO FRASER

(nodding)

Like seeing someone collapse in front of them, exactly the same way their father did.

LAILA FURNESS

And the point is that, at a subconscious level, Guy associated that event with the father he loved 'going away' and never coming back.

This is a little boy who was experiencing profound grief over the loss of his father. And not only had no one apparently noticed that fact, but the trauma he'd experienced at the time of that death had prevented his grief from being expressed in any remotely healthy way.

He was angry and bereft and confused. Nothing in his world made sense to him any more. The only thing that *did* make sense was that it was all fine until Luke came along; in his young mind, it was *all Luke's fault.*

And that night, deep in a dissociative state, he did something about it. He made Luke 'go away' too.

Cut back to: STUDIO.

Laila sits back and shakes her head; she looks deeply troubled.

LAILA FURNESS

I blame myself – I should have put all this together long before. All the signs were there – all those photos of him looking lost and unhappy, the disruptive behaviour, the 'daydreaming', even the damn cake—

She takes a deep breath and turns towards the screen.

Guy – trust me, you need to deal with this. Properly, this time. You need to talk to someone—

She stops.

The camera swings slowly round past the team so that we can see the screen; there's no one there.

The chair Guy was sitting on is empty.

CUT TO: FOOTAGE from Ep 1. Guy in the sitting room of Dorney Place, wearing a crisp white shirt and jeans, the expensive Breitling watch his mother gave him, the silver wrist chain. He looks happy and relaxed, on the brink of a life-changing opportunity.

NICK VINCENT (Producer) - off

So now its 2023 and it's been nearly twenty years since all this happened. Why are you revisiting it now?

GUY HOWARD

Because I want to know the truth. Because that's what I do, as a film-maker. And because my family has lived with this thing hanging over our heads for almost two decades and until someone finds out who did it and puts him away none of us will ever have any peace.

I want to find the truth.

Whatever that truth turns out to be.

FADE OUT

- end credits -

Episodes seven and eight

Broadcast

November 7

Date: Sun 26/11/2023, 9.18 **Importance:** High

From: Bill Serafini

To: David Shulman

Subject: Update

David,

Thanks for your time Monday. As agreed, now we know our con's real name was Jonah McKenna I'll step up my efforts on the dormant offshore and Swiss bank accounts, and engage a specialty consultancy with expertise in that area.

My immediate priority will be to find the sister, since Rebecca McKenna is almost certainly her brother's next of kin, and without her, our ability to engage meaningfully with any financial institution still holding assets in Jonah McKenna's name will be severely limited.

That said, Ms McKenna continues to prove elusive – not least because we can't be sure if she is still going by that name. Tarek Osman tells me his team have made no discernible progress with the international medical and nursing organizations, and I'm afraid law enforcement is unlikely to be much help either: even if the Brits decide to pursue a prosecution against Guy (which personally I doubt, given the lapse of time, his age when the crime was committed, and the mental health issues he was clearly laboring under at the time) I query whether the Met will think it's value for money spending taxpayer dollars running the sister down. They already have sufficient circumstantial evidence confirming McKenna's identity.

But there are still other options: I'm reaching out to my contacts at Interpol and in the specialist MissPers sector, to see if they might be able to assist. With that in mind, I'm in the process of organizing a range of high-quality age-progression images (i.e. with and without the glasses, with her original red hair color and with other dyes and lengths). We just have to hope we get a hit.

In the meantime, enjoy Jackson Hole. The weather forecast over the next few days is looking good, snow-wise.

Best wishes and happy holidays to the family,

Bill

The Times, 30 November 2023

Infamous director found dead after 'devastating' revelations

Luke Ryder case claims another victim

By Angela Odiwe

After the sensational ending to the Showrunner series Infamous, which aired on November 7th, the notorious Campden Hill murder case has taken yet another shocking turn.

Guy Howard, the director of the series and stepson of the victim, was revealed in the closing moments of the final episode to be the real killer of Jonah McKenna, who married Howard's mother as 'Luke Ryder' in 2001. Howard was arrested last week and released on police bail while the Crown Prosecution Service reviews the case in the light of new information uncovered by the series, which had initially implicated Howard's sister

One of the most shocking revelations of the final episode was the production team's discovery of a child's cricket bat, once the property of Mr Howard, which still bears traces of blood, and could therefore have been the weapon used to attack 'Luke Ryder' on the night of his death. Police sources have confirmed that this has been taken for a full forensic examination.

Avon and Somerset Police responded to a 999 call just after 3pm yesterday, when Howard's mother, Caroline Bowyer, who married former ambassador Jeremy Bowyer in 2009, returned from a doctor's appointment with her carer. Mrs Bowyer was taken to Yeovil hospital by ambulance after collapsing at the

Howard, 30, is believed to have died some time yesterday morning, after an apparent heart attack, which may have been the result of an overdose.

Although no suicide note was found, and the room was in some disarray with items possibly missing, it is understood that the police are not treating the death as suspicious. Friends of the film-maker told us that he was 'utterly devastated' by the revelations made in the programme, and had 'no memory' of any such assault.

A sighting by an elderly neighbour of a red-haired woman in glasses and a nurse's uniform going into the house has been discounted by police, after the agency providing Mrs Bowyer's care confirmed they made no visit yesterday, and have no staff answering that description.

The Flamborough Gazette, 27 June 2024

FLAMBOROUGH GAZETTE

Your Community Paper Since 1968

Newly painted hydrant on Little River Road, Flamborough. The project has taken two years to complete

All fire hydrants are now painted

MICHAEL LANDRY
Community correspondent

A project that started with a trucking accident has marked its completion with a special event at Flamborough Junior High School. When a truck wrecked a fire hydrant on Victoria Street in October 2021, just outside the school, pupils in the 7th grade class decided that they would make their own contribution to restoring and brightening up the area.

The replacement hydrant was painted that weekend, and since then local businesses have sponsored the children to repaint their local hydrants in bright colours, with the proceeds going to local charities.

Speaking at the event, head-teacher Matthew Surtees said "This has been a genuine community effort, and has shown the children the value of teamwork, and how even small positive acts can make a big difference."

Mystery watch still unclaimed

According to Sergeant Pierre Doucet of Flamborough County Police, a valuable watch found in the graveyard of St Laurence Church six months ago has still not been claimed. The man's watch, a Breitling Avenger, has a chrome strap, and was found lying on the memorial local children call 'Jonah and the whale'.

The engraving on the back has not been revealed, so the owner can be identified if they come forward, but it is believed to include a first name with the initial 'G' and reference to a 21st birthday. "Quite apart from the sentimental value it's such an expensive watch I can't believe it hasn't been missed," says Sergeant Doucet. "If you know who might have lost it, please get in touch with us at the Flamborough Police Station."

Acknowledgments

After six Adam Fawley books, *Murder in the Family* has been a first for me in lots of ways. Most obviously my first standalone, but also my first book with HarperCollins, my new publishers. I absolutely loved the idea of this, right from the start, and if my readers enjoy reading it even half as much as I enjoyed writing it, I'll be a very happy person.

Some things have remained the same, of course. My wonderful agent, Anna Power, continues to be an outstanding support in every way, and I also owe a great deal of gratitude to my team at Johnson & Alcock, especially Hélène Butler, Anna Dawson, Saliann St Clair, and Kroum Valtchkov.

My 'pro team' of advisers have once again been invaluable, so a huge thank-you to DI Andy Thompson, Joey Giddings, and Nicholas Syfret KC and also to Julie Stokes for her help on the psychological aspects of the story.

Many of my friends continue to be my 'first readers', and this time round some of them have also been kind enough to let me use their photos, either as the 'faces' of some of the *Infamous* team or elsewhere in the book: Stuart, Ben, Joey, Fabio, Rachel, and Hamish, I definitely owe you one! Thank you also – and always – to Simon, Sarah, Elizabeth, and Stephen.

I have a new publishing team this time round, and I'd like to thank my new editors in the UK and US, Julia Wisdom and

Rachel Kahan, Susanna Peden and the UK PR team, Olivia French and Roisin O'Shea for marketing, and especially the fabulous proof design, my copyeditor Janette Currie, Andy O'Neill and everyone at Palimpsest Book Production, and the brilliant Elizabeth Burrell and Angel Belsey for their work on the text. And finally, a big thank you to the lovely Phoebe Morgan, who was the one who made the move to HarperCollins a reality, and Kimberley Young, the Executive Publisher, for welcoming me to the Harper family.

About the Author

Cara Hunter is the author of the *Sunday Times* bestselling crime novels featuring DI Adam Fawley and his Oxford-based police team. Her books have sold over a million copies in the UK alone, and have been translated into 27 languages so far. Her third novel, *No Way Out*, was selected by the *Sunday Times* as one of the 100 best crime novels since 1945. Her first novel, *Close to Home*, sold over half a million copies, was a Richard and Judy Book Club pick and was shortlisted for Crime Book of the Year in the British Book Awards 2019. The fifth book, *The Whole Truth*, was a Richard and Judy summer pick for 2021. The series is now in script development for TV, and the screen rights to *Murder in the Family* have been acquired by Neal Street Productions.